A new "page-
from

CW01666544

In his electrifying
Blue Gold, Clive C
(*Chicago Tribune*) exploits of Kurt Austin,
NUMA's Special Assignments Team and a hero for our time. Now, he continues his reign as "just about the best storyteller in the business" (*New York Post*) with a novel that takes us from the depths of the ocean to the heights of adventure—to the dawn of mankind . . .

LOST CITY

An enzyme that could dramatically prolong life has been discovered in the North Atlantic—under two thousand feet of icy water in an area known as the "Lost City." But why are the people attempting to harvest its secrets dying mysteriously? Why are scientists from a remote Greek laboratory disappearing one by one? And what does all of this have to do with a body found frozen in the ice high up in the Alps?

To a family of ruthless French arms dealers, the Lost City is the key to world domination. To Kurt Austin, leader of NUMA's Special Assignments Team, and his colleague Joe Zavala, it's clear they have their work cut out for them. But this job may be even bigger than they think—in fact, it may be their greatest, and deadliest, challenge of all . . .

continued . . .

PRAISE FOR
CLIVE CUSSLER

"PURE ENTERTAINMENT . . . as reliable as Pitt's trusty Colt .45."
—*People*

"CLIVE CUSSLER HAS NO EQUAL."
—*Publishers Weekly*

"PURE CUSSLER, PURE FUN. The action just keeps accelerating."
—*The San Francisco Examiner*

"FULL OF ACTION, INTRIGUE, AND BEAUTIFUL WOMEN."
—*San Antonio Express-News*

"Nobody does it better than Clive Cussler. NOBODY!"
—Stephen Coonts

PRAISE FOR
CLIVE CUSSLER'S NUMA® SERIES

"A SPINE-TINGLING ADVENTURE ON THE HIGH SEAS."
—*Chicago Tribune*

"Cussler twists fact and fiction into a rope of tension that WILL LEAVE YOU DANGLING UNTIL THE LAST PAGE."
—*Tulsa World*

"ACTION-FUELED, RIP-ROARING . . . A roiling stew of seafaring adventure [and] cutting-edge science."
—*Publishers Weekly*

"MARVELOUS . . . simply terrific fun." —*Kirkus Reviews*

"YOU CAN'T GET MUCH MORE SATISFYING."
—*The Cleveland Plain Dealer*

"Audacious and WILDLY ENTERTAINING."
—*New York Daily News*

PRAISE FOR

CLIVE CUSSLER'S DIRK PITT® SERIES

VALHALLA RISING

"[A] NONSTOP THRILLER . . . CUSSLER SPEEDS AND TWISTS through the complex plot and hairbreadth escapes [with] the intensity and suspense of a NASCAR race."

—*Publishers Weekly*

"ACTION-FILLED ADVENTURE . . . GREAT FUN."

—*Library Journal*

"CLIVE CUSSLER . . . IS AT TOP FORM HERE."

—*Kirkus Reviews*

ATLANTIS FOUND

"A DELIGHTFUL PAGE-TURNER that is almost impossible to put down." —*The San Francisco Examiner*

"WICKEDLY ENGROSSING." —*Publishers Weekly*

"BY FAR THE BEST. *Atlantis Found* has wonderful characters and a plot that speeds along like a comet."

—*Tulsa World*

"THE FUNNEST DIRK PITT ADVENTURE SINCE *RAISE THE TITANIC!*." —*Rocky Mountain News*

"ENOUGH INTRIGUE TO SATISFY EVEN THE MOST DEMANDING THRILL-SEEKERS . . . An entertaining and exciting saga, full of techno details and narrow escapes." —*The Chattanooga Times*

Dirk Pitt® Adventures by Clive Cussler

TROJAN ODYSSEY
VALHALLA RISING
ATLANTIS FOUND
FLOOD TIDE
SHOCK WAVE
INCA GOLD
SAHARA
DRAGON
TREASURE
CYCLOPS
DEEP SIX
PACIFIC VORTEX
NIGHT PROBE
VIXEN 03
RAISE THE *TITANIC*!
ICEBERG
THE MEDITERRANEAN CAPER

Fiction by Clive Cussler with Paul Kemprecos

LOST CITY
WHITE DEATH
FIRE ICE
SERPENT
BLUE GOLD

Fiction by Clive Cussler and Craig Dirgo

SACRED STONE
GOLDEN BUDDHA

Nonfiction by Clive Cussler and Craig Dirgo

THE SEA HUNTERS II
THE SEA HUNTERS
CLIVE CUSSLER AND DIRK PITT REVEALED

LOST

A NOVEL FROM
THE NUMA® FILES

BERKLEY BOOKS • NEW YORK

CITY

CLIVE
CUSSLER
WITH PAUL KEMPRECOS

THE BERKLEY PUBLISHING GROUP
Published by the Penguin Group
Penguin Group (USA) Inc.
375 Hudson Street, New York, New York 10014, USA
Penguin Group (Canada), 10 Alcorn Avenue, Toronto, Ontario M4V 3B2, Canada
(a division of Pearson Penguin Canada Inc.)
Penguin Books Ltd., 80 Strand, London WC2R 0RL, England
Penguin Group Ireland, 25 St. Stephen's Green, Dublin 2, Ireland (a division of Penguin Books Ltd.)
Penguin Group (Australia), 250 Camberwell Road, Camberwell, Victoria 3124, Australia
(a division of Pearson Australia Group Pty. Ltd.)
Penguin Books India Pvt. Ltd., 11 Community Centre, Panchsheel Park, New Delhi—110 017, India
Penguin Group (NZ), Cnr. Airborne and Rosedale Roads, Albany, Auckland 1310, New Zealand
(a division of Pearson New Zealand Ltd.)
Penguin Books (South Africa) (Pty.) Ltd., 24 Sturdee Avenue, Rosebank, Johannesburg 2196,
South Africa

Penguin Books Ltd., Registered Offices: 80 Strand, London WC2R 0RL, England

This is a work of fiction. Names, characters, places, and incidents either are the product of the author's imagination or are used fictitiously, and any resemblance to actual persons, living or dead, business establishments, events, or locales is entirely coincidental.

LOST CITY

A Berkley Book / published by arrangement with Sandecker, RLLLP

PRINTING HISTORY
G. P. Putnam's Sons hardcover edition / July 2004
Berkley international edition / March 2005

Copyright © 2004 by Sandecker, RLLLP.
Cover design © 2004 by Lawrence Ratzkin.
Cover illustration © 2004 by Craig White.

All rights reserved.
No part of this book may be reproduced, scanned, or distributed in any printed or electronic form without permission. Please do not participate in or encourage piracy of copyrighted materials in violation of the author's rights. Purchase only authorized editions.
For information, address: The Berkley Publishing Group,
a division of Penguin Group (USA) Inc.,
375 Hudson Street, New York, New York 10014.

ISBN: 0-425-20364-6

BERKLEY®
Berkley Books are published by The Berkley Publishing Group,
a division of Penguin Group (USA) Inc.,
375 Hudson Street, New York, New York 10014.
BERKLEY is a registered trademark of Penguin Group (USA) Inc.
The "B" design is a trademark belonging to Penguin Group (USA) Inc.

PRINTED IN THE UNITED STATES OF AMERICA

10 9 8 7 6 5 4 3 2

If you purchased this book without a cover, you should be aware that this book is stolen property. It was reported as "unsold and destroyed" to the publisher, and neither the author nor the publisher has received any payment for this "stripped book."

Acknowledgments

Many thanks to Neal Iverson, associate professor of geology and atmospheric sciences at Iowa State University, for his guided tour of the Svartisen, Norway, subglacial observatory. The books of H. Rider Haggard and Ben Bova provided unique perspectives on the implications of immortality. And a thank-you is in order as well to the SEAmagine Hydrospace Corporation for the use of its remarkable SEAmobile.

PROLOGUE

THE FRENCH ALPS, AUGUST 1914

HIGH ABOVE the soaring majesty of the snow-capped mountains, Jules Fauchard was fighting for his life. Minutes before, his plane had slammed into an invisible wall of air with a force that jarred his teeth. Now updrafts and downdrafts were tossing the light aircraft about like a kite on a string. Fauchard battled the gut-wrenching turbulence with the skill that had been drilled into him by his strict French flying instructors. Then he was through the rough patch, luxuriating in smooth air, unaware that it would nearly prove his undoing.

With his plane finally stable, Fauchard had given in to the most natural of human impulses. He closed his weary eyes. His eyelids fluttered and drooped, then slammed shut as if weighted down with lead. His mind drifted into a shadowy, uncaring realm. His chin slumped onto his chest. His limp fingers relaxed their grip on the control stick. The diminutive red plane wavered drunkenly in what the French pilots called a *perte de vitesse*, or loss of way, as it slipped off on one wing in a prelude to a tailspin.

Fortunately, Fauchard's inner ear detected the change in equilibrium, and alarms went off in his slumbering brain. His head snapped up and he awakened in a daze, struggling to marshal his muddled thoughts. His nap had lasted only a few seconds, but in that time his plane had lost hundreds of feet of altitude and was about to go into a steep dive. Blood thundered in his head. His wildly beating heart felt as if it were about to explode from his chest.

The French flying schools taught student pilots to fly an airplane with the same light touch as a pianist's on the keys, and Fauchard's endless hours of drill proved their worth now. Using a feather touch on the controls, he made sure not to overcompensate and gently coaxed the plane back on an even keel. Satisfied that the plane was stabilized, he let out the breath he had been holding and gulped in air, the arctic cold striking his lungs like shards of glass.

The sharp pain jolted him from his lethargy. Fully awake again, Fauchard summoned up the mantra that had sustained his resolve throughout his desperate mission. His frozen lips refused to wrap themselves around the syllables, but the words screamed in his brain.

Fail, and millions die.

Fauchard clamped his jaws shut with renewed determination. He rubbed the frost from his goggles and peered over the cockpit cowling. The alpine air was as clear as fine crystal, and even the most distant detail stood out in sharp relief. Ranks of saw-toothed mountains marched off to the horizon, and miniature villages clung to the sides of verdant alpine valleys. Fluffy white clouds were stacked up like piles of newly picked cotton. The sky was luminous in its blue intensity. The summer snow capping the jagged summits was bathed in a soft sky-blue pink from the lowering sun.

Fauchard filled his red-rimmed eyes with the magnificent beauty, as he cocked his ear and listened to the exhaust sound produced by the eighty-horsepower, four-stroke Gnome rotary engine that powered the Morane-Saulnier N aircraft. All was well. The engine droned on as it had before his near-fatal nap. Fauchard was reassured, but his close call had shaken his self-confidence. He realized, to his astonishment, that he had experienced an unfamiliar emotion. *Fear.* Not of death, but of failure. Despite his iron resolve, his aching muscles further reminded him that he was a man of flesh and blood like any other.

The open cockpit allowed for little movement and his body was encased in a fur-lined leather coat over a thick Shetland wool sweater, turtleneck and long underwear. A woolen scarf protected his neck. A leather helmet covered his head and ears, and his hands were enclosed in insulated leather gloves. Fur-lined mountain climber boots of the finest leather were on his feet. Although he was dressed for polar conditions, the icy cold had penetrated to his bones and dulled the edge of his alertness. This was a dangerous development. The Morane-Saulnier was tricky to fly and required undivided attention.

In the face of the gnawing fatigue, Fauchard clung to his sanity with the single-minded stubbornness that had made him into one of the richest industrialists in the world. Fierce determination still showed in his flinty gray eyes and the stubborn tilt of his craggy chin. With his long aquiline nose, Fauchard's profile resembled that of the eagles whose heads graced the family crest on the plane's tail.

He forced his numbed lips to move.

Fail, and millions die.

The stentorian voice that had struck fear in the European halls of power emerged from his throat as a croak, the pitiful sound drowned out by the engine's roar and the rush of air past the fuselage, but Fauchard decided a reward was in order. He reached into the top of his boot and extracted a slim silver flask. He unscrewed the top with difficulty because of the thick gloves, and took a pull from the flask. The high-octane schnapps was made from grapes grown on his estate and was almost pure alcohol. Warmth flooded through his body.

Thus fortified, he rocked in his seat, wiggled his toes and fingers and hunched his shoulders. As the blood flowed back into his extremities, he thought of the hot Swiss chocolate and fresh-baked bread with melted cheese that awaited him on the other side of the mountains. The thick lips under the bushy handlebar mustache tightened in an ironic smile. He was one of the wealthiest men in the world, yet he was cheered by the prospect of a plowman's meal. So be it.

Fauchard allowed himself an instant of self-congratulation. He was a meticulous man and his escape plan had gone off like clockwork. The family had placed a watch on him after he had made his unwelcome views clear before the council. But while the council had pondered his fate, he'd evaded the watchers with a combination of diversion and luck.

He'd pretended to drink too much and told his butler, who was in the pay of his family, that he was going to bed. When all was quiet, he had quietly left his bedroom chamber, slipped out of the château and made his way to where a bicycle was hidden in the woods. Carrying his precious cargo in a backpack, he had ridden through the woods to the airfield. His plane was fueled and ready to go. He had taken off in the dawn's light, stopping twice at remote locations where his most loyal retainers had stockpiled fuel.

He drained the flask and glanced at the compass and clock. He was on course and only minutes behind schedule. The lower peaks ahead indicated that he was nearing the end of his long journey. Soon he would make the final approach to Zurich.

He was thinking about what he would say to the pope's emissary when it seemed as if a flight of startled birds took off from the starboard wing. He glanced to the right and saw, to his dismay, that the birds were actually shreds of fabric that had peeled off the airfoil, leaving a ragged hole several inches across. There could be only one explanation. The wing had been hit by gunfire, and the high-pitched roar of the engine had drowned out the noise.

Reacting instinctively, Fauchard banked the plane left, then right, twisting and turning like a swallow in flight. As his eyes scoured the skies, he glimpsed six biplanes flying in V formation below him. With uncanny calm, Fauchard switched off his engine as if he were preparing to volplane to the ground in an unpowered landing.

The Morane-Saulnier dropped like a stone.

Under ordinary circumstances, this would have been suicidal, placing him in his adversary's gunsights. But Fauchard had recognized the attacking planes as Aviatiks. The German-built plane of French design was powered by a Mercedes in-line engine and had originally been built for reconnaissance. More important, the machine gun mounted in front of the gunner could fire only upward.

After a fall of a few hundred feet, he gently adjusted the elevator and his plane came up behind the Aviatik formation.

He lined up his plane's nose on the closest Aviatik and squeezed the trigger. The Hotchkiss gun rattled and tracer bullets homed in on the target's tail. Smoke poured from the plane and then flames enveloped the fuselage.

The Aviatik began a long spiraling plunge to earth. A few well-placed volleys brought down another Aviatik as easily as a hunter bagging a tame pheasant.

Fauchard accomplished the kills so swiftly that the other pilots were unaware they were under attack until they saw the greasy black smoke trails from the plummeting planes. The precise formation began to come apart at the seams.

Fauchard broke off the attack. His targets were scattered and the element of surprise was no longer on his side. Instead, he put the Morane-Saulnier into a steep thousand-foot climb into the belly of a puffy cloud.

As the misty gray walls hid his plane from unfriendly eyes, Fauchard leveled off and performed a damage check. So much fabric had ripped off that the wooden ribs of the wing were exposed. Fauchard cursed under his breath. He had hoped to bolt from the cloud and outdistance the Aviatiks with his plane's superior speed, but the damaged wing was slowing him down.

Unable to run, he would have to stay and fight.

Fauchard was outgunned and outnumbered, but he was flying one of the most remarkable aircraft of its day. Developed from a racing plane, the Morane-Saulnier, though tricky to fly, was incredibly nimble and responsive to the lightest touch. In an era when most airplanes had at least two wings, the Morane-Saulnier was a midwinged monoplane. From the bullet-shaped propeller spinner to its triangular tail fin, the Morane-Saulnier was only twenty-two feet long, but it was a deadly gnat by any measure, thanks to a device that would revolutionize aerial warfare.

Saulnier had developed a synchronizing mechanism that allowed the machine gun to fire through the propeller. The system had outpaced the newfangled guns, though, which sometimes fired erratically, and since ammunition could hang fire, metal deflectors shielded the propeller blades from errant bullets.

Girding himself for battle, Fauchard reached under the seat and his fingers touched the cold metal of a strongbox. Next to the box was a purple velvet bag, which he pulled out and placed on his lap. Steering the plane with his knees, he extracted a steel helmet of ancient design from the bag and ran his fingers over the engraved surface. The metal was ice-cold to the touch, but heat seemed to radiate from it, surging through his whole body.

He placed the helmet on his head. It fit snugly over the leather covering, and was perfectly balanced. The helmet was unusual, in that its visor was made in the form of a human face whose mustache and raptor's nose resembled Fauchard's. The visor limited his visibility and he pushed it up above his brow.

Shafts of sunlight were filtering into the cloud dungeon as his cover thinned. He flew through the smoky wisps that marked the edge of the cloud and broke into full daylight.

The Aviatiks were circling below like a school of hungry sharks around a sinking ship. They spotted the Morane and began to climb.

The lead Aviatik slipped below Fauchard's plane and moved into firing range. Fauchard gave a sharp tug on his seat belt to make sure it was tight, and then he pulled the nose of his plane upward, climbing in a great backward loop.

He hung upside down in the cockpit, giving thanks to the French instructor who had taught him the evasive maneuver. He completed the loop and leveled out, placing his plane behind the Aviatiks. He opened fire on the nearest plane, but it peeled off and dove at a steep angle.

Fauchard stayed on the plane's tail, enjoying the thrill of being the hunter rather than the prey. The Aviatik leveled out and made a tight turn, trying to get behind Fauchard. The smaller plane easily matched him.

The Aviatik's move had put it at the mouth of a wide valley. With Fauchard giving the plane little room to maneuver, it flew directly into the valley.

Hoarding his ammunition like a miser, Fauchard fired short bursts from the Hotchkiss. The Aviatik rolled left and right and the tracers went to either side of the plane. It flew lower, trying to stay below Fauchard and his deadly machine gun. Again, Fauchard tried to line up a shot. Again, the Aviatik went lower.

The planes skimmed over the fields at a hundred miles an hour, staying barely fifty feet above the ground. Herds of terrified cows scattered like windblown leaves. The twisting Aviatik managed to stay out of Fauchard's sights. The rolling contours of the ground compounded the difficulty of a clear shot.

The landscape was a blur of rolling meadows and neat farmhouses. The farms were growing closer together. Fauchard could see the roofs of a town ahead where the valley narrowed to a point.

The Aviatik was following a meandering river that ran up the center of the valley directly toward the town. The pilot flew so low his wheels almost touched the water. Ahead, a quaint fieldstone bridge crossed the river as the waterway entered the town.

Fauchard's finger was tightening on the trigger, when an overhead shadow broke his concentration. He glanced upward and saw the wheels and fuselage of another Aviatik less than fifty feet above. It dropped lower, trying to force him down. He glanced at the lead Aviatik. It had started its climb to avoid hitting the bridge.

Pedestrians crossing the span had seen the trio of advancing planes and were running for their lives. The sleepy old plow horse pulling a wagon across the bridge reared up on its hind legs for the first time in years as the Aviatik skimmed a few yards over the driver's head.

The overhead plane dropped down to force Fauchard into the bridge, but at the last second he pulled back on his control stick and goosed the throttle. The Morane-Saulnier leaped upward and carried him between the bridge and the Aviatik. There was a huge explosion of hay as the plane's wheels clipped the wagon's load, but Fauchard kept his plane under control, guiding it up over the roofs of the town.

The plane on Fauchard's tail pulled up a second later.

Too late.

Less agile than the monoplane, the Aviatik smashed into the bridge and exploded in a ball of fire. Equally slow to climb, the lead Aviatik grazed a church steeple whose sharp spire gutted its belly. The plane came apart in the air and broke into a hundred pieces.

"Go with God!" Fauchard shouted hoarsely, as he wheeled his plane around and pointed it out of the valley.

Two specks appeared in the distance. Moving fast in his direction. They materialized into the last of the Aviatik squadron.

Fauchard aimed his plane directly between the approaching aircraft. His lips tightened in a grin. He wanted to make sure the family knew what he thought of their attempt to stop him.

He was close enough to see the observers in the front cockpits. The one on his left pointed what looked like a stick, and he saw a flash of light.

He heard a soft *tunk* and his rib cage felt as if a fiery poker had been thrust into it. With a chill, he realized that the observer in the Aviatik had resorted to simpler but more reliable technology—he had fired at Fauchard with a carbine.

He involuntarily jerked the control stick and his legs stiffened in a spasm. The planes flashed by on either side of him. His hand went limp on the control stick and the plane began to waver. Warm blood from his wound puddled in his seat. His mouth had a coppery taste and he was having trouble keeping things in focus.

He removed his gloves, unbuckled his seat belt and reached down under his seat. His weakening fingers grasped the handle of the metal strongbox. He placed it on his lap, took the V strap that ran through the handle and attached it to his wrist.

Summoning his last remaining reservoir of strength, he pushed himself erect and leaned out of the cockpit. He rolled over the coaming, his body hit the wing and bounced off.

His fingers automatically yanked the ripcord, the cushion he'd been sitting on burst open, and a silk parachute caught the air.

A curtain of blackness was falling over his eyes. He caught glimpses of a cold blue lake and a glacier.

I have failed.

He was more in shock than pain and felt only a profound and angry sadness.

Millions will die.

He coughed a mouthful of bloody froth and then he knew no more. He hung in his parachute harness, an easy target for one of the Aviatiks as it made another pass.

He never felt the bullet that crashed through his helmet and drilled into his skull.

With the sun glinting off his helmet, he floated lower until the mountains embraced him to their bosom.

1

THE SCOTTISH ORKNEYS, THE PRESENT

JODIE MICHAELSON was steaming with anger. Earlier in the evening, she and the three remaining contestants of the *Outcasts* TV show had had to walk in their heavy boots on a thick rope stretched out along a three-foot-high berm made of piled rocks. The stunt had been billed as the "Viking Trial by Fire." Rows of torches blazed away on either side of the rope, adding drama and risk, although the line of fire was actually six feet away. The cameras shot from a low side angle, making the walk seem much more dangerous than it was.

What wasn't phony was the way the producers had schemed to bring the contestants to near violence.

Outcasts was the latest offering in the "reality" shows that had popped up like mushrooms after the success of *Survivor* and *Fear Factor.* It was an accelerated combination of both formats, with the shouting matches of *Jerry Springer* thrown in.

The format was simple. Ten participants had to pass a gamut of tests over the course of three weeks. Those who failed, or were voted off by the others, had to leave the island.

The winner would make a million dollars, with bonus points, which seemed to be based on how nasty the contestants could be to one another.

The show was considered even more cutthroat than its predecessors, and the producers played tricks to ratchet up the tension. Where other shows were highly competitive, *Outcasts* was openly combative.

The show's format had been based in part on the Outward Bound survival course, where a participant must live off the land. Unlike the other survival shows, which tended to be set on tropical isles with turquoise waters and swaying palm trees, *Outcasts* was filmed in the Scottish Orkneys. The contestants had landed in a tacky replica of a Viking ship, to an audience of seabirds.

The island was two miles long and a mile wide. It was mostly rock that had been tortured into knobs and fissures aeons ago by some cataclysm, with a few stands of scraggly trees here and there and a beach of coarse sand where most of the action was filmed. The weather was mild, except at night, and the skin-covered huts were tolerable.

The speck of rock was so insignificant that the locals referred to it as the "Wee Island." This had prompted a hilarious exchange between the producer, Sy Paris, and his assistant, Randy Andleman.

Paris was in one of his typical raves. "We can't film an adventure show on a place called 'Wee Island,' for godsakes. We've got to call it something else." His face lit up. "We'll call it 'Skull Island.' "

"It doesn't look like a skull," Andleman said. "It looks like an overdone fried egg."

"Close enough," Paris had said, before dashing off.

Jodie, who had witnessed the exchange, elicited a smile from Andleman when she said, "I think it rather resembles the skull of a dumb TV series producer."

The tests were basically the kind of gross-out stunts, such as ripping live crabs apart and eating them or diving into a tank full of eels, that were guaranteed to make the viewer gag and watch the next installment, to see how bad things would get. Some of the contestants seemed to have been chosen for their aggressiveness and general meanness.

The climax would come when the last two contestants spent the night hunting each other using nightscopes and paint-ball guns, a stunt that was based on the short story "The Most Dangerous Game." The survivor was awarded another million dollars.

Jodie was a physical fitness teacher from Orange County, California. She had a killer body in a bikini, although her curves were wasted under her down-filled clothes. She had long, blond hair and a quick intelligence that she had hid to get on the program. Every contestant was typecast, but Jodie refused to play the bimbo role the producers had assigned to her.

In the last quiz for points and demerits, she and the others had been asked whether a conch was a fish, a mollusk or a car. As the show's stereotype blonde, she was supposed to say "Car."

Jeezus, she'd never live something like that down when she got back to civilization.

Since the quiz debacle, the producers had been making strong hints that she should go. She'd given them their chance to oust her when a cinder got in her eye and she'd failed the fire walk. The remaining members of the tribe had gathered around the fire with grave looks on their faces, and Sy Paris had dramatically intoned the order to leave the clan and make her entry into Valhalla. *Jeezus*.

As she headed away from the campfire now, she fumed at herself for failing the test. But there was still a bounce to her step. After only a few weeks with these lunatics, she was glad to be off the island. It was a rugged, beautiful setting, but she had grown weary of the backbiting, the manipulation and general sneakiness in which a contestant had to indulge for the dubious honor of being hunted down like a rabid dog.

Beyond the "Gate to Valhalla," an arbor made of plastic

whalebones, was a large house trailer that was the quarters for the production crew. While the clan members slept in skin tents and ate bugs, the crew enjoyed heat, comfortable cots and gourmet meals. Once a contestant was thrown out of the game, he or she spent the night in the trailer until a helicopter picked him or her up the next morning.

"Tough luck," said Andleman, who met her at the door. Andleman was a sweetheart, the complete opposite of his hard-driving boss.

"Yeah, *real* tough. Hot showers. Hot meals. Cell phones."

"Hell, we've got all that right here."

She glanced around at the comfortable accommodations. "So I noticed."

"That's your bunk over there," he said. "Make yourself a drink from the bar, and there's some terrific paté in the fridge that'll help you decompress. I've got to go give Sy a hand. Knock yourself out."

"Thanks, I will."

She went over to the bar and made herself a tall Beefeater martini, straight up. The paté was as delicious as advertised. She was looking forward to going home. The ex-contestants always made the rounds of the TV talk shows to rake over the people they'd left behind. Easy money. She stretched out in a comfortable chair. After a few minutes, the alcohol put her to sleep.

She awoke with a start. In her sleep, she had heard high-pitched screams like the sound of seabirds flocking or children in a playground, against a background of yells and shouts.

Peculiar.

She got up, went to the door and listened. She wondered if Sy had come up with yet another means of humiliation. Maybe he had the others doing a wild savage dance around the fire.

She walked briskly along the path that led to the beach. The noise grew louder, more frantic. Something was dreadfully wrong. These were screams of fright and pain rather than excitement. She picked up her pace and burst through the Gate to Valhalla. What she saw looked like a scene from a Hieronymus Bosch depiction of Hell.

The cast and crew were under attack by hideous creatures that seemed half man, half animal. The savage attackers were snarling, pulling their victims down and tearing at them with claws and teeth.

She saw Sy fall, then Randy. She recognized several bodies that were lying bloody and mauled on the beach.

In the flickering light from the fire, Jodie saw that the attackers had long, filthy white hair down to their shoulders. The faces were like nothing she had ever seen. Ghastly, twisted masks.

One creature clutched a severed arm which he was raising to his mouth. Jodie couldn't help herself, she screamed . . . and the other creatures broke off their ungodly feast and looked at her with burning eyes that glowed a luminous red.

She wanted to vomit, but they were coming toward her in a crouching lope.

She ran for her life.

Her first thought was the trailer, but she had enough presence of mind to know she'd be trapped there.

She ran for the high rocky ground, the creatures snuffing behind her like bloodhounds. In the dark, she lost her footing and fell into a fissure, but unknown to her the accident saved her life. Her pursuers lost her scent.

Jodie had cracked her head in the fall. She regained consciousness once, and thought she heard harsh voices and gunshots. Then she passed out again.

She was still lying unconscious in the fissure the next morning when the helicopter arrived. By the time the crew had scoured the island and finally found Jodie, they had come to a startling discovery.

Everyone else had vanished.

2

MONEMVASSIA, THE GREEK PELOPONNESE

IN HIS RECURRING nightmare, Angus MacLean was a staked goat being stalked by a hungry tiger whose yellow eyes stared at him from the jungle shadows. The low growls gradually grew louder until they filled his ears. Then the tiger lunged. He could smell its fetid breath, feel its sharp fangs sinking into his neck. He strained at his collar in a futile attempt to escape. His pathetic, terrified bleating changed to a desperate moan . . . and he awakened in a cold sweat, his chest heaving, and his rumpled blankets damp from perspiration.

MacLean stumbled out of his narrow bed and threw open the shutters. The Greek sunlight flooded the white-washed walls of what had been a monk's cell. He pulled on shorts and a T-shirt, slipped into his walking sandals and stepped outside, blinking his eyes against the shimmer of the sapphire sea. The hammering of his heart subsided.

He took a deep breath, inhaling the perfumelike fragrance of the wildflowers that surrounded the two-story stucco monastery. He waited until his hands stopped shaking, then he set off on the morning hike that had proven to be the best antidote for his shattered nerves.

The monastery was built in the shadow of a massive rock, hundreds of feet high, that tour books often referred to as "the Gibraltar of Greece." To reach the summit, he climbed along a path that ran along the top of an ancient wall. Centuries before, the inhabitants of the lower town would retreat to the ramparts to defend themselves from invaders. Only ruins remained of the village that had once housed the entire population in times of siege.

From atop the lofty perch offered by the crumbling foundation of an old Byzantine church, MacLean could see for miles. A few colorful fishing boats were at work. All was seemingly tranquil. MacLean knew that his morning ritual gave him a false sense of security. The people hunting him would not reveal themselves until they killed him.

He prowled among the ruins like a homeless spirit, then descended the wall and made his way back to the monastery's second-floor dining room. The fifteenth-century monastery was one of the traditional buildings the Greek government operated as guesthouses around the country. MacLean made a point of arriving for breakfast after all the other guests had left to go sightseeing.

The young man cleaning up in the kitchen smiled and said, "*Kali mera*, Dr. MacLean."

"*Kali mera*, Angelo," MacLean replied. He tapped his head with his forefinger. "Did you forget?"

Light dawned in Angelo's eyes. "Yes. I'm very sorry. *Mr.* MacLean."

"That's quite all right. Sorry to burden you with my strange requests," MacLean said in his soft Scottish brogue. "But as I said before, I don't want people thinking I can cure their upset stomachs and stomachaches."

"*Neh.* Yes, of course, *Mr.* MacLean. I understand."

Angelo brought over a bowl of fresh strawberries, honeydew melon and creamy Greek yogurt, topped with local honey and walnuts, and a cup of thick black coffee. Angelo was the young monk who served as resident hostler. He was in his early thirties, with dark curly hair and a handsome face that was usually wreathed in a beatific smile. He was a combination concierge, caretaker, chef and host. He wore ordinary work clothes and the only hint of his vows was the rope tied loosely around his waist.

The two men had struck up a strong friendship in the weeks MacLean had been a guest. Each day, after Angelo finished his breakfast work, they would talk about their shared interest, Byzantine civilization.

MacLean had drifted into historical studies as a diversion from his intense work as a research chemist. Years ago his studies had taken him to Mystra, once the center of the Byzantine world. He had drifted down the Peloponnese and stumbled upon Monemvassia. A narrow causeway flanked by the sea was the only access to the village, a maze of narrow streets and alleys on the other side of the wall whose "one gate" gave Monemvassia its name. MacLean had fallen under the spell of the beautiful place. He vowed to return one day, never thinking that when he came back he'd be running for his life.

The Project had been so innocent at first. MacLean had been teaching advanced chemistry at Edinburgh University when he was offered a dream job doing the pure research that he loved. He'd accepted the position and taken a leave of absence. He threw himself into the work, willing to endure the long hours and intense secrecy. He led one of several teams that were working on enzymes, the complex proteins that produce biochemical reactions.

The Project scientists were cloistered in comfortable dormitories in the French countryside, and had little contact with the outside world. One colleague had jokingly referred to their research as the "Manhattan Project." The isolation posed no problem for MacLean, who was a bachelor with no close relatives. Few of his colleagues complained. The astronomical pay and excellent working conditions were ample compensation.

Then the Project took a disturbing turn. When MacLean and the others raised questions, they were told not to worry. Instead, they were sent home and told just to wait until the results of their work were analyzed.

MacLean had gone to Turkey instead, to explore ruins. When he'd returned to Scotland several weeks later, his answering machine had recorded several hang-ups and a strange telephone message from a former colleague. The scientist asked if MacLean had been reading the papers and urged him to call back. MacLean tried to reach the man, only to learn that he had been killed several days before in a hit-and-run accident.

Later, when MacLean was going through his mail pile, he found a packet the scientist had sent before his death. The thick envelope was stuffed with newspaper clips that described a series of accidental deaths. As MacLean read the clips, a shiver ran down his spine. The victims were all scientists who had worked with him on the Project.

Scrawled on an enclosed note was the terse warning: "Flee or die!"

MacLean wanted to believe the accidents were coincidental, even though it went against his scientific instincts. Then, a few days after he read the clips, a truck tried to run his Mini Cooper off the road. Miraculously, he escaped with only a few scratches. But he'd recognized the truck driver as one of the silent guards who had watched over the scientists at the laboratory.

What a fool he had been.

MacLean knew he had to flee. *But where?* Monemvassia had come to mind. It was a popular vacation spot for mainland Greeks. Most of the foreigners who visited the rock came for day trips only. And now here he was.

While MacLean was pondering the events that had brought him there, Angelo came over with a copy of the *International Herald Tribune*. The monk had to run errands but he would be back in an hour. MacLean nodded and sipped his coffee, savoring the strong dark taste. He skimmed the usual news of economic and political crises.

And then his eye caught a headline in the international news briefs:

SURVIVOR SAYS MONSTERS
KILLED TV CAST, CREW

The dateline was a Scottish island in the Orkneys. Intrigued, he read the story. It was only a few paragraphs long, but when he was done, his hands were shaking. He read the article again until the words blurred.

Dear God, he thought. *Something awful has happened.*

He folded the newspaper and went outside, stood in the soothing sunlight and made a decision. He would return home and see if he could get someone to believe his story.

MacLean walked to the city gate and caught a taxi to the ferry office on the causeway, where he bought a ticket for the hydrofoil to Athens the next day. Then he returned to his room and packed his few belongings. What now? He decided to stick to his usual routine for his last day, walked to an outdoor café and ordered a tall glass of cold *limonade.* He was engrossed in his paper when he became aware that someone was talking to him.

He looked up and saw a gray-haired woman in flowered polyester slacks and blouse standing next to his table, holding a camera.

"Sorry to interrupt," she said with a sweet smile. "Would you mind? My husband and I—"

Tourists often asked MacLean to document their trips. He was tall and lanky, and with his blue eyes and shock of salt-and-pepper hair, he stood out from the shorter and darker Greeks.

A man sat at a nearby table, giving MacLean a buck-toothed grin. His freckled face was beet-red from too much sun. MacLean nodded and took the camera from the woman's hand. He clicked off some shots of the couple and handed the camera back.

"Thank you so much!" the woman said effusively. "You don't know what it means to have this for our travel album."

"Americans?" MacLean said. His urge to talk English overcame his reluctance to engage anyone in conversation. Angelo's English skills were limited.

The woman beamed. "Is it *that* obvious? We try so hard to fit in."

Yellow-and-pink polyester was decidedly not a Greek fashion statement, MacLean thought. The woman's husband was wearing a collarless white cotton shirt and black captain's hat like those sold mainly for the tourist trade.

"Came down in the hydrofoil," the man said with a drawl, rising out of his chair. He pressed his moist palm into MacLean's. "Hell, that was some ride. You English?"

MacLean responded with a look of horror.

"Oh no, I'm Scottish."

"I'm one-half Scotch and the other half soda," the man said with his horse grin. "Sorry about the mix-up. I'm from Texas. Guess that would be like you thinking we were from Oklahoma."

MacLean wondered why all the Texans he met talked as if everyone had a hearing problem. "I never would have thought that you were from Oklahoma," MacLean said. "Hope you have a nice visit."

He started to walk away, only to stop when the woman asked if her husband could take their picture together because he had been so kind to them. MacLean posed with the woman, then her husband.

"Thank you," the woman said. She spoke with a more refined air than her husband. In short order, MacLean learned that Gus and Emma Harris were from Houston, that Gus had been in the oil business, and she'd been a history teacher, fulfilling her lifelong dream to visit the Cradle of Civilization.

He shook hands, accepted their profuse thanks and set off along the narrow street. He walked fast, hoping they wouldn't be tempted to follow, and took a circuitous route back to the monastery.

MacLean closed the shutters so his room was dark and cool. He slept through the worst of the afternoon heat, then got up and splashed cold water on his face. He stepped outside for a breath of fresh air and was surprised to see the Harrises standing near the old whitewashed chapel in the monastery courtyard.

Gus and his wife were taking pictures of the monastery. They waved and smiled when they saw him, and MacLean went out and offered to show them his room. They were impressed by the workmanship in the dark wood paneling. Back outside again, they gazed up at the sheer cliffs behind the building.

"There must be a wonderful view from up there," Emma said.

"It's a bit of a hike to the top."

"I do a lot of bird-watching back home, so I'm pretty fit. Gus is in better shape than he looks." She smiled. "He used to be a football player, although it's hard to believe now."

"I'm an Aggie," Mr. Harris said. "Texas A and M. There's more of me now than there was back then. Tell you what, though, I'll give it a try."

"Do you think you could show us the way?" Emma asked MacLean.

"I'm sorry, I'm leaving on the hydrofoil first thing tomorrow." MacLean told them they might make the climb on their own if they got started early before the sun got too hot.

"You're a dear." She patted MacLean on the cheek in motherly fashion.

He was grinning, admiring their pluck as he watched them depart along the path that ran along the seawall in front of the monastery. They passed Angelo, who was coming back from town.

The monk greeted MacLean, then turned to look at the couple. "You have met the Americans from Texas?"

MacLean's grin turned to a puzzled frown. "How did you know who they were?"

"They came by yesterday morning. You were up there on your walk." He pointed to the old city.

"That's funny, they acted as if this was their first day here."

Angelo shrugged. "Maybe when we get old, we'll forget, too."

Suddenly, MacLean felt like the staked goat in his nightmare. A cold emptiness settled in his stomach. He excused himself and went back to his room, where he poured himself a stiff shot of ouzo.

How easy it would have been. They would have climbed to the top of the rock and asked him to pose for a photo near the edge. One shove and down he would go.

Another accident. Another dead scientist.

No heavy lifting. Not even for a sweet old history teacher.

He dug into the plastic bag he used for his dirty laundry. Buried at the bottom was the envelope full of yellowing newsclips, which he spread on the table.

The headlines were different, but the subject of each story was the same.

SCIENTIST DIES IN AUTO ACCIDENT. SCIENTIST KILLED IN HIT-AND-RUN. SCIENTIST KILLS WIFE, SELF. SCIENTIST DIES IN SKIING ACCIDENT.

Every one of the victims had worked on the Project. He reread the note: "Flee or die!" Then he put the *Herald Tribune* clip in with the others and went to the monastery's reception desk. Angelo was going through a pile of reservations.

"I must leave," MacLean said.

Angelo looked crestfallen. "I'm very sorry. How soon?"

"Tonight."

"*Impossible.* There is no hydrofoil or bus until tomorrow."

"Nevertheless, I must leave and I'm asking you to help me. I can make it worth your while."

A sad look came into the monk's eyes. "I would do this for friendship, not money."

"I'm sorry," MacLean said. "I'm a little upset."

Angelo was not an unintelligent man.

"This is because of the Americans?"

"Some bad people are after me. These Americans may have been sent to find me. I was stupid and told them I was going on the hydrofoil. I'm not sure if they came alone. They may have someone watching at the gate."

Angelo nodded. "I can take you to the mainland by boat. You will need a car."

"I was hoping you could arrange to rent one for me," MacLean said. He handed Angelo his credit card, which he had tried not to use before, knowing it could be traced.

Angelo called the car rental office on the mainland. He spoke a few minutes and hung up. "Everything is taken care of. They will leave the keys in the car."

"Angelo, I don't know how I can repay you."

"No payment. Give a big gift next time you're in church."

MacLean had a light dinner at a secluded café, where he found himself glancing with apprehension at the other tables. The evening passed without event. On the way back to the monastery, he kept looking over his shoulder.

The wait was agonizing. He felt trapped in his room, but he reminded himself that the walls were at least a foot thick and the door could withstand a battering ram. A few minutes after midnight, he heard a soft knock on the door.

Angelo took his bag and led the way along the seawall to a set of stairs that went down to a stone platform used by swimmers for diving. By the light of an electric torch, MacLean could see a small motorboat tied up to the platform. They got into the boat. Angelo was reaching for the mooring line when quiet footfalls could be heard on the steps.

"Out for a midnight cruise?" said the sweet voice of Emma Harris.

"You don't suppose Dr. MacLean was leaving without saying good-bye," her husband said.

After his initial surprise, MacLean found his tongue. "What happened to your Texas drawl, Mr. Harris?"

"Oh, *that.* Not very authentic, I must admit."

"Don't fret, dear. It was good enough to fool Dr. MacLean. Although I must admit that we had a little luck in completing our errand. We were sitting in that delightful little café when you happened by. It was nice of you to let us take your picture so we could check it against your file photo. We don't like to make mistakes."

Her husband gave an avuncular chuckle. "I remember saying, 'Step into my parlor . . .' "

" '. . . Said the spider to the fly.' "

They broke into laughter.

"You were sent by the company," MacLean said.

"They're very clever people," Gus said. "They knew you would be on the lookout for someone who looked like a gangster."

"It's a mistake a lot of people have made," Emma said, a sad note in her voice. "But it keeps us in business, doesn't it, Gus? Well. It was lovely traveling in Greece. But all good things must come to an end."

Angelo had listened to the conversation with a puzzled expression on his face. He was unaware of the danger they were in. Before MacLean could stop him, he reached over to untie the boat.

"Excuse us," he said. "We must go."

They were the last words he would ever utter.

There was the muffled *thut* of a silenced gun and a scarlet tongue of fire licked the darkness. Angelo clutched his chest and made a gurgling sound. Then he toppled from the boat into the water.

"Bad luck to shoot a monk, my dear," Gus said to his wife.

"He wasn't wearing his cassock," she said, with a pout in her voice. "How was I to know?"

Their voices were hard-edged and mocking.

"Come along, Dr. MacLean," Gus said. "We have a car waiting to take you to a company plane."

"You're not going to kill me?"

"Oh no," said Emma, again the innocent traveler. "There are other plans for you."

"I don't understand."

"You will, my dear. You will."

3

THE FRENCH ALPS

THE AEROSPATIALE ALOUETTE light utility helicopter threading its way through the deep alpine valleys appeared as insignificant as a gnat against the backdrop of towering peaks. As the helicopter approached a mountain whose summit was crowned with three uneven knobs, Hank Thurston, seated in the front passenger's seat, tapped the shoulder of the man sitting beside him and pointed through the canopy.

"That's *Le Dormeur*," Thurston said, raising his voice to be heard over the thrashing rotor blades. " 'The Sleeping Man.' The profile supposedly resembles the face of a sleeper lying on his back."

Thurston was a full professor of glaciology at Iowa State University. Although the scientist was in his forties, his face exuded a boyish enthusiasm. Back in Iowa, Thurston kept his face clean-shaven and his hair neatly trimmed, but after a few days in the field he began to look like a bush pilot. It was a look he cultivated by wearing aviator sunglasses, letting his dark brown hair grow long so gray strands would show and by shaving infrequently, so that his chin was usually covered with stubble.

"Poetic license," said the passenger, Derek Rawlins. "I can see the brow and the nose and chin. It reminds me of the Old Man of the Mountain in New Hampshire before it fell apart, except that the stone profile here is horizontal rather than vertical."

Rawlins was a writer for *Outside* magazine. He was in his late twenties, and with his air of earnest optimism and neatly trimmed sandy-blond hair and beard, he looked more like a college professor than Thurston did.

The crystal clarity of the air created an illusion of nearness, making the mountain seem as if it was only an arm's length away. After a couple of passes around the crags, the helicopter broke out of its lazy circle, scudded over a razorback ridge and dropped down into a natural bowl several miles across. The floor of the mountain basin was covered by an almost perfectly round lake. Although it was summer, ice cakes as big as Volkswagens floated on the mirrorlike surface.

"Lac du Dormeur," the professor said. "Carved out by a retreating glacier during the Ice Age and now fed by glacial waters."

"That's the biggest martini on the rocks I've ever seen," Rawlins said.

Thurston laughed. "It's as clear as gin, but you won't find any olive at the bottom. That big square structure built into the mountain off to the side of the glacier is the power plant. The nearest town is on the other side of the mountain range."

The aircraft passed over a wide, sturdy-looking vessel anchored near the shore of the lake. Cranes and booms protruded from the boat's deck.

"What's going on down there?" Rawlins said.

"Some sort of archaeological project," Thurston said. "The boat must have come up the river that drains the lake."

"I'll check it out later," Rawlins said. "Maybe I can pry

a raise out of my editor if I come back with two stories for the price of one." He glanced ahead at a wide ice floe that filled the gap between two mountains. "Wow! That must be our glacier."

"Yup. *La Langue du Dormeur*. 'The Sleeper's Tongue.' "

The helicopter made a pass over the river of ice that flowed down a wide valley to the lake. Rugged, snow-dusted foothills of black rock hemmed the glacier in on both sides, shaping it into a rounded point. The edges of the ice field were ragged where the flow encountered crevasses and ravines. The ice had a bluish tinge and was cracked along its surface like the parched tongue of a lost prospector.

Rawlins leaned forward for a better look. "The Sleeper should see a doctor. He's got a bad case of trench mouth."

"As you said, poetic license," Thurston said. "Hold on. We're about to land."

The helicopter darted over the leading edge of the glacier and the pilot put the aircraft into a slow banking turn. Moments later, the chopper's runners touched down on a brown grassy strip a couple of hundred feet from the lake.

Thurston helped the pilot unload a number of cartons from the helicopter and suggested that Rawlins stretch his legs. The reporter walked to the water's edge. The lake was unearthly in its stillness. No ripple of air disturbed the surface, which looked hard enough to walk across. He threw a stone to reassure himself that the lake wasn't frozen solid.

Rawlins's gaze shifted from the widening ripples to the boat anchored about a quarter mile from shore. He recognized the distinctive turquoise blue-green color of the hull immediately. He had encountered vessels of similar color while on writing assignments. Even without the letters numa painted in bold black letters on the hull, he would have known the boat belonged to the National Underwater and Marine Agency. He wondered what a NUMA vessel was doing in this remote place far from the nearest ocean.

There was definitely an unexpected story here, but it

would have to wait. Thurston was calling him. A battered Citroën 2C was hurtling toward the parked helicopter in a cloud of dust. The pint-sized auto skidded to a stop next to the chopper and a man who resembled a mountain troll emerged from the driver's side like a creature hatched from a deformed egg. He was short and dark-complexioned, with a black beard and long hair.

The man pumped Thurston's hand. "Wonderful to have you back, *Monsieur le professeur*. And you must be the journalist, Monsieur Rawlins. I am Bernard LeBlanc. Welcome."

"Thanks, Dr. LeBlanc," Rawlins said. "I've been looking forward to my visit. I can't wait to see the amazing work you're doing here."

"Come along then," LeBlanc said, snatching up the reporter's duffel bag. "Fifi awaits."

"Fifi?" Rawlins looked around as if he expected to see a dancer from the Follies Bergere.

Thurston irreverently jerked his thumb at the Citroën. "Fifi is the name of Bernie's car."

"And why shouldn't I give my car a woman's name?" LeBlanc said with a mock expression of pique. "She is faithful and hardworking. And beautiful in her own way."

"That's good enough for me," Rawlins said. He followed LeBlanc to the Citroën and got in the backseat. The boxes of supplies were secured to the roof rack. The other men got in the front and LeBlanc drove Fifi toward the base of the mountain that flanked the right side of the glacier. As the car began its ascent up a gravel road, the helicopter lifted off, gained altitude over the lake and disappeared behind the high ridge.

"You're familiar with the work being done at our subglacial observatory, Monsieur Rawlins?" LeBlanc said over his shoulder.

"Call me Deke. I've read the material. I know that your setup is similar to the Svartisen glacier in Norway."

"Correct," Thurston chimed in. "The Svartisen lab is seven hundred feet under the ice. We're closer to eight hundred. In both places, the melting glacier water is channeled into a turbine to produce hydroelectric power. When the engineers drilled the water conduits, they bored an extra tunnel under the glacier to house our observatory."

The car had entered a forest of stunted pine. LeBlanc drove along the narrow track with seemingly reckless abandon. The wheels were only inches from sheer drop-offs. As the incline became steeper, the Citroën's tiny workhorse of an engine began to wheeze.

"Sounds like Fifi is showing her age," Thurston said.

"It is her *heart* that is important," LeBlanc replied. Nevertheless, they were crawling at a tortoise pace when the road came to an end. They got out of the car and LeBlanc handed them each a shoulder harness, donning one himself. A box of supplies was strapped onto each harness.

Thurston apologized. "Sorry to recruit you as a Sherpa. We flew in supplies for the entire three weeks we're here, but we went through our *fromage* and *vin* faster than we expected and used the occasion of your visit to bring in more stuff."

"Not a problem," Rawlins said with a good-natured grin, expertly adjusting the weight so it rode easily on his shoulders. "I used to jackass supplies to the White Mountain huts in New Hampshire before I became an ink-stained hack."

LeBlanc led the way along a path that rose for about a hundred yards through scraggly pines. Above the tree line the ground hardened into flat expanses of rock. The rock was sprayed with daubs of yellow spray paint to mark the trail. Before long, the trail became steeper and smoother where the rocks had been buffed by thousands of years of glacial activity. Water from runoff made the hard surface slick and treacherous to navigate. From time to time they crossed crevasses filled with wet snow.

The reporter was huffing and puffing with exertion and altitude. He sighed with relief when they stopped at last on a shelf next to a wall of black rock that went up at an almost vertical angle. They were close to two thousand feet above the lake, which shimmered in the rays of the noonday sun. The glacier was out of sight around an escarpment, but Rawlins could feel the raw cold that it radiated, as if someone had left a refrigerator door open.

Thurston pointed to a round opening encased in concrete at the base of the vertical cliff. "Welcome to the Ice Palace."

"It looks like a drainage culvert," Rawlins said.

Thurston laughed and crouched low, ducking his head as he led the way into a corrugated metal tunnel about five feet in diameter. The others followed him in a stooping walk that was made necessary by their backpacks. The passage ended after about a hundred feet and opened into a dimly lit tunnel. The shiny wet orange walls of metamorphic rock were striped black with darker minerals.

Rawlins looked around in wonder. "You could drive a truck through this thing."

With room to spare. "It's thirty feet high and thirty feet wide," Thurston said.

"Too bad you couldn't squeeze Fifi through that culvert," Rawlins said.

"We've thought of it. There's an entrance big enough for a car near the power plant, but Bernie is afraid she'd get beat up running around these tunnels."

"Fifi has a very delicate constitution," LeBlanc said with a snort.

The Frenchman opened a plastic locker set against a wall. He passed around rubber boots and hard hats with miners' lights on the crowns.

Minutes later, they set off into the tunnel, the scuffle of their boots echoing off the walls. As they plodded along, Rawlins squinted into the gloom beyond the reach of his headlamp. "Not exactly the Great White Way."

"The power company put the lighting in when they drilled through. A lot of those dead bulbs haven't been replaced."

"You've probably been asked this, but what brought you into glaciology?" Rawlins said.

"That's not the first time I've heard the question. People think glaciologists are a bit odd. We study huge, ancient, slow-moving masses of ice that take centuries to get anywhere. Hardly a job for a grown man, wouldn't you say, Bernie?"

"Maybe not, but I met a nice Eskimo girl once in the Yukon."

"Spoken like a true glaciologist," Thurston said. "We have in common a love of beauty and a desire to get outdoors. Many of us were seduced into this calling by our first awe-inspiring view of an ice field." He gestured around at the walls of the tunnel. "So it's ironic that we spend weeks at a time *under* the glacier, far from the sunlight, like a bunch of moles."

"Look what it has done to me," LeBlanc said. "Constant thirty-five degrees and one hundred percent humidity. I used to be tall and blond-haired, but I have shrunk and become a shaggy beast."

"You've been a short shaggy beast for as long as I've known you," Thurston said. "We're down here for three-week stints, and I agree that we do seem a bit molelike. But even Bernie will agree that we're lucky. Most glaciologists only observe an ice field from above. We can walk right up and tickle its belly."

"What exactly is the nature of your experiments?" Rawlins asked.

"We're conducting a three-year study on how glaciers move and what they do to the rock they slide over. Hope you can make that sound more exciting when you write your article."

"It won't be too hard. With all the interest in global warming, glaciology has become a hot subject."

"So I hear. The recognition is long overdue. Glaciers are affected by climate, so they can tell us to within a few degrees what the temperature was on earth thousands of years ago. In addition, they trigger changes in the climate. Ah, here we are, Club Dormeur."

Four small buildings that looked like trailer homes sat end to end within a bay carved from the wall.

Thurston opened a door to the nearest structure. "All the comforts of home," he said. "Four bedrooms with room for eight researchers, kitchen, bath with shower. Normally, I've got a geologist and other scientists, but we're down to a skeleton crew consisting of Bernie, a young research assistant from Uppsala University and me. You can dump those supplies here. We're about a thirty-minute walk from the lab. We've got phone connections between the entrance, research tunnel and lab room. I'd better let the folks at the observatory know we're back."

He picked up a wall phone and said a few words. His smile turned into a puzzled frown.

"Say again." He listened intently. "Okay. We'll be right there."

"Is there anything wrong, professor?" LeBlanc said.

Thurston furrowed his brow. "I just talked to my research assistant. Incredible!"

"Qu'est-ce que c'est?" LeBlanc said.

Thurston had a stunned expression on his face. "He says he's found a man frozen in the ice."

4

TWO HUNDRED FEET below the surface of Lac du Dormeur in waters cold enough to kill an unprotected human, the glowing sphere floated above the gravelly bottom of the glacial lake like a will-o'-the-wisp in a Georgia swamp. Despite the hostile environment, the man and woman seated side by side inside the transparent acrylic cabin were as relaxed as loungers on a love seat.

The man was husky in build, with shoulders like twin battering rams. Exposure to sea and sun had bronzed the rugged features that were bathed in the soft orange light from the instrument panel, and bleached the pale, prematurely steely gray hair almost to the color of platinum. With his chiseled profile and intense expression, Kurt Austin had the face of a warrior carved on a Roman victory column. But the flinty hardness that lay under the burnished features was softened by an easy smile, and the piercing coral-blue eyes sparkled with good humor.

Austin was the leader of NUMA's Special Assignments Team, created by former NUMA director Admiral James Sandecker, now vice president of the United States, for undersea missions that often took place secretly outside the realm of government oversight. A marine engineer by education and experience, Austin had come to NUMA from the CIA, where he had worked for a little-known branch that specialized in underwater intelligence gathering.

After coming over to NUMA, Austin had assembled a team of experts that included Joe Zavala, a brilliant engineer specializing in underwater vehicles; Paul Trout, a deep-ocean geologist; and Trout's wife, Gamay Morgan-Trout, a highly skilled diver who had specialized in nautical archaeology before attaining her doctorate in marine biology. Working together, they had conducted many successful probes into strange and sinister enigmas on and under the world's oceans.

Not every job that Austin undertook was filled with danger. Some, like his latest assignment, were quite pleasant and more than made up for the bumps, bruises and scars he had collected on various NUMA assignments. Although he had known his female companion only a few days, he had become thoroughly entranced by her. Skye Labelle was in her late thirties. She had olive skin and mischievous violet-blue eyes that peered out from under the brim of her woolen hat. Her hair was dark brown, bordering on black. Her mouth was too wide to be called classical, but her lips were lush and sensual. She had a good body, but it would never make the cover of *Sports Illustrated*. Her voice was low and cool, and when she spoke it was obvious she had a quick intelligence.

Although she was striking rather than pretty, Austin thought she was one of the most attractive women he had ever met. She reminded him of a portrait of a young raven-haired countess he had seen hanging on the wall of the Louvre. Austin had admired how the artist had cleverly caught the passion and unabashed frankness in the subject's gaze. The woman in the painting had a deviltry in her eyes, as if she wanted to throw off her regal finery and run barefoot through a meadow. He remembered wishing he could have met her in person. And now, it seemed, he had.

"Do you believe in reincarnation?" Austin said, thinking about the museum portrait.

Skye blinked in surprise. They had been talking about glacial geology.

"I don't know. Why do you ask?" She spoke American English with a slight French accent.

"No reason." Austin paused. "I have another, more personal question."

She gave him a wary look. "I think I know. You want to know about my name."

"I've never met anyone named Skye Labelle before."

"Some people believe I must be named after a Las Vegas stripper."

Austin chuckled. "It's more likely that someone in your family had a poetic turn of mind."

"My crazy parents," she said, with a roll of her eyes. "My father was sent to the U.S. as a diplomat. One day he went to the Albuquerque hot air balloon festival and from that day on, he became a fanatical aeronaut. My older brother was named Thaddeus after the early balloonist Thaddeus Lowe. My American mother is an artist, and something of a free spirit, so she thought the idea of my name was wonderful. Father insists he named me after the color of my eyes, but everyone knows babies' eyes are neutral when they are first born. I don't mind. I think it's a nice name."

"They don't get any nicer than Beautiful Sky."

"*Merci*. And thank you for all this!" She gazed through the bubble and clapped her hands in childlike joy. "This is absolutely *wonderful*! I never dreamed that my studies in archaeology would take me under the water inside a big bubble."

"It must beat polishing medieval armor in a musty museum," Austin said.

Skye had a warm, uninhibited laugh. "I spend very little time in museums except when I'm organizing an exhibition. I do a lot of corporate jobs these days to support my research work."

Austin raised an eyebrow. "The thought of Microsoft and General Motors hiring an expert in arms and armor makes me wonder about their motives."

"Think about it. To survive, a corporation must try to kill or wound its competition while defending itself. Figuratively speaking."

"The original 'cutthroat competition,'" Austin said.

"Not bad. I'll use that phrase in my next presentation."

"How do you teach a bunch of executives to draw blood? Figuratively speaking, of course."

"They already have the blood lust. I get them to think 'out of the box,' as they like to say. I ask them to pretend that they are supplying arms for competing forces. The old arms makers had to be metallurgists and engineers. Many were artists, like Leonardo, who designed war engines. Weapons and strategy were constantly changing and the people who supplied the armies had to adjust quickly to new conditions."

"The lives of their customers depended on it."

"Right. I might have one group devise a siege machine while another comes up with ways to defend against it. Or I can give one side metal-piercing arrows while the other comes up with armor that works without being unwieldy. Then we switch sides and try again. They learn to use their native intelligence rather than to rely on computers and such."

"Maybe you should offer your services to NUMA. Learning how to blast holes in ten-foot-thick walls with a trebuchet sounds like a lot more fun than staring at budget pie charts."

A sly smile crossed Skye's face. "Well, you know, most executives *are* men."

"Boys and their toys. A surefire formula for success."

"I'll admit I pander to the childish side of my clients, but my sessions are immensely popular and very lucrative. And they allow me the flexibility to work on projects that might not be possible on my salary from the Sorbonne."

"Projects like the ancient trade routes?"

She nodded. "It would be a major coup if I could prove that tin and other goods traveled overland along the old Amber Route, through the Alpine passes and valleys to the Adriatic, where Phoenician and Minoan ships transported it to the eastern reaches of the Mediterranean. And that the trade went both ways."

"The logistics of your theoretical trade route would have been complex."

"You're a genius! Exactly my point!"

"Thanks for the compliment, but I'm just relating it to my own experiences moving people and material."

"Then you know how complicated it would be. People along the land route, like the Celts and the Etruscans, had to cooperate on trade agreements in order to move the materials along. I think trade was a lot more extensive than my colleagues would admit. All this has fascinating implications about how we view ancient civilizations. They weren't all about war; they knew the value of peaceful alliances a long time before the EU or NAFTA. And I mean to prove it."

"Ancient globalization? An ambitious goal. I wish you luck."

"I'll *need* it. But if I do succeed I'll have you and NUMA to thank. Your agency has been wonderfully generous in the use of its research vessel and equipment."

"It goes both ways. Your project gives NUMA a chance to test our new vessel in inland waters and to see how this submersible operates under field conditions."

She made a sweeping gesture with her hand. "The scenery is perfectly lovely. All we need is a bottle of champagne and foie gras."

Austin leaned over and handed a small plastic cooler to his companion. "Can't help you there, but how about a *jambon et fromage* sandwich?"

"Ham and cheese would be my second choice." She unzipped the cooler, extracted a sandwich, handed it to Austin and took one for herself.

Austin brought the submersible to a hovering stop. As

he chewed on his lunch, savoring the crusty baguette and the creamy slab of Camembert cheese, he studied a chart of the lake.

"We're here, alongside a natural shelf that roughly parallels the shoreline," he said, running his finger along a wavy line. "This could have been exposed land centuries ago."

"It goes along with my findings. A section of the Amber Route skirted the shore of Lac du Dormeur. When the waters rose, the traders found another route. Anything we find here would be very old."

"What exactly are we looking for?"

"I'll know it when I see it."

"Good enough for me."

"You're far too trusting. I'll elaborate. The caravans that plied the Amber Route needed places to stop for the night. I'm looking for the ruins of hospices, or settlements that may have grown up around a stopping place. Then I hope to find weapons that would flesh out the full trade story."

They washed their lunch down with Evian water, and Austin's fingers played over the controls. The battery-powered electrical motors hummed, activating the twin lateral thrusters that the sphere rested on, and the submersible continued its exploration.

The SEAmagine SEAmobile was fifteen feet long, about the length of a midsized Boston whaler, and only seven feet wide, but it was capable of carrying two people in one-atmosphere comfort to a depth of fifteen hundred feet for hours at a time. The vehicle had a range of twelve nautical miles and a maximum speed of 2.5 knots. Unlike most submersibles, which bobbed like a cork when they surfaced, the SEAmobile could be operated like a boat. It sat high in the water when it wasn't submerged, giving the pilot clear visibility, and could cruise to a dive site or edge up to a dive platform.

The SEAmobile looked as if it had been assembled from spare parts cast off from a deep submergence lab. The crystal ball cockpit was fifty-four inches in diameter and it was perched on two flotation cylinders the size of water mains. Two protective metal frames shaped like the letter *D* flanked the sphere.

The vehicle was built to maintain positive buoyancy at all times and the tendency to float to the surface was countered by a midship-mounted vertical thruster. Because the SEAmobile was balanced to remain level constantly, at the surface or under it, the pilot didn't have to fiddle around with pitch controls to keep it at a horizontal attitude.

Using a navigational acoustic Doppler instrument to keep track of their position, Austin guided the vehicle along the underwater escarpment, a broad shelf that gradually sloped down into the deeper water. Following a basic search pattern, Austin ran a series of parallel lines like someone mowing a lawn. The sub's four halogen lights illuminated the bottom, whose contours had been shaped by the advance and retreat of glaciers.

The sub tracked back and forth for two hours and Austin's eyes were starting to glaze from staring at the monotonous gray seascape. Skye was still entranced by the uniqueness of her surroundings. She leaned forward, chin on her hands, studying every square foot of lake bottom. In time, her persistence paid off.

"There!" She jabbed the air with her forefinger.

Austin slowed the vehicle to a crawl and squinted at a vague shape just beyond the range of the lights, then moved the submersible in for a closer look. The object lying on its side was a massive stone slab about twelve feet long and half as wide. The chisel marks visible along its edges suggested that it was not a natural rock formation. Other monoliths could be seen nearby, some standing upright; others topped with similar slabs like the Greek letter *pi*.

"Seems we took a wrong turn and ended up at Stonehenge," Austin said.

"They're burial monuments," Skye said. "The arches mark the way to a tomb for funeral processions."

Austin increased the power to the thrusters and the vehicle glided over six identical archways spaced thirty feet or so apart. Then the ground on either side of the archways began to rise, creating a shallow valley. The natural hillsides morphed into high cyclopean walls constructed with massive hand-hewn blocks.

The narrow canyon ended abruptly in a sheer vertical wall. Cut into the wall was a rectangular opening that looked like the door on an elephant house. A lintel about thirty feet wide topped the door opening and above the huge slab was a smaller, triangular hole.

"Incredible," Skye said in hushed tones. "It's a *tholos*."

"You've seen this before?"

"It's a beehive tomb. There's one in Mycenae called the 'Treasury of Atreus.' "

"Mycenae. That's Greek."

"Yes, but the design is even older. The tombs go back to 2200 B.C. They were used for communal burials in Crete and other parts of the Aegean. Kurt, do you know what this means?" Her voice quivered with excitement. "We could establish trade links between the Aegean and Europe far earlier than anyone has dared to suggest. I'd give *any*thing to get a close look at the tomb."

"My standard price for an underwater tomb tour is an invitation to dinner."

"You can get us inside?"

"Why not? We've got plenty of clearance on either side and above. If we go slowly—"

"The *hell* with slow! *Dépêche-toi. Vite, vite!*"

Austin laughed, and moved the submersible forward toward the dark opening. He was as eager as Skye, but he advanced with caution. The lights were beginning to probe the interior when a voice came over the vehicle's radio receiver.

"Kurt, this is support. Come in, please."

The words being transmitted through the water had a metallic vibrato, but Austin recognized the voice of the NUMA boat's captain.

He brought the submersible to a hovering stop and picked up the microphone. "This is the SEAmobile. Do you read me?"

"Your voice is a little faint and scratchy, but I can hear

you. Please tell Ms. Labelle that François wants to talk to her."

François Balduc was the French observer NUMA had invited aboard as a courtesy to the French government. He was a pleasant, middle-aged bureaucrat who stayed out of the way except at dinner, when he assisted the cook in turning out some memorable feasts. Austin handed the mike to Skye.

There was a heated discussion in French, which ended when Skye passed the microphone back.

"Merde!" she said with a frown. "We've got to go up."

"Why? We still have plenty of air and power."

"François got a call from a big shot in the French government. I'm needed immediately to identify some sort of artifact."

"That doesn't sound very urgent. Can it wait?"

"As far as I'm concerned it can until Napoleon returns from exile," she said with a sigh, "but the government is subsidizing part of my research here, so I'm on call, so to speak. I'm sorry."

Austin stared with narrowed eyes at the opening. "This tomb has been hidden from human view possibly for thousands of years. It's not going anywhere."

Skye nodded in agreement, although her heart clearly wasn't in it.

They looked longingly at the mysterious doorway, and then Austin put the submersible in a U-turn. Once they were clear of the canyon, he reached for the vertical thruster control, and the submersible began its ascent.

Moments later, the bubble cockpit popped out at the surface near the NUMA catamaran. He maneuvered the craft around behind the boat and drove it over a submerged platform between the twin hulls. The gate was raised and a winch hoisted the platform carrying the submersible up onto the deck.

François was awaiting their arrival, an anxious expression on his usually bland face. "I'm so sorry to interrupt your work, Mademoiselle Skye. The *cochon* who called me was most insistent."

She pecked him lightly on the cheek. "Don't worry, François; it's not your fault. Tell me what they want."

He gestured toward the mountains. "They want you over there."

"The *glacier*? Are you sure?"

He nodded his head vigorously. "Yes, yes, I asked the same thing. They were very clear that they needed your expertise. They found something in the ice. That's all I know. The boat is waiting."

Skye turned to Austin, an anxious look on her face. He anticipated her words. "Don't worry. I'll wait until you get back before I dive on the tomb."

She embraced Austin in a warm hug and kissed him on both cheeks.

"*Merci*, Kurt. I really appreciate this." She shot him a smile that was only a few BTUs short of seduction. "There's a nice little bistro on the Left Bank. Good value for the money." She laughed at his blank look. "Don't tell me you've forgotten your dinner invitation? I accept."

Before Austin could reply, Skye climbed down the ladder into the waiting powerboat, the outboard motor buzzed, and the shuttle headed toward shore. Austin was an attractive and charming man, and he had met many fascinating and beautiful women in his career. But as leader of NUMA's Special Assignments Team, he was on call day or night. He was seldom home and his globe-hopping lifestyle was not conducive to a long-term relationship. Most encounters were all too brief.

Austin had been attracted to Skye from the start, and if he read the signals in her glance and smile and voice correctly, the feeling was mutual. He chuckled ruefully at the turnabout. Usually he was the one who went charging off when duty called, while his romantic interest of the moment cooled her heels. He gazed off at the boat making its way toward shore and wondered what sort of artifact could have created so much excitement. He almost wished that he had accompanied Skye.

Within a few hours, he would be thanking the gods that he *didn't* go along for the ride.

5

LEBLANC MET SKYE on the beach and correctly sized up her sour mood. But the Frenchman's unkempt appearance masked his considerable Gallic charm and wit. Minutes after Skye got into the car, the troll-like man had her laughing with his stories about the temperamental Fifi.

Skye saw that the Citroën was heading to one side of the ice field and said, "I thought we were going to the glacier."

"Not *to* the glacier, mademoiselle. We will be going *under* it. My colleagues and I are studying the movement of the ice at an observatory eight hundred feet beneath Le Dormeur."

"I had no idea," Skye said. "Tell me more."

LeBlanc nodded and launched into an explanation of his work at the observatory. As Skye listened intently, her scientific curiosity took the edge off her irritation at being drawn away from the ship.

"And what is the nature of *your* work on the lake?" LeBlanc said when he was through. "We emerged from our cave one day and *voilà*! The submersible had appeared like magic."

"I'm an archaeologist with the Sorbonne. The National Underwater and Marine Agency was kind enough to provide a vessel for my research. We traveled up the river that runs into Lac du Dormeur. I hope to find evidence of old Amber Route trading posts under the waters of the lake."

"Fascinating! Have you come across anything of interest?"

"Yes. That's why I'm anxious to get back to the project as soon as possible. Could you tell me why my services are so urgently required?"

"We found a body frozen in the ice."

"A *body*?"

"We think it is the corpse of a man."

"Like the Ice Man?" she said, recalling the mummified body of a Neolithic huntsman found in the Alps some years earlier.

LeBlanc shook his head. "We believe this poor fellow is of more recent origin. At first we thought he was a climber who had fallen into a crevasse."

"What made you change your mind?"

"You'll have to see."

"Please don't play games with me, Monsieur LeBlanc," Skye snapped. "My specialty is ancient arms and armor, not old bodies. Why am I being called into this?"

"My apologies, mademoiselle. Monsieur Renaud has asked us not to say anything."

Skye's mouth dropped open. "*Renaud?* From the state archaeological board?"

"One and the same, mademoiselle. He arrived hours after we notified the authorities of the discovery and has put himself in charge. You know him?"

"Oh *yes*, I know him." She apologized to LeBlanc for jumping down his throat and sat back in her seat, arms folded across her chest. I know him *very* well, she thought.

Auguste Renaud was a professor of anthropology at the Sorbonne. He spent little time in teaching, which was a godsend for the students, who despised him, and instead devoted his energy to playing politics. He had built up a cadre of cronies, and with his connections he had risen to a place in the state's archaeological establishment, where he used his influence to reward and punish. He had stymied several of Skye's projects, hinting that they could be put on a fast track if she would sleep with him. Skye had told him she would rather sleep with a roach.

LeBlanc parked the Citroën and led Skye to the tunnel entrance. He scrambled into the entry culvert and, after a moment's hesitation, she followed him to the main tunnel. LeBlanc fitted Skye out with a hard hat and headlamp and they began walking. Five minutes later, they were at the living quarters. LeBlanc used a telephone to call ahead to let the lab know that they were on their way. Then they started off on their half-hour trek.

As they hiked through the tunnel, their footsteps echoed off the dripping walls. Skye glanced around at their damp surroundings and said, "This is like the inside of a wet boot."

"Not exactly the Champs-Elysées, I agree. But the traffic is not as bad as in Paris."

Skye was awestruck at the engineering accomplishment the tunnel represented and kept up a barrage of questions about the details as they trudged deeper into the tunnel. At one point, they came upon a square section of concrete surrounding a steel door in the tunnel wall.

"Where does that door go?" she inquired.

"It leads to another tunnel that connects to the hydroelectric system. When the flow through the tunnels is slow earlier in the year, we can open the door, ford a little stream, and go places farther into the system. But this time of year, the water rises, so we keep the door shut."

"You can get to the power plant from here?"

"There are tunnels all through the mountain and under the ice cap, but only the dry ones are accessible. The others carry the water to the plant. A regular river flows under the glacier and the current can become quite brisk. We don't normally work this late in the season. Melting water flows in the natural cavities between the ice and the rock, creates pockets and slows down our research. But our work took longer this spring than we thought it would."

"How do you get air down here?" Skye said, sniffing at the dampness.

"If we were to keep going past the lab and under the glacier for another kilometer more or less, eventually we would come to a large opening on the far side of the ice. It was used to bring in the trailers for the lab and staff. It's been left open like a mine entrance. Air flows in from there."

Skye shivered in the dank cold. "I admire your determination. This is not the most pleasant place to work."

LeBlanc's deep laugh echoed off the dripping walls. "It's most *un*pleasant, very boring, and we're always soaked to the bone. We take a few trips into the sunlight during our three-week stays here, but it's depressing to have to return to the caves, so we tend to stay in the lab, which is dry and well lit. It's equipped with computers, vacuum pumps for filtering sediments, even a walk-in freezer so we can work on ice samples without having them melt. After working an eighteen-hour day, you shower and crawl into bed, so the time goes by fast. Ah, I see that we're almost there."

Like the living quarters, the lab trailers were nestled in a carved-out section of wall. As LeBlanc stepped up to the nearest lab, the door opened and a tall thin figure stepped out. The sight of Renaud rekindled Skye's simmering wrath. He actually resembled a praying mantis more than a roach. He had a triangular face, wide at the top, with a pointed chin. His nose was long and his eyes small and close together. His thinning hair was a pallid red.

Renaud greeted Skye with the limp, moist handshake that had triggered her revulsion the first time she met him.

"Good morning, my dear Mademoiselle Labelle. Thank you for coming to this damp, dark cave."

"You're welcome, Professor Renaud." She glanced around at the inhospitable surroundings. "This environment must suit you well."

Renaud ignored the veiled suggestion that he had crawled out from under a rock and ran his eyes up and down Skye's well-put-together body as if he could see through her heavy clothing. "*Any*place where you and I are together suits me well."

Skye stifled her gag reflex. "Perhaps you can tell me what was so important that you had to pull me away from my work."

"With pleasure." He reached over to take her by the arm. Skye stepped out of reach and linked her arm through LeBlanc's.

"Lead on," she said.

The glaciologist had been watching the verbal fencing with mirthful eyes. His mouth widened in a toothy grin and he and Skye walked arm in arm to a steep flight of rough wooden stairs. The stairs led up to a tunnel about twelve feet high and ten feet wide.

Approximately twenty paces from the stairs, the tunnel branched out into a *Y.* LeBlanc escorted Skye down the right-hand passageway. Water was streaming along a shallow channel that had been cut in the tunnel floor for drainage. A black rubber hose about four inches in diameter ran alongside one wall.

"Water jet," LeBlanc explained. "We collect the drainage water, heat it up and spray it on the ice to melt it. The ice is like putty at the bottom of the glacier. We're constantly melting it, otherwise it would re-form at the rate of two to three feet a day."

"That's very fast," Skye said.

"*Very.* Sometimes we go as far as fifty meters into the glacier and we have to be alert so the ice doesn't close behind us."

The tunnel ended in an icy slope about ten feet high. They clambered up the slippery rock surface on a ladder and entered an ice cave with space enough to hold more than a dozen people. The walls and ceiling were bluish white except for areas that were covered with dirt scraped up by the movement of the glacier.

"We're at the bottom of the glacier," LeBlanc said. "There is nothing but ice above our heads for eight hundred feet. This is the dirtiest part of the ice floe. It gets cleaner the more you drill into it. I must leave now to do an errand for Monsieur Renaud."

Skye thanked him and then her attention was drawn to the far wall where a man in a raincoat was spraying the ice with a hot water hose. The melting ice generated clouds of steam, which made the damp air in the room even harder to breathe. The man turned off the jet when he saw he had visitors and came over to shake hands.

"Welcome to our little observatory, Mademoiselle Labelle. Hope the trip from the outside wasn't too arduous. My name is Hank Thurston. I'm Bernie's colleague. This is Craig Rossi, our assistant from Uppsala University," he said, gesturing at a young man in his early twenties, "and that's Derek Rawlins, who's writing about our work for *Outside* magazine."

As Skye shook hands, Renaud brushed by the others and went over to the wall to examine a vaguely human figure that was locked in the ice.

"As you can see, this gentleman has been frozen for some time," Renaud said. Glancing at Skye, he said, "Not unlike some of the women I have encountered."

No one laughed at the joke. Skye stepped past Renaud and ran her fingers around the perimeter of the dark shape. The limbs were twisted in grotesque positions.

"We found him when we were enlarging the cave," Thurston explained.

"He looks more like a bug on a windshield than a man," Skye said.

"We're lucky he's not just a big greasy smear," Thurston said. "He's in pretty good shape, considering. The ice at the bottom of a glacier, and anything in it, is squeezed like putty by hundreds of tons of pressure."

Skye peered at the vague form. "Are you assuming that he was on top of the glacier at one point?"

"Sure," Thurston said. "With a valley glacier like Le

Dormeur or some of the others you'll find in the Alps, a reasonable amount of snowfall moves pretty fast through the ice."

"How long would it take?"

"My guess is that it would take a hundred years, more or less, to get from the top to the bottom of Le Dormeur." It would only work for an object near the head of the glacier high in the mountains, where ice flows vertically as well as horizontally."

"Then it's possible that he was a climber who fell into a crevasse?"

"That's what we thought at first. Then we took a closer look."

Skye put her face closer to the ice. The body was dressed almost entirely in dark leather, from his boots to the snug Snoopy-type cap. Tufts of fur lining poked out here and there. A gun holster, pistol still in it, hung from a belt.

Her gaze moved up to the face. The features were unclear through the ice, but the skin was burnished to a dark copper color, as if he had lain out in the sun too long. The eyes were covered with a pair of goggles.

"Incredible," she whispered, then stepped back and turned to Renaud. "But what does this have to do with me?"

Renaud smiled and went over to a plastic storage container and reached inside. He grunted as he lifted out a steel helmet. "This was found near the man's head."

Skye took the helmet and studied the intricate design engraved on the metal, pursing her lips in thought. The visor was formed into the face of a man with a large nose and a bushy mustache. The crown was engraved with ornate, interlocking flowers and stems, and mythical creatures revolved like planets around a stylized three-headed eagle. The eagle's mouths were open in a defiant scream and bundles of spears and arrows were clutched in its sharp claws.

"We actually discovered the helmet first," Thurston said. "We shut down the pump immediately and luckily we didn't damage the body."

"A wise decision," Renaud said. "An archaeological site

is vulnerable to contamination, very much like a crime scene."

Skye poked her fingers through a rough opening in the right side of the helmet. "This looks like a bullet hole."

Renaud snorted. "Bullet hole! A spear or an arrow would be more appropriate."

"It's not unusual to see proof marks, dents in armor where it was tested against firearms," Skye said. "The hole is unusually clean. This steel is of exceptionally high quality. Look, except for a few scratches and dings it's hardly damaged after being squeezed by the ice. You've called in a forensics expert?" she said.

"He should be here tomorrow," Renaud said. "We don't need a specialist to tell us this fellow is dead. What can you tell us about this helmet?"

"I can't place it," she said, with a shake of her head. "The general shape resembles some I have seen, but the markings are unknown to me. I'd have to look for an armorer's mark and check it against my database. There are many contradictions here." She gazed at the body. "The clothing and the gun look twentieth century. He appears to be an aviator, judging from his uniform and the goggles. Why would he be wearing an old helmet, if that is the case?"

"Very interesting, Mademoiselle Labelle," Renaud said with an impatient sigh, "but I expected you to be more help." He took the helmet from her hands and replaced it in the container after first pulling out a small riveted strongbox. He cradled the battered metal box like a baby. "This was near the body. What we find inside may identify this person and tell us how he got here. In the meantime," he said to Thurston, "I would like you to continue melting the ice around the body in case there are other identifying objects. I will take full responsibility."

Thurston gave him a skeptical look, and then shrugged. "This is your country," he said, and started the hot water hose again. He melted another few inches of ice on either side of the body, but found nothing. After a while they went back to the lab for some nourishment and to warm up, then returned to the ice cave and resumed their explorations. When Renaud said he would stay in the lab while the others went back to the ice cave, no one protested.

Thurston had worked on the ice for a while longer before Renaud showed up and clapped his hands for attention. "We must stop for now. We have visitors."

Excited voices echoed along the passageway. A moment later, a trio of men carrying video and still cameras and notebooks burst into the cave. Except for a tall man, who held politely back, they noisily jostled each other and bumped shoulders in their zest to film the body.

Skye grabbed Renaud by the sleeve and pulled him aside. "What are these reporters doing here?" she demanded.

He looked down his long thin nose. "*I* invited them. They are part of a press pool chosen by lot to cover this great discovery."

"You don't even know what this discovery *is*," she said with unveiled contempt in her voice. "And you just lectured *us* against contaminating the site."

He dismissed her protest with an airy wave of his hand. "It's important to let the world know about this wonderful find." Renaud raised his voice to gain the reporters' attention. "I'll answer your questions about the mummy as soon as we move outside the tomb," Renaud said, leading the way out of the cave. Skye simmered with anger.

"Jeezus!" said Rawlins. "Mummy. Tomb. He's making himself sound like he just found King Tut."

The photographers took another battery of shots and moved out of the chamber, except for the tall man. He was around six and a half feet tall, his face was a pasty white and he had a muscular build that matched his height. A camera hung around his neck and slung from his shoulder was a large canvas gear bag. He stared impassively at the body for a moment, and then he followed after the others.

"I overheard what you said to Renaud," Thurston said to Skye. "The site will start freezing up again soon and maybe that will protect it."

"Good. Let's see what that idiot is cooking up in the meantime."

They hurried from the cave and down the ladder and the wooden stairs to the main tunnel. Renaud stood outside a lab building, holding the strongbox high above his head.

"What's in it?" a reporter called out.

"We don't know. We will have to open it under controlled circumstances so as not to damage the contents."

He spun around on his heel so everyone could get a shot. The big man with the camera around his neck failed to take advantage of the photo op, however. Instead, he shouldered his way past the others, ignored the murmurs of protest from his fellow reporters and planted himself directly in front of Renaud.

"Give the box to me," he said in an impassive tone, extending his large hand.

Renaud looked startled. Then, thinking the man was joking, decided to play along with the game. He grinned and hugged the box tightly to his chest. "Not on your life," he said.

"No," the man said, without raising his voice. "Not on *your* life!"

He reached inside his coat, brought out a pistol and slammed the barrel down on Renaud's knuckles. The expression in Renaud's eyes went from amusement to surprise to pain. He collapsed to his knees, clutching his mangled fingers.

The man caught the box before it fell to the ground. Then he wheeled around and waved the gun at the reporters, who fell over themselves trying to back up, before he strode off down the tunnel.

"Stop him!" Renaud said through his pain, holding his crushed fingers.

"What about that telephone?" one reporter said.

Thurston snatched the telephone off the wall and held it to his ear. "Dead," he said with a frown. "The line must have been cut. There's no one back at the living quarters anyhow. We'll hike to the entrance and call for help."

Thurston and LeBlanc helped Renaud to his feet. They administered first aid to his hand with a kit from the lab while the reporters speculated as to the identity of the big man. None of them recognized him. He had simply appeared bearing the proper credentials and been given a seat on the floatplane that dropped them off at the edge of the lake where LeBlanc had picked them up.

LeBlanc and Skye said they would join Thurston. The reporters decided to stay put after Thurston warned that the gunman might be waiting in the tunnel. They walked briskly for several minutes, their headlamps stabbing the semidarkness. Then they walked at a slower pace and more deliberately, as if they expected the big man to leap out of the darkness. They listened for footsteps, but all they heard was the dripping of water off the ceiling and walls.

Suddenly, a loud hollow explosion came from the dark tunnel ahead, followed by an earthshaking shock. Almost simultaneously, a blast of hot air surged through the tunnel. They hit the ground, trying to bury their faces into the wet floor as the pressure wave swept over them.

When it seemed safe, they stood and wiped the muck off their faces. Their ears were ringing, so they had to shout to be heard.

"What was *that*?" LeBlanc said.

"Let's take a look." Thurston started forward, fearing the worst.

"Wait!" Skye said.

"What's wrong?" Thurston said.

"Look at your feet."

Light from their headlamps began to reflect off something that was sparkling and moving on the tunnel floor.

"Water!" Thurston yelled.

The torrent rushed toward them.

They turned and ran deeper into the tunnel, with waves lapping at their heels.

6

THROUGH HIS BINOCULARS Austin had watched Skye get into a car and followed the vehicle as it climbed the slope to one side of the glacier and disappeared behind the trees. It was as if the earth had swallowed her up. As he leaned against the ship's railing, his eyes were drawn to La Langue du Dormeur. With its mottled surface and the dark brooding peaks on both sides, the glacier looked like a scene from the planet Pluto. Sun glistened on the ice, but it did little to alleviate the waves of cold that poured off the surface and rolled across the mirror-flat lake surface.

Thinking back to Skye's theory, that caravans using the Amber Route had made their way around the edge of the lake, he tried to put himself in the boots of the ancient travelers and wondered what they would have made of a natural phenomenon as big and implacable as the glacier. More than likely, they would have taken it as a creation of the gods, who had to be appeased. Maybe the underwater tomb had something to do with the glacier. He was as anxious to explore the tomb as she was. It would take little effort to launch the submersible and take a solo run, but she would never forgive him. And he wouldn't blame her.

Austin decided to make sure the submersible was ready for a dive when Skye did return. As he checked out the SEAmobile with a fine-tooth comb, Austin could hear his father's voice in his head reminding him to make sure of every detail. His father, the wealthy owner of a marine salvage company based in Seattle, had taught Kurt basic seamanship and given him a couple of nuggets of nautical advice. Never tie a knot that can't be undone with a flip of the line, even when the line was wet. And always keep your boat "shipshape and Bristol fashion."

Austin had taken his father's words to heart. The knots he learned through constant practice never snagged. He made sure the lines on the sailing pram his father built for him were neatly coiled, and the brightwork polished and metal kept clean of corrosion. The advice stayed with him when he went on to college. While studying for his master's degree in systems management at the University of Washington, he also attended a highly rated diving school in Seattle and trained as a professional diver, attaining high proficiency in a number of specialized areas.

After college he worked on North Sea oil rigs for two years and returned to his father's salvage company for six years, before being lured into government service by a little-known branch of the CIA that specialized in underwater intelligence-gathering. At the end of the Cold War, the CIA closed down the undersea investigation branch and he moved over to NUMA.

As a lover of philosophy, with its search for truth and hidden meanings, Austin knew the Old Man's advice went beyond the practical tasks associated with running a boat. His father was telling him in simple terms about life, and the need to be ready and prepared for the unexpected. It was advice Austin took seriously, and his attention to detail had saved his life and those around him on more than one occasion.

He tested the batteries, made sure the air tanks had been replaced with fresh ones, and examined the vehicle with a practiced eye. Satisfied with his inspection, he gently rapped his knuckles against the transparent dome. "Shipshape and Bristol fashion," he said with a smile.

Austin climbed down from the submersible onto the deck of the *Mummichug*. The twin-hulled, eighty-foot craft was the smallest NUMA research vessel he had ever worked on. Like the tiny fish that was its namesake, the *Mummichug* was at home in fresh or salt water. It was a modified version of a vessel designed for inshore duty in the cantankerous waters along the New England coast.

It was seaworthy and fast, driven by powerful diesel engines that gave it a cruising speed of 20 knots. It slept eight and was ideal for short missions. Despite its size, the *Mummichug*'s winches and A-frame could haul heavy loads. And a larger vessel would not have been able to navigate the winding river to the glacier.

Finding himself at loose ends without Skye to talk to, Austin grabbed a mug of coffee in the galley, and then went below to the remote sensing lab. It was a small space crammed with several computer monitors set up on tables. Like everything else on the ship, the lab was understated, although electronic nerves and ganglions connected the monitors to a sophisticated array of sensing instruments.

He plunked himself down in a chair in front of a screen, took a sip of coffee and called up the file on the side-scan sonar display. Dr. Harold Edgerton had pioneered side-scan sonar in 1963 when he'd mounted a sonar transducer on the side rather than the bottom of his survey boat. The discovery, which allowed surface vessels to cover large areas of bottom, would revolutionize underwater search techniques.

When the *Mummichug* had first arrived on site, Skye had asked for a survey along the shore across the lake from the glacier, which would have presented a formidable roadblock to caravans. She reasoned that travelers would have lingered near the river before fording it and a settlement might have built up nearby. The waterway itself may have been used as a tributary of the Amber Route.

While the submersible had carried out its underwater mission, the ship had continued its sonar survey along the lake's perimeter. Austin wanted to see what the scan had picked up. He put the screen in a slow scroll and the high-resolution sonar image flowed down from the top of the monitor like twin amber waterfalls. Displayed on the right side of the screen were latitude, longitude and position.

Interpreting sonar images requires a practiced eye, but it is not the most exciting occupation. With its flat, gravelly bottom, Lac du Dormeur was even more monotonous than some. Austin found his thoughts drifting off. His eyelids had dropped to half-mast, but they snapped open when an anomaly caught his attention. He scrolled back, leaned forward to examine the dark cross etched against the monotone background, then, with a click of the computer mouse, zoomed in on the image and enhanced the details.

He was looking at a plane; he could even see the cockpit. He clicked on the print icon and a few seconds later a picture rolled off the printer. He studied the image under a strong light. Part of a wing seemed to be missing. He rose from his seat and was headed for the door, intending to alert the captain to his find, when François burst into the lab. He was obviously agitated. The French observer usually wore an imperturbable smile, but he looked as if he had just heard that the Eiffel Tower had fallen.

"Monsieur Austin, you must come quickly to the bridge."

"What's wrong?" Austin said.

"It's Mademoiselle Skye."

Austin's stomach did a flip-flop. "What about her?"

An incomprehensible mishmash of *Franglais* streamed from the man's mouth. Austin brushed past the sputtering Frenchman and climbed two steps at a time to the bridge. The captain was in the pilothouse, talking into the radio microphone. When he saw Kurt, he said, *"Attendez,"* and set the mike aside.

Captain Jack Fortier was a slightly built man of French-Canadian origin who had become a U.S. citizen so he could work for NUMA. His ability to speak French had come in handy on the expedition, although some of the locals he encountered snickered behind his back at his strong Quebecois accent. Fortier told Austin that the derision didn't bother him because his language was the purer, unsullied by regional accents, as in France. Not much seemed to bother the captain, which is why Austin was surprised to see Fortier's brow furrowed with worry.

"What's happened to Skye?" Austin said, getting right to the point.

"I'm on the phone with the supervisor of the power plant. He says there has been an accident."

A chill danced up and down Austin's spine. "What sort of accident?"

"Skye and some other people were in a tunnel under the glacier."

"What was she doing there?"

"There's an observatory under the ice where scientists can study the movement of the glacier. It's part of the tunnel system the power company built to use water coming off the glacier. Apparently something went wrong and water flooded the tunnel."

"Has the power plant been able to make contact with the observatory?"

"No. The telephone line is down."

"So we don't know if they're dead or alive."

"Apparently not," Fortier said in a half whisper.

The news rocked Austin back on his heels. He took a deep breath and exhaled slowly as he collected his thoughts.

Rallying, he said, "Tell the plant supervisor I want to meet with him. Tell him to have detailed plans of the tunnel system ready. And rustle up a boat to get me to shore." Austin paused as he realized that he was barking orders at the captain. "Sorry," he said. "I didn't mean to sound like a marine drill sergeant. This is your ship. Those were only suggestions."

"Suggestions well taken," the captain replied with a smile. "Don't worry about it. I don't have a clue what to do next. The ship and crew are at your command."

Captain Fortier picked up the mike and began to speak French.

Austin stared at the glacier through the pilothouse window. He was as still as a bronze statue, but his calmness was deceiving. His nimble mind was racing ahead, exploring strategies. But he knew it was all mental smoke and mirrors for now because he couldn't come up with a plan until he knew exactly what he had to deal with.

He thought of the beguiling expression on Skye's face as she left the ship. He knew the odds were against it, but he vowed to see that enchanting smile again.

7

A TRUCK AWAITED AUSTIN on the beach. The driver tore up the hill to the plant at breakneck speed. As the truck approached the block-shaped gray concrete structure, which was built into the base of a steep mountain wall, Austin could see someone pacing back and forth in front of the entrance. The truck skidded to a stop and the man rushed over, opened the door for Austin and extended his hand in greeting.

"*Parlez-vous Français*, Monsieur Austin?"

"I *parle* a little," Austin replied as he got out of the truck.

"*D'accord.* Okay," the man said with an indulgent smile. "I speak enough English. My name is Guy Lessard. I am the plant supervisor. This is a terrible business."

"Then you must know that time is of the essence," Austin said.

Lessard was a short wiry man with a precisely trimmed mustache adorning his thin face. He had an air of nervous energy, as if he had tapped into one of the power lines that streamed from the plant on high metal towers.

"Yes, I understand. Come. I'll explain the situation." Walking briskly, he led the way through the door.

Austin glanced around at the small plain lobby. "Somehow I expected a larger facility."

"Don't be deceived," Lessard replied. "This is a portal building. It's used mostly as office space and living quarters. The plant itself extends deep into the mountain. Come."

They passed through another door on the far side of the lobby and stepped into a large, brightly lit cavern.

"We took advantage of the natural rock formations to give us a start on the drilling," Lessard said, his voice bouncing off the walls and ceiling. "There are some fifty kilometers of tunnels running under the mountain and beneath the glacier."

Austin let out a low whistle. "There are highways in the States that aren't that long," Austin said.

"It was a formidable achievement. The engineers used a tunnel-boring machine with a diameter of nearly thirty feet. It was a simple matter to drill the research tunnel."

He led the way across the cavern to a tunnel entrance. Austin's ears picked up a low hum, like the sound of a hundred beehives.

"That noise must be your generator," he said.

"Yes, we only have one turbine now, but there are plans to build a second one." He paused at a door in the tunnel wall. "Here we are in the control room."

The plant's nerve center was a sterile chamber about fifty feet square, that looked like the inside of a giant slot machine. Arrayed along three walls were banks of blinking lights, electrical dials, gauges and switches. Lessard went over to a horseshoe-shaped console that dominated the center of the room, sat down in front of a computer monitor and motioned for Austin to take the chair beside him.

"You know what we do at this plant?" he said.

"In general. I've been told that you tap the melting water from the glacier for hydroelectric power."

Lessard nodded. "The technology is relatively uncomplicated. Snow falls from the sky and builds up on the glacier. In warm weather the glacier ice melts, forming water pockets and rivers. The torrent is channeled through the tunnels to the turbine. *Voilà!* You have electricity. Clean and cheap and renewable." Lessard's routine explanation couldn't hide the pride in his voice.

"Simple in theory, but impressive in execution," Austin said as he pictured the system in his mind. "You must have a large crew."

"There are only three of us," Lessard said. "One for each shift. The plant is almost entirely automated and could probably run itself without us."

"Could you show me a diagram of the system?"

Lessard's hands played over the keyboard. A diagram flashed onto the screen, similar to the display in a metropolitan traffic control center. The intersecting colored lines reminded Austin of the map for the London Underground.

"Those lines that are blinking blue represent tunnels that have water running through them. The red ones are dry conduits. The turbine is here."

Austin stared at the lines, trying to make sense of the confusing display. "Which tunnel was flooded?"

Lessard tapped the screen with a fingertip. "This one. The main access to the observatory." The line was blinking blue.

"Is there any way to shut down the flow?"

"We tried when we detected water getting into the research tunnel. Apparently, the concrete wall between the research and water tunnels has been breached. By diverting the flow in the other tunnels, we were able to contain it. The research tunnel remains filled with water."

"Do you have any idea how this wall you mentioned was breached?"

"A gate at this intersection provides access from one tunnel to another. It's closed this time of year as a safeguard because the water is high. The gate is made to withstand tons of pressure. I don't know what could have happened."

"Is there any way to drain that tunnel water off?"

"Yes, we could seal off some tunnels and pump the water out eventually, but it would take days," came the devastating reply.

Austin indicated the glowing screen in front of them. "Even with this extensive network of tunnels?"

"I'll show you what the problem is."

Lessard led the way out of the control room and they walked along a tunnel for several minutes. The omnipresent hum of the turbine was overpowered by another sound like a strong wind blowing through the trees. They climbed a flight of metal stairs on the other side of a steel door to an observation platform protected by a watertight plastic-and-metal canopy. Lessard explained that they were in one of several off-site control rooms. The rushing noise had become a roar.

Lessard flicked a wall switch and a floodlight illuminated a section of tunnel where a torrent raged. The foaming water level almost reached the observation bubble. Austin stared at the white water, sensing its vast power.

"This time of year water melts from huge pockets in the ice," Lessard shouted over the racket. "They add to the normal flow. It's like the floods you get in swollen rivers when the mountain snow melts too quickly in the spring." Lessard had a pained expression on his narrow face. "I'm sorry we can't help you or the people trapped inside."

"You've helped me a great deal already, but I'll need to see a detailed diagram of the research tunnel."

"Of course." As Lessard led the way back to the control room, he decided he liked this American. Austin was thorough and methodical, qualities Lessard prized above all others.

Back in the main nerve center, Austin glanced at the wall clock and saw that precious minutes had gone by since the tour began. Lessard went over to a metal cabinet, slid open a wide shallow drawer and pulled out a set of blueprints.

"Here is the main entrance to the research tunnel. It's not much more than a culvert. These rectangles are the living quarters for the scientists. The lab is about a mile from the main entrance. As you can see in this side view, there are stairs that run up through the ceiling to another level, where there is a passage that leads to the subglacial observatory itself."

"Do we know how many people could be trapped?"

"There were three in the scientific team most recently. Sometimes, when they get sick of being underground, we get together to drink a few glasses of wine. Then there is the woman from your ship. A floatplane brought some people in before the accident, but I don't know how many it had aboard when it took off a short while ago."

Austin leaned over the diagram, his eyes taking in every detail. "Suppose the people under the glacier made it to the observatory. The air trapped in this passageway would keep the water from inundating the observatory area."

"That's true," Lessard said with little enthusiasm.

"If there is air, they could still be alive."

"Also true, but their supply of air is limited. This may be a case of the living envying the dead."

Austin didn't have to be reminded of the gruesome fate that awaited Skye and the others. Even if they had survived the flood, they faced a slow and uneasy death from lack of oxygen. He concentrated on the diagram and noticed that the main tunnel continued on for some distance beyond the observatory. "Where does this go?"

"It continues about 1.5 kilometers, rising gradually to another entrance."

"Another culvert?"

"No. There is an opening like a mine entrance in the side of the mountain."

"I'd like to see it," Austin said. A plan was forming in his mind. It was based on conjecture and assumption, and would need a healthy dose of luck to work, but it was all he had.

"It's on the other side of the glacier. The only way to get to it is by air, but I can show you where it is from here."

Minutes later, they were on the flat roof of the power plant. Lessard pointed to a ravine on the far side of the glacier. "It's right near that little valley."

Austin followed the pointing finger with his eyes, and then glanced toward the sky. A big helicopter was lumbering toward the power plant.

"Thank God!" Lessard said. "At last, someone has answered my call for help."

Hurrying downstairs, the two men emerged from the power plant as the helicopter dropped out of the sky. The truck driver and another man Austin assumed to be the plant's third shift were outside, watching the helicopter touch down on a landing pad a few hundred feet from the plant's front door. As the rotors whirled to a halt, three men emerged from the chopper. Austin frowned. This was no rescue party. All three men were wearing dark suits that had middle management written all over them.

"It is my superior, Monsieur Drouet. He *never* comes here," Lessard said, unable to contain the awe in his voice.

Drouet was a portly man with a Hercule Poirot mustache. He hustled over and in an accusatory tone said, "What is going on, Lessard?"

While the plant supervisor explained the situation, Austin checked his watch. The hands seemed to be flying around the dial.

"What effect has this incident had on production?" Drouet said.

Austin's smoldering temper erupted. "You might be more interested in what effect it has on the people trapped inside that glacier."

The man tilted his chin, managing to look down his nose at Austin even though he was shorter by several inches.

"*Who* are you?" he said, like the caterpillar addressing Alice from the mushroom.

Lessard intervened. "This is Mr. Austin with the American government."

"American?" Austin could swear he heard the man sniff. "This is none of your business," Drouet said.

"You're wrong. It is very *much* my business," Austin replied in a level voice that cloaked his anger. "My friend is in that tunnel."

Drouet was unmoved. "I have to wait for orders from my superior after I report to him. I'm not without sympathy. I'll order a rescue attempt immediately."

"That's not soon enough," Austin said. "We have to do something *now*."

"Nevertheless, it's the best I can do. Now, if you'll excuse me."

With that, he and the other suited men filed into the power plant. Lessard glanced at Austin, shook his head sadly and trailed after them.

Austin was trying to stifle the impulse to drag the bureaucrat back by the collar when he heard the sound of an engine and saw a dot in the sky. The dot grew larger and became a helicopter, smaller than the first. It shot across the lake, circled once around the power plant, then set down next to the other chopper in a cloud of dust.

Even before the rotors stopped, a slim, dark-complexioned man hopped out and gave Austin a wave. Joe Zavala strode over with an easy lope and a slight athletic swing to his shoulders, his relaxed walk a holdover from his boxing days, when he fought professionally as a middleweight to earn his way through college. His handsome, unmarred features testified to the success of his time in the ring.

The gregarious, soft-spoken Zavala had been recruited by Admiral Sandecker as soon as he graduated from the New York Maritime College, and he had been an invaluable member of the Special Assignments Team, working with Austin on many jobs. He had a brilliant mechanical mind and was a skilled pilot, with thousands of hours flying helicopters, small jets and turboprop aircraft.

Several days earlier, they had traveled to France together. While Austin flew on to the Alps to hook up with the *Mummichug*, Joe had stopped in Paris. As an expert in the design and building of underwater vehicles, he had been asked to join a panel on manned versus unmanned submersibles sponsored by IFREMER, the French Institute of Marine Research and Exploration.

Austin had called Zavala on his cell phone after learning about the tunnel accident. "Sorry to break up your trip to Paris," he had said.

"You broke up more than that. I met a member of the National Assembly who showed me the town."

"What's his name?"

"*Her* name is Denise. After a tour of Paris, we decided to head for the mountains where the young lady has a chalet. I'm in Chamonix."

Austin was not surprised to hear Zavala's story. With his soulful eyes and thick black hair combed straight back, Joe resembled a younger version of screen and TV actor Ricardo Montalban. The combination of good looks, good-humored charm and intelligence made him an object of desire to many of the single women around Washington, and the same qualities attracted females wherever he went. Sometimes it could be a distraction, especially on a mission, but in this case it was a godsend. Chamonix was only a few mountains away.

"Even better. I need your help."

Zavala could tell by the urgency in his friend's voice that the situation was serious. "I'm on my way," Zavala said.

Reunited on the barren hill overlooking the lake, they shook hands and Austin apologized again for putting a damper on his friend's love life. A slight smile cracked the ends of Zavala's lips.

"No problem, pal. Denise is a fellow public servant and

understood completely when I said duty called." He glanced at the helicopter. "She also pulled strings to get me transportation."

"I owe your young lady a bottle of champagne and some flowers."

"I always knew that you were a true romantic at heart." Zavala gazed around and said, "Beautiful scenery, even if it's a little bleak. What's going on?"

Austin headed for the helicopter. "I'll fill you in on the way."

MOMENTS LATER, they were airborne. As they flew over the glacier, Austin gave Zavala a *Reader's Digest*–style condensed version of events.

"Hell of a mess," Zavala said when he heard the story. "Sorry about your friend. Skye sounds like someone I'd like to meet."

"I hope you'll have that pleasure," Austin said, although he knew the odds were long and becoming longer with every passing minute.

He directed Zavala to the valley Lessard had pointed out from the roof of the power plant. Zavala landed at a spot of ground that was more or less level among the ledges and crags. They took an electric torch from the helicopter's emergency kit and walked up a gradual slope. The damp cold radiating from the glacier penetrated their thick jackets. A concrete casing framed the entrance to the tunnel. The area in front of the opening was washed out and dozens of miniature canyons ran down the slope. They stepped into a tunnel similar in size to those Austin had seen behind the power plant. The slanting floor was wet, and after they had gone in a few yards, water lapped at their toes.

"Not exactly the tunnel of love, is it?" Zavala said, peering into the darkness.

"It's what I would expect the river Styx to look like."

Austin stared at the black water for a moment, and then a bolt of energy seemed to pass through his body. "Let's get back to the power plant."

Drouet and his companions emerged from the plant building after Zavala's helicopter touched down. Drouet hurried over to greet Austin.

"I must apologize for my earlier behavior," he said. "I didn't have all the facts about this horrible situation. I have since talked to my superiors and the American embassy, which told me about you and NUMA, Monsieur Austin. I didn't know there were French citizens trapped under the glacier."

"Should their nationality have made any difference?"

"No, of course not. *Inexcusable*. You will be happy to know I have sent for help. A rescue team is on its way."

"That's a start. How long before they get here?"

Drouet hesitated, knowing the answer was unsatisfactory. "Three or four hours."

"You must know that will be too late."

Drouet wrung his hands in anguish. He was obviously distressed. "At least we can recover the bodies. It's the best I can do."

"It's not the best *I* can do, Monsieur Drouet. We're going to try to bring them back alive, but we'll need your help."

"You're not serious! Those poor people are trapped under eight hundred feet of ice." He studied the silent determination in Austin's face and arched an eyebrow. "Very well. I'll knock heads together to get you anything you need. Tell me what I must do."

Austin was pleasantly surprised to learn that Drouet's plump exterior hid a layer of steel.

"Thank you for your offer. First, I'd like to borrow your helicopter and pilot."

"Yes, of course, but I see your friend has a helicopter."

"I'll need a bigger one."

"I don't understand. These unfortunate people are trapped in the *ground*, not the air."

"Nevertheless." Austin gave Drouet a hard look that said he was through wasting time.

Drouet nodded vigorously. "Very well. You have my full cooperation."

While Drouet scurried over to talk to his pilot, Austin called the NUMA vessel's captain on a hand radio and spent several minutes sketching out his plan. Fortier listened carefully.

"I'll get right on it," he said.

Austin thanked him and gazed at the glacier, sizing up the adversary he was about to tackle. He had no room in his scheme of things for self-doubt. He knew plans could go awry, and had scars all over his body to prove it. He also knew that problems could be fixed. He was certain that, with luck, his scheme would work. What he *wasn't* sure of was whether Skye was still alive.

8

SKYE WAS VERY much alive. Renaud, who was feeling the full force of her fury, could attest to that. After Renaud had made one of his self-serving comments, Skye had snapped. She had laced into the hapless Frenchman, her eyes bright with tears of rage as she tongue-lashed him for ruining the biggest discovery of her career. Renaud finally summoned up the courage to croak a protest. Skye had exhausted her repertoire and lung power by then and cut him short with a withering glare and a well-chosen word.

"Idiot!"

Renaud tried to play on her sympathy. "Can't you see I'm injured?" He held his bruised and lacerated hand.

"It's your own stupid fault," she said coldly. "How in God's name could you allow a man with a gun to come into this place?"

"I thought he was a reporter."

"You have the brain of an amoeba. Amoebas don't think. They *ooze*."

"Mademoiselle, please," LeBlanc entreated. "We have only so much air to breathe. Save your strength."

"Save it for *what*?" She pointed to the ceiling. "It may have escaped your attention, but we are stuck under a very large glacier."

LeBlanc put his finger to his lips.

Skye glanced around at the cold and frightened faces and saw she was making the others even more miserable. She realized, too, that her tirade against Renaud was a product of her fear and frustration. She apologized to LeBlanc and clamped her lips tightly together, but before she did so, she muttered, "He *is* an idiot."

Then she went over and plunked down next to Rawlins, the magazine writer, who was sitting with his back against a wall, writing in a notebook. He had bunched a plastic tarp together and was using it to insulate his posterior from contact with the wet floor. She snuggled close for warmth, saying, "Pardon me for being forward, but I'm freezing."

Rawlins blinked in surprise, set the notebook aside and then gallantly wrapped an arm around her shoulder.

"You were pretty hot a minute ago," he said.

"Sorry for losing my temper in front of everyone," she murmured.

"I don't blame you, but try to look on the bright side. At least we've got lights."

The floodwaters must have missed the wires that ran along the top of the tunnel to the power plant. Although the lights had flickered a few times, the power was still on. The wet and weary survivors were crowded into the stretch of tunnel that ran between the ice cave and the stairs.

Despite his optimistic observation, Rawlins knew they were short on time. He and the others were finding it more difficult to breathe. He attempted to divert his thoughts.

"What was that scientific discovery you were talking about?" he asked Skye.

A dreamy look came into her eyes. "I found an ancient tomb under the waters of the lake. I think it may have had something to do with the Amber Route, which means that trade contacts between Europe and the Mediterranean countries go further back than anyone has ever imagined. To Minoan or Mycenaean times maybe."

Rawlins groaned.

"Are you all right?" Skye said.

"Yeah, I'm fine. Oh hell, no, I'm not. The only reason I'm here was to do a story on the subglacial observatory. Then they found the body in the ice, which would have been a major exclusive. Then a thug posing as a reporter pistol-whips your pal Renaud and floods the tunnel. Wow! My stuff would have been picked up all over the world. I would have been the next Jon Krakauer. Publishers would be pounding on my door with book deals. Now, you tell me about the Minoan angle."

"I don't know that it's Minoan," Skye said, trying to ease his distress. "I could be wrong."

He shook his head sadly.

The TV reporter, who had been listening to the conversation, said, "Don't blame you for feeling bad, but put yourself in my place. I've got video of the body and the French guy getting smacked with the gun."

The other reporter tapped his tape recorder. "Yeah, and I got the voices all on tape."

Rawlins stared at the fire hose snaking past their feet. "I wonder if we could use a water jet to melt a tunnel through the glacier."

Thurston was sitting next to Rawlins. He chuckled and said, "I've already done some calculations in my head. It will take us about three months if we work steadily."

"Do we get time off for Sundays and holidays?" Rawlins asked.

Everyone laughed, except for Renaud.

Rawlins's offbeat humor reminded Skye of Austin. How long had it been since she left the ship? She glanced at her watch and realized that only a few hours had elapsed. She had been eagerly looking forward to their date. She'd been entranced by the rugged profile, the pale, almost white hair, but it went beyond physical attraction.

He was interesting, a study in contrasts. Austin had a quick sense of humor and he could be warm and gentle, but she detected diamond hardness behind the twinkle in those blue eyes. And, of course, there were those magnificent shoulders. She wouldn't be surprised if he could walk on the bottom of the sea.

Her eyes shifted to Renaud, who was at the far end of the attractiveness spectrum. He sat on the other side of the tunnel, nursing his swollen hand. She frowned, thinking that the worst part of this whole affair was being entombed with an insect like Renaud. The thought depressed her, so she rose and walked to the staircase that led down to the main tunnel. Black water lapped over the top of the staircase. Not a chance of escape. She became depressed again. Looking for a diversion, she sloshed through puddles and climbed the ladder to the ice cave.

The glacier was already starting to retake its lost territory. New ice had formed in jagged icicles where there was none before. The ice had thickened and the body was no longer visible in its tomb. The helmet was still in its container. She picked it up and held it under a light where she could see the etchings. They were intricate and finely executed. The work of a master. The design struck her as not being simply decorative. There was a rhythm to it, as if it were telling a story. The metal seemed to pulsate with a life of its own. She got a grip on her rampaging thoughts. Lack of air was making her imagine things. If only she had more time, she could figure it out. *Damn* that Renaud.

She carried the helmet back into the tunnel. The walk in the thin air had exhausted her. She found a spot against the wall, propped the helmet beside her and sat down. The others had stopped talking. She could see their chests heaving as they sucked the anorexic air into their lungs. She found that she was doing the same, gulping like a fish out of water, but still not meeting the demands of her lungs. Her chin dropped, and she fell asleep.

When she awoke, the lights had finally gone out. So, she said to herself, we will die in darkness after all. She tried to call out to the others, to wish them a farewell, but she didn't have the strength. She fell asleep again.

9

AUSTIN STRAPPED THE last waterproof stuff bag onto the SEAmobile's flat rear deck behind the bubble cockpit and stepped back to inspect the job. The vehicle looked more like a mechanical pack mule than a high-tech submersible, but the jerry-rigged arrangement would have to do. With no idea how many people were trapped under the glacier, he had rounded up every set of scuba equipment and backup gear he could find and simply hoped for the best.

Austin gave an okay sign to François. The government observer had been standing by with a hand radio, acting as a combined liaison and translator between the ship and the helicopter. François returned the gesture and spoke into the hand radio. The pilot of the French helicopter was waiting for the call.

Within minutes, the helicopter was lifting off the beach. It flew out to the NUMA boat, where it hovered and dropped a cable down to the deck. Austin ducked his head against the blast from the spinning rotors, grabbed the hook at the end of the cable and attached it to a four-point harness system. He and the crew had already secured the trailer and submersible so the load could be lifted in one piece.

He gave the pilot a thumbs-up. The cable went taut and the helicopter rose slightly and hung in space with its rotors madly slashing the air. Despite the ear-shattering racket, the submersible and trailer only lifted a few inches off the deck. The combined weight of the sub, trailer and cargo were beyond the aircraft's lifting capacity. Austin signaled the chopper to ease off. The line went slack and the load thumped back onto the deck.

Austin pointed to the helicopter and shouted in François's ear.

"Tell them to stay where they are until I figure this out."

As François translated, Austin got on his own radio and called Zavala, whose helicopter had been circling high above the ship.

"We've got a problem," Austin said.

"So I see. Wish this chopper was a sky crane," he said, referring to the huge industrial helicopters that were designed to hoist big loads.

"We may not need one." Austin laid out what he had in mind.

Zavala laughed and said, "My life must have been very dull before I met you."

"Well?"

"Tricky," Zavala said. "Dangerous as hell. Audacious. But possible."

Austin never doubted his partner's flying skills. Zavala had thousands of hours as a pilot in helicopters, small jet and turboprop aircraft. It was the vagaries, the unexpected that bothered him. A shift of the wind, human inattention or equipment failure could turn a carefully calculated risk into a disaster. In this case, the job could end with a mix-up in translation. He had to be sure the message was clear.

He pulled François aside and told him what he wanted the French pilot to do. Then he made him repeat his instructions back to him. François nodded in understanding.

He spoke into his radio and the French helicopter moved off to the side so that the lifting line was at an angle.

Zavala's chopper darted in and dropped a line, which Austin quickly spliced onto the harness. He gave the choppers a visual check, making sure there was plenty of space between the two aircraft. They would be pulled together by the weight they were lifting and he didn't want the helicopters tangling rotors.

Once more, Austin gave the signal to lift. The rotors churned away in earsplitting concert and this time the submersible and trailer seemed to leap skyward. A foot. Two feet. A yard. Two yards. The pilots were well aware of the fact that the helicopters were of unequal size and power, and adjusted for the difference with amazing skill.

They rose in slow motion, the strange load swinging between them until they were a couple of hundred feet above the lake's surface, and then they flew toward land until they were lost against the dark rock of the mountains. Zavala kept up a running commentary over the radio. He had to break off a couple of times to correct his position.

Austin didn't breathe easily until he heard Zavala's laconic announcement: "The eagles have landed."

Austin and several crewmen scrambled into a small boat and were on shore waiting when the helicopters came back, flying side by side, and landed on the beach. Austin climbed into Zavala's chopper and the French helicopter took on crew from the *Mummichug*.

Minutes later, they dropped down for a landing near the bright yellow SEAmobile, which was on its trailer in front of the tunnel entrance. Austin supervised the crew as they adjusted the sub's load. Then the trailer was backed into the sloping tunnel to the water's edge. Chocks were inserted behind the wheels, while Austin left the tunnel to confer with Lessard. At Austin's request, the plant supervisor had retrieved another blueprint from his trove. He spread it out on a flat rock.

"These are the internal aluminum supports I told you about. You'll encounter them a few hundred feet inside the tunnel. There are twelve sets laid three abreast, approximately ten yards between one set and the other."

"The submersible is less than eight feet wide," Austin said. "I've figured out that I'll only have to cut one column in each set to squeeze through."

"I suggest that you stagger your cuts. In other words, don't cut the same column position in every set. As you can see by this diagram, the ceiling is the thinnest here of any place within the tunnel. You've got hundreds of tons of ice and rock pressing down on the tunnel."

"I've figured that into the equation."

Lessard's eyes bored into Austin's face. "I called Paris after you posed your plan and talked to a friend in the state power company. He said this end of the tunnel was built to move the lab trailers into place. It was discarded as prime access because as time went on there was danger of the roof collapsing. The columns were installed to keep the tunnel open as a ventilating airshaft. This is what worries me," he said, drawing his finger across the top of the tunnel drawn on the blueprint. "There's a large unstable pocket of water here. Because of the lateness of the season, it is even bigger than usual. If there is a weakness in the support system, the whole ceiling could come down."

"It's worth the risk," Austin said.

"You've considered the possibility that you're risking your lives in vain, that the people are already dead."

Austin replied with a grim smile, "We won't know that until we take a look, will we?"

Lessard regarded Austin with an expression of admiration. The American with the pale hair and arresting blue eyes was either insane or supremely confident in his abilities. "You must like this woman very much."

"I only met her a few days ago, but we have a dinner date in Paris and I intend to keep it."

Lessard replied with a shrug. Gallantry was something a Frenchman could appreciate. "The first few weeks are the time of maximum attraction between a man and a woman, before they know each other well. Well, *bonne chance, mon ami.* I see your friend wants your attention."

Austin thanked Lessard for his advice and went over to where Zavala was standing in front of the tunnel entrance.

"I've gone over the sub's control system. Pretty simple stuff," Zavala said.

"I knew you wouldn't have a problem." Austin took a last glance around. "Time to vamoose, amigo."

Zavala gave him a sour look. "You've been watching too many reruns of the Cisco Kid."

Austin pulled on an insulated one-piece dry suit. Looking like a big Day-Glo Gumby, he led the way into the tunnel and slipped a helmet containing an underwater acoustic transceiver onto his head. Zavala helped him on with his air tank and weight belt, and then gave him a hand climbing onto the back of the submersible.

He sat behind the bubble using the waterproof stuff bags as a seat and pulled on his fins. A crewman handed up a lightweight underwater cutting torch and oxygen tank, which Austin secured to the deck with bungee cords. Zavala got into the cabin and gave Austin the high sign.

"Ready to roll?" Austin said, testing his headset.

"Sure, but I feel like the bubble boy."

"You can trade places with me anytime you'd like, Bubble Boy."

Zavala chuckled. "Thanks, but I'll pass on the generous offer. You look natural riding shotgun, Tex."

Austin rapped on the bubble. He was ready.

The launch crew lifted the trailer hitch and slowly let the trailer roll into the water, keeping its speed under control with a pair of launching lines, until the wheels were submerged. As soon as the vehicle started to float, the crew jerked on the pull lines and pushed the vehicle at the same time. The SEAmobile floated free of the trailer and the motors came alive.

Zavala used the lateral thrusters on the tail section to put the SEAmobile into a 360-degree turn, facing the vehicle into the tunnel. He moved the vehicle forward until the water was deep enough to submerge. Using a light touch on the vertical thruster, he pushed the sub down until the hull was under water. The tail thrusters whirred again, the submersible moved forward, going deeper, and the water washed over Austin and the bubble.

The quartet of halogen lights in the front of the vehicle played off the orange walls and ceiling, and the reflected light gave the water a brownish cast.

Zavala's metallic voice came over Austin's earphones.

"This is like diving into a bucket of chocolate mole sauce."

"I'll remember that the next time I eat in a Mexican restaurant. I was thinking about something more poetic and Dante-ish, like a descent into Hades."

"At least Hades is warm and dry. How far are the first support columns?"

Austin stared into the murk beyond the reach of the lights and thought he saw a dull glint of metal. He stood up and leaned against the bubble, holding onto the D-shaped protective bars that flanked the cabin.

"I think they're coming up now."

Zavala slowed the submersible to a stop a few yards from the first set of aluminum columns, each about six inches across, that barred the way. Carrying the torch and tank, Austin swam to the base of the middle column. He ignited the torch and the sharp blue flame quickly cut through the metal close to the base. At the top of the column he made another cut, and then he yelled "Timber!" and pushed the middle section out. He motioned for Zavala to follow, directing him through the gap with hand signals, like an airport worker guiding a plane to its gate. Then he went on to the next set of columns.

As he swam, he cast a wary glance above his head and tried not to think of the thousands of gallons of water and tons of ice pressing down on the thin rock ceiling. Heeding Lessard's advice, he cut the right-hand column on the second set. Again Zavala moved the vehicle through. Austin cut a middle column, then a left-hand one on the next set. Then he started the process over again.

The work went smoothly. Before long, twelve columns lay on the tunnel floor. Austin resumed his seat on the back of the submersible and told Zavala to go at the vehicle's top speed of 2.5 knots. Although they were moving at a brisk walk, the darkness and the closeness of the walls combined made it seem to Austin as if he were on Neptune's chariot flying down to the Abyss.

With nothing to do but hold on, he extended his thoughts to the difficult task ahead. Lessard's words echoed in his ears. The Frenchman was right about maximum attraction. He might also be right about everyone in the tunnel being dead.

It had been easier being optimistic while he was in daylight. But as they plunged deeper into the stygian darkness, he knew that the rescue attempt could be in vain. He had to admit that there was little chance that anyone could remain alive for long in this dreadful place. Reluctantly, he steeled himself for the worst.

10

IN HER DREAM, Skye was having dinner with Austin in a Parisian bistro near the Eiffel Tower and he was saying, "Wake up," and she was answering with no little irritation, "I'm not asleep."

Wake up, Skye.

Austin again. Irritating man.

Then Austin was reaching across the table, past the wine and paté, gently slapping her cheek, and she was getting angrier. She opened her mouth. "Stop!"

"That's better," Austin said.

Her eyelids popped open like a pair of broken window shades and she turned her face away from the blinding light. The light shifted and she saw Austin's face. He looked worried. He gently squeezed her cheeks until she opened her mouth, then she felt the hard plastic mouthpiece of a scuba regulator between her teeth.

Air flowed into her lungs, reviving her, and she saw that Austin was kneeling by her side. He was wearing an orange dry suit and some strange sort of headgear. He took her hand and gently wrapped her fingers around the small air tank that fed the regulator.

He removed the regulator from his own mouth.

"Can you stay awake for a minute?" he said.

She nodded.

"Don't go away. I'll be right back."

Then he stood and walked toward the staircase. In the brief instant before he descended into the water with his electric torch, she saw the others who'd been trapped with her, all looking like derelicts sleeping off a cheap wine binge in an alley.

Moments later, the water in the stairway emitted an eerie glow and Austin reappeared holding a line slung over one shoulder. He dug his feet in and hauled on the line like a Volga boatman. The floor was treacherous underfoot and he slipped to his knee, but he was up immediately. A plastic bag that was attached to the line came out of the water and slid across the floor like a big fish. More bags followed.

Austin quickly unzipped the bags and handed out the air tanks that they contained. He had to shake a few people into a groggy consciousness, but when they got their first breath of air, they revived quickly. As they greedily sucked down the life-giving air, the metallic sound of the regulator valves was loud in the confined space.

Skye spit out the mouthpiece. "What are *you* doing here?" she said, like a society doyenne addressing a party crasher.

He hoisted Skye gently to her feet and kissed her on the forehead. "Never let it be said that Kurt Austin let a little hell or high water stand in the way of our dinner date."

"Dinner! But—"

Austin tucked the regulator back between Skye's lips. "No time for talking."

Then he was opening the other bags and pulling out dry suits. Rawlins and Thurston were both certified divers, as it turned out, and they helped the others get into their suits and scuba gear. Before long, the survivors were suited up. Not exactly a SEAL team, Austin thought, but with a lot of luck they might make it.

"Ready to go home?" he asked.

The muted chorus that echoed in the cave was incomprehensible but enthusiastic.

"Okay," he said. "Follow me."

Austin led the pitiful-looking cave dwellers down the staircase and into the flooded tunnel. More than one eyebrow was raised at the strange vision of Zavala waving at them from inside his glowing bubble.

Austin had foreseen that his passengers would need something to hold on to during their ride. Before he and the *Mummichug*'s crew had piled the dive gear bags onto the sub, they had stretched fishing net over the SEAmobile's deck. With vigorous use of hand signals, pushes and prods, Austin arranged the cave survivors facedown on the deck in rows of three like sardines in a can.

He put Renaud, with his bad hand, in the first row, right behind the bubble, between the reporters. Skye was in the middle row between Rawlins and Thurston, who were the most experienced in the water. He would be behind her in the third row between LeBlanc, who seemed strong as a bull, and Rossi, the young research assistant.

As insurance, Austin ran lines over the backs of his passengers as if he were securing any bulky cargo. The submersible was practically invisible under the tightly packed bodies, but the arrangement was the best he could think of with the limited space available. Austin swam to the rear, where he put himself behind Skye. He would have to move freely from his perch later, so he left himself unfettered.

"All our ducks are lined up in a row," he said over the communicator. "Tight quarters back here, so I'd advise against picking up hitchhikers."

With a whirr of electric motors, the SEAmobile inched forward at a crawl, then sped up to a walk. Austin knew the survivors must be weary beyond words. Although he had cautioned the group to be patient, the vehicle's slow pace was maddening and he was having trouble abiding by his own advice.

At least he could talk to Zavala. The others were alone with their thoughts. The submersible plowed through the tunnel as if it were being pulled by a team of turtles. At times, the submersible seemed to be standing still and the tunnel walls were moving past them. The only sounds were the monotonous hum of the motor and the burble of escaping air bubbles. He almost yelled for joy when Zavala announced, "Kurt, I can see the columns dead ahead."

Austin lifted his head. "Stop before you get to them. I'll bird-dog you through the slalom course."

The SEAmobile coasted to a halt. Austin detached himself from the deck and rose above the bubble. The first set of supports gleamed about thirty feet ahead. With easy, rhythmic kicks of his fins, Austin swam toward the supports and passed through the gap he had cut in the columns. Then he spun around and waved Zavala through like a traffic cop, directing him to the right or left as needed.

The submersible eased slowly through the opening. Zavala veered from his straight course to steer through the next opening and that's when he got into trouble. The overburdened submersible responded sluggishly and skidded into a slide. Using a steady hand on the thruster controls, he arrested the sideways momentum and headed the submersible toward the opening. But as the vehicle passed through the breach, he tried to compensate and the sub clipped a column and began to fishtail.

Austin swam off to one side and plastered himself against a tunnel wall until Zavala prudently brought the SEAmobile to a stop. Austin swam up to the cabin.

"You really have to do something about your driving, old pal."

"Sorry," Zavala said. "With all the weight in the back, this thing handles like a bumper boat."

"Try to remember that you're not behind the wheel of your Corvette."

Zavala smiled. "I wish I were."

Austin inspected the passengers, saw that they were holding up, and swam ahead to the next set of columns. He held his breath as the vehicle and its load eased through without incident. Zavala was getting the hang of controlling the sub and they successfully navigated several more sets of columns. Austin kept a count in his head. Only three more sets of pillars to go.

As he approached the next set of columns he noticed something was off-kilter. He squinted through his mask and was not reassured by what he saw. He had cut the middle column out and now the supports on either side of the opening looked like a pair of bowed legs. A quick movement caught his eye and he glanced upward. Bubbles were streaming through a narrow fissure in the ceiling.

Austin didn't have to be a structural engineer to figure out what was happening. The ceiling weight was too much for the remaining supports to bear. They could collapse any second, entombing the submersible and its passengers in the tunnel forever.

"Joe, we've got a problem ahead," Austin said, doing his best to keep his voice calm.

"I see what you mean," Zavala replied, leaning forward to peer through the bubble. "Those columns look like a cowboy's legs. Any advice on how we navigate this mousetrap?"

"The same way porcupines make love. *Carefully.* Make sure you walk in my footprints."

Austin swam toward the bowed supports and easily passed through with space on either side. He turned and shielded his eyes against the sub's bright halogen lights, then waved Zavala ahead. Zavala successfully maneuvered the vehicle through the opening without touching either column. But he ran into trouble from an unexpected quarter. Part of the net trailing off the rear end of the submersible snagged on the stub of the column Austin had cut. Zavala felt the tug and instinctively applied power without thinking.

It was the worst possible thing he could have done.

The vehicle hesitated as the thrusters dug in, then the net tore free and the sub lurched ahead out of control, smashing into the right-hand column of the next set with all of its substantial weight. Zavala quickly compensated for the wild swing. But it was too late. The damaged column buckled.

Austin watched the slow-motion disaster unfold. His

eyes darted to the ceiling, suddenly obscured by a massive cloud of bubbles.

"Move out!" Austin shouted. "The roof's coming down!"

Curses in Spanish filled Austin's earphones.

Zavala applied full power to the thrusters and aimed for the next gap. The vehicle passed within feet of Austin. With perfect timing, he reached out and grabbed on to the fishnet, dangling like a Hollywood stuntman on a runaway stagecoach.

Zavala was more intent on haste than precision and didn't bother to fine-tune his steering. The vehicle clipped a column. It was only a tiny dent, but the column bent and snapped. Austin had managed to scramble back on to the deck by then and he held on grimly as the vehicle spun completely around and regained its proper heading.

One more opening loomed ahead.

The submersible made a clean pass through the space without touching a column. But the damage had already been done.

The ceiling burst asunder and crashed down in a crushing avalanche of huge boulders, releasing the water stored in the glacial pocket. Thousands of gallons of water poured into the confined space of the tunnel. A powerful pressure wave hit the SEAmobile and pushed it through the tunnel like a leaf through a sluice.

The wave rushed toward the entrance, carrying the vehicle on its crest.

Unaware of the drama unfolding in the dark recesses below the glacier, the support crew had drifted back to the helicopters. The lone crewman who'd been keeping watch for the vehicle had stepped outside the tunnel for air when he heard the roar issue from the bowels of the earth. His legs reacted before his brain did and carried him away from the tunnel mouth. He was off to one side, hiding behind a boulder, when the vehicle shot out of the tunnel's entrance into the open air.

The wave's full force expended itself outside the cave,

leaving the vehicle high and dry. Dazed and battered passengers untied the lines that held them and dropped off the deck. They spit out the regulators and sucked fresh air into their lungs in great coughing gulps.

Zavala was out of the cabin running back toward the tunnel. He stepped aside when a secondary, weaker wave burst from the tunnel, surged around the vehicle and disgorged a struggling figure in an orange suit. Austin's cracked face mask was askew. The communicator helmet had been ripped from his head and the force of the wave was rolling him like a ball caught in the surf.

Zavala reached down, caught Austin in midroll and helped him to his feet.

He was as unsteady as a drunk and his eyes were as glassy as marbles. Austin spit out a mouthful of foul water and barked like a wet dog.

"Like I said, Joe. You really have to do something about your driving."

THE FRENCH rescue team arrived an hour later. The helicopter dropped down in front of the power plant like an osprey on a fish. Even before its runners had touched the ground, six dashing and rugged mountain climbers piled out the door, lugging carabiners and coils of rope. Their leader explained that they brought mountain-climbing equipment because they understood people were trapped *on* the glacier, not under it.

When the leader learned that his team's services were not needed, he shrugged and admitted philosophically that even a crack mountain team would have been useless in a water rescue. Then he broke out a couple of bottles of champagne he had brought along. Raising his glass high in a toast, he said there would be other opportunities; people were always getting into trouble in the mountains.

After the impromptu celebration, Austin supervised the submersible's return to the *Mummichug*, and then he returned to the power plant with Zavala. The survivors had been shuttled to the plant for showers and hot food. Dressed in a motley assortment of borrowed clothes, they had gathered in the plant's recreation room to tell their story.

The reporters ran the videotapes of the attack on Renaud, but they were of poor quality and showed only a blurred glimpse of the gunman's face. The audiotape revealed little except for the brief exchange between Renaud and his assailant.

Austin was nursing his bumps and bruises with a bottle of Belgian beer from the power plant's larder. He sat with his chin cradled in his hand, feeling his anger grow as Skye and the others trapped in the tunnel described details of the cold-blooded act that almost condemned several innocent people to a horrible death under the ice.

"This is a matter for the police," said Drouet, the power plant supervisor, after he had heard the full story. "The authorities should be notified immediately."

Austin held his tongue. By the time the gendarmes arrived, the trail would be colder than the beer in his hand.

Renaud was anxious to leave. Brandishing his hand as if it were a fatal wound, he bullied his way and found a seat on the power plant helicopter. Rawlins and the reporters were eager to file details of their story, which had gone far beyond the discovery of the frozen body. The reporters called in the chartered floatplane that had delivered them to the glacier.

The plane's pilot cleared up one mystery. He said he'd been waiting on the lake for the reporters to return from the glacier, when a big man he had brought in showed up at the beach in LeBlanc's Citroën. The man said the other reporters were staying overnight, and that he needed a ride out immediately.

Skye watched the floatplane skim across the lake for a takeoff and she broke into laughter. "Did you see Renaud? He was using his injured hand to push other people out of the way so he could get on first."

"The mocking tone of your voice suggests that you are not sorry to see Renaud leave," Austin said.

She pretended she was washing her hands. "Good riddance to bad rubbish, as my father used to say."

Lessard was standing next to Skye, and he had a sad look in his eyes as he watched the floatplane leap from the lake and head toward a valley between two mountain peaks.

"Well, Monsieur Austin, I must go back to work," he said in a mournful voice. "Thank you for the excitement you and your friends have brought to this lonely outpost."

Austin grasped Lessard's hand in a firm grip. "The rescue would have been impossible without your help," Austin said. "I don't think you'll be alone for long. When the story gets out, you'll be inundated with reporters. The police will be sniffing around here as well."

Lessard looked more pleased than annoyed. "You *think* so?" He beamed. "If you'll excuse me, I'd better get back to my office to prepare for visitors. I'll have a truck drive you back to the lake if you'd like."

"I'll walk with you," Skye said. "I've got to pick up something I left in the plant."

Zavala said of Lessard, "That gentleman apparently isn't content with his fifteen minutes of fame. Now, if you are through with my services—"

Austin put his hand on Zavala's shoulder. "Don't tell me you want to leave this garden spot so you can to get back to Chamonix and your French pastry."

Zavala's eyes followed Skye. "It appears I'm not the only one partaking of the local delicacies?"

"You're way ahead of me, Joe. The young lady and I haven't even had our first date yet."

"Well, I'm the last guy to stand in the way of true romance."

"Nor am I," Austin said, walking Zavala to the helicopter. "See you in Paris."

11

THE TRAFFIC JAM was horrendous even by Washington standards. Paul Trout had been sitting behind the steering wheel of his Humvee, staring with glazed eyes at the wall-to-wall carpet of cars clogging Pennsylvania Avenue, when he turned suddenly to Gamay and said, "My gills are starting to close up."

Gamay rolled her eyes in the way of a wife long used to her husband's eccentricities. She knew what was coming. Paul's family said only half-jokingly that if a Trout stayed away from his ancestral home for too long, he would start gasping for breath like a fish out of water. Therefore she wasn't surprised when he made an illegal U-turn, displaying the contempt for rules of the road that seems born into Massachusetts drivers.

While Paul drove as if he were on Desert Storm maneuvers, she used her cell phone to call the airline for reservations and to let their NUMA office know they would be away for a few days. They whirled through their Georgetown town house like twin tornadoes, packed their overnight bags and dashed to the airport.

Less than two hours after their shuttle flight landed in

Boston, they were on Cape Cod, strolling along Water Street in the village of Woods Hole, where Trout had been born and raised. Woods Hole's main thoroughfare is about a quarter of a mile long, squeezed between a salt pond and a harbor, and bordered on both sides by buildings that house organizations devoted to marine and environmental science.

The most conspicuous of these is the world-renowned Woods Hole Oceanographic Institution. Nearby, in a vintage brick-and-granite edifice, is the Marine Biological Laboratory, whose research programs and library of nearly two hundred thousand volumes attract scholars from around the globe. Within walking distance of the MBL is the National Marine Fisheries aquarium. On the outskirts of the village are the U.S. Geological Survey and dozens of sea education institutions and private companies that produce the high-tech underwater gadgets used by ocean scientists the world over.

A breeze was coming off the harbor from the direction of the Elizabeth Islands. Trout paused on the tiny drawbridge that separates Eel Pond and Great Harbor and he filled his lungs with salty air, thinking that there must be some truth to the gill-closing story. He could actually breathe again.

Trout was the son of a local fisherman and his wife, and his family still owned the low-slung Cape Cod cottage where he had been raised. His intellectual home was the Oceanographic Institution. As a boy he used to run errands for some of the scientists who worked at the institution and it was at their encouragement that he had specialized in deep-ocean geology, a move that would bring him eventually to NUMA and its Special Assignments Team.

Within hours of their arrival, Paul had checked on his house, touched base with several relatives and stopped off for lunch with Gamay at a local watering hole where he knew everyone at the bar. Then he began to make the rounds. He was visiting the Institution's Deep Submergence Lab where an old colleague was bringing him up-to-date on the latest in autonomous underwater vehicles, when the phone rang.

"It's for you," his colleague said, handing Trout the phone.

A voice boomed on the line. "Hello, Trout. This is Sam Osborne. Heard down at the post office that you were back in town. How are you and your lovely wife?"

Osborne was a phycologist, one of the world's foremost experts in the science of algology, or the study of algae. After years of teaching, he still talked in a range that was two or three decibels above that of a normal human being.

Trout didn't bother asking how Osborne had tracked him down. It was impossible to keep anything secret in a village the size of Woods Hole. "We're fine, thank you. Nice of you to give me a call, Dr. Osborne."

Osborne cleared his throat. "Well, er, actually I wasn't calling you. I wanted to speak to your wife."

Trout smiled. "I don't blame you for that. Gamay is much prettier than I am."

He handed the phone to his wife. Gamay Morgan-Trout was an attractive woman, not gorgeous or overly sexy, but appealing to most men. She had a flashing smile with a slight gap in her upper teeth like the model-actress Lauren Hutton. She was tall, five feet ten, and 135 pounds, slim for her height. Her hair, which was long and generally worn swirled, was dark red, the reason her father, a wine connoisseur, had named her after the grape of Beaujolais.

More open and vivacious than her husband, she worked well with men, a talent that went back to her tomboy days in Wisconsin. Her father was a successful developer who had encouraged her to compete with men, teaching her to sail and shoot skeet. She was an expert diver and marksman.

Gamay listened for a moment, and then said, "We'll be right over." Hanging up, she said, "Dr. Osborne has asked us to come by the MBL. He says it's urgent."

"*Every*thing is urgent to Sam," Paul said.

"Now, now. You needn't be snide just because he wanted to talk to me."

"I don't have a snide bone in my body," Paul said, linking arms with Gamay.

He bid good-bye to his colleague in the Submergence Lab and he and Gamay set off along Water Street. A few minutes later, they were climbing the wide stone steps at the Lillie Research Building, where they went through an arched doorway into a quiet lobby.

Dr. Osborne was waiting for them just inside. He pumped Paul's hand and embraced Gamay, whom he'd had as a student when she was studying marine biology at the Scripps Institute of Oceanography in California. Osborne was in his mid-fifties, and his receding, curly white hair seemed to be slipping off the back of his skull. He had a big-boned physique and large workman's hands that looked more suitable for handling a pickax than the delicate strands of marine vegetation that were his specialty.

"Thanks for coming over," he said. "I hope that this is no imposition."

"None at all," Gamay said sweetly. "Always a pleasure to see you."

"You may not think so when you hear what I have to tell you," Osborne said with an enigmatic smile.

Without further explanation, he led them to his office. Although the MBL was known all over the world for its research facilities and library, the Lillie Building lab was an unprepossessing place. Exposed pipes ran along the ceilings, the doors lining the hallways were of dark wood with pebbled glass panels, and in general it looked exactly like what it was, a venerable old lab building.

Osborne ushered the Trouts into his office. Gamay had remembered Osborne as fanatically neat and organized, bordering on the anal, and she saw that he hadn't changed. Where many professors of his stature surrounded themselves with piles of paper and reports, his office consisted of a computer table and chair and a couple of folding chairs for visitors. His only luxury was a tea maker, which he had picked up in Japan.

He poured three cups of green tea and after a brief exchange of pleasantries, he said, "Pardon me for being so brusque, but time is short, so I'll get right to the point." He leaned back in his chair, tented his fingers and said to Gamay, "As a marine biologist, you're acquainted with *Caulerpa taxifolia*?"

Gamay had received a degree in marine archaeology from the University of North Carolina before changing her field of interest and enrolling at Scripps, where she'd attained a doctorate in marine biology. Gamay smiled inwardly as she remembered being a student in Osborne's class. He typically asked questions in the form of a statement.

"*Caulerpa* is an alga that's native to the tropics, although it's often seen in home aquariums."

"Correct. And you know that the cold-water strain that thrives so well in aquaria has become a major problem in certain coastal areas?"

Gamay nodded. "Killer seaweed. It's destroyed large expanses of the seabed in the Mediterranean and has spread to other places as well. It's a strain of a tropical alga. Tropical algae don't normally live in cold water, but this strain has adapted. It could spread anywhere in the world."

Osborne turned to Paul. "The weed we're talking about was inadvertently released into the water beneath the Oceanographic Museum of Monaco in 1984. Since then it has spread to thirty thousand hectares in the coastal floor off six Mediterranean countries, and it's a problem off Australia and San Diego. It spreads like wildfire. The problem goes beyond speed. The *Caulerpa* colonies are extremely invasive. The weed spreads out with runners and forms a dense green carpet that crowds out other flora and fauna, depriving plants and animals of sunlight and oxygen. Its presence destroys the base of the marine food web, damages native species with devastating consequences for ecosystems."

"Isn't there any way to fight this stuff?"

"In San Diego, they've had some success using tarpaulins to quarantine patches of weed, while pumping chlorine into the water and the mud that anchors the plants. This technique would be useless with a widespread infestation. There has been an effort to educate aquarium dealers who sell *Caulerpa* or deal in rocks that might be contaminated with organisms."

"No natural enemies?" Trout said.

"Its defense mechanisms are amazingly complex. The weed contains toxins that deter herbivores. It does not die back in winter."

"Sounds like a real monster," Trout said.

"Oh it *is*. It is. A tiny fragment can start a new colony. Its only weakness is that it can't reproduce sexually, like its wild relatives. But think what might happen if it were to disperse eggs over long distances."

"Not a pleasant thought," Gamay said. "It could become unstoppable."

Osborne turned to Paul. "As an ocean geologist, you're familiar with the area of the Lost City?"

Trout was glad to get out of the realm of biology and into his area of expertise. "It's an area of hydrothermal vents along the Atlantic Massif. The material spewing from the sea bottom has built up tall mineral towers that resemble skyscrapers, hence the name. I've read the research on it. Fascinating stuff. I'd like to get out there sometime."

"You may soon get your chance," Osborne said.

Paul and Gamay exchanged puzzled glances.

Osborne chuckled, noting their befuddled expressions.

"Perhaps you'd better come with me," he said.

They left the office and after several twists and turns found themselves in a small laboratory. Osborne went over to a padlocked metal storage cabinet. He unlocked the door with a key hung from his belt and extracted a cylindrical glass phial about twelve inches tall and six inches in diameter. The top was sealed tight. He placed the phial on the table under a lab light. The container seemed to be filled from top to bottom with a thick grayish-green substance.

Gamay leaned forward to examine the contents and said, "What is this gunk?"

"Before I answer your question, let me give you a little background. A few months ago, MBL participated in a joint expedition to the Lost City with the Woods Hole Oceanographic. The area is rife with unusual microbes and the substances they produce."

"The combinations of heat and chemicals have been compared to the conditions that prevailed when life began on earth," Gamay said.

Osborne nodded. "On that expedition, the submersible *Alvin* brought up samples of seaweed. This is a dead sample of what you're looking at."

"The stem and leaf looks vaguely like *Caulerpa*, but different somehow," Gamay said.

"Very good. The genus has more than seventy *Caulerpa* species, including those you find in pet shops. Invasive behavior had been documented in five of those, although few of the species are well studied. This is a totally unknown species. I've named it *Caulerpa Gorgonosa*."

"Gorgonweed. I like it."

"You won't like it after you've become as well acquainted with this infernal freak as I have. Scientifically speaking, we're looking at a mutant strain of *Caulerpa*. Unlike its cousins, though, this species *can* reproduce sexually."

"If that's true, this Gorgonweed can spread its eggs over long distances. That could be a serious matter."

"It already is. Gorgonweed has intermingled with *taxifolia*, and is now displacing that weed. It has shown up in the Azores, and we're seeing samples along the coast of Spain. Its growth rate is nothing short of phenomenal. There has been a burst of growth that is extraordinary. Great patches of weed are floating in the Atlantic. Soon they will join in a single mass."

Paul let out a low whistle. "It could take over the entire ocean at that rate."

"That's not the worst of it. *Taxifolia* creates a smothering carpet of alga. Like the Medusa whose gaze could turn men into stone, Gorgonweed becomes a thick, hard biomass. Nothing can exist where it is present."

Gamay gazed at the phial with the horror brought on by her knowledge of the world's oceans. "You're basically talking about the world's oceans solidifying."

"I can't even comprehend a worst-case scenario, but I do know this. Within a short time, Gorgonweed could spread along temperate coasts and cause irreparable ecological damage," Osborne said, his voice an uncharacteristic whisper. "It would affect the weather, possibly causing famine. It could bring ocean commerce to a stop. Nations that depend on ocean protein could go hungry. There would be political disruptions around the world as the haves and the have-nots fight over food."

"Who else knows about this?" Paul said.

"Ships have reported the weed as a nuisance, but outside of this room only a few trusted colleagues in this and other countries are aware of the gravity of the situation."

"Shouldn't people know about the threat so they can get together to fight it?" Gamay said.

"Absolutely. But I didn't want to sow seeds of panic until my research was complete. I was in the process of preparing a report which I will submit next week to pertinent organizations such as NUMA and the UN."

"Is there any chance you could do it sooner?" Gamay said.

"Oh yes, but here's the problem. When the issue is biological control, there is often a tug-of-war between eradication interests and scientific study. The eradicators understandably want to attack the problem quickly with every weapon at their command. If this news gets out, research will be quarantined for fear their work will spread the weed." He glanced at the phial. "This creature is not some sort of oceanborne crabgrass. I'm convinced we can successfully deal with it once we have more weapons at our disposal. Unless we know exactly what we're dealing with, no eradication method will work."

"How can NUMA help?" Gamay said.

"Another Lost City expedition is under way. The Oceanographic research vessel *Atlantis* will be on site this week with the *Alvin*. They will attempt to explore the area of the sea where the weed appears to have mutated. Once we determine the conditions that led to this aberration, we can work to defeat it. I've been trying to figure out how I can finish my work here and go on the expedition. When I heard you two were in town, I took it as a sign from the gods. You bring the perfect blend of expertise. Would you consider joining the expedition in my stead? It would only be a few days."

"Of course. We'd have to get permission from our superiors at NUMA, but that will present no problem."

"I can trust you to be discreet. Once we have samples in hand, I will release my report simultaneously with my colleagues worldwide."

"Where is the *Atlantis* now?" Paul said.

"Returning from an unrelated mission. It is stopping in the Azores tomorrow to refuel. You can join the ship there."

"It's doable," Paul said. "We can be back in Washington tonight and on our way in the morning." He glanced at the phial. "We're going to have a real problem if that thing in there gets out of the bottle."

Gamay had been staring at the greenish blob. "The genie is already *out* of the bottle, I'm afraid. We're going to have to figure out how to get it back *in*."

12

GORGONWEED?" Austin said. "That's a new one. Is this stuff as bad as your friend says it is?"

"It could be," Gamay said. "Dr. Osborne is quite concerned. I respect his judgment."

"What do you think?"

"It's cause for worry, but I can't say definitively until we have more evidence from the Lost City."

Gamay had called Austin aboard the *Mummichug*. She apologized for getting him out of bed, but said she and Paul were en route to the Lost City and wanted to make sure that he knew what they were up to.

"Thanks for filling me in. We'd better alert Dirk and Rudi," he said, referring to Dirk Pitt, who had succeeded Admiral Sandecker as head of NUMA, and Rudi Gunn, who was in charge of the agency's day-to-day operations.

"Paul has talked to both of them. NUMA already had some biologists working on the *Caulerpa* problem."

Austin smiled. "Why am I not surprised that Dirk is one step ahead of us?"

"Only *half* a step. He was unaware of the Lost City connection. He'll be waiting for a report on our dive."

"Me, too. Good luck. Keep in touch."

As Austin hung up, the words of T. S. Eliot came to mind. "This is the way the world ends/Not with a bang but a whimper."

A soggy whimper at that.

Paul and Gamay could handle the situation and there was nothing he could do in the meantime, so he busied himself with a stem-to-stern inspection of the SEAmobile. Aside from a few dents and scrapes, the vehicle was in better shape than he was, Austin concluded. He sat in the bubble cabin and went through a checklist. Satisfied all systems were working, he picked up two mugs of coffee from the galley, went below and knocked softly on the door to Skye's stateroom.

Recognizing that the *Mummichug* was a relatively small vessel, the boat's designers had factored in small individual cabins where crew members could enjoy their privacy. Skye was up and dressed. She opened the door immediately and smiled when she saw Austin.

"Good morning," he said. As he handed Skye a steaming mug, he noticed the dark circles under her eyes. "Did you sleep well?"

"Not very. I kept dreaming I was being smothered under tons of ice."

"I have a proven cure for nightmares. How would you like to explore an underwater tomb?"

Her face lit up. "How could any woman in her right mind refuse such an enticing offer?"

"Follow me then. Our chariot waits without."

With Austin and Skye on board, the submersible was lowered into the water between the catamaran's twin hulls. Once free of the support vessel, the sub cruised along the surface to a position whose coordinates had been recorded into the navigation system, and Austin put the SEAmobile into a dive.

The clear lake waters enveloped the cockpit bubble as the submersible sank into the lake, and within minutes they were following the line of megaliths to the tomb. Austin stopped the submersible at the entrance, made sure the vehicle's cameras were operating, and then goosed the horizontal thrusters. A second later, the vehicle slipped through the opening into the ancient sepulchre.

The powerful lights failed to reach the far wall of the chamber, indicating that it was huge, with ceilings so high they couldn't be seen. As the SEAmobile slowly made its way into the chamber, Austin panned the sub's movable light along the right wall, and saw that it was decorated with a carved bas-relief.

The skillfully executed and detailed renderings showed sailboats, houses, pastoral scenes with palm trees and flowers, dancers and musicians. There were flying fish and frolicking dolphins. The boats looked quite ancient. The people depicted were well dressed and seemed to be enjoying a prosperous life.

Skye leaned forward in her seat, her face pressed against the plastic bubble like a child at Christmas.

"I see *wonderful* things," she said, quoting Howard Carter's first words at the discovery of King Tut's tomb.

Austin had been thinking that there was something hauntingly familiar about the scenes. "I've been here before," he said.

"*Here*, in this tomb?"

"No. But I've seen drawings similar to these carvings in a cave in the Faroe Islands, in the North Atlantic. The style and subject was very much the same. What do you make of them?"

"I'm probably foolish for guessing, but they look Minoan, similar to the drawings excavated at Akrotiri, on the island of Santorini, or in Crete. The Minoan civilization flourished around 1500 B.C." The significance of what she was saying dawned on her. "Do you know what this means?" she said with excitement. "These drawings and the ones you saw would indicate that the Minoans went much farther afield than most people suspect."

"Which makes them the missing link in your international trade theory?"

"That's right," she said. "This confirms that east-west trade is far older and more extensive than anyone thought it was." She clapped her hands. "I can't wait to show this video to my smug-faced colleagues back in Paris."

The submersible came to the end of the wall, turned a corner and started down another side of the rectangular chamber. The scenes were of Lac du Dormeur and the glacier. But instead of barren shore, there were buildings, even what appeared to be a rendering of the tomb, complete with arches, and the glacier, as silent and implacable as ever.

"It appears you were right about settlements around the lakeshore and the mouth of the river."

"This is marvelous! We can use these carvings to make site maps of ruin locations."

In the sculpted scene, the ice field had covered even more of the valley centuries before when it was carved by some unknown artist. The sculptor had managed to imbue his work with a majesty and power that went beyond a mere objective rendering of what he saw. They made several sweeps of the chamber and found no markers or a sarcophagus.

"I was all wrong about this place," she said. "It's not a tomb. It's a *temple*."

"A reasonable assumption given the lack of bodies. If we're done here, I'd like to unravel another lake mystery." He unfolded the side-scan sonar printout he'd brought with him and pointed at the anomaly on the lake's bottom.

"It looks like a plane," Skye said. "What's a plane doing down here? *Wait.* The man in the ice?"

Austin answered with an enigmatic smile, the sub's horizontal thrusters whirred and they whisked through the temple door back out into the lake. He slowed the sub when they neared the position designated on the printout and kept his eyes peeled. Before long, a cigar-shaped object came into view.

As they drew closer, Austin saw that the cylindrical wood framework was partially covered with tattered and faded red fabric. The conical engine housing had been torn off and lay on the bottom and the engine gleamed in the sub's lights. The cold lake temperatures had kept the fuselage clear of marine vegetation that would have covered it in warmer climes. The propeller was gone, probably snapped off in the crash. He circled around the fuselage and found what was left of the missing wing several yards away. Then he brought the sub back to the plane.

Skye pointed to the emblem painted on the tail. "I saw that same design—the triple-headed eagle—on the helmet that was found under the glacier."

"Too bad we don't have the helmet now."

"But we *do.* I brought it out with me. It's on the ship."

Austin remembered Skye clutching a bag as she climbed aboard the SEAmobile. He was learning quickly that this attractive woman with the smile like a sunny day was not someone to be underestimated. Austin stared at the eagle, and then let his gaze shift to the empty cockpit.

"Now we know where the Ice Man came from. He must have bailed out and his plane crashed in the lake."

Skye responded with an evil laugh. "I was thinking of Renaud. He said that the Ice Man didn't just drop out of the sky. He was wrong. From what you've found, that's *exactly* what happened."

The submersible circled the wreck, with Austin shooting video and digital photos of the wings and surrounding bottom, and then headed for the surface. Before long, they were stepping out of the cockpit onto the deck. Skye had been babbling with excitement about their find, but she went silent when she caught a glimpse of the glacier. She walked over to the rail and stared off at the ice field.

Sensing her change in mood, Austin put his arm around her shoulders.

"Are you all right?"

"It was so peaceful underwater. Then we surfaced and I

saw the glacier." She shuddered. "It reminded me that I almost died under that thing."

Austin studied the troubled expression in Skye's lovely eyes, which were fixed in the hundred-yard stare that shell-shocked troops sometimes get. "I'm not a shrink, but I've always found it helpful to confront my demons," he said. "Let's go for a boat ride."

The unexpected suggestion seemed to bring her back to reality. "Are you serious?"

"Grab a couple of bagels and a thermos of coffee from the mess and I'll meet you at the skiff. I like my bagels with raisins, by the way."

Skye was skeptical, but she had come to have a great deal of confidence in Austin, and would probably have followed him to the moon on a pogo stick if he asked. Austin got the power skiff ready while she rounded up coffee and bagels from the galley and they set off for shore. They dodged floating chunks of ice and pulled the boat up at a dark gravel beach a few hundred yards from where the glacier narrowed and broke up in pieces as it encountered the lake.

A short hike along the shore brought them to the glacier's sidewall. The icy bulwark rose several stories above the plain; its surface was pockmarked with caves and craters and twisted free-form sculptures created by freezing, melting and unimaginable pressures. The ice was covered with dirt and a deep, unearthly blue light emanated from the wrinkles and grottos.

"There's your demon," Austin said. "Now, go up and touch it."

Skye smiled wanly, approached the glacier as if it were alive and reached out and touched an icy knob with a fingertip. Then she placed both palms on the glacier and leaned her weight against the ice, eyes closed, as if she were hoping to push it away.

"It's cold," she said with a smile.

"That's because your demon is nothing but a big ice cube. It's the same way I think about the sea. It's not out to get you. It doesn't even know you exist. You touched it. You're still breathing." He lifted the pack he'd been carrying. "Consultation has ended. Time for brunch."

Near the edge of the lake they found a couple of flat rocks to use as chairs and sat facing the water. Skye doled out the bagels and said, "Thanks for the exorcism. You were right about facing your fears."

"I've had good experience in that area."

She arched a brow. "Somehow I don't see you being afraid of anything."

"That's not true. I was very afraid that I would find you dead."

"I appreciate that, and I owe you my life. But I meant it in a different way. You seem fearless when it comes to your own well-being."

He leaned close to her ear and whispered, "Would you like to know my secret?"

She nodded.

"I put on one hell of a good act. How's your bagel?"

"Fine, but my head is awhirl. What do you make of this craziness?"

Austin stared off at the anchored NUMA boat, thinking of Coleridge's description of a painted ship on a painted sea, and tried to put events in order.

"Let's deal with what we know for starters." He sipped his coffee. "The scientists working the glacier find a man's body frozen in the ice, and it has been there for some time. An old helmet and a strongbox are found near the body. A man posing as a reporter takes the box at gunpoint and floods the tunnel. Apparently, he knows nothing about the helmet."

"That's where my logical mind bogs down. Why did he try to kill us? We were in no position to do him any harm. By the time we got out of the tunnel, he would have been long gone."

"I think he flooded the tunnel to cover up the Ice Man. You and the others happened to be in the way. Like the glacier. Nothing personal."

She nibbled thoughtfully on her bagel. "That makes morbid sense, I suppose."

Skye paused, her eyes going past Austin's shoulder. A cloud of dust was approaching at a high rate of speed. As the cloud neared, they could see that a Citroën was kicking up the dust. Fifi. The car skidded to a stop, and LeBlanc, Thurston and Rawlins got out and came over.

"I'm so glad we caught you," LeBlanc said, his broad face wreathed in a smile. "I called the ship from the power plant and they said you had gone ashore."

"We wanted to say good-bye," Thurston said.

"You're leaving?" Skye said.

"Yes," the glaciologist said, waving in the direction of the glacier. "There's no point in staying here with our observatory underwater. We're heading back to Paris. A helicopter will run us to the nearest airport."

"Paris?" Skye said. "Do you have room for me?"

"Yes, of course," LeBlanc said. He extended his hand. "Thank you again for saving our lives, Monsieur Austin. I would not like Fifi to be an orphan. She will stay at the power plant with Monsieur Lessard. We're going to talk to the power company about draining the observatory. Perhaps we can return next season."

"I'm so sorry to be running off like this," Skye said to Austin. "But there's nothing more to be done here and I want to compile all my data for analysis."

"I understand. The *Mummichug*'s project is coming to an end. I'll stay on board to write up my report while the ship's heading back up the river. Then I'll catch a ride to the nearest railroad station and take the high-speed train to Paris for our dinner date."

"*Bien.* Under one condition. I'm buying."

"How could anyone in his right mind refuse an enticing offer like that? You can show me the town."

"I'd like that," she said. "I'd like that very much."

Austin brought Skye back to the ship to collect her belongings and gave her a ride to the beach where the helicopter awaited. She kissed him on both cheeks and on the lips, made him promise to call when he got to Paris, and climbed into the helicopter. Austin was on his way across the lake when the chopper passed overhead and he saw Skye waving at him from a window.

Back on board, Austin unloaded the videocassette and digital disk from the submersible's cameras. He took them into the ship's dry lab and fed the digital images into a computer. He ran off prints showing the design on the plane's fuselage and examined them. Next, he zeroed in on the photos he had taken of the plane's engine until he found the one he was looking for. It showed markings on the engine block.

He selected the engraved area with his cursor, zoomed in, refining the image as he enlarged it, until he could see the name of the manufacturer and a serial number. He leaned back in his chair and stared at the image for a moment, and then he reached for a phone that could connect him anywhere in the world and punched out a number.

"Orville and Wilbur's flying bike shop," said a reedy voice.

Austin smiled as he pictured the hawk nose and narrow face of the man at the other end of the line. "You can't fool me, Ian. I happen to know that the Wright Brothers closed their bicycle shop a long time ago."

"Hell, Kurt, can't blame me for trying. I've been up to my earlobes trying to raise private funds for the Udvar-Hazy Center out at Dulles airport and I don't want to waste my time with small talk."

Ian MacDougal was a former marine fighter pilot in charge of the archives division at the Smithsonian's Air and Space Museum. He was the airborne equivalent of St. Julien Perlmutter, whose extensive library of nautical books was the envy of many academic institutions, and whose grasp of sea history was known the world round. The tall and lean MacDougal was the physical antithesis of the rotund Perlmutter, and he was far less flamboyant, but his encyclopedic knowledge of aircraft and their history matched St. Julien's grasp of the sea.

"You can rely on me for a hefty contribution, Ian, and I'll try to spare the small talk," Austin said. "I'm in France and I need to identify a plane I found at the bottom of a glacial lake in the Alps."

"I can always depend on you for a challenge." MacDougal sounded delighted to be distracted from fund raising. "Tell me about it."

"Crank up your computer and I'll send you some digital photos."

"Consider it cranked."

Austin had already programmed the photos for transmission, and the pictures taken at the lake bottom whisked on cyber wings across the Atlantic in a millisecond. MacDougal had stayed on the line and Austin could hear him muttering to himself.

"Well?" Austin said after a few moments.

"I'm taking a guess, but from the distinctive cone-shaped engine housing, I'd say we're looking at a Morane-Saulnier. She was a World War One mono-wing fighter plane based on a racing plane. The little buzzard could outfly and outmaneuver almost any other fighter aircraft of the day. The gun and propeller synchronization setup was truly revolutionary. One of the Allied planes crashed, unfortunately, and Fokker copied the system and improved upon it. There's a moral there somewhere."

"I'll let you deal with the moral complexities. Given what you know, do you have any idea how this plane got to the bottom of the lake?"

"Fell out of the sky, obviously, which is what planes sometimes do. I can guess on the rest, but I'd probably be wrong. I do know someone who might be able to help you. He's only a couple of hours from Paris."

Austin jotted down the information. "Thanks," he said. "I'll get my museum contribution to you as soon as I get back to Washington. In the meantime, give my regards to Wilbur and Orville."

"I'll be glad to oblige."

Austin hung up, and a moment later he was calling the number Ian had given him.

13

SKYE SLAMMED the cover down on the thick reference book she had been reading and shoved it across her desk to join a tall stack of similar well-worn volumes. She hunched her shoulders and stretched her arms to work the kinks out of her muscles, and then leaned back in her chair, lips pursed, and stared at the helmet in front of her. She had always considered ancient weapons and armor simply as tools, nothing more than inanimate objects used in the bloody business of war, but this thing made her shiver. The oxidized black surface seemed to exude a malevolence she had never before encountered.

After she had returned to Paris, Skye had taken the helmet to her office at the Sorbonne expecting that identification would be easy with the reference tools at her command. She had photographed the helmet, fed the images into her computer and searched through an extensive database compiled from hundreds of sources. She had started with her French archives, and then moved on to Italy and Germany, the countries that were once the primary armor centers.

Finding no match, she'd expanded the country search to

take in all of Europe, and when that search had bottomed out she moved to Asia and the rest of the world. She combed records going back as far as the Bronze Age. After the computer search fell flat, she turned to the printed page and exhumed every musty reference book in her library. She pored over old prints, manuscripts and ivory and metal carvings. In desperation, she researched the Bayeux Tapestry, but the conical headgear its warriors wore in battle bore no resemblance to the helmet sitting in front of her.

The helmet was a contradiction. The workmanship was extraordinary and more characteristic of an ornamental than a war helmet, although the nicks and gouges marring the surface suggested that it could have been worn in battle. The apparent bullet hole was a puzzle all to itself.

The design suggested an early origin. The weight was borne by the head as in the earlier helmets. Later models had an *armet*, the flared bottom that allowed the weight to be transferred to the shoulders via a collar called a *gorget*. The helmet was topped with a fan-shaped crest, another later innovation that added protection from a mace or sword.

Helmet style evolved from the conical shape in the eleventh century to rounded helms in the twelfth century. The nose guards had expanded to protect the face, developing eye slits known as "sights," and ventilation openings called "breaths" came into being. German helmets tended to be heavy and spiky; the Italian models were rounder, reflecting the Renaissance influence.

The most extraordinary thing about this helmet was the metal. Steel manufacture had started as early as 800 B.C., but it took hundreds of years to develop metal of such high quality. Whoever had forged this metal was a master. The strength built into this helmet's steel was evident in the dent in the crown known as a "proofmark." Someone had tested the metal with a pistol, or *arquebus*, and it had proved itself impenetrable. But as the bullet hole showed, each rise in the efficiency of defense produced a corresponding response in the effectiveness of attack. Armor finally became obsolete in the 1522 Battle of Bicocca. The enemy was gravity, rather than projectiles; armor simply became too heavy to wear.

The face embossed on the visor was typical of sixteenth-century Italian armor. Artisans avoided embossing in combat helmets. Surface features had to be smooth and round, or shaped with planes to offer a glancing blow. Embossing could destroy the effectiveness of a glancing surface. She picked up her letter opener, actually an Italian dagger, and tried to catch the edge and point in the helmet. Despite the embossing and etching that covered the helmet, the metal had been cleverly fashioned to shed the blows.

She came back to the steel again. No detail distinguished one armorer from another more than his ability to temper metal. She rapped her knuckles on the helmet, which gave forth a clear, bell-like sound, and then with her forefinger she traced a five-point star with "legs." She turned the helmet around. Seen from another angle the etching depicted a shooting star. She recalled seeing a sword from an English collection that had been made with iron from a meteorite. The steel was capable of being sharpened to a razor's edge. Why not a helmet? She made a note to have a metallurgist check it out.

Skye rubbed her tired eyes, and with a resigned sigh she reached for the phone and punched out a number. A man's voice came on the line. It was deep, and pleasantly cultivated.

"*Oui. Darnay Antiquités.*"

"Charles. It's Skye Labelle."

"Ah, Skye!" Darnay was clearly glad to hear her voice. "How are you, my dear? How is your work going? Is it true that you were in the Alps?"

"Yes. That's why I'm calling. I came across an old helmet during my expedition. It's quite extraordinary and I'd like you to look at it. It has me stumped."

"What about your wonderful computer?" Darnay teased.

Darnay and Skye had had friendly arguments over the

technological tools she used. He felt empirical experience gained through constant handling of artifacts was more valuable than browsing any database. She countered that the computer saved her valuable time.

"Nothing is wrong with my computer," she said with mock indignation. "I've looked through every book in my library as well. I can't find an exact match."

"I'm very surprised." Darnay was acquainted with Skye's reference library and knew it was one of the best he had ever seen. "Well, I'd love to look at it. Come over now if you'd like."

"*Bien.* I'll be right along."

She wrapped the helmet in a pillowcase, then put it in a shopping bag from *Au Printemps* and headed out for the nearest Métro station. Darnay's shop was on the Right Bank, down a narrow street next to a *boulangerie* that sent out mouthwatering aromas of baking bread. Printed in small gilt letters on the shop's door was the word ANTIQUITÉS. In the window was an odd, dust-covered assortment of powder horns, flintlock pistols and a few rusty swords. It was not a display that would entice anyone into the shop, which was Darnay's intention.

The door bell tinkled as she entered the shop. The dingy interior was dark and narrow, and empty except for a rusty suit of armor and some flyspecked cabinets holding a few poor replicas of antique daggers. A velvet curtain at the rear of the shop parted, and a wiry man dressed in black emerged from the widening ribbon of light. He cast a furtive glance at Skye, brushed by as silently as a shadow and left the shop, quietly shutting the door behind him.

Another man stepped out of the back room. He was short, and in his seventies, and resembled the old film actor Claude Rains. He was impeccably attired in a dark blue suit and stylish red silk tie, but would have projected an air of elegance if he had been in a workman's smock. His dark eyes sparkled with intelligence. His hair and thin mustache were silver-gray and he was smoking a Gauloises in a cigarette holder, which he removed from his lips so he could kiss Skye on both cheeks.

"That was fast," he said with a smile. "This helmet of yours must be a very important find."

She returned the kisses. "That's for you to tell me. Who's that man who just left?"

"He is one of my, er, suppliers."

"He looks like a sneak thief."

An alarmed expression crossed Darnay's face. Then he laughed. "Of course. That's what he is."

Darnay flipped the sign on his door to CLOSED, and then led her past the curtain to his office. In stark contrast to the worn-at-the-heels seediness of his showroom, the office-workshop was well lit by track lights and the desk and work space were of contemporary design. The walls were hung with weapons, but most of them were inferior items that he sold to less knowledgeable collectors. His top-grade inventory he kept safe in a warehouse.

Although he teased Skye about her reliance on technology, he did business mostly through the Internet, and a glossy catalog, mailed to an exclusive list of buyers, that was hungrily awaited by dealers and collectors worldwide.

Skye had first sought Darnay out for advice in spotting forgeries. She soon learned that his knowledge of old arms and armor surpassed that of some academics, including herself. They had become good friends, although it became apparent that he dealt in the shadowy world of illegal antiquities. In short, he was a crook, but a classy one.

"Let's see what you have, my dear." He pointed to a brightly lit table that was used to photograph objects for the catalog.

Skye removed the helmet from the bag and set it on the table, then pulled off the pillowcase with a flourish.

Darnay gazed with reverence at the object. Then he walked around the table; puffing on his cigarette, bending low, with his face inches from the metal. After going through the dip-and-stand routine, he picked the helmet up, hefted the weight, held it high and then put it on his head.

Wearing the helmet, he walked over to a cabinet and pulled out a bottle of Grand Marnier.

"Brandy?" he offered.

Skye laughed at the sight and shook her head. "Well, what do you think?"

"Extraordinaire." He put the helmet back on the table and poured himself a brandy. "Where did you get this lovely objet d'art?"

"It was frozen into Le Dormeur glacier."

"A *glacier*? Even *more* extraordinary."

"That's not half the story. It was found near a body that was embedded in the ice. The body may have been in the glacier less than a hundred years. The man probably parachuted from a plane whose wreckage was found in the nearby lake."

Darnay poked his forefinger through the hole in the helmet. "And this?"

"I think it's a bullet hole."

The antiquities dealer didn't seem surprised. "Then this Ice Man could have been wearing the helmet?"

"Possibly."

"It's not a failed proofmark?"

"I don't think so. Look at the hardness of that steel. Musket balls would have bounced off the metal like peas. The hole was made by a more modern firearm."

"So we have a man flying over a glacier wearing an old helmet, shot with modern weapons."

She shrugged. "It seems so."

Darnay sipped his brandy. "Fascinating, but it all makes little sense."

"*Nothing* about this whole affair makes sense."

She settled into a chair and told Darnay about Renaud's summons to the cave and her harrowing rescue. Darnay listened with furrowed brow.

"Thank God you're safe! This Kurt Austin is an *homme formidable.* Handsome, too, I suppose."

"Very much so." She felt herself blushing.

"I owe him my gratitude. I have always thought of you

as a daughter, Skye. I would have been devastated if anything had happened to you."

"Well, nothing did, thanks to Mr. Austin and his colleague Joe Zavala." She gestured at the helmet. "Well?"

"I believe it's older than it looks. As you say, the steel is extraordinary. The metal used in its manufacture may very well have been forged in the stars. The fact that this is the only one of its kind that I have ever seen, and that you found no reference to it in your library, leads me to think it might have been a prototype."

"If the features were so innovative, why weren't these ideas picked up sooner?"

"You know the nature of arms and men. Good sense does not always prevail over intransigence. The Polish insisted on using horse cavalry against armored panzer divisions. Billy Mitchell had an uphill fight convincing the army hierarchy of the value of aerial bombardment. Maybe someone looked at this and said the old equipment was preferable to the untested."

"Any thoughts on the eagle motif I saw here and on the plane?"

"Yes, but none of them are scientific."

"I'd be interested to hear them anyhow. And perhaps I'll take that offer of brandy."

Darnay poured another snifter and they tapped glasses. "I'd say the eagle represents the joining together, an alliance of some sort, of three different groups into one. *E pluribus unum.* 'Out of many, one.' It was not an easy arrangement. The eagle seems to be pulling itself apart, yet it must hang together or die. The weapons it is clutching in its claws would lead me to believe that this alliance has something to do with war."

"Not bad for an unscientific guess."

He smiled. "If we only knew who your Ice Man was." He glanced at his watch. "Excuse me, Skye, but I have a conference call with a dealer in London and a buyer in the United States. Would you mind if I kept this piece here for a few hours so I could study it further?"

"Not at all. Just call when you want me to pick it up. I'll either be at my office or my apartment."

A cloud passed over his brow. "My dear girl, there is more here than meets the eye. Someone was willing to kill for this artifact. It must have great value. We must be very careful. Does anyone know you have it?"

"Kurt Austin, the NUMA man I told you about. He's trustworthy. Some of those who were in the cave would know of it. And Renaud."

"Ah, Renaud," he said, drawing out the name. "That's not good. He'll want it back."

Her dark eyes snapped with anger. "Over my dead body." She smiled nervously, realizing the implication of her words. "I can stall him, say the helmet is at the metallurgist."

Darnay's phone rang. "That is my call. We'll talk later."

After leaving the shop, she went to her apartment instead of her office. She wanted to check her answering machine, hoping she would hear from Austin. Her discussion with Darnay had given her the jitters. She had the feeling that danger was lurking nearby, and hearing Austin's voice would have offered some reassurance. When she got home, she played her messages, but there was no word from Kurt.

She felt weary from her work. She lay down on the sofa with a fashion magazine, intending to relax before going back to the office. But after a few minutes the magazine fell from her fingers to the floor and she drifted off into a deep sleep.

SKYE WOULD have slept less soundly if she knew what Auguste Renaud was up to. He sat in his office in a dangerous fury, head bent over his desk, compiling a list of complaints against Skye Labelle. His hand was mending, but his pride was still gravely wounded.

All his ill will centered on that insolent woman. He would pull every political string at his command, call in every IOU owed him to destroy her, ruin her career and that of anyone who had been even vaguely friendly to her. She had humiliated him in front of others and ignored his authority. She virtually ignored his demand that she produce the helmet. He would have her thrown out of the Sorbonne. She'd *beg* for mercy. He pictured himself as the Creator in one of those Renaissance paintings of God chasing Adam and Eve from the Garden of Eden with his flaming sword.

He had encountered her in the elevator that morning. She had said good morning and smiled at him, sending him off into a simmering rage. He had his anger under control by the time he got to his office and was directing it to the list of complaints he had in front of him. He was writing a detailed description of her loose morals when he heard a soft shuffle. The chair creaked in front of his desk. He assumed it was his assistant.

Head still bent to his work, he said, "Yes?"

When no one answered, he looked up and his bowels turned to ice water. The chair had been turned around. Sitting in it was the big puffy-faced man who had attacked him under the glacier.

Renaud was adept at survival. He pretended that he hadn't recognized his visitor.

He cleared his throat. "How can I help you?" he said.

"You don't know me?"

"I don't believe so. You have business with the university?"

"No, I have business with *you.*"

Renaud's heart sank.

"I'm sure you must be mistaken."

"You were on television," the man said.

Even before Renaud had arrived back in Paris, he had called a favored television reporter and arranged an interview in which he took complete credit for finding the Ice Man, and suggested that he was responsible for the rescue as well.

"Yes. You saw the interview?"

"You told the reporter that you found *objects* under the glacier. The box was one object. What were the others?"

"There was only one, a helmet. Apparently, it was very old."

"Where is the helmet now?"

"I thought it was left in the cave. But a woman smuggled it out."

"Who is this woman?"

A malicious gleam came to Renaud's eye. Maybe this cretin would leave him alone if he had a more tempting target. He could get rid of him and Skye at the same time.

"Her name is Skye Labelle. She's an archaeologist. Do you want her name and number?" He reached for the faculty directory and opened it. "She has an office on the floor below this one. The number is 216. Anything you do to her is all right with me." He tried to hide his joy. He'd give almost anything to see Skye's face when this madman arrived at her doorstep.

The man slowly stood up. Good, he was leaving.

"Is there anything else you want?" Renaud said with a magnanimous smile.

The big man smiled slowly in return.

From under his coat, he drew a .22 caliber pistol that had a silencer attached to the barrel.

"Yes," he said. "I want to die."

The gun coughed once. A round red hole appeared in Renaud's forehead. He fell forward onto his desk, his smile frozen on his face.

The big man picked up the directory, tucked it in his pocket and without looking back at the lifeless body slumped over the desk, left the office as silently as he had entered.

14

THE ANTIQUE PLANE high above Austin's head danced in a graceful sky ballet in seeming defiance of the laws of gravity and physics. He watched in amazement from the edge of the grassy airfield south of Paris as the plane did an aerial spiral, then a half upward loop and half roll, reversing direction in a perfectly executed Immelmann.

Austin tensed as the plane dove and swooped in low over the field. The plane was going too fast for a safe landing. It was coming in like a guided missile. Seconds later, the aircraft's bicycle-style landing gear hit the ground and the plane bounced a yard or two in the air, but then it touched down again and taxied up to the hangar with a guttural roar of its engine.

As the two-blade wooden propeller spun to a stop, a middle-aged man climbed out of the cramped cockpit, removed his goggles and strode over to Austin, who was standing near the hangar. He was grinning from ear to ear. If he had been a puppy, he would have been wagging his tail with joy.

"Sorry the plane has only one seat, Monsieur Austin. It

would be a pleasure to take you up for a ride."

Austin eyed the tiny airplane, taking in the bullet-shaped engine cover, the wood-and-fabric fuselage and the triangular fin and rudder with the skull and crossbones painted on it. Metal stringers that supported the stubby wings ran in parasol fashion from an A-shaped strut just forward of the cockpit.

"With all due respect, Monsieur Grosset, your airplane hardly looks big enough for *one* person."

Laugh lines crinkled the Frenchman's weathered face. "I don't blame you for being skeptical, Monsieur Austin. The Morane-Saulnier N looks as if a schoolboy put it together in his basement. Only twenty-two feet long, with a wingspan of twenty-seven feet. But this little mosquito was one of the deadliest planes of its day. It was fast—over one hundred miles an hour—and amazingly maneuverable. In the hands of a skilled pilot, it was an extremely efficient killing machine."

Austin walked to the plane and ran his hand over the fuselage. "I was surprised at the streamlined fuselage and the single-wing design. When it comes to World War One, I usually picture blunt-nosed biplanes."

"And with very good reason. Most planes used in the war had two wings. The French were ahead of the other countries in developing the monoplane. This model was, for a time, the most aerodynamically advanced aircraft of the war. Its main advantage over the biplane was its ability to climb more quickly, although this shortcoming was overcome later with the Sopwith and the Nieuport."

"Your Immelmann was beautifully done."

"Merci," Grosset said with a bow. "Sometimes it is not as easy as it appears. This little plane weighs less than a thousand pounds fully loaded, but it is powered by the 116-horsepower I Rhone engine. It is tricky to handle and a delicate hand is needed on the controls." He grinned. "One pilot said that the major danger in flying the N was not combat but landing. You may have noticed that my approach speed was high."

Austin chuckled. "You have a talent for understatement, Monsieur Grosset. I thought you were going to drill a hole in the ground."

"I would not be the first to do so," Grosset said, with an easy laugh. "My task was a simple one compared to the old pilots. Picture yourself coming in with your wings full of bullet holes and the fabric in tatters. Maybe you have been wounded so you're weak from loss of blood. Now, *there* is a challenge."

Austin detected a hint of nostalgic envy in Grosset's tone. With his fine features and thin mustache, the Frenchman was the epitome of the dashing escadrille daredevils who buzzed German trenches in defiance of antiaircraft fire. Austin had called Grosset, the director of the air museum, after speaking to Ian MacDougal, and asked him to look at the pictures of the lake plane. Grosset said he would be glad to help out if he could. True to his word, he'd called back with a tentative ID shortly after receiving the digital photos over the Internet.

"Your plane is in many pieces," he'd said, "but I agree with Monsieur Ian that it is a World War One–era aircraft called a Morane-Saulnier N."

"I'm afraid my knowledge of early aircraft is on the sketchy side," Austin had replied. "Can you tell me more about it?"

"I can do better," Grosset had said. "I can *show* you one. We have an N in our air museum."

Earlier that day, after checking into his Paris hotel, Austin had caught a high-speed train that had taken him to the museum faster than if he had flown in Grosset's plane. The museum was situated in a hangar complex at the edge of the airfield less than fifty miles south of Paris.

After the demonstration of his plane's capabilities, Grosset invited Austin to his office for a glass of wine. The office was tucked into a corner of the hangar, which was filled with vintage airplanes. They walked past a Spad, a Corsair and a Fokker into a small room whose walls were festooned with dozens of airplane pictures.

Grosset poured a couple of glasses of Bordeaux and toasted the Wright Brothers. Austin suggested that they raise their glasses as well to Alberto Santos-Dumont, an early Brazilian air pioneer who had lived in France for many years and was considered French by many.

Printouts of the photos Austin had sent Grosset were spread out on top of an old wooden desk. Austin picked up a picture of the wrecked plane, studied the broken framework and shook his head in wonderment.

"I'm amazed that you were able to identify the plane from this mess."

Grosset set his glass aside and fanned out the photos until he came to one he wanted.

"I wasn't sure at first. I had my suspicions, but as you say, this is a mess. I recognized the machine gun here as a Hotchkiss, but they were commonly used by the early warplanes. And the distinctive conical engine housing was a strong clue. Then I noticed something quite interesting." He shoved the photo across the desk and handed Austin a magnifying glass. "Take a close look at this."

Austin examined the rounded wood shape. "It looks like a propeller blade."

"Correct. But not just any propeller blade. See here, there is a metal plate fastened to the propeller. Raymond Saulnier devised a true synchronizing gear early in 1914, which allowed him to fire a Hotchkiss machine gun through a spinning propeller. Ammunition would sometimes hang fire, so he fitted crude metal deflectors to the propeller blades."

"I've heard of that. A low-tech solution to a complex problem."

"After a few test pilots were killed by ricocheting bullets, the idea was temporarily abandoned. Then came the war and with it the impetus to come up with new ways to kill your enemy. A French ace named Roland Garros met with Saulnier, and they fitted his plane with steel deflector plates that worked as designed. He had several kills before his plane fell behind enemy lines. The Germans used his system to develop the Fokker synchronizing gear."

Austin picked up another photo and pointed to a small light-colored rectangle in the cockpit. "What do you make of this? It looks like a metal plaque."

"You have sharp eyes," Grosset said with a smile. "It is a manufacturer's code." He passed over another photo. "I enlarged the picture on the computer. The letters and numbers are a little fuzzy, but I enhanced the resolution and you can make them out well enough. I was able to match them with the records in the museum's archives."

Austin looked up from the picture. "Were you able to trace its ownership?"

Grosset nodded. "There were forty-nine Ns built. After seeing how successful Garros was, other French pilots obtained the plane and used it with deadly efficiency. The English bought some of these 'Bullet' planes, as they called the model, and the Russians as well. They performed better than the Fokker, but many pilots were wary of their high landing speed and sensitivity. You say you found this wreckage in the Alps?"

"Yes, at the bottom of a glacial lake near the Dormeur glacier."

Grosset sat back in his chair and tented his fingers. "Curious. Some years ago I was called into that area to look over the wreckage of some old planes, scattered at various locations. They were a type known as an Aviatik, primarily used for scouting and reconnaissance. I talked to some of the local residents who said there were stories told by their grandparents of an air battle. It would have happened around the start of World War One, although I could not pinpoint an actual date."

"Do you think this aerial dogfight had anything to do with this latest find?"

"Perhaps. It may be yet another piece of a puzzle nearly a hundred years old. The mysterious disappearance of Jules Fauchard. He was the owner of the plane you found."

"The name doesn't ring a bell."

"Fauchard was one of the wealthiest men in Europe. He disappeared in the year 1914, apparently while flying his

Morane-Saulnier. He was in the habit of flying around his vast estate and vineyards. One day, he simply never came back. A search was launched within the probable range of his plane, but no trace was ever found. Within a few days, the war began and his disappearance, while regretful, became a mere historical footnote."

Austin tapped the photo that showed the machine gun. "Fauchard must have worried a lot about his grapes. How did a citizen come to be flying a warplane?"

"Fauchard was an arms manufacturer with strong political connections. It would have been nothing for him to have a plane diverted from the French arsenal. The larger question is how he got to the Alps."

"Lost?"

"I don't think so. His plane would not have made it to Lac du Dormeur on a tank of fuel. In those days airports were few. He would have had to stockpile fuel supplies along his route. This suggests to me that his flight was part of a deliberate plan."

"Where do you think he was headed?"

"The lake is near the Swiss border."

"And Switzerland is known for secret banking. Maybe he was on his way to Zurich to cash a check."

Grosset responded with a soft chuckle. "A man of Fauchard's position had no use for cash." His face grew serious. "You have seen the television reports about the body that was found in the ice?"

"No, but I talked to someone who saw the body. She said he appeared to be wearing a long leather coat and a close-fitting cap like those worn by early aviators."

Grosset leaned forward, excitement in his eyes. "This would *fit*! Fauchard could have bailed out. He landed on the glacier and his plane crashed in the lake. If we could only retrieve the body."

Austin thought back to the dark, water-filled tunnel. "It would be a monumental task to pump the tunnel dry."

"So I understand." He shook his head. "If anyone could accomplish the task, it would be the Fauchards."

"His family is still around?"

"Oh yes, although you wouldn't know it. They are fanatical about their privacy."

"Not surprising. Many wealthy families don't like attention."

"It goes deeper than that, monsieur. The Fauchards are what are called 'Merchants of Death.' Arms dealers on a vast scale. Armaments are regarded by some as an unsavory business."

"The Fauchards sound a bit like a French version of the Krupps."

"They have been compared to the Krupps, although Racine Fauchard would argue that."

"Racine?"

"She would have been Jules's grandniece. A *femme formidable*, from what I am told. She still runs the family business."

"I would imagine that Madame Fauchard would like to know the fate of her long-lost ancestor."

"I agree, but it would be difficult for an ordinary mortal to get past the lawyers, public relations people and bodyguards that protect a person of her wealth." He thought about it for a moment, and then he said, "I have a friend who is a director at the company. I can call him with this information and see where it leads. Where can I reach you?"

"I'm taking the train back to Paris; I'll give you my cell phone number."

"Bien," Grosset said. He called a taxi to take Austin back to the train station. Then they walked past the antique planes to the front of the museum to wait for the ride.

They shook hands and Austin said, "Thanks for your help."

"My pleasure. May I ask what interest NUMA has in this situation?"

"None, actually. I discovered the plane as I was working on a NUMA-sponsored project, but I'm pursuing it on my own, primarily out of curiosity."

"Then you won't be using intermediaries in any dealings you might have with the Fauchards?"

"I hadn't intended to."

Grosset mulled over Austin's reply. "I was in the military for years and you seem to be a man who can take care of himself, but I would warn you to be very careful in any dealings you might have with the Fauchards."

"Why is that?"

"The Fauchards are not just any wealthy family." He paused, trying to choose his words carefully. "It is said that they have a *past.*"

Before Austin could ask Grosset what he meant, the car pulled up, they said their adieus and he was on his way to the train station. As Austin sat back in his seat, he pondered the Frenchman's warning. Grosset seemed to be saying that the Fauchards had more than one skeleton in the family closet. The same thing could be said about any rich family on the face of the earth, Austin mused. The fortunes that built grand houses and status were often based on a foundation of slavery, opium dealing, smuggling or organized crime.

With nothing more to go on than nuance, Austin turned his thoughts to meeting Skye once more, but Grosset's words continued to echo in his mind like the tolling of a distant church bell.

It is said that they have a past.

15

SKYE HAD HER OFFICE in the Sorbonne science center, a Le Corbusier–influenced edifice of glass and concrete that was sandwiched between some art nouveau buildings near the Pantheon. The street was normally quiet except for the gaggles of university students who used it as a shortcut. But as Skye turned the corner, she saw police cars blocking both ends of the avenue. More official cars were lined up in front of the building and police officers swarmed around the entrance.

A portly policeman manning a barricade raised his hand to bar her way. "Sorry, mademoiselle. You cannot pass."

"What has happened, monsieur?"

"There has been an accident," he said.

"What *kind* of an accident?"

"I don't know, mademoiselle," the policeman said, with an unconvincing shrug.

Skye pulled her university ID card from her pocketbook and brandished it under the officer's nose. "I work in that building. I would like to know what is going on and whether it concerns me."

The police officer glanced from Skye's face to the ID

picture and said, "You had better talk to the inspector in charge." He led Skye over to a man in plainclothes who was standing next to a police car, talking to a couple of uniformed police officers.

"This woman says she works in the building," the policeman explained to the inspector, a dumpy middle-aged man whose face had the world-weary expression of someone who has seen too much of the underside of life.

The inspector studied Skye's identification card with baggy, red-rimmed eyes and handed it back after jotting her name and address down in his notebook.

"My name is Dubois," he said. "Please come with me." He opened the police car door, motioned for her to get in the backseat and slid in beside her. "When was the last time you were in your office building, mademoiselle?"

She checked her watch. "About two or three hours ago. Maybe a little more."

"Where did you go?"

"I am an archaeologist. I took an artifact to an antiques expert for him to look at. Then I went to my apartment for a nap."

The inspector made a few notes. "When you were in the building, did you notice anyone or anything that struck you as strange?"

"No. All was normal as far as I know. Could you tell me what has happened?"

"There has been a shooting. Someone was killed. Did you know a Monsieur Renaud?"

"*Renaud?* Of course! He was my department head. You say he's dead?"

Dubois nodded. "Shot by an unknown assailant. When was the last time you saw Monsieur Renaud?"

"When I came to work around nine o'clock. We were in the elevator. My office is on the floor below his. We said a good morning and went on our separate ways."

Skye hoped that the slight shading of the truth didn't show in her face. When she'd greeted Renaud, he had simply glowered back at her without speaking.

"Can you think of anyone who would harm Monsieur Renaud?"

Skye hesitated before replying. She suspected that the inspector's basset hound expression was a mask meant to lull suspects into making self-incriminating statements. If he had talked to others, he would have learned that Renaud was universally loathed within his department. If she said anything to the contrary, he would wonder why she was lying.

"Monsieur Renaud was a controversial figure in the department," she said after a moment. "Many people didn't like the way he ran things."

"And *you*, mademoiselle? Did you like the way he ran things?"

"I was among a number of people on the faculty who thought he was not the person for his post."

The lieutenant smiled for the first time. "A most diplomatic response, mademoiselle. May I ask where exactly you have been before coming here?"

Skye gave him Darnay's name and the address of the antique shop, and her home address, which he duly noted, reassuring her that it was routine procedure. Then he got out of the car, opened the door and handed her his business card.

"Thank you, Mademoiselle Labelle. Please call me if you can think of anything else regarding this matter."

"Yes, of course. I have a favor to ask, Lieutenant. May I go to my office on the second floor?"

He thought about it for a moment. "Yes, but you must be accompanied by one of my men."

They got out of the car and Inspector Dubois called over the police officer Skye had first spoken to and instructed him to escort her through the police cordon. Every policeman in Paris seemed to have converged on the crime scene. Renaud was a scoundrel, but he was a prominent figure at the university and his murder would cause a sensation.

More police officers and technicians were working inside the building. Forensics people were dusting for fingerprints and photographers scurried around snapping pictures. Skye led the way to her second-floor office with the policeman close behind, stepped inside and looked around. Although all her furnishings and papers appeared to be in place, she had the strange feeling that something was amiss.

Skye's eyes scanned the room, and then she went to her desk. She was compulsively neat when it came to her paperwork. Before leaving her office, she had stacked her reference books, papers and files with micrometer precision. Now the edges were ragged, as if they had been hurriedly re-stacked.

Someone had been at her desk!

"Mademoiselle?"

The police officer was giving her an odd look and she realized that she had been staring blankly into space. She nodded, opened a desk drawer and extracted a file. She tucked the file under her arm without bothering to see what it contained.

"I'm through here," she said with a forced smile.

Skye resisted the impulse to bolt from the office and tried to walk at her usual pace, but her legs seemed made of wood. Her calm façade gave no hint of her racing pulse and her heartbeat seemed to thunder in her ears. She was thinking that the same hand that had disturbed her papers could have held the gun that killed Renaud.

The policeman escorted her from the building and past the barricade. She thanked him and walked home in a daze, crossing streets without looking either way, a near-suicidal move in Paris. She paid no attention to the screech of brakes, the cacophony of blaring horns and the shouted curses.

Her full-blown panic attack had subsided by the time she turned the corner of the narrow street to where her apartment was located. She wondered if she had done the right thing not telling Inspector Dubois that her office had been searched. In her mind she could see the inspector thinking that this crazy paranoid woman must go on the list of suspects.

Skye lived in a nineteenth-century, mansard-roofed house in Mouffetard, on the fringes of the Quartier Latin. She enjoyed the busy neighborhood, with its shops and restaurants and street jazz musicians. The old town house had been turned into three apartments. Skye's was on the third floor and her wrought-iron balcony gave her a view of the street life and the ubiquitous Parisian chimney pots. She sprinted up the stairs. Relief washed over her as she opened the door. She felt safe back in her apartment, but the feeling of security lasted only until she walked into the living room. She couldn't believe the sight that greeted her.

The room looked as if a bomb had gone off. Chair and sofa cushions were strewn about the floor. Her coffee table was swept clear of magazines. Books had been pulled from their shelves and thrown about haphazardly. The kitchen was even worse. Cabinets were wide open and the floor was covered with broken glass and dishes. Moving like a sleepwalker, she went into the bedroom. Drawers had been yanked from their dressers and their contents dumped everywhere. The bedcovers and sheets had been yanked off the bed and the mattress sliced open, spilling out the stuffing.

She went back into the living room and gazed at the mess. She was shivering with anger at the violation of her privacy. She felt as if she had been raped. The anger gave way to fear as she realized that the person who wrecked her apartment might still be in there. She hadn't checked the bathroom. She grabbed a poker from the fireplace, and with her eyes glued to the bathroom door, she began to back out of the apartment.

The floor creaked behind her.

She whirled and raised the poker over her head.

"Hul-lo," Kurt Austin said, his coral-colored eyes wide in surprise.

Skye almost fainted. She dropped the poker by her side. "I'm sorry," she said.

"I should apologize for creeping up on you. The door was open, so I stepped inside." He noticed Skye's ashen face. "Are you all right?"

"I'm fine now that you're here."

Austin surveyed the living room. "I didn't know you had tornadoes in Paris."

"I think the person who killed Renaud did this."

"Renaud? Not the man who was trapped under the glacier with you?"

"Yes. He was shot to death in his office."

Austin's jaw hardened. "Have you checked the other rooms?"

"Every one except the bathroom. I haven't dared look in the closets."

Austin took the poker from her hand. "Insurance," he said.

He went into the bathroom and came out a minute later.

"Do you smoke?" Austin said.

"Not for many years. Why?"

"You were right to worry." He produced a cigarette butt. "I found a pile of these in the bathtub. Someone was waiting for you to come home."

Skye shuddered. "Why did he leave?"

"Whatever the reason, it was lucky for you that he did. Tell me about Renaud."

They cleared off the sofa and Skye recounted the details of her visit to the university office building. "Am I crazy connecting this disaster and the search of my office to Renaud's murder?"

"You'd be crazy *not* to make the connection. Is there anything missing from your apartment?"

She looked around the living room and shook her head. "It's impossible to tell." Her eye fell on the telephone answering machine.

"Strange," she said. "When I left the apartment, there were only two messages on the machine. Now there are four."

"One is from me. I called as soon as I got into Paris."

"Someone must have listened to the last two messages, because the light isn't blinking."

Austin hit the PLAY button and heard his recorded voice saying that he couldn't reach her at her office, and was going to drop by her apartment on the chance she might be between home and work. He hit the play button again. Darnay's voice came on.

"Skye. It's Charles. I was wondering if I could take the helmet with me to my villa. It's proving more challenging than I anticipated."

"Dear God," she said, her face waxen. "Whoever was waiting for me must have heard the message."

"Who is Charles?" Austin said.

"A friend. He is a dealer in rare arms and armor. I left the helmet with him to examine. Wait—" She salvaged her address book from a pile of papers and looked under the *D*s. A page was torn out. She showed the book to Austin. "Whoever was here has tracked down Darnay."

"Try to warn him."

She picked up the telephone, dialed a number and listened for several moments. "No one is answering. What should we do?"

"The smart thing would be to call the police."

She frowned. "Charles wouldn't like that. He operates his business on the fringes of the law and sometimes beyond that. He'd never forgive me if the police descended on his place and started poking around."

"What if his life depended on it?"

"He didn't answer the phone. Maybe he's not even there. Maybe we're worrying for nothing."

Austin was less optimistic, but he didn't want to waste precious time in a fruitless argument. "How far is the shop from here?"

"On the Right Bank. Ten minutes by taxi."

"I've got a car outside. We'll do it in five."

They ran for the stairs.

• • •

THE ANTIQUE SHOP window was dark and the door was locked. Skye produced one of the few keys Darnay had entrusted to outsiders, and opened the door. A line of light seeped out from under the office curtains.

Austin cautiously pushed the curtain aside. The bizarre scene that greeted him looked like an exhibition in a wax museum. A kneeling gray-haired man had his chin resting on a wooden shipping container, like a condemned man with his head on the chopping block. His hair was disheveled; he was bound hand and foot, his mouth gagged with duct tape.

A big man stood over him like an executioner, leaning on a long two-handed broadsword, a black mask covering the upper part of his face. The executioner looked up and smiled at Austin. He pulled the mask off, threw it aside and raised the sword over Darnay's neck. The light gleamed wickedly on the double-edged blade.

"Please stay," he said in a voice that was surprisingly high-pitched for his size. "Your friend here would simply lose his head if you left."

Skye dug her fingers into Austin's arm, but he hardly noticed. Austin remembered the descriptions he had heard and knew that he was looking at the fake reporter who had flooded the glacial tunnel.

"Why would we leave?" Austin said nonchalantly. "We just got here."

The dough-faced man smiled, but his sword remained poised over Darnay's neck.

"This man has been very foolish," he said. He glanced at a shelf lined with old helmets. "He refuses to tell me which of these head pots is the one I'm looking for."

Darnay's stubbornness had probably saved his life, Austin thought. The old man must have known he'd be killed as soon as his assailant got what he came for.

"I'm sure any one of them would fit you," Austin said helpfully.

The man ignored the suggestion and fastened his gaze on Skye. "*You'll* tell me, won't you? You're the expert on these things."

"You killed Renaud, didn't you?" Skye said.

"Don't shed any tears for Renaud. He told me where to find you," the man said. The sword elevated a few inches. "Show me the helmet you removed from the glacier and I'll let you all go."

Not likely, Austin thought. Once Renaud's killer had the helmet, he would dispatch all three of them. Austin decided to make a move even though it meant gambling with Darnay's life. He'd been eyeing a battle-ax on a wall a few feet away. He stepped over and snatched the weapon off its hooks.

"I'd suggest you put that sword down," he said, his voice low and cool.

"Would you like me to put it down on Monsieur Darnay's neck?"

"You could do that," Austin said, his eyes locked on the man's face so there would be no miscalculation. "But then your fat bald head would be rolling on the floor next to his."

He hefted the ax for emphasis. The weapon was primitive but fearsome. The carbon steel head was elongated and designed so it could be used as a spear. A spike stuck out from behind the ax head like the sharp beak of a stork. Metal *langelets* extended from the ax head to protect the hardwood shaft.

The man pondered Austin's taunt. He knew from the uncompromising tone of Austin's voice that if he killed Darnay or Skye, he'd be a dead man. He would have to take care of Austin first, and then deal with the others. Austin had anticipated the move, actually welcomed it. In his experience, big men sometimes underestimated lesser human beings.

The man took a step toward Austin, raised the sword high and quickly brought it down in a blurry arc. Austin was unprepared for the move and realized it was he who had underestimated his opponent. Despite his large physical bulk, the man moved with feline quickness. Austin's reflexes took hold before his mind had time to process the metallic blur. His arms came up, holding the ax levelly in front of him.

The sword blade clanged against the ax shaft's protective sheathing. Shards of pain stabbed Austin's arms from the shock of the powerful blow and the blade stopped mere inches above his head, but he pushed the sword off, slid his hand down the shaft and swung the ax like a Louisville Slugger. It was an aggressive move fueled in part by the urgent need to defend his life. There was another reason; he simply didn't like this guy.

The deadly ax blade would have eviscerated the big man had he not seen the windup and leaned back at the waist. Austin was learning the hard way that there was more to medieval arm-to-arm combat than sheer muscle. The weight of the ax head whipped him around like a centrifuge. He spun in a full circle before he was able to check his swing.

Doughboy was driven back by the unexpected ferocity of the attack, but he recovered quickly. Seeing that Austin's wild swing had thrown him off balance, he changed tactics. He held the sword straight out in front of him and lunged.

It was a clever move. The sword point only needed to penetrate Austin's defense by a few inches to kill him. Austin sucked his chest in and sprang back, turning his side to his attacker. He evaded the main thrust, which slipped past the upraised ax, but the sword tip punched a hole in his shirt and drew blood. Austin whacked the sword aside and responded with a jabbing attack of his own.

Austin was starting to get the feel of the ax. The weapon was the M-16 rifle of its day. With it, an infantryman could hook a knight off his horse, hack through his armor and stab him to death. The long shaft gave Austin an edge and he found that short swings and jabs were the deadliest way to use the weapon.

Doughboy was learning as well. He slashed ineffectively at the sharp tip as he backed up in the face of

Austin's resolute advance. He stopped with his back to the table that was piled high with helmets. Unable to retreat farther, he brought his sword up in preparation for a slashing counterattack. Austin beat him to the punch with a sudden forward lunge. The big man backed into the table and the helmets clattered to the floor.

Doughboy tripped over a helmet before regaining his footing. He roared like a wounded lion and came at Austin, slashing from every direction with wild swings that were practically impossible to anticipate. Sweat dripped into Austin's eyes, blurring his vision, and he retreated under the fierceness of the attack until he had his back to the wall.

Seeing that Austin could go no farther, Doughboy snarled in triumph and raised his sword, preparing to bring it down in a swing that used every muscle at his command. Austin saw the blow coming and knew he'd never be able to stop it with the ax or get in a swing of his own.

He went on the offensive. Holding the ax high, he surged forward and with a straight-armed thrust that drove the leveled shaft into Doughboy's Adam's apple, hit him broadside across the throat. The man's eyes bulged and he let out a strangled grunt.

Austin had checked the attack, but the move had put him in a vulnerable position. Doughboy was gasping for breath, but the fat around his thick neck had kept his windpipe from being crushed completely. He removed his left hand from the sword hilt and grabbed onto the ax shaft. Austin tried to jam the shaft into the man's throat again. When that didn't work, he jerked the weapon back, but the man had a lock grip on the shaft and wouldn't let go.

Austin lifted his knee and drove it into the man's crotch, but his opponent only grunted. *He must have testicles of iron,* Austin thought, and he used his two-handed leverage and attempted to twist the ax handle out of the man's hand. That ploy ended when Doughboy dropped the sword completely and grabbed onto the shaft with his right hand. They were like two boys fighting over a baseball bat, but the loser in this deadly game would go home in a casket.

Doughboy's superior strength and weight began to tell. His hands were on the outside of the shaft where he had the advantage of leverage as well. His manic grin changed to a feral croak of triumph and he twisted the ax out of Austin's hand.

Austin glanced around. There were weapons all over the workshop, but none within ready reach. Doughboy smiled and began to advance. Austin backed up until he was up against a wall and could go no farther. Doughboy smiled and raised the ax for a swing that would cleave Austin in two.

Seeing that the man's midsection was temporarily exposed, Austin used his powerful legs to drive his head into the man's gut with battering ram force. The man let out a sound like a squeezed bellows and the ax dropped from his hands.

Austin came out of his bounce with legs spread apart, ready to drive his fists into the doughy face. Austin's head butt had clearly hurt Doughboy. His pale face was even pastier than normal and he was gasping for breath.

He must have decided that whatever the pleasures of slicing and dicing Austin, dead was dead. He reached under his jacket and his hand came out filled with a pistol with a silencer mounted on the barrel. Austin braced himself for the impact of a bullet at close range. But the man's smile faded, to be replaced by a look of perplexity. A feathered stick had appeared like magic and was protruding from his right shoulder. The gun fell from his fingers.

Austin turned and saw Skye holding a crossbow. She had fitted another shaft to the weapon and was frantically winding back the bow string. Doughboy's eyes went to Austin, who was scrambling for the fallen gun, then back to Skye. He opened his mouth and bellowed. Stopping only to snatch a helmet from the pile of those littering the floor, he lurched toward the shop door and tore the curtain aside in his haste to escape.

With the pistol in his hand, Austin cautiously followed. He heard the tingle of the front door bell, but by the time he stepped out onto the sidewalk the street was deserted. He went back inside, making sure to lock the front door. Skye had cut Darnay's bonds.

Austin helped Darnay to his feet. The antiques dealer was bruised from being slapped around and stiff from kneeling, but otherwise he seemed all right. Austin turned to Skye and said, "You never told me you were a dead shot with a crossbow."

Skye had a stunned look on her face. "I can't believe I hit him. I closed my eyes and just pointed in the general direction." She saw his bloodstained shirt. "You've been hurt."

Austin inspected the wound. "It's only a scratch, but someone owes me a new shirt."

"You wielded a *fauchard* very well," Darnay said, as he dusted his knees and elbows.

"What did you say?" Austin replied.

"That weapon you handled so deftly. It's a *fauchard*, a fifteenth-century pole arm similar to the *glaive*. There was a move to abolish it in the Middle Ages because of the terrible wounds it produced. Your weapon was a combination between a *fauchard* and a battle-ax. You look puzzled?"

"It's just that I've been hearing that name a lot lately."

"I find this weapons discussion fascinating," Skye said, "but could anyone suggest what do we do now?"

"We can still call in the police," Austin said.

Darnay looked alarmed. "I'd rather not have the gendarmes here. Some of my dealings—"

"Skye has already filled me in. But you're right; the police might have a hard time buying a story about a big bad man who attacked us with a sword."

The antiques dealer heaved a sigh of relief and glanced around at the wreckage. "I never thought my office would be used for a reenactment of the Battle of Agincourt."

Skye was inspecting the pile of helmets. "It's not here," she said, a bleak expression on her face.

Darnay replied with a smile, went over to a wall and pressed a wooden panel. A rectangular section swung open to reveal a large safe, which he opened with a few clicks of the combination lock. He reached inside and pulled out Skye's helmet. "This little item seems to produce a lot of excitement."

"I'm sorry I brought you into this," Skye said. "That awful man was waiting for me at my apartment and he heard your call. I never dreamed—"

"It's not your fault. As I said on the phone, I need to examine this beauty further. I'm thinking that it might be prudent to close shop for a while and do business from my villa in Provence. I'd love to have you as my guest. I'd worry about you as long as that *gros cochon* is on the loose."

She thought about it. "Thank you, but I have too much work to do. The department is going to be in chaos with Renaud gone. Keep the helmet as long as you wish."

"Very well, but consider spending the night at my apartment."

"You might want to accept Monsieur Darnay's invitation," Austin said. "We can sort things out in the morning."

Skye thought about it again and said she would have to go back to her apartment first to pick up some clothes. Austin made her wait in the hall while he made sure her apartment was safe. He didn't think Doughboy would be feeling too frisky with the crossbow bolt in his shoulder, although the big man seemed to have a high pain threshold and a talent for the unexpected.

Skye was almost through packing her overnight bag when Austin's cell phone twittered.

Austin talked to someone on the other end for a few moments, and when he hung up he had a grin on his face. "Speak of the devil. That was Racine Fauchard's appointments secretary. I've been summoned to an audience tomorrow with the grand dame herself."

"Fauchard? I couldn't help noting your reaction when Darnay identified the poleax. What's going on?"

Austin gave Skye a quick reprise of his visit to the air museum and the connection between the Ice Man and the Fauchard family.

Skye snapped her bag shut. "I want to go with you."

"I don't think that's a good idea. It might be dangerous."

Skye replied with a derisive laugh. "An old lady? *Dangerous?*"

"It does sound silly," Austin admitted, "but this whole business with the body in the ice, the helmet and that goon who killed Renaud seems to go back to the Fauchards. I don't want to involve you."

"I'm *already* involved, Kurt. *I* was the one trapped under the glacier. It was my office and this apartment that man searched, obviously looking for the helmet I brought out from under the glacier. It was my friend Darnay who would have been killed if not for you." She crossed her arms and made her strongest point. "Besides, I'm an arms expert and my knowledge might come in handy."

"Persuasive arguments." Austin pondered the pros and cons. "All right. Here's the deal. I introduce you as my assistant, and we'll use an assumed name."

Skye leaned over and pecked Austin on the cheek. "You won't regret this."

"Right," Austin said. He didn't sound convinced, although he knew Skye had some valid points.

Skye was an attractive woman and time spent in her company was never wasted. There was no direct connection linking the Fauchards and the violent man he had nicknamed Doughboy. At the same time, Grosset's warning about the Fauchard family echoed in his brain like a warning bell tolling in the night.

It is said that they have a past.

16

THE FARMER WAS singing a tearful version of "Le Souvenir" when the red blur filled his windshield and his truck's cab reverberated with an ear-shattering roar. He jerked the wheel to the right and sent the heavily laden vehicle nose first into a drainage ditch. The truck slammed into an embankment, catapulting the load of wooden cages onto the ground. The impact smashed the cages into splinters and freed hundreds of squawking chickens. The driver extricated himself from the truck and shook his fist at the crimson plane with the eagle insignia on the tail. He scurried for cover amid an explosion of feathers as the aircraft buzzed his truck again.

The plane climbed into the sky and did a triumphant rollover. The pilot was laughing so hard he almost lost control of the aircraft. He wiped the tears from his eyes with his sleeve and flew low over the vineyards that stretched for hundreds of acres in every direction. With a flick of a switch he sent a cloud of pesticides spraying out from the twin pods under the plane's wings. Then he peeled off in a new direction. The vineyard valleys changed to brooding forest and dark-water lakes that gave the land below a particularly melancholy aspect.

The plane skimmed the treetops, heading toward four distant spikes that rose above the forest on a hill. As the plane drew nearer, the spikes became guard towers that anchored the corners of a thick, crenellated stone wall. A wide moat filled with stagnant green water surrounded the wall and was in turn bordered by extensive formal gardens and woodland paths. The plane buzzed the roof of the imposing château within the walls, and then it flew out over the woods, dropped down onto a green swath of grass and taxied up to a Jaguar sedan parked at the edge of the airstrip. As the pilot climbed from the cockpit, a ground crew materialized out of nowhere and pushed the plane into a small flagstone hangar.

Ignoring the crew, Emil Fauchard strode to the car, walking with an athletic grace, muscles rippling under his flying suit of black Italian leather. He whipped his goggles off and handed them to the waiting chauffeur along with his gloves. Still chuckling over the expression on the truck driver's face, he settled into the plush backseat and poured himself a shot of cognac from a built-in bar.

Fauchard had the classic features of a silent film star and a profile the Barrymore family would have been proud of. For all his physical perfection, however, Fauchard was a repellent man. His arrogant dark eyes had all the warmth of a cobra's. With his handsome, almost perfect face, he was like a marble statue that had been given life but not humanity.

The local farmers whispered that Fauchard had the look of a man who had made a pact with the devil. Maybe he *was* the devil, others said. The more superstitious took no chances and made the sign of the cross when he passed by, a holdover from the days of the evil eye.

The Jaguar followed a driveway that ran under a long tunnel-like tree canopy, then ascended to the main entrance of the château. The car drove over an arched bridge that spanned the moat, then through the wall gate into an expansive cobblestone courtyard.

The Fauchard château was feudal in silhouette and had none of the architectural finesse seen in castles of Renaissance design. It was a stolid, squatting edifice of great size, anchored in place by medieval towers at each corner, mimicking the placement of turrets in the outer wall. Large windows had replaced some of the arrow slits in the exterior, and low-relief ornamentation had been added here and there, but the cosmetics could not hide the brooding, militaristic aspect of the building.

A burly man with a shaved head and a face like a pit bull stood sentry in front of the château's ornately carved double doors. He had somehow crammed a body shaped like a refrigerator into the black suit of a butler.

"Your mother is in the armory," the man said in a rasping voice. "She has been expecting you."

"I'm sure she has, Marcel," Emil said, brushing past the butler.

Marcel was in charge of the small army that surrounded his mother like a Praetorian guard. Even Emil couldn't get near her without being intercepted by one thuggish servant or another. Many of the scar-faced retainers who filled posts normally reserved for household servants were former enforcers for the French mob, although she favored ex–Foreign Legionnaires like Marcel. They stayed out of sight for the most part, but Emil always sensed they were there, watching, even when he couldn't see them. He despised his mother's bodyguards. They made him feel like a stranger in his own house, and even worse, he had no power over them.

He entered a spacious vestibule hung with ornate tapestries and walked down a portrait gallery that stretched along one wall of the château and seemed to go on forever. Hundreds of portraits lined the gallery. Emil hardly glanced at his ancestors, who had no more meaning to him than faces on postage stamps. Nor did he care that many of those ancestors had died violent deaths in this very house.

The Fauchards had been in the château for centuries, since assassinating its former owner. There was hardly a pantry, bedroom or dining hall where some member of the Fauchard family, or one of their enemies, had not been garroted, stabbed or poisoned. If the château were still haunted by the ghosts of those murdered within its walls, every corridor in the vast edifice would have been crowded with restless wraiths.

He went through a high arched door into the armory, an immense, vaulted hall whose walls were hung with weapons that spanned the centuries, from heavy bronze swords to automatic rifles, grouped according to time period. The focal point of the armory was a display of fully armored mounted knights in full charge against an unseen enemy. Enormous stained-glass windows that depicted warriors rather than saints lined one wall of the hall, imparting a religious atmosphere, as if the armory were a chapel dedicated to violence.

Emil went through another door into a library of military history that adjoined the armory. Light streaming through an octagon oculus illuminated the large mahogany desk at the center of the book-lined room. In contrast to the prevailing militant theme, the dark wood desk was carved with flowers and woodland nymphs. A woman wearing a dark business suit sat behind the desk going over a pile of papers.

Although Racine Fauchard was no longer youthful, she was still strikingly beautiful. She was as slender as a fashion model and in contrast to some women, who bend in on themselves as they grow older, she was as straight as a candle. Her skin was covered with fine wrinkles, but her complexion was as flawless as fine porcelain. Some people compared Racine's profile to that of the famous Nefertiti bust. Others said she looked more like the hood ornament on a classic car. Those meeting her for the first time might have guessed from her silver hair that she was of middle age.

Madame Fauchard looked up at her son's entry and gazed at him with eyes the hue of burnished steel.

"I've been waiting for you, Emil," she said. Her voice was soft but the unyielding authority in it was unmistakable.

Fauchard plunked into a fourteenth-century leather chair that was worth more than many people earned in a decade.

"Sorry, Mother," he said, with a careless expression on his face. "I was up dusting the grapes in the Fokker."

"I heard you rattle the roof tiles." Racine arched a finely shaped brow. "How many cows and sheep did you terrify this morning?"

"None," he said, with a satisfied smile, "but I did strafe a convoy and freed some Allied prisoners." He broke into laughter at her blank stare. "Well, all right. I buzzed a chicken truck and drove it into a ditch."

"Your aerial antics are most amusing, Emil, but I'm tired of paying the local farmers for the damage your exploits cause. There are more serious matters that deserve your attention. The future of the Fauchard empire, for one."

Fauchard caught the icy tone in the voice and straightened up in his chair, like a malicious schoolboy who'd been scolded for a prank. "I know that, Mother. It's just my way of blowing off steam. I *think* better up there."

"I hope you have thought about how you might deal with the threats to our family and way of life. You are the heir to all that the Fauchards have built up through many centuries. It is not a duty you should take lightly."

"And I don't. You must admit we have buried a potentially embarrassing problem under thousands of tons of glacial ice."

Racine's lips parted in a thin smile, revealing her perfect white teeth. "I doubt whether Jules would have liked being called an 'embarrassing problem.' Sebastian deserves no credit. Due to his clumsiness, we almost lost the relic for all time."

"He never knew it was under the ice. He was intent on bringing out the strongbox."

"An exercise in futility." She flipped the cover open on the battered metal box that sat on her desk. "The potentially incriminating documents in here were ruined by water leakage years ago."

"We didn't know that."

She ignored his excuse. "Nor did you know the woman archaeologist escaped with the relic. We *must* get the helmet back. The success or failure of our whole enterprise now rests on its recovery. That fiasco at the Sorbonne was handled badly and brought in the police. Then Sebastian botched another attempt to retrieve our property. The helmet he brought us from the antiques dealer was nothing more than a cheap trinket manufactured in China for the theater."

"I am looking into that—"

"You must stop looking and *act.* Our family has never allowed failure of any kind. We can never show weakness or we will be destroyed. Sebastian has become a liability. He may have been seen at the Sorbonne. Take care of it."

Emil nodded. "I'll deal with him."

Racine knew her son was lying. Sebastian was like a mastiff trained to kill on command and was loyal only to her son. Having a servant like that in the superheated pressure chamber that was the Fauchard family could not be allowed, for very practical reasons. She knew that familial ties had never blocked a fatal dagger blow or fended off a smothering pillow when power and fortune were at stake.

"See that you do, and make it soon."

"I will. Our secret is safe in the meantime."

"Safe! We were nearly exposed by a chance discovery. The key to the family's future is in the hands of a stranger. I tremble to think how many other minefields are out there. Follow my lead. When my wayward chemist Dr. MacLean strayed from the reservation, I brought him back with a minimum of fuss."

Emil chuckled. "But, Mother, you were the one who had all the project scientists except MacLean encounter 'accidents' before their work was done."

Racine pinioned her son with a cold stare. "A miscalculation. I never said I was infallible. It is a mark of maturity to admit mistakes and rectify them. Dr. MacLean is at work on the formula as we speak. In the meantime, we must retrieve the relic so we can make our family whole again. Have you made any progress?"

"The antiquities dealer, Darnay, has disappeared. We are trying to track him down."

"What about the woman archaeologist?"

"She seems to have vanished from Paris."

"Keep looking. I have sent my personal agents to find her. We must move quietly. In the meantime, there is the threat to our larger enterprise. The Woods Hole Oceanographic Institution is working with NUMA to explore the Lost City."

"Kurt Austin, that man who rescued the people from under the glacier, was from NUMA. Is there any connection?"

"Not that I know of," Racine said. "The joint expedition was in the works before Austin appeared on the scene. I'm concerned that the expedition could see the results of our work and questions would be raised."

"We can't afford that."

"I agree. That's why I have put a plan in place. The deep-sea vehicle *Alvin* is scheduled to make several dives. It will vanish on the first."

"Is that wise? It would provoke a large search-and-rescue effort. Investigators and reporters will swarm over the site."

A humorless smile came to Racine's lips. "True, but only if the disappearance is reported to the outside world. The support ship will vanish as well, with all its crew, before the *Alvin*'s disappearance is reported. Searchers will have thousands of square miles of ocean to contend with."

"A vanished ship and crew! Your talents have always awed me, Mother, but I never knew you were a magician."

"Learn from me, then. Use failure as a stepping-stone to success. A ship is steaming toward the Lost City with a hold full of our *mistakes*. It will be remotely controlled by another vessel several miles away. It will anchor near the dive site. Once the submersible has been launched, the ship will call a Mayday, a fire aboard will be reported, the research vessel will send a boat over to investigate. The boarding crew will be greeted by our hungry lovelies. Once they have finished their work, the freighter will be moved hull to hull with the research vessel and the explosives aboard detonated by remote control. Both ships will disappear. No witnesses. We don't want a repeat of the situation with those television people."

"A near disaster," Emil admitted.

"True reality television," she said. "We were lucky that the sole survivor is thought to be a babbling lunatic. One more thing. Kurt Austin has asked for a meeting. He says he has information that might be of interest to our family regarding the body in the glacier."

"He knows about Jules?"

"We will find out. I have invited him here. If I see that he knows too much, I will place him in your hands."

Emil rose and came around the desk. He gave his mother a peck on the cheek. Racine watched him as he left the armory, thinking how well Emil embodied the Fauchard spirit. Like his father, he was brilliant, cruel, sadistic, homicidal and greedy. And also like his father, Emil lacked common sense and was impulsive. These were the same characteristics that had caused Racine to kill her husband many years before when his actions were about to jeopardize her plans.

Emil wanted to assume her mantle, but she feared for the future of the Fauchard empire and her carefully laid plans. She also knew that Emil wouldn't hesitate to kill her when the time came, which was one reason she had kept Emil in the dark as to the real significance of the relic. She would hate to have to dispose of her only offspring, but one had to be careful when a viper lived in the house.

She picked up the phone. The chicken farmer Emil had driven off the road must be found and compensated for the damage to his chicks and dignity.

She sighed heavily, thinking that a mother's work is never done.

17

BLESSED WITH smooth seas and fair winds, the research vessel *Atlantis* rapidly covered the distance from the Azores Islands and dropped anchor north of the Mid-Atlantic Ridge over a submerged sea mountain called the Atlantic Massif. The seamount rises sharply from the ocean floor about fifteen hundred miles east of Bermuda and just south of the Azores. In the distant past, the massif protruded from the ocean, but now its flat top is some twenty-five hundred feet below the waves.

Alvin was scheduled to dive the next morning. After dinner, Paul and Gamay got together with the other scientists on board to discuss the dive. They decided to gather rock, mineral and plant samples in the area around the Lost City and to record as many visual observations as possible.

The Alvin Group, a seven-member team of pilots and engineers, was up at dawn and by six o'clock they were starting to go through a fourteen-page checklist. By seven, they were swarming over the submersible, checking its batteries, electronics and other systems and instruments. They loaded still and video cameras on board along with lunches and extra warm clothing for the pilot and scientists.

Then they placed stacks of iron bars on the outside of the hull to make the submersible heavy enough to sink to the bottom. The *Alvin*'s trip to the ocean floor was more a free-fall descent than an actual dive. When it was time to come up, the submersible would drop the ballast weights and float to the surface. For safety purposes, the manipulator arms could be dropped if they became entangled, and if the submersible got into trouble it could jettison the fiberglass outer hull, allowing the personnel sphere to rise to the surface on its own. If the submersible got itself into dire straits, the crew had seventy-two hours of life support.

Paul Trout was a veteran fisherman who understood the quirky nature of the ocean. He had checked the weather reports, but he relied mostly on his own instincts and experience. He surveyed the weather and sea conditions from the deck of the *Atlantis.* The deep-blue sky was unmarred by clouds except for a few wispy mares' tails, and he had seen rougher seas in a bathtub. Conditions were perfect for a dive.

As soon as it was light, the dive team had dropped two transponders to the ocean floor in the general area of the *Alvin*'s dive. The transponders sent out a *ping* sound that allowed the submersible to keep track of its position in a dark world where there were no street signs and the ordinary techniques of surface navigation were practically useless.

Gamay stood nearby, engrossed in a phone conversation with Dr. Osborne. They were discussing the latest satellite photos of Gorgonweed infestation.

"The weed is spreading more rapidly that we calculated," Osborne said. "Great masses of it are headed toward the east coast of the United States. And spots have begun to show up in the Pacific."

"We're about to launch the *Alvin*," Gamay said. "We're in a quiet period, so the water should be relatively clear."

"You'll need all the visibility you can get," Osborne said. "Keep a sharp eye out for areas of growth. The infestation source may not be readily apparent."

"The cameras will be rolling every minute and we may pick up something when we look at the pictures," Gamay said. "I'll send photos back as soon as we have something."

After Gamay hung up, she relayed Osborne's words to Paul. It was time to go. A crowd of people gathered on the fantail to watch. One of them was a trim man with salt-and-pepper hair who came over and wished them well. Charlie Beck was the leader of a team that had been training the ship's crew in security procedures.

"You've got a lot of guts going down in that thing," he said. "The SEAL delivery vehicles always made me claustrophobic."

"It will be a little tight," Gamay said, "but it's only for a few hours."

When it wasn't diving, the submersible was housed on the aft deck in a special building known as the *Alvin* hangar. Now the hangar doors opened and the *Alvin* emerged, moving toward the stern on a set of rails, finally coming to a halt under the A-frame. The Trouts and the pilot climbed a set of stairs and walked across a narrow bridge to the sub's red-painted top, or "sail," as it was called. They took their shoes off and squeezed through the twenty-inch hatch.

Two escort divers climbed onto the submersible and attached a winch line from the A-frame. While this was happening, a small inflatable boat was launched over the side. Controlled by an engineer on the "Dog House," a small room atop the hangar, the A-frame winched the eighteen-ton vehicle off the deck and lowered it into the ocean with the escort divers still hanging on. The divers removed the lines securing the tool basket at the bow end of the submersible, made one last check and said their good-byes down the hatch, then they swam to the inflatable to be taken back to the ship.

They took their seats in the submersible's tight cabin, a titanium pressure sphere eighty-two inches in diameter. Practically every inch of the sphere's interior was covered with panels that contained switches for power activation, ballast control, monitors for oxygen and carbon dioxide, and other instruments. The pilot sat on a low raised stool where she could control the vehicle with the joystick in front of her.

The Trouts squeezed into the tight space on either side of the pilot, sitting on cushions that provided a modicum of comfort. Despite the tight quarters, Trout was excited. Only his New England reserve kept him from shouting with joy. For a deep-ocean geologist, the cramped quarters of the *Alvin* were better than a deluxe stateroom on the *QE2*.

Since its construction for the U.S. Navy in 1964, the *Alvin*'s exploits had made it the world's most famous submersible. The stubby twenty-five-foot-long little vehicle with the singing chipmunk's name could dive as deep as fourteen thousand feet. The vehicle had made international headlines after it found a lost hydrogen bomb off the coast of Spain. On another expedition, it transported the first visitors to the grave of the *Titanic*.

Seats on the *Alvin* were difficult to come by. Trout considered himself extremely lucky. If not for the urgent nature of the expedition, he might have waited years to go on a dive, even with his impressive NUMA credentials and inside connections.

The pilot was a young marine biologist from South Carolina whose name was Sandy Jackson. With her calm, cool demeanor and laconic drawl, Sandy seemed like a younger version of the legendary aviatrix Jacqueline Cochran. She was a slim woman in her thirties, and under her jeans and wool sweater was the wiry physique of a marathon runner. Hair the hue of raw carrots was tucked under the tan *Alvin* baseball cap, which she wore with its navy blue visor backward.

While Gamay had settled for a functional one-piece jumpsuit, Trout saw no reason to change his sartorial habits for a deep-sea dive. He was impeccably dressed, as usual. His stonewashed jeans were tailored, his button-down shirt came from Brooks Brothers and he wore one of the large colorful bow ties that he collected. This one had a sea-horse pattern. His bomber jacket was made of the finest Italian leather. Even his silk long underwear was custom-made. His light brown hair was carefully parted down the middle and swept back at the temples, making him look like a character from an F. Scott Fitzgerald novel.

"This is an easy trip," Sandy said as the tanks filled with water and the submersible began its twenty-five-hundred-foot dive. "*Alvin* dives around a hundred feet a minute, which means we'll be on the bottom in less than a half hour. If we were diving to the fifteen-thousand-foot max, we'd drop for an hour and a half. We usually play classical music on the way down and soft rock on the ascent," Sandy said, "but it's up to you."

"Mozart would set the proper mood," Gamay said.

A moment later, the cabin was filled with the lilting strains of a piano concerto.

"We're about midway," Sandy said after fifteen minutes.

Trout greeted the announcement with a broad grin. "Can't wait to see this underwater metropolis."

While the *Alvin* sank into the depths, the *Atlantis* moved in a slow circle above the dive area and the support crew gathered with the chief scientist in the top lab, between the bridge and the chart room, where the dive is monitored.

Sandy reported their progress with the acoustic telephone, acknowledged the garbled reply, then turned to the Trouts.

The submarine continued its descent.

"What do you folks know about the Lost City?" she said.

"From what I've read, it was found by accident in the year 2000. The discovery apparently came as quite a surprise," Gamay said.

Sandy nodded. "*Surprise* doesn't begin to describe our reaction. *Shell-shocked* would be a more accurate term. We were towing the *Argo II* behind the ship looking for volcanic activity on the mid-ocean ridge. Around midnight, the second shift leader saw what looked like frozen white Christmas trees on the video monitor screens and realized we'd hit hydrothermal vents. We didn't see tube worms or clams like those found at other ocean vent areas. Word spread like wildfire. Before long, everyone on the ship was trying to squeeze into the control van. By then, we were starting to see the towers."

"I heard one scientist say that if the Lost City were on land, it would be a national park," Trout said.

"It wasn't just *what* we found but where we found them. Most of the vents that have previously been discovered, like the 'black smokers' for instance, were near mid-oceanic ridges formed by tectonic plates. The Lost City is nine miles from the nearest volcanic center. We sent the *Alvin* down the next day."

"I understand some columns are nearly twenty stories high," Trout said.

Sandy switched on the outside floodlights and glanced through her view port. "See for yourself."

Paul and Gamay peered through the circular windows. They had seen the still photos and videos of the Lost City, but nothing could have prepared them for the primordial scene that unfolded before them. Paul's large hazel eyes blinked in excitement as the vehicle glided over a fantastic forest of lofty columns. Gamay, who was equally enthralled, said the columns reminded her of the "snow ghosts" that form atop mountains where supercooled fog forms tufts of rime on the tree branches.

The carbonate and mica pillars ranged in color from stark white to beige. Gamay knew from her research that the lighter-colored columns were active while the darker ones were extinct. The towers soared to multiple, feathery spires at their summits. Delicate white flanges jutted out from the sides the way mushrooms grow on old tree trunks. New crystals were continuously forming, giving the edges the appearance of Spanish lace.

At one point Sandy slowed the *Alvin*'s descent and the submersible hovered near a chimney whose flat top was at least thirty feet across. The tower seemed to be alive and moving. The chimney was covered with mats of growth that undulated in the bottom currents as if in rhythm to music from the speakers.

Gamay let out the breath she'd been holding. "This is like being in a dreamscape."

"I've seen it before and I'm still in awe," Sandy said. She steered the *Alvin* close to the top of the tall column. "This is where it gets *really* interesting. The warm water coming from below the sea bottom rises and becomes trapped under those flanges. Those mats you see are actually dense microbe communities. The flanges trap the 160-degree alkaline fluids that stream up the chimneys from below ocean crust that is 1.5 billion years old. The water carries methane, hydrogen and minerals emitted by vents. Some people think we may be looking at the beginnings of life," she said in a hushed voice.

Trout turned to his wife. "I'm strictly a rock-and-gravel guy," he said. "As a biologist, what do you think of that theory?"

"It's certainly possible," Gamay said. "The conditions out there could be similar to what they were in the early days of the earth. Those microbes living around the columns resemble the first life-forms to evolve in the sea. If this process can occur *without* volcanoes, it greatly increases the number of locations on the seafloor of early earth where microbial life could have started. Vents like these could be incubators for life on other planets as well. The moons of Jupiter may have frozen oceans that could be teeming with life. The Mid-Atlantic Ridge is hundreds of miles long, so the potential for new discoveries is endless."

"Fascinating," Trout said.

"Where's the Gorgonweed epicenter from here?" Gamay asked.

Sandy squinted at her instruments. "A little east of here. The *Alvin*'s speed is rather underwhelming—two knots tops—so sit back and enjoy the ride, as the airline pilots say."

The towers thinned out and began to vanish as the submersible moved out of the Lost City. Eventually, however, the lights began to pick out more spires.

Sandy let out a low whistle. "Wow! It's a whole new Lost City. Unbelievable!"

The submersible wove its way through a thicket of towers that extended in every direction beyond the range of the vehicle's bright lights.

"This makes the original Lost City look like East Podunk," Trout said, as he peered with wondering eyes through the view port. "We're talking about real skyscrapers here. That one looks like the Empire State Building."

"Ugh," Gamay said a moment later. "Guess this is the place. Reminds me of kudzu."

They were coming up on a dark green curtain of algae that floated like a smoky pall among the pinnacles.

The *Alvin* rose about thirty feet, passed over the cloud, then dropped back down once they were clear.

"Funny to see stuff like that at this depth," Gamay said, with a shake of her head.

Trout was staring out his view port. "That's not *all* that's funny," he murmured. "Am I seeing things off to the right?"

Sandy steered the *Alvin* so the full force of the klieg lights was directed at the sea bottom.

"It *can't* be!" she said, as if she had seen a McDonald's on a corner of the newly discovered undersea metropolis. She brought the submersible to within a few yards of the bottom. Two lines of parallel tracks at least thirty feet apart led off into the darkness.

"Seems we're not the first visitors," Trout said.

"It looks as if a giant bulldozer passed this way," Sandy said. "But that's impossible." She paused, and then in a hushed tone, said, "Maybe this really *is* the lost city of Atlantis."

"Nice try, but these tracks look too recent," Paul said.

The tracks went straight for a while, and then curved between two towers that soared for nearly three hundred feet.

At several points along the way, they came upon towers lying on their sides like toppled bowling pins. Other pillars had been ground to powder by giant treads. Something very large and powerful had cut a swath through the new Lost City.

"It looks like an undersea clear-cutting operation," Trout said.

Gamay and Paul worked the video and still cameras to record the scene of destruction. They were at least a half mile into the new vent field. The original Lost City was like a pine woods compared to a redwood forest. Some of the towers were so tall that their summits were invisible. From time to time, they had to detour around great blobs of algae.

"Thank goodness for those cameras," Sandy said. "The folks on the surface would never believe what we're seeing."

"I don't quite believe it myself," Trout said. "I—What was *that*?"

"I saw it, too," Gamay said. "A big shadow passed over us."

"A whale?" Trout said.

"Not at this depth," Gamay replied.

"What about a giant squid? I've heard they can dive deeper than whales."

"*Any*thing is possible in a place like this," Gamay said.

Trout asked Sandy to put the vehicle into a slow spin.

"No problem," Sandy said, working the controls. The vehicle slowly began to pivot. They were in the middle of a tight concentration of towers that obscured sight in every direction.

The towers directly in front of the *Alvin* seemed to be vibrating like strings in a piano. Then two or three of the spires crumbled in slow motion and disintegrated in a smoky cloud. Trout had a vague impression that something black and monstrous in size was emerging from the smoke screen and heading directly for them.

Trout yelled at Sandy to put the *Alvin* in reverse, knowing that it was too slow to evade anything faster than a jellyfish, but the pilot was transfixed by the advancing behemoth and didn't respond until it was too late.

The vehicle shuddered and a loud metallic clunk rattled the pressure hull.

Sandy tried to move the submersible backward, but there was no response from the controls.

Trout glanced through the view port again.

Where an instant before, the lights had illuminated a forest of white and beige towers, a monstrous mouth yawned ahead.

Inexorably, the *Alvin* was drawn into the great glowing maw.

18

THE *ALVIN* HAD failed to answer the call, and though it was not yet due to surface, concern was mounting aboard the *Atlantis* with each passing moment. There had been little apprehension at first. The submersible had an impeccable safety record and carried reliable backup systems in case of an emergency. Tension had already ratcheted up to a high peak when the strange ship showed up.

Charlie Beck leaned against the rail, examining the vessel through his binoculars. It was a small freighter well past her prime. Its hull was splotched with cancerous rust spots and was badly in need of a coat of paint. The ship seemed haunted by a general air of neglect. Painted below the name on the scarred hull was the country of registration, Malta.

Beck knew that the freighter was probably neither Celtic nor Maltese, and that these were designations of convenience. The ship's name could have been changed five times in the last year. Its crew would undoubtedly be low-paid sailors from third or fourth world countries. It was the perfect example of a potential pirate ship or terrorist ship, what some in the maritime security business call the "Al Qaeda navy."

As a professional warrior, Captain Charlie Beck lived in a relatively uncomplicated world. Clients gave him jobs to do, and he did them. In his rare reflective moments, Beck thought that one day he should erect a memorial paying homage to Blackbeard the pirate. Had it not been for William Teach and the bloodthirsty brethren who succeeded him, Beck reasoned, he would not have his Mercedes, his speedboat on Chesapeake Bay or his trophy house in Virginia horse country. He'd be a broken-down paper-pusher, sitting behind a desk in the Pentagon labyrinth, staring at his service pistol and thinking about putting a bullet in his brain.

Beck was the owner of Triple S, shorthand for Sea Security Services, a specialized consulting firm that hired out to shipowners who were worried about the threat of piracy. His security teams ranged around the world, teaching ship crews how to recognize and defend themselves against attacks at sea. In highly dangerous waters, heavily armed Triple S teams rode shotgun as well.

The company had started with a few former navy SEALs who missed being in action. Business had grown briskly, fueled by the rapid growth of piracy. But the World Trade Center attacks had heightened awareness of terrorism threats, and Beck soon found himself at the head of a far-flung, multimillion-dollar corporation.

Commercial shipowners had always worried about piracy, but it was the attack on the research vessel *Maurice Ewing* that provided a wake-up call for the scientific community. The *Ewing* was on an oceanographic expedition off the coast of Somalia when a group of men in a small boat raked the vessel with gunfire and launched a rocket-propelled grenade at the research ship.

The grenade missed the *Ewing* and the ship made a safe getaway, but the incident demonstrated that a research ship on a peaceful, scientific expedition was considered as much a prize as a container ship carrying valuable cargo.

To a pirate, a research vessel was a floating mother lode. A pirate could sell a stolen laptop computer on the black market for more money than he might earn in a year at a respectable job.

As an acute businessman, Beck saw a niche to be filled. Business was only part of his motivation. Hard-nosed as Beck might be, he was not without sentiment. He had a particular love of the sea, and attacks against scientific oceanic inquiry were personally offensive to him.

Beck's company had developed a program specifically aimed at security for research vessels, which were particularly vulnerable to attacks because they anchored for long periods of time to conduct ocean drilling and to provide support for tethered vehicles or submersibles. A stationary ship was a sitting duck for pirates.

Beck and a team of SEALs had come aboard the research vessel *Atlantis* through a previous arrangement with the shop operations division at the Woods Hole Oceanographic Institution. After stopping for a few days to make the Lost City probe, the *Atlantis* had planned to sail to the Indian Ocean and hired a Triple S team to go along. Beck, who went on operations whenever he could, wanted the ship's crew and his men to be prepared. He'd read about the Lost City in a scientific journal and was eager to join the expedition.

Beck was in his late fifties and his hair had gone to salt-and-pepper, and squint wrinkles framed his gray eyes. He waged a constant battle through diet and exercise with a persistent middle-aged paunch. Yet he still maintained the snapping turtle attitude and hard leanness that had got him through the challenging, sometimes brutal SEAL training, and he ran his company with military discipline.

On the trip out, Beck and his three-man team of former SEALs had put the crew and scientists through the usual training exercises. They'd taught the scientific team that speed and surprise were a pirate's greatest allies. The crews learned how to vary schedules, restrict access in port, travel in daylight, how to spot a potential threat, aim searchlights, keep their night watches on high alert and how to repel boarders with fire hoses. And if all that failed, they were to give the pirates what they wanted. No ship's computer was worth someone's life.

The training had gone well, but as the scientific activity on board increased, thoughts of security were put aside. Unlike Southeast Asia and Africa, the waters around the Mid-Atlantic Ridge were not considered pirate country. There was some excitement when the *Alvin* was launched, but there was nothing much to do until it resurfaced.

Then the strange ship hove into sight in the midst of the *Alvin* crisis. It seemed too much of a coincidence to Beck.

Although he knew the *Atlantis* was not in usually dangerous waters, and there was nothing overtly threatening about the ship or its behavior, he watched with careful eyes after it stopped dead in the water, and then he climbed to the bridge to consult with the captain. As Beck entered the wheelhouse, he could hear a voice squawking over the radio.

"Mayday, Mayday. Come in."

The captain had the mike in his hand and was trying to return the call. "Mayday received. This is the research ship *Atlantis*. Please state the reason for your Mayday."

The distress call repeated with no elaboration.

As the captain tried to make contact, again without success, greasy black smoke rose from the ship's deck.

The captain examined the ship through his binoculars. "Looks like a fire in one of the holds."

He ordered the helmsman to move closer to the other vessel. The distress call kept repeating. *Atlantis* came to a stop a couple of hundred yards from the freighter. Beck scanned the ship's deck. Smoke still poured out of the hold, but he was surprised not to see anyone on deck. With a fire on board, crewmen should have been crowding the rails trying to get attention, climbing into lifeboats, or jumping over the side.

Beck's antennae began to quiver.

"What do you make of it?" he asked the captain.

The captain lowered his binoculars. "Can't figure it. A fire wouldn't have incapacitated the whole crew. Someone was operating the ship until a few minutes ago. And there's apparently someone in the bridge sending the Mayday. I'd better send a party over to investigate. Maybe the crew is incapacitated or trapped below."

Beck said, "Use my men. They're trained in boarding and in medical treatment." He grinned. "Besides, they've been getting lazy and could use the exercise."

"Be my guest," the captain said. "I've got enough on my mind with the *Alvin*." He ordered his first mate to ready a small shuttle boat.

Beck's men had been on deck, their eyes glued to the dramatic sight of the burning vessel. He ordered them to round up their weapons and ammo.

"You guys have been getting flabby," he said. "Think of this as an exercise, but keep your weapons loaded. Heads-up at all times."

The team snapped into action. The men had become bored with inactivity and welcomed the diversion. Navy SEALs are known for their unconventional dress. A sharp eye would have recognized the "drive-on rag," headbands, the unofficial headgear many SEALs preferred to the traditional floppy hat. But they had traded in their camouflage uniforms for denims and work shirts.

Even a small SEAL team like Beck's could produce an amazing measure of firepower. They kept their weapons wrapped in cloth and out of sight. Beck favored the short-barreled 12-gauge shotgun that could cut a man in half. His men carried the black Car-15, a compact version of the M-16 favored by many SEALs.

Beck and his men climbed into an outboard-powered inflatable boat and quickly covered the distance between the two ships. Beck, who was at the helm, made a feint toward the ship. When he failed to draw fire, he went in for a closer look, eventually heading toward a ladder that hung down the side of the hull near the bow.

Sheltered under the steep sides of the ship, they pulled

on their gas masks and shouldered their weapons. Then they climbed to the smoke-filled deck. Beck paired off with his least experienced man and sent the rest of the team to the other side with orders to make their way to the stern.

They rendezvoused a moment later without seeing a soul and began to make their way to the bridge. They leap-frogged up companionways, with each two-man team covering the other.

"Mayday, Mayday. Come in."

The voice was coming through the open door of the wheelhouse. But when they stepped inside, the wheelhouse was empty.

Beck went over and examined the tape recorder next to the microphone. It had been set to play the same message over and over again. Alarm bells went off in his head.

"Goddamnit!" one of his men said. "What the hell's that *stink*?"

The stench was coming through their masks.

"Never mind the smell," Beck said quietly, cocking his shotgun. "Back to the boat. Double time."

Beck's words had barely left his lips when a bloodcurdling shriek filled the wheelhouse. A terrifying apparition had launched itself through the open door. Acting on pure instinct, the captain brought the gun up in a single motion and fired from his hip.

There were more shrieks intermingled with the shouts of his men, and blurred glimpses of long white hair, yellow teeth, glowing red eyes and lunging bodies.

His shotgun was knocked from his hands. Withered hands clawed at his throat. He was thrown to the deck and the overpowering smell of decaying flesh filled his nostrils.

19

THE ROLLS-ROYCE Silver Cloud raced through the sun-drenched French countryside, passing a blur of farmhouses, rolling green fields and yellow haystacks. Darnay had offered the use of his car before he flew off to Provence. Unlike his colleague Dirk Pitt, who favored exotic cars, Austin drove a nondescript vehicle from the NUMA motor pool back home. As the Rolls whisked over hill and dale, Austin felt as if he were at the controls of a flying carpet.

Skye sat beside him, her hair playfully tousled by the warm breeze flowing through the open windows. She noticed the faint smile on his lips. "A penny for your thoughts."

"I was congratulating myself on my good luck. I'm driving a magnificent car through countryside that could have inspired a Van Gogh painting. There's a lovely woman at my side. And I'm on the NUMA payroll."

Skye gazed with longing at the passing scenery. "It's unfortunate that you *are* being paid. Otherwise, we could forget about the Fauchards and go off on our own. I'm so sick of this whole sordid business."

"This shouldn't take long," Austin said. "We passed a charming *auberge* a while back. After we visit *chez* Fauchard, we could stop and have the dinner we've been putting off."

"All the more reason to wrap up our visit as quickly as possible." The car was approaching a crossroad. Skye consulted a map. "We should be turning off not far from here."

Several minutes later, Austin wheeled the car onto a narrow strip of macadam. Hard dirt tracks branched off from the road and provided access to vineyards stretching as far as the eye could see. The vineyards eventually thinned out and the car came to an electrified chain-link fence. NO TRESPASSING signs in several languages hung from the fence. The gate was open so they kept on going and plunged into a dense forest. Thick tree trunks hugged the road on both sides and the dense canopy filtered the sun's rays.

The temperature dropped several degrees. Skye crossed her arms and hunched her shoulders.

"Cold?" Austin said. "I can roll up the windows."

"I'm fine," she said. "I wasn't prepared for the abrupt change from the lovely farmland and vineyards. This forest is . . . so foreboding."

Austin glanced at the dense woods. He saw only shadows beyond the phalanx of trees. Occasionally, the woods opened to reveal a dank marsh. He flicked on the headlights, but they only served to intensify the gloominess.

Then the scenery began to change. The road widened and was bordered on both sides by tall oaks. Their branches interlocked high above, creating a long tree tunnel that went on for at least a mile before ending quite suddenly. The road began to rise.

"Mon Dieu!" Skye exclaimed when she saw the massive granite pile that loomed ahead on a low hill.

Austin's eyes took in the conical turrets and the high, crenellated walls.

"We seem to have passed through a time warp into fourteenth-century Transylvania."

Skye said in hushed tones, "It's magnificent in an ominous sort of way."

Austin was less enthralled with the château's architecture. He gave her a sidelong glance. "They used to say the same thing about Castle Dracula."

He wheeled the Rolls onto a white gravel driveway that encircled an ornate fountain whose motif was a group of armor-clad men hacking each other to death in bloody combat. The bronze faces on the struggling warriors were twisted in agony.

"Charming," Austin said.

"*Ugh!* It's absolutely grotesque."

Austin parked the Rolls near an arched bridge that spanned a wide moat. A swampy odor rose from the greenish-brown surface of the stagnant water. They walked across the bridge and drawbridge and passed through a gate into the expansive cobblestone-paved courtyard that surrounded the château and separated the building from the encircling walls. No one came to greet them so they made their way across the courtyard and climbed the stairs to a terrace that ran along the front of the house.

Austin put his hand on the massive knocker that decorated the iron-banded wooden door. "Does this look familiar?"

"It's the same eagle design as on the helmet and the plane."

Nodding in agreement, Austin lifted the knocker and let it drop twice.

"I predict that a toothless hunchback named Igor will open the door," he said.

"If that happens, I'm running for the car."

"If that happens, I'd advise you not to get in my way," Austin said.

The man who answered the doorbell's ring was neither toothless nor hunched. He was tall and blond and dressed in white tennis clothes. He could have been in his forties, or fifties, although it was hard to tell his age because his face was unlined and he was as trim as a professional athlete.

"You must be Mr. Austin," the man said with a bright smile, his hand extended in greeting.

"That's right. And this is my assistant, Mademoiselle Bouchet."

"I'm Emil Fauchard. A pleasure to meet you. You're very kind to come all the way from Paris. My mother has been eagerly awaiting your arrival. Please come this way."

He ushered his guests into a commodious foyer and led the way at a brisk pace along a carpeted hallway. Painted on the high vaulted ceilings were mythological scenes showing nymphs, satyrs and centaurs in unearthly woodland settings. As they followed their guide, Skye leaned into Austin's ear.

"So much for your Igor theory."

"It was only a hunch," Austin said with a straight face.

Skye rolled her eyes, the only appropriate response to Austin's pun.

The hallway seemed endless, although it was hardly a boring walk. Decorating the dark wood-paneled walls were enormous tapestries of medieval hunting scenes showing life-sized figures of nobles and squires whose arrows were making pincushions out of hapless deer and wild boar.

Fauchard stopped at a door, which he opened, and gestured for them to enter.

The chamber they stepped into was a stark contrast to the château's oversized architecture. It was small and intimate and with its low beamed ceilings and walls lined with antiquated books, it was like a room in a country cottage. A woman sat in a leather chair in a corner of the room, reading by the light streaming through a tall window.

"Mother," Fauchard softly called out. "Our visitors have arrived. This is Mr. Austin and his assistant, Mademoiselle Bouchet." Skye had chosen her alias out of the Paris phone book.

The woman smiled and put her book down, then stood to greet them. She was tall and almost military in her posture. A black business suit and lavender scarf set off her pale complexion and silver hair. Moving as gracefully as a ballerina, she came over and shook hands. Her grip was unexpectedly strong.

"Please sit down," she said, indicating two comfortable leather chairs. Glancing at her son, she said, "Our guests must be thirsty after their long drive." She spoke English with no accent.

"I'll attend to it on my way out," Emil said.

Moments later, a servant appeared bearing cold bottled water and glasses on a tray. Austin studied Madame Fauchard as she dismissed the servant and poured their glasses full. As with her son, it was difficult to guess her age. She could have been anywhere from forty to sixty years old. Whatever her age, she was quite beautiful in a classic sense. Except for a spidery network of wrinkles, her complexion was as flawless as a cameo and her gray eyes were alert and intelligent. Her smile ranged from beguiling to the mysterious, and when she spoke her voice had only a few of the cracks in it that can come with old age.

"It was very kind of you and your assistant to travel all the way from Paris, Mr. Austin."

"Not at all, Madame Fauchard. You must be very busy with your duties and I'm pleased that you were able to see us on such short notice."

She threw her hands up in a gesture of astonishment.

"How could I *not* see you after hearing about your discovery? Frankly, I was stunned when I learned that the body found in Le Dormeur glacier could be that of my great-uncle, Jules Fauchard. I have flown over the Alps many times, never suspecting that an illustrious member of my family lay frozen in the ice below. Are you quite certain it's Jules?"

"I never saw the body, and can't be sure about the identity," he said. "But the Morane-Saulnier airplane I discovered in the glacial lake was traced to Jules Fauchard through a manufacturer's serial number. Circumstantial evidence, but compelling nonetheless."

Madame Fauchard stared off into space. "It could only be Jules," she said, more to herself than to her guests. Rallying her thoughts, she said, "He disappeared in 1914 after taking off from here in his plane, a Morane-Saulnier. He loved to fly and had gone to French military flying schools, so he was quite accomplished at it. Poor man. He must have run out of fuel or encountered severe weather in the mountains."

"This is a long way from Le Dormeur," Skye said. "What could have possessed him to fly all the way to the Alps?"

Madame Fauchard responded with an indulgent smile. "He was quite mad, you know. It happens in the best of families." She turned back to Austin. "I understand you are with NUMA. Don't look surprised, your name has been all over the newspapers and television. It was very clever and daring of you to use a submarine to rescue the scientists trapped under the glacier."

"I didn't do it alone. I had a great deal of help."

"Modest as well as clever," she said, gazing at him with an expression that signified more than casual interest. "I read about the horrible man who attacked the scientists. What could he have wanted?"

"A complicated question with no easy answers. He evidently wanted to make sure no one could ever retrieve the body. And he took a strongbox that may have held documents."

"A pity," she said with a sigh. "Perhaps those documents could have shed light on my great-uncle's strange behavior. You asked what he was doing in the Alps, Mademoiselle Bouchet. I can only guess. You see, Jules suffered a great deal."

"Was he ill?" Skye said.

"No, but he was a sensitive man who loved art and literature. He should have been born into another family. Jules had problems being part of a family whose members were known as 'Merchants of Death.' "

"That's understandable," Austin said.

"We've been called worse, monsieur. Believe me. In one of those ironies of fate, Jules was a natural businessman.

He was devious and his behind-the-scenes schemes would have done credit to a Machiavelli. Our family company prospered under his hand."

"That image doesn't seem to fit with what you've told me about his gentle character."

"Jules hated the violence that was implicit in the wares he sold. But he reasoned that if we didn't make and sell arms, someone else would. He was a great admirer of Alfred Nobel. Like Nobel, he used much of the family fortune to promote peace. He saw himself as a balance of natural forces."

"Something must have unbalanced him."

She nodded. "We believe it was the prospect of World War One. Pompous and ignorant leaders started the war, but it is no secret that they were pushed over the precipice by the arms merchants."

"Like the Fauchards and the Krupps?"

"The Krupps are *arrivistes*," she said, wrinkling her nose as if she smelled something rotten. "They were nothing but glorified coal miners, parvenus who built their fortunes on the blood and sweat of others. The Fauchards had been in the arms business for centuries before the Krupps surfaced in the Middle Ages. What do you know about our family, Mr. Austin?"

"Mostly that you're as secretive as an oyster."

Madame Fauchard laughed. "When you're dealing with arms, *secrecy* is not a dirty word. However, I prefer to use the word *discreet*." She angled her head in thought then rose from her chair. "Please come with me. I'll show you something that will tell you more about the Fauchards than a thousand words."

She guided them along the corridor to a set of tall arched doors emblazoned with a three-headed-eagle emblem in black steel.

"This is the château's armory," she said, as they stepped through the doorway. "It is the heart and soul of the Fauchard empire."

They were in an immense chamber whose walls soared

to high, ribbed ceilings. The room seemed to be laid out in the shape of a cathedral. They were standing in a long, column-lined nave that was crossed by a transept, with the altar section behind it. The nave was lined with alcoves, but instead of statues of saints, the niches contained weapons apparently grouped according to time period. More armor and weapons could be seen on a second level that wrapped around the perimeter of the room.

Directly in front of them, caught in midcharge, were four lifelike knights and their huge stuffed mounts, all in full armor, lances extended as if defending the armory from interlopers.

Skye surveyed the array with a professional eye. "The scope and extent of this collection is breathtaking."

Madame Fauchard went over and stood next to the mounted knights. "These were the army tanks of their day," she said. "Imagine yourself as a poor infantryman, armed only with a lance, who sees these gentlemen bearing down on you at full gallop." She smiled, as if relishing the prospect.

"*Formidable,*" Skye said, "but not invincible as weapons and tactics advanced. The longbow had arrows that could puncture some armor at long range. A halberd could penetrate armor and a two-handed cutting sword of war could dispatch a knight if he could be pulled off his horse. All their armor would have been useless against firearms."

"You have hit upon the heart of our family's success. Every development in weaponry would eventually be overcome with more advanced weaponry. Mademoiselle sounds as if she knows what she's talking about," Madame Fauchard said, raising a finely arched brow.

"My brother made a hobby of ancient weapons. I couldn't help learning from him."

"You learned well. Every piece in here was produced by the Fauchard family. What do you think of our family's artistry?"

Skye examined the display in the nearest alcove and

shook her head. "These helmets are primitive but extremely well made. Perhaps more than two thousand years old."

"Bravo! They were produced in pre-Roman times."

"I didn't know the Fauchards went back that far," Austin said.

"I wouldn't be surprised if someone discovered a cave drawing of a Fauchard making a flint spearhead for a Neolithic client."

"This château is quite a leap in time and geography from a Neolithic cave."

"We have come a long way since our humble beginnings. Our family were armorers based in Cyprus, a crossroad of the commerce in the Mediterranean. The Crusaders arrived to build outposts on the island and they admired our craftsmanship. It was the custom of wealthy nobles to retain household armorers. My ancestors moved to France and eventually organized a number of craftsmen's guilds. The guild families intermarried and formed alliances with two other families."

"Hence the three eagles on your coat of arms?"

"You're quite observant, Monsieur Austin. Yes, but in time the other families were marginalized and the Fauchards eventually dominated the business. They controlled different specialty shops and sent agents throughout Europe. There was no end to the demand, from the Thirty Years War to Napoleon. The Franco-Prussian War was lucrative and set the stage for World War One."

"Which brings us full circle to your great-uncle."

She nodded. "Jules became morose as war seemed inevitable. By then we had grown into a cartel of arms and took on the name of Spear Industries. He tried to persuade our family to pull out of the arms race, but it was too late. As Lenin said at the time, Europe was like a barrel of gunpowder."

"Which needed only the assassination of the Grand Duke Ferdinand to provide a spark."

"The Grand Duke was a lout," she said, with a wave of her long fingers. "His death was less a spark than an excuse. The international arms industry had interlocking agreements and patents. Every bullet fired or bomb exploded by either side meant shared profits for the owners and stockholders. The Krupps made money from German deaths and Spear Industries from the death of French soldiers. Jules foresaw this would be the situation and the fact that he was ultimately responsible is probably what unhinged him."

"Another casualty of the war?"

"My great-uncle was an idealist. His passion brought him a premature and senseless death. The sad part of all this is that his death made no more difference than some poor soldier being gassed in the trenches. Only a few decades later, our leaders dragged us into another world war. Fauchard's factories were bombed to dust, our workers killed. We rapidly recouped our losses in the Cold War. But the world has changed."

"It was still a pretty dangerous place the last time I looked," Austin said.

"Yes, the weapons are more deadly than ever, but conflicts are more regional and shorter in length. Governments, like your own, have replaced the major arms dealers. Since I inherited the leadership of Spear Industries, we have divested our factories and we're essentially a holding company that subcontracts for goods and services. With the fear of rogue nations and terrorists, our business remains steady."

"An amazing story," Austin said. "Thank you for being so forthcoming with your family history."

"Back to the present," she said, with a nod of her head. "Mr. Austin, what are the prospects of retrieving the plane that you found in the lake?"

"It would be a delicate job, but not impossible for a competent salvager. I can recommend a few names, if you'd like."

"Thank you very much. We'd like to retrieve *any* property that is rightfully ours. Do you plan on returning to Paris today?"

"That was our intention."

"*Bien.* I'll show you the way out."

Madame Fauchard led them along a different corridor whose walls were covered with hundreds of portraits. She paused in front of a painting of a man in a long leather coat.

"This is my great-uncle Jules Fauchard," Madame Fauchard said.

The man in the painting had an aquiline nose and a mustache and stood in front of a plane similar to the one Austin had seen at the French air museum. He was wearing the same helmet Skye had turned over to her friend Darnay.

A soft gasp escaped from Skye's throat. It was barely audible, but Madame Fauchard stared at Skye and said, "Is there a problem, mademoiselle?"

"No," Skye said, clearing her throat. "I was admiring that helmet. Is it in your armory collection?"

Racine gave Skye a hard stare.

"No. It is not."

Austin tried to divert the direction of the conversation.

"There is not much family resemblance to you or your son," he said.

Racine smiled. "The Fauchards were coarse-featured, as you can see. We favor my grandfather, who was not a Fauchard by blood. He married into the Fauchard family and took their name as his. It was an arranged marriage, done to bring together two families in an alliance of convenience. There was no male heir to the Fauchards at the time, so they manufactured one."

"You have a fascinating family," Skye said.

"You don't know the half of it." She gazed thoughtfully at Skye for a moment and smiled. "I just had a wonderful idea. Why don't you stay for dinner? I'm having a few guests over anyhow. We are putting on a masque, as in the old days. A little costume party."

"It's a long drive back to Paris. Besides, we didn't bring costumes," Austin said.

"You can stay here as our guests. We always have a few extra costumes. We'll find something appropriate. We have everything you'd need to make yourselves comfortable. You can get an early start in the morning. I won't take no for an answer."

"You're very gracious, Madame Fauchard," Skye said. "We wouldn't want to impose."

"No imposition at all. Now, if you'll excuse me, I will talk to my son about tonight's arrangements. Please feel free to wander about the first floor of the château. The upper floors are living quarters."

Without a further word, Madame Fauchard whisked off along the corridor, leaving them with only the Fauchard ancestors for company.

"What was that all about?" Austin said, as Madame Fauchard disappeared around a corner. Skye clapped her hands and rubbed them together.

"My plan worked! I purposely babbled on about my arms expertise in the armory to get her attention. Once I set the hook, I reeled her in. Look, Kurt, you said that the Fauchard family was the key to this business under the glacier and the attack at Darnay's shop. We couldn't simply leave with empty hands. What's the problem?"

"You could be in danger. *That's* the problem. Your mouth dropped open when you saw the portrait of good ol' Jules. She knows you've seen the helmet."

"That wasn't planned. I was really startled when I saw Jules wearing the helmet I recovered from the glacier. Look, I'm willing to take the chance. Besides, a costume party might be fun. She wouldn't try anything with guests around. She seems quite gracious and not the dragon lady I expected."

Austin wasn't convinced. Madame Fauchard was a charming woman, but he suspected her Whistler's mother act was pure theater. He had seen the cloud pass over her face at Skye's reaction to the portrait above their heads. Madame Fauchard, not Skye, had set the hook and reeled them in. Warning bells were chiming in his brain, but he smiled anyway. He didn't want to alarm Skye.

"Let's look around," he said.

It took them an hour to explore the first floor. It covered several acres, but mostly what they saw of it was corridors. Every door they tried was locked. As they made their way through the labyrinth of passageways, Austin tried to memorize the layout. Eventually they came back to the front door vestibule. His unease grew.

"Odd," he said. "A building this size must require a large support staff, but we haven't seen a single soul outside of the Fauchards and the servant who brought us the water."

"That is strange," Skye said. She tried the front door and smiled. "Look here, Mr. Worrywart. We can leave anytime we want to."

They stepped out onto the terrace and walked across the courtyard to the gate. The drawbridge was still down, but the portcullis, which had been up when they entered, had been lowered. Austin put his hands on the bars and gazed through the iron grating.

"We won't be leaving anytime soon," he said with a grim smile.

The Rolls-Royce had vanished from the driveway.

20

THE *ALVIN* HAD RISEN like a seagull atop a rolling billow before it dropped in a free fall that ended with a bone-jarring clang of metal against metal. The impact threw the three people inside the *Alvin* from their seats. Trout tried to avoid a collision with Gamay and the small-framed pilot, but his six-foot-eight physique was ill suited for acrobatics and he slammed into the bulkhead. Galaxies whirled around inside his head and when the stars cleared he saw Gamay's face close to his. She looked worried.

"Are you all right?" she said with concern in her voice.

Trout nodded. Then he pulled himself back into his seat and gingerly explored his bruised scalp with his fingers. The skin was tender to the touch, but he was not bleeding.

"What happened?" Sandy said.

"I don't know," Trout said. "I'll take a look."

Trout tried to ignore the sick feeling in his gut and crawled over to a view port. For an instant, he wondered if the bump on his head was making him see things. The scowling face of a man stared at him. The man saw Trout. He tapped on the acrylic view port with the barrel of a gun and jerked his thumb upward. The message was clear. Open the hatch.

Gamay had her face pressed against another view port. "There's a real ugly guy out there," she whispered. "He's got a gun."

"Same here," Trout said. "They want us to climb out."

"What should we do?" Sandy said.

Someone started banging on the hull.

"Our welcoming party is becoming impatient," Gamay said.

"So I see," Trout said. "Unless we can figure out how to turn the *Alvin* into an attack sub, I suggest that we do whatever they want us to."

He reached up and opened the hatch. Warm, damp air rushed in and the same face he had seen in the view port was framed in the circular opening. The man gestured at Trout and pulled out of view. Trout stuck his head and shoulders through the hatch and saw that the *Alvin* was surrounded by six armed men.

Moving slowly, Trout climbed out onto the sub's hull. Sandy emerged and the color drained from her face when she saw the reception party. She froze in place until Gamay gave her a nudge from below and Trout helped her down to the metal deck.

The *Alvin* had come to rest in a brightly lit compartment as big as a three-car garage. The air was heavy with the smell of the sea. Water dripped from the *Alvin*'s hull and gurgled down drains in the deck. The muted hum of engines could be heard in the distance. Trout surmised that they were in the air lock of an enormous submarine. At one end of the chamber, the walls curved to meet each other in a horizontal crease like the inside of a large mechanical mouth. The submarine must have gulped the *Alvin* down like a grouper eating a shrimp.

A guard punched a wall switch and a door opened in the bulkhead opposite the mechanical mouth. The same guard pointed the way with the barrel of his gun. The prisoners stepped through the doorway into a smaller room that looked like a robot factory. Hanging from wall racks were at least a dozen "moon suits," whose thick joined arms ended in grasping claws. From his work with NUMA, Trout knew that the suits were human-shaped submersibles used for diving for long periods at extreme depths.

The door hissed shut and the prisoners marched along a passageway between three guards in front and three taking up the rear. The navy-blue jumpsuits the guards wore had no identification markings of any sort. The men were muscular, hard-looking types with close-cropped hair, and they moved with the assurance of trained military men. They were in their thirties and forties—too old to be raw recruits. It was impossible to guess their nationalities because they had kept silent, preferring to communicate their wishes with gun gestures. Trout guessed they were mercenaries, probably special warfare types.

The parade made its way through a network of passageways. Eventually, the prisoners were shoved into a cabin and the door clicked shut behind them. The small stateroom had two bunks, a chair, an empty closet and a head.

"Cozy," Gamay said, taking in the tight accommodations.

"This must be the third-class cabin," Trout said. He had a dizzy spell and put his hand against the bulkhead to steady himself. Seeing the concern in Gamay's face, he said, "I'm okay. But I need to sit down."

"You need some first aid," Gamay said.

While Trout sat on the edge of a bunk, Gamay went into the head and ran cold water over a towel. Trout placed the towel on his temple to keep the swelling down. Sandy and Gamay took turns going back to the sink to replenish the cold-water compress. Eventually, the swelling was reduced. With great care, Trout adjusted his bow tie, which was hanging half off his neck, and he combed his hair with his fingers.

"Better?" Gamay said.

Newly refreshed, Trout grinned and said, "You always told me that I'd get a big head someday."

Sandy laughed in spite of her fears. "How can you two be so calm?" she said in wonder.

Trout's unflappability was less bravado than pragmatism and faith in his own abilities. As a member of NUMA's Special Operations Team, Trout was not unused to danger. His laid-back academic demeanor disguised an innate toughness passed down by his hardy New England forebears. His great-grandfather had been a surfman in the Lifesaving Service, where the motto was "You have to go out, but you don't have to come back." His fishermen grandfather and father had taught him seamanship and respect for the sea, and Trout had learned to rely on his own ingenuity.

With her slim athletic body and graceful movements, her luxuriant dark red hair and flashing smile, Gamay was sometimes mistaken for a fashion model or an actress. Few would have believed that she had been a tomboy growing up in Wisconsin. Although she had grown into a woman who possessed every desirable feminine trait possible, she was no hothouse flower. Rudi Gunn, the assistant director at NUMA, had recognized her intelligence when he suggested she be brought into the agency with her husband. Admiral Sandecker readily accepted Gunn's suggestion. Since then, Gamay had displayed her intelligence and cool resourcefulness on many missions with the Special Assignments Team.

"Calmness has nothing to do with it," Gamay said. "We're simply being practical. Like it or not, we're stuck here for the time being. Let's use deductive reasoning to figure out what happened."

"Scientists are not supposed to draw any conclusions until we're ready to support them with facts," Sandy said. "We don't have all the facts."

"You learned the scientific method well," Trout said. "As Ben Jonson said, there's nothing like the prospect of a hanging to focus a person's mind. Since we don't have all the facts, we can use scientific dead reckoning to get us where we want to go. Besides, we don't have anything else to do. First, we know for sure that we've been kidnapped and we're being held prisoner in a large submarine of curious design."

"Could this be the vehicle that made those tracks through the Lost City?" Sandy said.

"We don't have the facts to support that theory," Trout said. "But it wouldn't be impossible to design a submersible that could crawl along on the sea floor. NUMA had something like that a few years ago."

"Okay, then what's it doing here? Who are these people? And what do they want with us?"

"I have the feeling that those questions will soon be answered," Gamay said.

"You're talking more like a swami than a scientist," Sandy said.

Gamay touched her finger to her lips and pointed at the door. The handle was turning. Then the door opened and a man stepped into the cabin. He was so tall he had to duck his head under the jamb. The newcomer was dressed in a jumpsuit like the others, except for its lime-green color. He closed the door quietly behind him and gazed at the captives.

"Please relax," he said. "I'm one of the good guys."

"Let me guess," Trout said. "Your name is Captain Nemo and this is the *Nautilus*."

The man blinked in surprise. He had expected the prisoners to be cowed.

"No, it's Angus MacLean," he said with a soft Scottish burr. "*Dr.* MacLean. I'm a chemist. But you're right about this submarine. It's every bit as wonderful as Nemo's vessel."

"And we're all characters in a Jules Verne novel?" Gamay said.

MacLean replied with a heavy sigh. "I wish it were that easy. I don't want to unduly alarm you," he said with a quiet seriousness, "but your lives may depend upon our conversation in the next few minutes. Please tell me your names and what your profession is. I plead with you to be truthful. There is no brig on this vessel."

The Trouts understood the unspoken message. No brig

meant no prisoners. Trout looked into MacLean's kindly blue eyes and decided to trust him.

"My name is Paul Trout. This is my wife, Gamay. We're both with NUMA. This is Sandy Jackson, the pilot of the *Alvin.*"

"What's your scientific background?"

"I'm an ocean geologist. Gamay and Sandy are both marine biologists."

MacLean's serious face dissolved into a smile of relief. "Thank God," he murmured. "There's hope."

"Perhaps you'll answer a question for me," Trout said. "Why did you kidnap us and hijack the *Alvin*?"

MacLean replied with a rueful chuckle. "I had nothing to do with it. I'm as much a prisoner on this vessel as you are."

"I don't understand," Sandy said.

"I can't explain now. All I can say is that we are fortunate that they can use your professional expertise. Like me, they will keep you alive only as long as they need you."

"Who are *they*?" Trout asked.

MacLean ran his long gray fingers through his graying hair. "It would be dangerous for you to know."

"Whoever you are," Gamay said, "please tell the people who kidnapped us and took our submersible that our support ship will have people looking for us the second we're missed."

"They told me that won't be a problem. I've no reason to disbelieve them."

"What did they mean?" Trout said.

"I don't know. But I do know that these people are ruthless in the pursuit of their goals."

"What *are* their goals?" Gamay said.

The blue eyes seemed to deepen. "There are some questions it is not wise for you to ask or for me to answer." He rose from his chair and said, "I must report the results of my interrogation." He pointed at the light fixture and touched his fingers to his lips in a clear warning of a hidden microphone. "I'll return shortly with food and drink. I suggest you get some rest."

"Do you trust him?" Sandy said after MacLean left them alone once more.

"His story seems crazy enough to be true," Gamay said.

"Do you have any suggestions on what we should do?" Sandy said, looking from face to face.

Trout lay back in a bunk and attempted to stretch out, although his long legs hung off the edge of the mattress. He pointed to the light fixture and said, "Unless someone wants this bunk, I'm going to do as MacLean suggested and get some rest."

MacLean returned about half an hour later with cheese sandwiches, a thermos of hot coffee and three mugs. More important, he was smiling.

"Congratulations," he said, handing around the sandwiches. "You are now officially employed in our project."

Gamay unwrapped her sandwich and took a bite. "What exactly *is* this project?"

"I can't tell you everything. Suffice it to say that you are part of a research team. You will each be working on a need-to-know basis. I've been allowed to give you a tour as a way of acclimating you to the task ahead. I'll explain on the way. Our babysitter is waiting for us."

He rapped on the door, which was opened by a grim-faced guard who stood aside to let MacLean and the others out. With the guard trailing behind, MacLean led the way along a network of corridors until they came to a large room whose walls were covered with television monitors and glowing arrays of electronic instrument panels. The guard took up a position where he could keep a close eye on them, but otherwise didn't interfere.

"This is the control room," MacLean said.

Trout glanced around. "Where's the crew?"

"This vessel is almost entirely automated. There is only a small crew, a contingent of guards and the divers, of course."

"I saw the moon suits in the room near the air lock."

"You're very observant," MacLean said with a nod of

his head. "Now if you look at that screen, you'll see the divers at work."

A wall screen showed a picture of a column typical of the Lost City. As they watched, there was movement at the bottom of the screen. A diver clad in a bulbous moon suit was rising up the side of the column, propelled by vertical thrusters built into the suit. He was followed by three other divers, similarly equipped, all clutching thick rubber hoses in the mechanical manipulators that served as their hands.

Soundlessly, the grotesque figures floated up until they were near the top of the screen. Like bees collecting nectar, they stopped under the mushroom-shaped mantle rocks.

"What are they doing?" Trout said.

"I know," Sandy said. "They're collecting bio-organisms from the microbe colonies that live around the vents."

"That's correct. They are removing entire colonies," MacLean said. "The living material and the liquid it grows in are transported through the hoses to holding tanks."

"Are you saying this is a *scientific* expedition?" Gamay said.

"Not exactly. Keep watching."

Two divers had broken off from the others and moved on to the top of another column; the pair that was left began to dismantle the column itself, using handsaws.

"They're destroying the columns," Sandy said. "This is *criminal*!"

MacLean glanced over at the guard to see if he had noticed Sandy's outburst. He was leaning against the wall with a bored, detached expression on his face. MacLean waved to get the guard's attention and he pointed at a door off the control room. The guard yawned and nodded his approval. MacLean escorted the others through the door, which opened into a room full of large circular plastic vats.

"We can talk here," MacLean said. "These are storage vats for the biological material."

"The holding capacity must be huge," Gamay observed.

"It's very hard to keep the organisms alive away from their natural habitat. That's why they're taking down some of the columns. Only a small percentage of the harvest will be useful by the time we get back to land."

"Did you say *land*?" Trout said.

"Yes, the collected specimens are ultimately processed in a facility located on an island. We make periodic trips to unload the tanks. I'm not sure where it is."

MacLean saw the guard looking at them. "Sorry. Our babysitter seems to have stirred from his lethargy. We'll have to continue our discussion later."

"Quickly tell me about the island. It may be our only chance to escape."

"Escape? There's no hope of escape."

"There's always hope. What's it like on this island?"

MacLean saw the guard walking toward them and lowered his voice, making his words sound even more ominous. "It's worse than anything Dante could have imagined."

21

AS AUSTIN'S GAZE swept the steep walls and sturdy battlements that enclosed the Fauchard château, he felt an enormous respect for the artisans who had layered the heavy blocks into place. His admiration was tempered by the knowledge that the efficient killing machine those long-dead craftsmen had built to keep attackers at bay worked equally well to prevent those inside from getting out.

"Well," Skye said. "What do you think?"

"If Alcatraz were built on land, it would look something like this."

"Then what do we do?"

He hooked his arm in hers. "We continue our stroll."

After they had discovered the portcullis closed and their car gone, Austin and Skye had sauntered around the courtyard perimeter like tourists on a holiday. From time to time, they would stop and chat before ambling on. The casual veneer was meant to deceive. Austin hoped that anyone watching would think they were completely at ease.

As they walked, Austin's coral-blue eyes probed the enclosure for weaknesses. His brain cataloged every minute detail. By the time they had circled the courtyard and returned to their starting point, he could have drawn an accurate diagram of the château complex from memory.

Skye stopped and rattled a wrought-iron gate blocking a narrow stairway to the battlements. It was bolted shut. "We're going to need wings to get over these walls," she said.

"My wings are at the dry cleaner's," Austin replied. "We'll have to think of something else. Let's go back inside and nose around."

Emil Fauchard greeted them on the terrace. He flashed his toothy smile and said, "Did you have a pleasant tour of the château?"

"They don't build them like this anymore," Austin said. "By the way, we noticed our car was gone."

"Oh yes, we moved it out of the way to make room for our arriving guests. The keys were in the ignition. We'll pull it around when you're ready to leave. I hope you don't mind."

"Not all," Austin said with a forced grin. "Saves me the trouble of doing it myself."

"Splendid. Let's go inside then. The guests will be arriving soon."

Emil ushered them back into the château and up the wide staircase in the veranda to the second floor and showed them to adjoining guest rooms. Austin's room was actually a suite with bedroom, bath and sitting area, decorated in Baroque, heavy on the scarlet plush and gilt, like a Victorian brothel.

His costume was laid out on the canopied bed. The costume fit well except for snugness around his broad shoulders. After glancing at himself in a full-length mirror, he knocked on the door connecting his suite to Skye's. The door opened partway and Skye poked her head through. She broke into laughter when she saw Austin wearing the black-and-white-checked costume and belled cap of a court jester.

"Madame Fauchard has more of a sense of humor than I gave her credit for," she said.

"My teachers always said I was the class clown. Let's see how you look."

Skye stepped into Austin's room and spun around slowly like a fashion model on a runway. She was dressed in a tight-fitting black leotard that showed off every curve and mound of her figure. Her feet and hands were encased in furry slippers and gloves. Decorating her hair was a headband that had a pair of large pointed ears attached to it.

"What do you think?" she said, pirouetting once more.

Austin looked at Skye with an unabashed male appreciation that was just short of lust. "I believe you're what my grandfather used to call 'the cat's meow.' "

There was a light knock at the door. It was the bullet-head servant Marcel. He leered at Skye like a lion eyeing a tasty wildebeest, then his small eyes took in Austin's costume and his lips curled in a smile of unmistakable contempt.

"The guests are arriving," Marcel said in a voice like gravel sliding off a shovel. "Madame Fauchard would like you to follow me to the armory for cocktails and dinner." His gangsterish intonation was strangely at odds with his butler's formality.

Austin and his feline companion donned their black velvet masks and followed the burly servant down to the first floor and through the maze of corridors. They could hear voices and laughter long before they stepped into the armory. About two dozen men and women dressed in fantastic costumes milled around a bar that had been set up in front of a display of spiked maces. Servants who looked like clones of Marcel threaded their way through the crowd carrying trays of caviar and champagne. A string quartet dressed as rodents was playing background music.

Austin snatched two flutes of bubbly from a passing tray and offered one to Skye. Then they found a vantage point under the lances of the mounted knight display where they could sip their champagne and watch the crowd. The guests were equally divided between men and women, although it was hard to tell because of the variety of costumes.

Austin was trying to figure out the party's theme when a portly black bird approached, weaving like a ship in a heavy sea. The bird wobbled on its yellow legs and leaned forward, its shiny black beak dangerously close to Austin's eye, and drunkenly intoned in a slurred British accent, "*Once upon a midnight dreary* . . . damn, how does the rest of it go?"

Nothing harder to understand than an upper-class Brit with a snootful of booze, Austin thought. He picked up the rest of the verse, "*while I pondered, weak and weary* . . ."

The bird clapped its wings together, and then plucked a champagne glass from a passing tray. The long beak got in the way when he tried to drink so he pushed it up onto his forehead. The florid, jowly face hidden behind the beak reminded Austin of cartoons he had seen of the English symbol, John Bull.

"Always a pleasure to meet a lit'rate gen'lman," the bird said.

Austin introduced Skye and himself. The bird extended a winged hand. "I'm called 'Nevermore,' for the purposes of tonight's festivities, but I go by the name of Cavendish when I'm not running around as Poe's morose bird. *Lord* Cavendish, which shows you the sorry state of our once proud empire when an old sot like me is made a knight. Pardon, I see my glass is empty. Never more, old chap." He belched loudly and staggered off in pursuit of another glass of champagne.

Edgar Allan Poe. Of course.

Cavendish was a rather drunken Raven. Skye personified *The Black Cat.* Austin was the jester from *The Cask of Amontillado.*

Austin studied his fellow guests. He saw a corpselike woman wearing a soiled and bloodied white shroud. *The Fall of the House of Usher.* Another woman wore a garment covered with miniature chimes. *The Bells.* An ape was leaning against the bar, guzzling a martini. *The Murders in the Rue Morgue.* The ape was talking to an oversized beetle with a death's-head on his carapace. *The Gold-Bug.* Madame Fauchard not only had a sense of humor, Austin thought, she had an appreciation for the grotesque.

The music stopped and the room went silent. A figure stood in the doorway, about to enter the armory. Cavendish, who had returned with drink in hand, murmured, "Dear God!" He merged back with the other guests as if seeking the protection of the crowd.

All eyes were fixed on the tall woman who looked as if she had been exhumed from a grave. Blood splattered her long shroud and her gaunt white corpse's face. The lips were withered and the eyes set deep into skeletal sockets. There were gasps as she stepped into the room. She paused once again and stared into the eyes of each guest. Then she made her way across the floor as if she were floating on a cushion of air. She stopped in front of a giant ebony clock and clapped her hands.

"Welcome to the Masque of the Red Death," she said in the clear voice of Racine Fauchard. "Please continue your celebration, my friends. Remember"—her voice gaining a melodramatic quiver—"life is fleeting when the Red Death stalks the land."

The wrinkled lips widened in a hideous smile. Nervous laughter rippled through the crowd and the quartet resumed its playing. Servants who had been frozen in midstride continued on their rounds. Austin expected Madame Fauchard to greet her guests, but to his surprise the apparition came his way and removed the grisly mask to reveal her normal cameo features.

"You look quite handsome in your belled cap and tights, Monsieur Austin," she said, a seductive inflection in her tone.

"Thank you, Madame Fauchard. And I've never met a more charming plague."

Madame Fauchard cocked her head coquettishly. "You have a courtier's way with words." She turned to Skye. "And you make a lovely black cat, Mademoiselle Bouchet."

"*Merci*, Madame Fauchard," Skye said with a thin smile. "I'll try not to eat the string quartet, as much as I love mice."

Madame Fauchard studied Skye with the envy an aging beauty reserves for a younger woman. "They are rats, actually. I wish we had been able to give you more of a choice of costumes. But you don't mind playing the fool, do you, Mr. Austin?"

"Not at all. Court jesters once advised kings. Better to *play* the fool than to be one."

Madame Fauchard laughed gaily and glanced toward the doorway. "*Bien*, I see that Prince Prospero has arrived."

A masked figure dressed in tights and tunic of purple velvet, trimmed with gold, and a mask to match was making his way toward them. He removed his velvet cap with a flourish and bowed before Madame Fauchard.

"A lovely entrance, Mother. Our guests were properly terrified."

"As they should be. I will pay my respects to the others after I talk to Mr. Austin."

Emil bowed again, this time to Skye, and took his leave.

"You have interesting friends," Austin said, scanning the crowd. "Are these people your neighbors?"

"To the contrary. These are the remnants of the great arms families of the world. Immense wealth is represented in this room, all of it built on a foundation of death and destruction. Their ancestors fashioned the spear- and arrowheads that killed hundreds of thousands, built the cannon that devastated Europe in the last century and manufactured the bombs that leveled entire cities. You should be honored to be in such august company."

"I hope you won't be insulted when I say I'm not impressed."

Madame Fauchard replied with a sharp laugh. "I don't blame you. These prancing, chattering fools are decadent eurotrash living on the riches earned by the sweat of their forebears. Their once-proud companies and cartels today are nothing but faceless corporations traded on the New York Stock Exchange."

"What about Lord Cavendish?" Austin said.

"Even more pitiful than the others, because he has only

his name and no riches. His family once held the secret of forged steel before the Fauchards stole it."

"What about the Fauchards? Are they immune from decadence?"

"No one is immune, not even my family. That's why I will control Spear Industries as long as I live."

"Nobody lives forever," Skye said.

"What did you say?" Madame Fauchard's head snapped around and she pinioned Skye with eyes that blazed like fanned coals.

Skye had made a casual observation and wasn't prepared for the heat in Madame Fauchard's reaction.

"What I meant to say is that we're all mortal."

The flame in Racine's eyes flickered and died. "True, but some of us are more mortal than others. The Fauchards will prosper for decades and centuries to come. Mark my words. Now, if you'll excuse me I must tend to my guests. Dinner will be served shortly."

She replaced the hideous mask and glided off to rejoin her son.

Skye seemed shaken. "What was *that* all about?"

"Madame Fauchard is touchy about getting old. I don't blame her. She must have been a beauty in her day. She would have caught my eye."

"If you like making love to a corpse," Skye said with a toss of her head.

Austin grinned. "It seems the pussycat has claws."

"Very sharp ones, and I'd love to use them on your lady friend. I don't know why you were so worried. I'm bored to pieces."

Austin had been watching the arrival of more servants. A dozen or so hard-looking men had slipped quietly into the armory and taken up positions next to every door leading in or out of the great chamber.

"Sit tight," Austin murmured. "I have a feeling that the real party has yet to begin."

22

CAVENDISH WAS superbly intoxicated. The Englishman had shoved his raven's beak onto the top of his head to allow his rosebud mouth unimpeded access to his wine goblet. He had been gurgling wine throughout the medieval-style dinner, washing down the exotic game dishes—everything from lark to boar—like a human garbage disposal. Austin picked at his food to be polite, took an occasional sip of wine and advised Skye to do the same. They would need clear heads if his instincts were on the mark.

As soon as the dessert dishes were removed, Cavendish staggered to his feet and tapped the side of his water glass with a spoon. All eyes turned in his direction. He raised his goblet. "I would like to offer a toast to our host and hostess."

"Hear, hear," his fellow guests replied in boozy acknowledgment, lifting their drinks as well.

Encouraged by the response, Cavendish smiled. "As many of you know, the Fauchard and the Cavendish families go back centuries. We all know how the Fauchards, ah, borrowed the Cavendish process for forging steel on a mass basis, thus assuring their own rise while my people faded into the sunset."

"The fortunes of war," said the ape from *The Murders in the Rue Morgue*.

"I'll drink to that." Cavendish took a swig from his goblet. "Unfortunately, or *fortunately*, given the tendency of Fauchards to meet fatal accidents, we never married into their family."

"The fortunes of love," said the woman draped in bells. The guests around the table roared their drunken approval.

Cavendish waited for the laughter to die down, then said, "I doubt if the word *love* was ever uttered in this household. But *any*one can love. How many families can boast that they single-handedly started the War to End All Wars?"

A heavy silence descended on the table. The guests glanced furtively at Madame Fauchard, who had been sitting at the head of the table with her son seated to her right. She maintained the waxen smile she had held throughout the oration, but her eyes radiated the same heat Austin had seen when Skye mentioned her mortality.

"Monsieur Cavendish is most flattering, but he exaggerates the influence of the Fauchard family," she said in a cool voice. "There were many causes for the Great War. Greed, stupidity and arrogance, to name a few. Every family in this room joined the jingoistic pack in urging on the war that made us all fortunes."

Cavendish would not be discouraged. "Take credit where credit is due, my dear Racine. It is true that we arms people owned the newspapers and bribed the politicians who howled for war, but it was the Fauchard family, in its infinite wisdom, that paid to have the Grand Duke Ferdinand assassinated, thus plunging the world into a bloody brawl. We all know the rumors that Jules Fauchard bolted the pack, thus ensuring his untimely departure from the earth."

"Monsieur Cavendish," Madame Fauchard said, her voice a warning growl. But the Englishman was on a roll.

"But what many don't know," he said, "is that the Fauchards also bankrolled a certain Austrian corporal throughout his political rise and encouraged members of the Japanese Imperial Army to take on the United States." He paused to take a drink. "That turned out to be more than you bargained for and things got a bit out of your control, what with your slave factories bombed to dust. But as someone said a moment ago, 'the fortunes of war.'"

The chamber was gripped by an almost unbearable tension.

Madame Fauchard had removed her plague mask and the loathing etched in her face was even more terrible than the Red Death. Austin had no doubt that if Racine had been capable of telekinesis the weapons would have jumped off the walls and hacked Cavendish to bits.

One of the guests broke the heavy silence. "Cavendish. You've said enough. Sit down."

For the first time, Cavendish became aware of Madame Fauchard's withering stare. The Englishman's brain had caught up with his mouth and he knew he had gone too far. His foolish grin vanished and he wilted like a flower under the heat of a sunlamp. He sat down ponderously, more sober than when he had stood only moments before.

Madame Fauchard rose like a cobra uncoiling and raised her glass. "*Merci.* Now I will offer a toast to the great, *late* House of Cavendish."

The Englishman's ruddy complexion turned the color of paste. He mumbled his thanks and said, "You must excuse me. I don't feel well. Touch of the indigestion, I fear."

Rising from his chair, he made his way toward the exit and disappeared through the doorway.

Madame Fauchard glanced at her son. "Please see to our guest. We wouldn't want him to fall in the moat."

The lighthearted comment seemed to break the tension and conversation resumed as if the previous few minutes had never happened. Austin was less sanguine. As he watched Cavendish leave the room, he thought the Englishman had signed his own death warrant.

"What's going on?" Skye said.

"The Fauchards don't take well to having their dirty laundry hung out in public, especially when strangers are present."

Austin watched Madame Fauchard lean over to say something to her son. Emil smiled and rose from the table. He collected Marcel and together they left the armory. After-dinner brandy was being served when Emil returned about ten minutes later without Marcel. He gazed directly at Austin and Skye as he whispered in his mother's ear. Madame Fauchard nodded her head, her face impassive. The move was subtle, but Austin didn't miss the implication. His name and Skye's had just been added to the Cavendish death warrant.

Several minutes later, Marcel returned from his mission. Emil saw that he was back, then stood and clapped his hands. "Ladies and gentlemen of the Masque of the Red Death, Prince Prospero has prepared a memorable entertainment to cap off the evening's festivities."

He signaled a servant, who lit a torch from the flames of a brazier and handed it to Emil. With great ceremony, Emil produced a large skeleton key from the folds of his tunic and led the way along the nave, crossing the transept to the rear of the armory. He paused to insert the key in a low wooden door carved with skulls and human bones. As he opened the door, his torch flared and sputtered in the cool musty air that flowed through the portal.

"Follow me if you dare," Emil said with a smirking leer on his face, and then he ducked under the jamb.

Laughing giddily, the guests paused, then with wine goblets in hand they filed after Emil like the children of Hamlin following the Pied Piper. Austin put his hand on Skye's arm and kept her from going with the others.

"Make believe you're drunk," Austin said.

"I wish I *were* drunk," Skye said. "*Merde.* Here comes the dragon lady."

Madame Fauchard glided over and said, "The Red Death must take its leave, Monsieur Austin. Sorry we couldn't get to know each other better."

"I am, too. That was an interesting toast Sir Cavendish gave," he said, slurring his words.

"Great families are often the subject of malicious gossip." She turned to Skye. "The masquerade is at an end. I believe you have a relic that belongs to my family."

"What are you talking about?"

"Don't toy with me. I know you have the helmet."

"Then it was *you* who sent that awful man."

"Sebastian? No, he is my son's lapdog. If it's any consolation to you, he will be eliminated as a result of his failures. Never mind, we will persuade you to tell us where our property is. As for you, Monsieur Austin, I must bid you farewell."

"Until we meet again," Austin said, swaying slightly.

She gazed at him with a look approaching sadness. "Yes. Until we meet again."

Escorted by an entourage of servants, Madame Fauchard headed for the exit. Marcel had been standing nearby. Now he came over and curled his lip in his movie gangster's smile. "Monsieur Emil would be heartbroken if you missed the entertainment he has prepared for you."

"Wouldn't miss it for the world," Austin said, deliberately slurring his words.

Marcel lit another torch and gestured toward the door. Austin and Skye caught up with the tail end of the raucous crowd. Marcel took up the rear to make sure they didn't stray.

The procession descended a short stone staircase to a passageway about six feet wide. As the guests plunged deeper into the bowels of the château, the laughter began to ebb. The merriment died completely, along with conversation, when the guests entered a section of tunnel lined with eye-level stone shelves that overflowed with human bones. Emil stopped in front of a shelf, picked out a skull at random and held it above his head, where it grinned down at the guests as if amused by their clever costumes.

"Welcome to the catacombs of Château Fauchard," Emil proclaimed with the cheerfulness of a Disney World tour guide. "Meet one of my ancestors. Pardon if he is a bit reserved. He doesn't get many visitors."

He tossed the skull back into a recess, where it started a small avalanche of femurs, ribs and clavicles. Then he forged ahead, exhorting the guests to hurry or they would miss the show. The tunnel entered a series of large, barred rooms that Emil explained were the dungeons and torture chambers. Braziers had been set up in each room so their flickering light was filtered through stained-glass screens of different colors.

The strange colored light illuminated the wax faces of figures that looked so lifelike no one would have been surprised if they had moved. In one chamber, a great ape was stuffing a woman up a chimney. In another, a man was digging himself out of a grave. Every room had a scene from a Poe story.

Emil drifted back to Austin. The torchlight gave his mordant features a Satanic cast that fit in with the surroundings.

"Well, Monsieur Austin, what do you think of my little show so far?"

"Haven't had so much fun since I went to Madame Tussaud's wax museum."

"You flatter me. Bravo! The best is yet to come."

Emil kept going until he came to a chamber whose crimson light made all within its special radiance look like victims of the Red Death. In the floor of the room was a circular pit. A razor-sharp pendulum was swinging above a wooden framework. Strapped down on the framework, with rats crawling over his chest, was a large black bird. It was the scene from the *The Pit and the Pendulum*, where the victim is being tortured by the Spanish Inquisition.

Only in this instance the victim was Cavendish, who was tied down and gagged on the table.

"You will notice some differences in this scene," Emil said. "The rats you see scurrying around the dungeon are real. And so is the victim. Mr. Cavendish is a good sport, as the English would say, and he has gracefully agreed to participate for our amusement."

As Emil led the guests in a polite applause, Cavendish struggled against the bonds that held him.

The pendulum swung lower until it was only inches from the heaving chest. "He's going to be killed!" a woman screamed.

"Sliced and diced," Emil said with an incongruous cheeriness. He lowered his voice to a stage whisper. "Lord Cavendish is a ham at heart, I fear. Don't worry, my friends. The blade is made of wood. We wouldn't want our guest to go to pieces. But if it worries you . . ."

He snapped his fingers and the swinging pendulum slowed to a stop. Cavendish gave a violent convulsion and lay still.

Emil led the guests into the last dungeon. Although there was no scene set up in the chamber, in some ways it was the most frightening of all. The walls were covered in black velvet that stole what light escaped through the opaque black screen. The atmosphere was the most oppressive. There was a collective sigh of relief when Emil told his guests to follow a passageway that would lead from the dungeon. When Austin and Skye went to follow, he barred their way.

Austin stumbled drunkenly and whipped his cap off in a grand sweep. "After you, Gaston."

Emil had shed his foppish Prospero act and now his voice was businesslike and as hard-edged as cold steel.

"While Marcel leads our guests out of the catacombs, I have something special to show you and the young lady," he said, lifting a fold of black velvet draped against a wall. Behind the cloth was a cleft in the stones about two feet wide.

Austin blinked. "What's going on? Is this part of the show?"

"Yes," Emil said with a hard smile. "This is part of the show." He produced a pistol.

Austin looked at the gun and gave a soggy laugh. "Hell of a show," he said, shaking his head so the bells jangled.

He stepped through the opening, with Skye, then Emil behind her. They descended two more sets of stairs. The temperature dropped and the air became swamplike. Water glistened on the walls and dripped down on their heads. They continued down until Emil finally ordered them to stop in front of a recess about five feet wide and four feet deep.

He thrust the torch into a sconce and pulled a cloth off a pile of bricks. A trowel and a bucket of mortar sat on the floor next to the bricks. From a niche he extracted a wine bottle whose dark green glass was covered with dust and cobwebs. The bottle was stopped up with a cork, which Emil removed with his teeth. He handed the bottle to Austin

"Drink, Monsieur Austin."

Austin stared at the bottle. "Maybe we should let it breathe for a while."

"It has had centuries to breathe," Fauchard said. He gestured with his gun. "Drink."

Austin grinned foolishly as if he thought the gun was a toy and put the bottle to his mouth. Some of the wine dribbled down his chin and he wiped it away. He offered the bottle to Fauchard, who said, "No, thank you. I prefer to remain conscious."

"Huh?"

"You have caused us a great deal of trouble," Emil said. "My mother said to dispose of you in the most fitting way I could think of. A good son always does what his mother tells him to. Sebastian, say hello again to 'Ms. *Bouchet.*' "

A figure stepped from the shadows and the torch light illuminated the pale features of the man Austin had dubbed Doughboy. His right arm was in a sling.

"I believe you've met Sebastian," Emil said. "He has a gift for you, mademoiselle."

Sebastian threw a crossbow bolt at Skye's feet. "This is yours."

"What's going on?" Austin said.

"Your wine contained a paralytic substance," Emil said. "Within moments you will be unable to move, but all your other senses will function fine and you will know what is happening to you." He produced a pair of manacles from under his cloak and dangled them in front of Austin's face. "Maybe if you say 'For the love of God, Montresor,' I'll let you go."

"You bastard," Austin said. He leaned against the wall with his hand as if the strength were ebbing from his legs, but his eyes were fixed on the crossbow bolt a few feet away.

Skye had gasped in fright when she first saw Sebastian. Now, seeing Austin's plight, she lunged for Fauchard's gun hand and grabbed him by the wrist. Sebastian stepped in from behind and wrapped his good arm around her throat. Although he was operating with one arm in a sling, his strength was still formidable and she began to black out for lack of air.

Austin suddenly straightened up. Holding the bottle by the neck, he brought it down on Sebastian's head. The bottle broke in a shower of glass and wine. Sebastian released Skye, who fell to the floor, then stood for a few seconds, an expression of wonder in his eyes, and toppled like a fallen redwood tree.

Emil stepped aside to avoid Sebastian's crashing body and the ugly muzzle of the gun swung toward Austin. Austin threw a body block and slammed Emil into the recess. He groped for Emil's gun hand, but Fauchard got off a shot. The shot went wild and the bullet hit the wall inches from Austin's face. Stone fragments peppered Austin's cheek and he was blinded temporarily by the close muzzle flash. He tripped over the bricks and went down onto his knees. Fauchard danced out of the way.

"Too bad you won't have the lingering death I planned for you," he heard Fauchard say. "Since you're on your knees, why don't you try begging for your life?"

"I don't think so," Austin said. His fingers curled around a narrow wooden shaft. He scooped up the crossbow bolt and brought the point down on Emil's foot.

The sharp point easily passed through the gold slipper. Emil let out a mighty scream that echoed throughout the vault and he dropped the gun.

By then, Austin was back on his feet. He picked out a point on Emil's jaw and put all his weight and power behind a hard right cross that almost separated Fauchard's head from its shoulders. The gun dropped to the floor and Emil crumpled in a heap next to his companion. Austin helped Skye up. She had her hand to her bruised throat and was having trouble catching her breath.

He made sure she could breathe, then he bent over the dough-faced man.

"Looks like Sebastian let the wine go to his head."

"Emil said the wine was drugged. How—"

"I let it dribble down my chin. Wine that old probably tastes like vinegar."

Austin grabbed Emil by the ankles and pulled him into the recess. Then he cuffed one end of the manacles to Fauchard's wrist and the other to a wall ring. As he took his jester's cap off and pulled it down over Fauchard's ears, he said, "For the love of God, Montresor."

Austin removed the torch from its sconce and led the way along the tunnel. Despite his drunken act, he had tried to memorize every foot of the route they had followed. Before long they were back in the dungeons, looking down on Cavendish's body. The rats had scurried off at their approach. The Englishman's plump face was frozen in a rictus of horror.

Austin placed his fingers against Cavendish's neck, but he felt no pulse. "He's dead."

"I don't understand," Skye said. "There's no blood."

Austin ran his thumb along the edge of the blade, which was touching the feathers on Cavendish's chest. "Fauchard was telling the truth for a change. The blade is made of wood. Emil failed to let Cavendish in on his joke. I think our friend here was scared to death. C'mon, there's nothing we can do for him."

They continued along the passageway to a steep, narrow, winding staircase. The atmosphere in the tunnel became less musty as they climbed, and soon fresh air was blowing in their faces. They came to a door that opened into the courtyard and followed the laughter around to the front of the château, where the guests were being ushered under the open portcullis.

Walking slowly and weaving as if they were intoxicated, Austin and Skye caught up with the others. They melded into the crowd, passed through the gate, then walked across the arched stone bridge. Cars were lining up in the circular driveway to pick up the guests, who were effusively bidding one another good-night. Soon all the guests had departed and only Austin and Skye were left. One more car was coming around. It was Darnay's Rolls-Royce. The driver must have thought the car belonged to a guest. Austin stepped to the rear and opened the door for Skye.

He heard someone shout in French and turned to see Marcel running across the bridge. A servant who had been standing nearby heard Marcel's command and stepped in between Austin and the car. The guard was reaching under his tuxedo jacket when Austin demolished him with a short right to the midsection, then yelled at Skye to get in the backseat. He ran around to the other side of the car, yanked the door open, pulled the driver out, dispatched him with an elbow to the jaw and slid in behind the steering wheel.

He snapped the car into gear and stomped the accelerator. The Rolls took off, its tires kicking up a shower of gravel, and skidded around the fountain. Austin saw movement off to his left. Someone was running toward the car. He jerked the wheel in the opposite direction. Another guard stepped into the glare of the headlights. He had a gun clutched in both hands.

Austin ducked behind the dashboard and nailed the gas pedal. The man bounced over the hood and into the windshield, before rolling off. But the windshield was a network of spiderweb cracks from the impact with the man's body. Then the window on the passenger's side disintegrated. Austin saw muzzle flashes ahead and heard a sound like someone whacking a jackhammer against the chrome grille. He yanked the wheel over, felt the impact of another body and jerked the wheel in the opposite direction.

A light burned into his face and made it impossible to see through the damaged windshield. Austin hit the gas again, thinking he was headed for the exit drive, but his sense of direction had been thrown off. The Rolls left the ground at the edge of the moat, soared through the air and splashed down in the water. The air bag had activated and as he fought to push it aside, he could feel the water pouring through the window onto his legs. Bullets peppered the roof of the sinking car but the water dampened their effectiveness. Austin scrunched behind the dashboard and filled his lungs with air. A second later, the car went under completely.

23

THE ROLLS-ROYCE angled its long hood into the water like a submarine making a crash dive, and seconds later the car settled into the mud and detritus built up through the centuries. Austin crawled into the spacious backseat, his hands blindly extended in front of him like antennae on a foraging lobster. His groping fingers encountered soft flesh. Skye grabbed his wrists and pulled him up into a shallow pocket of air. He could hear her frenzied breathing.

He spit out a mouthful of putrid water. "Can you hear me?"

The gurgled reply could only have been a yes.

The water was up to his chin. He stretched his neck to keep his mouth and nose elevated and blurted out quick instructions.

"Don't panic. Stay with me. Squeeze my hand when you need air. Understand?"

Another gurgle.

"Now take three deep breaths and hold the last one."

Hyperventilating in unison, they filled their lungs to the limit, just as the air pocket disappeared and they were totally immersed. Austin tugged Skye to the door and shoved it open with his shoulder. He slithered out and pulled Skye with him. The water glowed green from the electric torches playing on the surface of the water. He and Skye would be dead the second they showed their heads. He gripped Skye's hand tightly in his and pulled her away from the dancing circles of light.

They had gone only a few yards before Skye squeezed his hand. Austin squeezed back and kept on swimming. Skye mashed his fingers again. She had already run out of air. Austin angled upward toward a patch of darkness. He cocked his head as it came out of the water, keeping his profile low so that only an ear and an eye were exposed. Marcel and his men were firing their guns at the bubbles rising from the drowned car. He yanked Skye up beside him and she wheezed like a broken bilge pump. Austin gave her a moment to fill her lungs and pulled her under again.

By swimming and surfacing, they had put distance between themselves and their pursuers, but Marcel and his men were starting to widen the search. Lights bobbed along the edge of the moat and beams probed the water. Austin swam closer to the château wall. His left arm was outstretched, and he was using the slimy stones of the château's submerged bulwarks as a guide. They swam around one of the buttresses that jutted out from the château's fortifications and hid in the shadow of the big stone knee.

"How much longer?" Skye said, barely able to get the words out, although she spoke with a healthy hint of anger in her voice.

"One more dive. We've got to get out of the moat."

Skye swore in French. Then they dove again and swam across to the other side and surfaced under a thick clump of bushes that overhung the bank.

Austin released Skye's wrist, reached up and grabbed two fistfuls of branches. Tucking his toes into the seams in the stone blocks lining the moat, he pulled himself up like a rock climber assaulting a headwall. Then he turtle-crawled on his belly to the edge, stretched his arms down. As he yanked Skye onto dry land, the bush blazed with light.

They rolled into the shadows, but it was too late. There was a chorus of shouts and footfalls pounded the earth as Marcel's men moved in from both sides in a pincers movement. Fearful of shooting each other, they were holding their fire. The only avenue of escape was into the woods ringing the château.

Austin headed for a break in the forest, whose silhouette was visible against the blue-black night sky. A pale slash of white stood out against the blackness. It was a gravel path into the woods. Their wet clothes and general weariness prevented them from breaking any Olympic records, but desperation gave wings to their feet.

Marcel's men were yelling with excitement with their prey in sight. The path led to a junction where three other lanes came together in a four-lane intersection.

"Which way?" Skye said.

The choices were limited. Voices were coming from the paths on either side.

"Straight," he said.

Austin sprinted across the intersection with Skye on his heels. As they ran, he scanned the woods, looking for an opening, but the trees grew close together and impenetrable brush and thornbushes blocked the way. Then the trees ended suddenly and the path plunged between hedges at least ten feet tall. They came to another intersection, this one with two lanes. Austin started down one, then came back and took a few steps down another. Both were flanked by tall hedges, almost as impenetrable as the château's walls.

"Uh-oh," he said.

"*Qu'est-ce que c'est* 'Uh-oh'?"

"I think we're in a garden maze."

Skye looked around. "Oh, *merde*!" she said. "*Now* what do we do?"

"We don't have a lab rat to lead us through this thing, so I'd suggest that we keep moving until we find our way out."

Since it didn't seem to make any difference, they took the left-hand path along a long curved stretch of hedge that swirled back on itself before branching out into two more lanes. The maze was going to be a challenge, Austin thought. It was laid out in a freehand design with circles and flourishes rather than with the right angles of a crossword puzzle grid. They would round a sharp corner only to find they were heading back in roughly the same direction.

Marcel's men were in the maze now. A couple of times, Austin and Skye stopped and held their breath until the voices faded on the other side of a hedge. They were within a few feet of each other, separated only by shrubbery.

Austin knew that Marcel would bring in more reinforcements and it would only be a matter of time before they were caught. There was simply no happy ending to their story unless they found their way out of the green labyrinth. If he were Marcel, he'd be guarding every escape route from the maze.

Damn!

Austin had stubbed his toe on a hard object. He went down on one knee and let loose with a string of quiet curses. But his anger turned to a muted joy when he discovered he had tripped over a wooden ladder that had probably been left by a gardener.

He lifted the ladder off the ground, leaned it against the hedge and climbed to the flat top. He crawled belly down, and as the sharp branches stabbed through his thin jester's costume he had the sensation of lying on a spongy bed of nails. But the hedge held his weight.

Lights were moving at several points in the maze. A search party was coming along the path toward Skye. He called down in a soft voice and told Skye to climb up the ladder onto the hedge. Then he pulled the ladder up and they lay on top of it. Not a moment too soon. They could hear boots crunching in the gravel and heavy breathing and whispers.

Austin waited until the searchers had gone down another lane, then he moved the ladder so that the other end rested on the closest hedge, bridging the space between. He crawled across the ladder and held it steady for Skye to follow. They repeated the process with the next hedge.

As long as they stayed in a straight line, they could work their way out of the maze. They worked as a team, placing their improvised bridge, crawling across it, watching for searchers and then doing it again. The branches tore at their palms and knees, but they ignored the discomfort.

Austin could see the black line of trees in the darkness—with only a few more hedgerows to bridge—when they heard the *thrump* of helicopter rotors coming from the direction of the château. The helicopter was a few hundred feet in the air, moving toward the maze. Then a twin pair of searchlights came on and scanned the ground below.

Austin did a quick ladder shift to the next hedge, but in his haste he misjudged the distance. When he crawled across the ladder, it slipped from the furthermost hedge and he tumbled onto the gravel path. He sprang to his feet, climbed back onto the hedge next to Skye and placed the ladder with more care this time. Then he was across, quickly followed by Skye.

The mistake had cost them precious time. The helicopter was making its first pass over the maze, the brilliant searchlights turning night into day. Austin bridged the last path and turned back to help Skye. Her foot slipped off one of the rungs about midway and he reached across to pull her toward him.

The helicopter was moving closer.

With Skye beside him, Austin slid the ladder down the outside of the last hedgerow. She climbed to the ground with the speed of a spider monkey. Her agility might have been due in part to avoid having Austin step on her hands. As soon as he hit the ground, Austin pulled the ladder down and shoved it close to the base of the hedge. Then he and Skye stretched out beside it.

The helicopter roared overhead.

They could feel the downdraft as the chopper executed a tight turn and came back over the maze and moved back and forth over the hedgerows. After a minute, the chopper darted off and began a sweep of the woods.

In its quick swing, the chopper's lights had illuminated an opening in the tree line. Austin helped Skye to her feet and they ran along the gravel path that surrounded the hedge, then they sprinted along a grassy path into the woods, unsure of where they were going but grateful to be out of the maze.

Several minutes later, they broke out into the open. They were at the edge of a meadow or field, but Austin was more interested in the ghostly outline of a building near the edge of the woods.

"What *is* it?" Skye whispered.

"Any port in a storm," he whispered.

He told her to stay put and loped across the field in the silver moonlight.

24

AUSTIN MADE IT across the moonlit field without incident and edged his way along the wall of the fieldstone building. He found an unlocked door and stepped into the dark interior, where his nostrils picked up the garage odors of oil and gasoline. He allowed himself a measure of optimism; a garage might house a car or truck. His groping fingers found a light switch and he discovered a second later that he was not in a garage, but in a small hangar.

The bright red biplane had swept-back wings and a heart-shaped tail decorated with a black three-headed-eagle design. He ran his fingers along the fabric fuselage, admiring the painstaking restoration that had gone into the aircraft. Attached to the underside of each wing was a torpedo-shaped metal tank. A skull and crossbones was stenciled on the outside of the containers. Poison.

He peered into the twin cockpits. The pilot's controls in the rear cockpit consisted of a single lever in front of the seat and a foot bar that controlled the rudder for steering. The forward-and-back movement of the stick would control the elevator. Moving it from side to side worked the ailerons at the ends of the wings, which tilted the plane for a turn. The system was primitive, but at the same time it was a miracle of simplicity that allowed the plane to be flown with one hand.

The cockpit housed an array of instruments that hadn't come with the original model, boasting handy devices like an up-to-date radio, a modern compass and GPS navigation system. Earphones connected the cockpits. Austin made a quick inspection of the hangar. The walls were hung with tools and spare parts. He peeked into a storeroom filled with plastic containers that were marked with skull and crossbones. The labels identified the contents of the containers as pesticide.

Austin snatched an electric torch from a wall bracket, turned the lights off and went to the door. All was quiet. He clicked the light on and off three times, and then watched as a shadow darted from the woods and made its way silently across the field to the hangar. He scanned the meadow and woods to make sure Skye hadn't been seen, and then pulled her into the hangar and shut the door.

"What took you so long?" she said with irritation in her voice. "I was worried when I saw the lights go on and off."

Austin didn't mind Skye's accusatory tone and took it as a sign that she had regained her natural spunkiness. He kissed her on the cheek. "My apologies," he said. "There was a line at the reservations counter."

She blinked at the darkness. "What *is* this place?"

Austin switched the torch on and let the beam play the length of the plane's fuselage, from the wooden propeller to the coat of arms on the tail.

"You're looking at the Fauchard family air force. They must use this to crop-dust the vineyards."

"It's beautiful," she said.

"It's more than beautiful. It's our ticket out of here."

"Can you fly that thing?"

"I think so."

"You *think* so?" She shook her head in disbelief. "Have you ever flown anything like this?"

"Dozens of times." He noted the skepticism in her eyes and said, "Okay. Once, at a county fair."

"A county fair," she echoed in a leaden tone.

"A *big* county fair. Look, the planes I've flown had somewhat more sophisticated control systems, but the principles are the same."

"I hope you fly better than you drive."

"It wasn't my idea to go for a midnight swim. You'll recall that I was distracted by Fauchard's goons."

She pinched his cheek. "How could I forget, *cheri*? Well, what are we waiting for? What do I have to do?"

Austin pointed to a bank of wall switches labeled in French. "First, I'd like you to tell me what these are for."

Austin listened as Skye translated the labels, then he took her around to the front of the plane. He placed her hands on the propeller and told her to jump back as soon as she had spun the blades. Then he climbed into the pilot's cockpit, quickly checked out the controls, and gave Skye the thumbs-up. Skye grabbed the propeller in both hands, gave the blades a spin and leaped back as instructed. The engine coughed a couple of times but failed to catch.

Austin adjusted the throttle slightly and told her to try again. Grim determination was reflected in Skye's face as she summoned every ounce of strength at her command. She put all her weight into the effort. This time the engine caught and burst into a roar that was amplified by the walls.

Skye dashed through the purple exhaust smoke and hit the switches to open the door and turn on the landing field lights. Then she clambered into the cockpit. She was still buckling her seat belt as the plane rolled out of the hangar.

Austin wasted no time taxiing before taking off. He gunned the engine and the plane began to pick up speed, advancing across the field between the double lines of lights. He tried to keep a gentle touch on the controls, but under his inexperienced hand the plane fishtailed and the waddling motion slowed the plane's acceleration.

He knew that if the plane didn't reach takeoff speed

soon, it would crash into the trees at the end of the airstrip. Austin willed himself to relax, letting the controls tell his hands and feet what to do. The plane straightened out and picked up speed. Austin gave the elevator a slight pull. The wheels left the ground and the plane began its climb, but it was still too low to clear the trees.

Austin willed a few more feet of lift from the wings. The doughty biplane must have heard his prayers because it seemed to rise slightly and grazed the treetops with its landing gear. The wings wagged from the impact, but the plane regained its even keel.

Austin kept the plane in a steady climb and glanced off to the left and right to get his bearings. The countryside was mostly in darkness except for Château Fauchard, whose sinister turrets were lit up by floodlights. He tried to draw a map in his mind using his recollections of the drive in from the main road. He could see the circular driveway with its odd fountain, and the lantern-lit drive leading down the hill into the long tree tunnel.

He banked the plane around to pick up the road through the vineyards, heading east at an altitude of about a thousand feet. He was bucking a slight breeze that kept the plane's speed down to a subsonic eighty miles per hour. Satisfied that he was on a course that would take them back to civilization, he picked up the microphone connected to Skye's cockpit.

"Sorry for the rough takeoff," he shouted over the engine roar. "Hope it didn't shake you up too much."

"I'll be fine once I put my teeth back in my head."

"Glad to hear that. You'll need your dentures when we have dinner."

"Truly a man with a one-track mind. Do you have any idea where we're going?"

"We're headed in roughly the same direction we came in. Keep a sharp eye out for lights. I'll try to land on a road near a town and hope there isn't too much traffic this time of night. Sit back and enjoy the ride."

Austin turned his attention to the task of getting them

down safely. Despite his cavalier attitude, he had no illusions about the difficulties that lay ahead. He was flying essentially blind, over unknown territory, in an antique aircraft he had no business operating, despite his extensive county fair experience. At the same time, he was enjoying the simple reliability built into the old aircraft. This was true seat-of-the-pants piloting. No cockpit bubble separated him from the cool wind. He was practically sitting on top of the engine and the noise was earsplitting. He had renewed respect for the men who'd flown these relics in combat.

He would have liked to wring a few more knots from the plane, which seemed to grind its way through the night sky. He was heartened when, after several minutes of flying, he began to see pinpoints of light in the distance. The plane was approaching the perimeter of Fauchard's vast holdings. His complacency was shattered by Skye's voice, shouting in his earphones.

At the same time he saw movement out of the corner of his eye and glanced to the left. The helicopter that had hunted for them in the maze had materialized about thirty feet away as if by magic. The cockpit lights were on, and he could see one of the Château Fauchard guards sitting in the passenger's seat. He had an automatic weapon on his lap, but he made no attempt to shoot the plane down, although it would have been an easy target.

A moment later, the now-familiar voice of Emil Fauchard crackled over the plane's radio.

"Good evening, Mr. Austin. How nice to see you again."

"What a pleasant surprise, Emil. I don't see you in the helicopter."

"That's because I'm in the château's security control center. I can see you quite clearly on the helicopter's camera."

Austin glanced at the camera pod slung under the helicopter's belly and gave it a friendly wave.

"I thought you would still be in the dungeon with the rest of the rats."

Emil ignored the insult. "How do you like my Fokker Aviatik, Austin?"

"I'd have preferred an F-16 loaded with air-to-air missiles, but this will do for now. Nice of you to let me use it."

"Not at all. We Fauchards are most generous when it comes to our guests. Now, I must ask you to turn around or you will be shot down."

The man in the helicopter stirred and aimed what looked like an AK-47 through the cockpit opening.

"You've obviously been tracking us. Why didn't you shoot us down when you had the chance?"

"I would prefer to keep my plane intact."

"Boys and their toys."

"What?"

Austin let the biplane drift a few yards. The helicopter veered off to avoid a collision.

"Sorry," Austin said. "I'm not used to this plane."

"Your childish maneuvers will get you nowhere. I'm intimately acquainted with the capabilities of the Aviatik. I would hate to lose it, but I'm willing to suffer the loss of the plane if necessary. Watch."

Emil must have given his pilot an order because the helicopter rose above the Aviatik and dropped until its runners were a few feet above Austin's head. The biplane pitched and yawed dangerously under the powerful downdraft. Austin pushed the plane's nose down and the helicopter followed, staying with the aircraft to show that escape was impossible. After a few seconds, the helicopter pulled away and began to pace the plane again.

Emil's voice came over Austin's earphones. "As you see, I can force you down anytime. Turn around or you and your lady friend will die."

"I might not be of any use to you, but if she goes, the secret of the helmet goes with her."

"It's a risk I'm willing to take."

"Maybe you should ask your mother first," Austin said.

Emil cursed in French, and seconds later the helicopter appeared over the biplane. The runners came down hard on the Aviatik's wings above Austin's head and pushed the biplane down. The chopper lifted off and hammered the Aviatik again. Austin fought to keep control. It was an unequal contest. The fabric-and-wood plane was no match for the faster and more maneuverable helicopter. Emil could pummel the plane until it crashed or fell apart.

Austin grabbed the mike. "You win, Emil. What do you want me to do?"

"Head back to the landing strip. Don't try any tricks. I'll be waiting for you."

I bet you'll be waiting, Austin thought.

Austin banked the plane and brought it around. Skye had been listening to the conversation on her earphones. "Kurt, we can't go back," she said over the intercom. "He'll kill you."

"If we don't go back, he'll kill both of us."

"I don't want you doing this for me."

"I'm not. I'm doing it for *me*."

"*Damnit*, Austin. You're as stubborn as a Frenchman."

"I'll take that as a compliment. But I draw the line at eating snails and frog's legs."

"All right, I give up," she said with exasperation. "But I'm not going down without a fight."

"Neither am I. Make sure your seat belt is tight."

He clicked the intercom off and concentrated on the ominous towers that marked the ancestral home of the man who wanted to kill him. As the biplane neared the château, Austin could see the twin lines of light that marked the airfield. He put the Aviatik in a banking turn as if he were heading toward the lights, but as he neared the château, he turned in the opposite direction and flew directly toward the nearest turret.

The helicopter kept pace. Emil's voice came over the radio. He was shouting in French. Austin shrugged, turned down the radio and turned his full attention to the task ahead.

The helicopter peeled away just when it seemed the plane would smash into the tower. With a few yards to spare, Austin veered off, missing the turret by yards, and flew over the château itself, in a diagonal line toward the opposite tower. He put the plane in a tight circle around the tower and came back over the complex in a figure eight. Then he flew around the next tower and executed the same pattern. He could only imagine what Emil's reaction would be, but he didn't care. He was wagering that Fauchard wouldn't try to force him down as long as he stayed over the château.

Austin knew he couldn't run figure eights forever. Nor did he intend to. With each banking turn, his eyes had swept the grounds beyond the moat. He switched the radio back on. Then he rounded the tower and started another figure eight, but halfway through it he veered off, passed over the circular driveway with its bizarre fountain and headed toward the lights that marked the long drive.

The helicopter had been circling high above. Once Austin was clear of the walls, the helicopter swooped down until it was directly over the Aviatik. Austin put the plane into a deep glide until the wheels were only a few yards over the pavement. Fauchard's pilot could have forced him down at any time, but he probably thought that Austin was going to land in the driveway so held off. The moment of indecision cost him dearly.

Instead of landing, Austin flew into the tunnel of trees.

The chopper climbed, its runners clipping the treetops. The pilot executed a g-force turn and circled.

Austin heard Fauchard's voice on the radio. He was shouting, "Get him! Get him!"

Following Fauchard's orders, the helicopter pilot followed the Aviatik into the arbor like a hound chasing a fox down a hole.

With its superior speed, the helicopter quickly caught up with the plane. Austin heard the thrashing of rotors over the sound of the Aviatik engine. His lips widened in a tight smile. He'd been worried that the helicopter would simply fly over the woods and wait for him to emerge from the other end of the tunnel. The insult about Fauchard's mother must have angered Emil beyond reason, as Austin hoped it would. No one liked being called a mama's boy, especially when it was true.

Austin was keeping the plane's wheels six feet above the road. He had a few yards of clearance above and on either side, but it was a tight fit and a slight deviation would leave the plane wingless or Austin headless.

The helicopter was right on his tail, but Austin tried to put his pursuer out of his mind. He kept his attention fixed on the distant dark spot that marked the other end of the tunnel. About halfway through the tunnel, Austin calmly reached out and pulled the lever that activated the spray pods.

Pesticide sprayed from the wing tanks in toxic twin streams, expanding into a noxious white cloud. The poisonous liquid coated the helicopter's windshield and blinded the pilot, then flowed through the open vent windows, transforming the chopper's cockpit into a flying gas chamber.

The pilot screamed in pain and took his hands off the controls to wipe the stinging liquid from his eyes. The helicopter slipped sideways, the rotors clipping the trees. The blades disintegrated, and the fuselage whipped around, careened into the woods and broke apart. Spraying fuel ignited and the chopper exploded in a huge orange-and-white fireball.

Flying ahead of the blast, Austin came out of the tunnel like a cannonball. He pulled back on the elevator and the plane rose out of the woods. As the Aviatik slowly gained altitude, Austin looked over his shoulder. Smoke and fire belched from the mouth of the tunnel and the blaze had spread to the trees.

He switched the intercom back on. "We're in the clear," he said.

"I've been trying to talk to you," Skye said. "What *happened* back there?"

"I was doing a little pest control," Austin said.

In the distance he could see beads of light marking roads and towns. Before long, car headlights were moving below them. Austin searched until he found a road that was well lit enough to land on, yet empty of traffic, and brought the plane down in a bumpy but safe landing. He taxied the plane off the highway and left it at the edge of a meadow.

As soon as their feet were back on ground, Skye embraced Austin and planted her lips on his in a kiss that was more than friendly. Then they began to walk. Despite their cuts and bruises, they were in a lighthearted mood after their escape. Austin breathed in the smell of grass and barns, and put his arm around Skye.

After about an hour of walking, they came upon a quaint *auberge*. The night clerk was half-asleep, but he sat up at full attention when Austin and Skye walked into the lobby and asked if they could have a room.

He stared at Austin's torn jester costume, and then at Skye, who looked like an alley cat that'd been in a fight, then back at Austin.

"Americain?" he said.

"Oui," Austin said with a weary grin.

The clerk nodded his head sagely and pushed the guest book across the desk.

25

TROUT WAS STRETCHED out on the cramped bunk with his hands behind his head when he sensed that a barely audible vibration had replaced the low-end rumble of the sub's engines. He felt a soft jolt, as if the submarine had come to a cushioned stop. Then there was silence.

Gamay, who was dozing off on the top bunk, said, "What was that?"

"I think we've docked," Trout said.

Prying his long body off the tight sleeping platform, Trout got up and pressed his ear to the door. He heard nothing, and he surmised that the sub had reached its destination. Minutes later, two armed guards unlocked the cabin door and told them to get moving. Sandy was waiting in the corridor under the watchful eyes of a second pair of guards. She had been moved to another cabin and it was the first time they had seen the *Alvin*'s pilot since MacLean's visit.

Trout gave Sandy a wink of reassurance and she greeted him with a nervous smile. Sandy was holding up well, but Trout wasn't surprised at her resilience. Anyone who piloted a deep submergence vehicle on a regular basis might be frightened, but not intimidated. With guards in front and behind, they climbed several levels to a hatchway that took them out onto the submarine's deck forward of the conning tower.

The sub was around four hundred feet long. It was anchored in a cavernous submarine pen that had a high arched roof. At the far end of the chamber, an intricate system of conveyor belts and ladder hoists disappeared into the wall. The guards prodded them across a gangway. MacLean was waiting on the dock.

"Good day, my fellow passengers," the chemist said, with a genial smile. "Follow me, if you will, as we enter the next phase of our adventure."

MacLean led the way to a large freight elevator. As the door closed, he glanced at his watch and his smile vanished.

"You've got about thirty-two seconds to talk," he said.

"I only need two seconds to ask you where we are," Trout said.

"I don't know where it is, but I suspect from the climate and the terrain that it's in the North Sea or Scandinavia. Maybe even Scotland." He checked his watch again. "Time's up."

The elevator door hissed open and they stepped out into a small room. The armed guard who was waiting for them barked into his walkie-talkie, then ushered them outside to a waiting minibus. The guard motioned for them to climb aboard, and then he followed, sitting in the back where he could keep an eye on the passengers. Before the guard pulled the window blinds down, Trout caught a glimpse of a long narrow cove far below the edge of the road.

After a ride of about twenty minutes over unpaved roads, the bus stopped and the guard ordered them off. They were in a complex of buildings surrounded by high barbed wire fence topped with electrical transformers. There were guards everywhere and the complex was disturbingly reminiscent of a concentration camp. The guard pointed toward a squat concrete building about the size of a warehouse. To get to it, they had to pass through more barbed wire. As they neared the building's entrance, an unearthly scream from inside the structure pierced the air. A chorus of shrieking howls followed.

Sandy's face registered her alarm. "Is this a zoo?" she said.

"I suppose you could say so," MacLean said. His grim smile was not especially reassuring. "But you'll find creatures here that the London Zoo never dreamed existed."

"I don't understand," Gamay said.

"You will."

Trout grabbed the chemist by the sleeve. "Please don't play games with us."

"Sorry at the poor attempts at humor. I've been through this little orientation one too many times and it's starting to get to me. Try not to be too alarmed at what you're about to see. The little dog and pony show is not meant to harm you, only to scare you into submission."

Trout gave him a faint smile. "You don't know how good that makes us feel, Dr. MacLean."

MacLean raised a bushy eyebrow. "I can see that you're not without a bleak sense of humor yourself."

"It's my Yankee upbringing. Our long crummy winters discourage a sunny view of the world."

"Good," MacLean said. "You'll need every bit of pessimism you can summon if you are to survive this hellhole. Welcome to the strange island of Dr. Moreau," he said, referring to the fictional story of the mad scientist who transformed men into beasts.

The guard had opened the double steel security doors and the stench that poured from inside the building overpowered all thoughts. The foul odor was a minor annoyance compared with the sounds and sights in the large room.

The walls were lined with cages occupied by manlike beasts that clawed and bit at the bars. The cages held twenty-five to thirty of the creatures. They stood on two legs and wore filthy rags, and were stooped over in a half crouch. Their long stringy white hair and beards obscured much of their faces, but there were glimpses of wizened and wrinkled features, the skin covered with dark age spots. Their mouths were open in a feral howl of rage and anger, displaying ragged and stained teeth. Their eyes were blood red and glowed with a terrifying luminosity.

Sandy had had enough. In a display of common sense, she bolted for the door, only to be blocked by a tall man dressed in army camouflage. He easily caught her by the arm and led her back into the building. He had a large nose, a sharply tapered chin and a leering mouth filled with gold teeth. A black beret was perched rakishly on his head. His presence had a strange effect on the caged creatures. They went silent at his arrival and retreated to the back of their cages.

"Good day, Dr. MacLean," he said, speaking in a European accent. He eyed the Trouts, letting his gaze linger on Gamay. "These are our newest recruits?"

"They are experts in our fields of study," MacLean said.

There was a flurry of activity at the door.

"What luck. You and our new guests arrived at feeding time."

A crew of guards entered, pushing a dolly stacked high with rat traps, the humane type that catches rodents without killing them. The guards unloaded the dolly, carried the traps and their squeaking occupants to the cages and released the rats.

Eyes glittering like rubies, the white-haired creatures had returned to the front of the cages. They must have been familiar with the drill because they were ready when the rats darted out of the traps. They pounced on the unfortunate rodents with the speed of panthers. Growling ferociously, they ripped the rats to pieces and devoured them with all the gusto of a gourmet in a five-star restaurant.

Sandy ran for the door again. This time, the man wearing the beret stood aside and let her go, roaring with laughter. Gamay was tempted to follow, but she knew she would rip the man's arm off if he laid a hand on her.

"The young lady evidently does not appreciate our recycling system. We control our rat infestation and feed our pets at the same time." Turning to MacLean, he said, "I hope you have told our guests what a lovely place this is."

"You are far more eloquent and persuasive than I could ever be, Colonel," MacLean said.

"That is true," the man said. He turned to face Trout. "I am Colonel Strega, the commander of this laboratory facility. The filthy devils you see enjoying their fine meals were once men like you. If you and the ladies do not do as you are told, we can make you into one of these fine-mannered fellows. Or we can feed you to them. It will all be according to my mood and generosity. The rules here are simple. You will work without complaint and in return you will be allowed to live. Do you understand?"

Trout was trying his best to ignore the gnawing and belching that issued from the cages. "I understand, Colonel, and I'll pass your message along to my weak-stomached friend."

Strega stared at Trout with his wolfish yellow eyes as if trying to memorize his face. Then he gave Gamay a 14-karat smile, clicked his heels, wheeled about and headed for the door. The guards prodded the Trouts out of the building, although they didn't need any persuasion. Strega was getting into a Mercedes convertible. Sandy was leaning against the building, vomiting. Gamay went over and put her arm around the *Alvin*'s pilot.

"Sorry about all that," MacLean said. "Strega insists on this orientation for newcomers. It's guaranteed to scare the pants off them."

"It scared more than that off me," Sandy said. "Next time I'll know to wear a diaper."

MacLean sighed. "We've all had a hard day. Let's get you settled in your quarters. After you've had a chance to shower and change, we'll get together for a drink at my place."

The bus went another half mile, passing through more

barbed and electrified fence, finally stopping at a complex laid out with a large round-roofed building surrounded by small flat-roofed structures.

"That's the lab where we'll be working," MacLean said. He pointed to a building set off by itself. "That's Strega's place. The guards have their quarters right next door. The cottages are for scientific staff. They look like bunkers, but you'll find them quite comfortable."

The guard ordered everyone off the bus and pointed the Trouts and Sandy to a pair of adjoining cottages. MacLean's place was next door. Trout and Gamay went to their quarters, basically one room with an iron bed, a small table and chair and a bathroom. It was spartan but clean. They shed their clothes and took long hot showers. Trout shaved with the dull disposable razor left for him.

Two lime-colored one-piece coveralls lay neatly folded on the bed. They had no desire to get into a prison uniform, but their own clothes had smelled vile even before they visited the animal house. Trout's coveralls were somewhat short in the sleeves and legs, but not uncomfortable. The bow tie didn't match but he wore it anyhow. Gamay would have looked glamorous even in sackcloth.

They went next door to get Sandy, but she was sleeping and they decided not to awaken her. MacLean welcomed them to his cottage, which was identical to the others except for its well-stocked bar. He insisted that they call him Mac, then he poured three glasses of Scotch whiskey and took the bottle with him when they went outside. The air was cool but not uncomfortable.

"I think my quarters may be bugged," MacLean explained. "Colonel Strega is a resourceful man."

"I'm not sure I care for his sense of humor," Gamay said.

"He's better known for his other qualities. The World Court would like to talk to him in regard to some mass graves in Bosnia. How's your drink?"

"Fine. We couldn't do better at Club Med," she said.

"When I get too depressed, I pretend I'm on vacation in an out-of-the-way resort," MacLean said.

"At the resorts I've visited, lunch wasn't delivered in rat traps," Trout said.

There was an awkward silence, which was broken by Gamay. "What, or who were those loathsome creatures in those cages?"

MacLean took his time answering. "Those were *mistakes*."

"As a fellow scientist, you'll understand when we say you have to be more specific," Trout said.

"Sorry. Maybe I had better start at the beginning."

MacLean poured more whiskey into his glass, took a hearty swallow and stared into space with a far-off look in his eyes.

"It seems so long ago, but it's only been three years since I was hired by a small research company outside of Paris to work with enzymes, the proteins that are produced by living cells. We were interested in the role that enzymes play in the aging process. Our company had only limited resources, so we were ecstatic when a large conglomerate absorbed our lab."

"Who was behind this conglomerate?" Trout asked.

"We didn't know and we didn't care. It didn't even have a name. We received substantial raises. We were promised greater funding and resources. We didn't mind when new conditions were imposed."

"What sort of conditions?"

"Under our new management, guards constantly watched us. Men in lab coats and suits, but guards nonetheless. Our movements were restricted. We lived in housing close to the lab. Company vehicles picked us up every morning and night. Those with families were allowed visitors from time to time, but all of us were warned of the secrecy of our work. We even signed contracts agreeing to the strict rules, but you have to understand, we were giddy. We were on a quest for the true Philosopher's Stone."

"I thought you were a chemist, not an alchemist," Gamay said. "As I recall, the Philosopher's Stone was a substance that could transform base metals like lead into silver or gold."

MacLean nodded. "That's a common *mis*conception. Many ancients believed that the stone was the legendary 'elixir of life.' If you mixed this wonderful substance with wine, the solution could heal wounds, restore youth and prolong life. *That's* the stone we were looking for."

"The quest for immortality," Trout mused. "It might have been easier to turn lead into gold."

A faint smile crossed MacLean's lips. "Many times during our research I had the same thought. I often pondered the impossibility of the task we had set ourselves."

"You're not the first to fail in that quest," Trout said.

"Oh *no,* Dr. Trout. You misunderstand. We *didn't* fail."

"Hold on, Mac. You're saying the elixir of life exists?"

"Yes. We discovered it at the bottom of the sea in the hydrothermal vents of the Lost City."

They stared at MacLean, wondering if the insanity of this island had turned the Scotsman into a madman.

"I've been poking my proboscis into sea mud for a long time," Trout said after a moment. "I've yet to discover anything that resembles the Fountain of Youth."

Gamay shook her head. "You'll have to excuse my skepticism. As a marine biologist, I'm more familiar than Paul with the vents, and to be honest, I don't have a clue what you're talking about."

MacLean's blue eyes sparkled with amusement. "You know more than you *think* you do, lass. Please explain why scientists around the world are excited about the microbes that have been found around the vents."

"That's easy," Gamay said, with a shrug of her shoulders. "Those bacteria are like nothing that's ever been found before. They're 'living fossils.' The conditions in the Lost City are similar to those that existed at the dawn of life on earth. If you figure out how life evolved around the vents, you can see how it could have started on earth, or even other planets."

"Exactly right. My work started with a simple premise. If you had something involved in the creation of life, maybe it could *extend* life as well. Our company had access to samples taken on earlier expeditions to the Lost City. The enzyme these microbes produced was the key."

"In what way?"

"Every living creature on earth is programmed for one task, to reproduce itself as many times as possible. Once its job is done, it becomes redundant, thus all organisms have a built-in self-destruct gene that dispatches them to make way for future generations. In human beings, sometimes the gene is activated prematurely and you have Werner's progeria, where an eight-year-old child looks like an eighty-year-old. We reasoned that if this gene can be switched on, it could be switched off, with the result that you slow aging."

"How would you test something like that?" Trout said. "You'd have to give it to test subjects and wait decades to see if they lived longer than your control group."

"That's a good point. There would be patent issues as well. Your patent could expire before you got your product on the market. But this enzyme not only switches the gene off, it serves as a super antioxidant, disarming free radicals. Not only can it retard the chemical processes that lead to aging, it can *restore* youth as well."

"The Philosopher's Stone?"

"Yes. Now you understand."

"You actually succeeded in doing this?" Trout said.

"Yes, in lab animals. We took mice that were senior citizens by human standards and restored their youth dramatically."

"How dramatically?"

"We had mice whose age in human years was ninety and reduced it to forty-five."

"You're saying you reversed the animal's age in half?"

"*Absolutely.* Muscle tone. Bone structure. Energy levels. Reproductive capacity. The mice were even more surprised by it than we were."

"That's a remarkable achievement," Gamay said, "but human beings are a lot more complicated than mice."

"Yes," he said with a sigh. "We know that now."

Gamay picked up on MacLean's unspoken message. "You experimented on human beings, didn't you?"

"Not my original team. It would have been years before we conducted trials involving humans. We would have done it under the most stringent of conditions." He gulped his drink, as if it could wash away unpleasant memories. "My team presented its preliminary findings and we heard nothing for a while. Then we were informed that the team was being disbanded, the lab broken up. It was all quite civilized. A handshake and a smile. We even received bonuses. Some time later, while he was clearing off his computer files, a colleague came across a videotape detailing human experiments. They were being conducted on an island somewhere."

Trout pointed to the ground at their feet. "Here?"

"A reasonable assumption, wouldn't you say?" MacLean said.

"What happened next?"

"We made a second fatal mistake in underestimating the ruthlessness of these people. We went back to the company as a group and demanded that they stop. We were told that the subjects were all volunteers, and that it was none of our business anymore. We threatened to go public with the information. They asked us to wait. Within a week, members of my former team began to have fatal 'accidents.' Hit-and-run. Fires. Electrocuted by unwise use of home appliances and tools. A few healthy men had heart attacks. Twenty-one in all."

Trout let out a low whistle. "You think they were murdered?"

"I *know* they were murdered."

"Did the police suspect foul play?" Gamay asked.

"Yes, in a few cases, but they could never prove anything. My colleagues had gone home to a number of different countries. And as I said, we were working in secret."

"Yet you survived," she said.

"Sheer luck. I was away on an archaeological dig. Hobby of mine. When I came home, I found a message from a colleague, since murdered, warning me my life was in danger. I ran off to Greece, but my former employers tracked me down and brought me here."

"Why didn't they kill you, too?"

MacLean laughed without humor. "They wanted me to lead a reconstituted research team. Seems they were too smart for their britches. After they killed off the original team, flaws began to surface in the formula. It was inevitable with research this complex. You saw their mistakes dancing around in their cages a little while ago."

"You're saying that this youth elixir created those snarling beasts?" Trout said.

MacLean smiled. "We told the fools that more work was needed. The enzyme has a different effect on humans. We're complicated creatures, as you say. There was a delicate balance involved. In the wrong mix, the chemical simply killed the subject. In others it triggered progeria. With those poor brutes you saw, the substance reached back in time and brought out the aggressive traits that served our ancestors well when they were reptiles or apes. Don't let their appearance deceive you. They still have human intelligence, as Strega learned."

"What do you mean?"

"There are two types of creatures. The Alphas were part of the original experiment, which I'm told started many years ago. The Betas were created in the most recent round of experimentation. Not long ago, a number of them managed to escape. Apparently, they were led by the Alphas. They constructed a crude raft and landed on another island, where they killed a number of people. Strega hunted them down and brought them back. He subjected some of the Alphas to the most awful tortures before killing them in view of others as a lesson."

"If they're so much trouble, why do they keep them around?" Gamay said.

"Apparently, our employers believe they have some value. A bit like us. Disposable tools. The latest test subjects were illegal immigrants from poor countries who thought they were going to Europe or America for jobs and a better life."

Trout's jaw hardened. "That's one of the most monstrous schemes I've ever heard of. One thing I can't figure. Why did these goons hijack the *Alvin* and kidnap us?"

"The enzyme has a short shelf life. They built the sub so the enzyme can be extracted as soon as it is harvested. It's separated from the microbes. Once it is stabilized, the submarine transports the finished product here for further research and development. They knew about your expedition. They must have been afraid their undersea mining project would be discovered. By chance, you were within minutes of discovering it."

"It wasn't chance at all. We were looking for the source of Gorgonweed," Gamay said.

"Now it's my turn to be puzzled. What is Gorgonweed?"

"It's a mutated form of a common alga," Gamay said. "It's been causing havoc around the world. The source of this mutation was traced back to the Lost City. We were trying to pinpoint its exact cause. We didn't advertise this part of the expedition because we didn't want to panic people. The situation is far worse than anyone has said in public."

"In what way?"

Gamay said, "If the weed is allowed to proliferate, the oceans would become nothing but huge soggy mats of vegetation. Ocean commerce would be impossible. Ports would be closed. Most species of fish would die, creating a huge disruption of the food chain that is bound to affect land production. The weather created by normal ocean cycles would become chaotic. Governments will fall. There will be disease and famine. Millions of people would die."

"Dear God. I was afraid something like that could happen."

"What do you mean?" Gamay said.

"The microbes were perfectly harmless in their natural habitat. There was always the possibility that they would migrate once we disturbed their habitat. They have evidently mutated the genes of higher organisms."

"Can it be reversed?"

"There is a good chance we could apply the work we're doing now to the solution."

"Do you think Colonel Strega would be open to a suggestion that we direct our energies toward saving the world from a Gorgonweed infestation?" Trout said.

MacLean laughed. "Colonel Strega believes this camp *is* the world. And that he is God."

"All the more reason to escape," Trout said.

"These people that kidnapped us must have known that a massive search would be launched for the *Alvin*," Gamay said.

MacLean looked into his empty glass, and then his eyes met hers. "According to Strega, the situation would be taken care of. He didn't go into details, but a number of the mutants were removed from the island not long ago. I think they had something to do with the plan."

"No details?"

MacLean shook his head.

Trout forced himself to deal with the problem at hand. "You said you were brought back here to reconstitute a scientific team," he said.

"Yes, there are six other unfortunate souls who were lured here, like the immigrants, with promises of work. You'll meet them at dinner. Our employer took great pains to make sure they were single people with little or no family attachments."

"How long do we have?"

"We have all known that we will be killed as soon as we extract the pure elixir. We've dragged our heels as much as we can, while showing some progress. It's been a delicate balance. A shipment of the elixir went out while we were on the sub."

"What does that mean for us?"

"We'll become redundant after the formula gets to its destination and our employers see if it will work."

"Will it?"

MacLean nodded. "Oh yes. The initial results will be quite swift and dramatic. Once Strega gets the word, he will start throwing us to the animals, one by one." He shook his head. "I'm afraid I rescued you only to bring you into a situation with no hope."

Trout rose from his chair and gazed around the camp, thinking that the rugged beauty of the island was out of place with the horrors he had seen.

"Any ideas?" he said.

"I think it would be helpful if Mac told us everything he knows about this place," Gamay said. "Every detail, no matter how silly or stupid it seems."

"If you're still thinking of escape, forget it," MacLean said bleakly. "There's no way."

Gamay glanced at her husband. "There's *always* a way," she said with a smile. "We just don't know what it is."

26

SKYE HAD SLIPPED into a deep slumber by the time Austin had crawled into the warm *auberge* featherbed. She clung to his side throughout the night, her sleep frequently disturbed by feverish murmurings of red death and dark water. Austin's nerves were on edge as well. Several times, he pried himself loose from Skye's hot grip and went to the window. Except for the moths fluttering around the inn's lighted sign, all was still. But Austin was far from complacent. The Fauchard family had a long reach.

After a fitful night's sleep, they were awakened by bright sunlight flooding their room. They put on the terry cloth bathrobes that Skye found in a closet and they had breakfast sent up to their room. Austin had tossed their tattered costumes into the trash. They recruited the maid who brought their food and sent her to shop for clothes. Fortified with a cup of strong coffee, Skye regained her usual sparkle, but Château Fauchard still weighed heavily on her mind.

"Should we report the Fauchards to the authorities?" she asked.

"The Fauchards are a rich and powerful family," Austin said.

"That doesn't mean they're above the law," she said.

"I agree with you. What part of our story do you think the police would believe? *The Pit and the Pendulum* or *The Cask of Amontillado*? If we make a fuss, we might even be accused of stealing Emil's plane."

"I see what you mean," she said with a frown. "Well then, what *do* we do?"

"Go back to Paris. Regroup. Dig out every bit of dirt we can on the Fauchards." Austin cleared his throat. "Who's going to tell your friend Darnay that his bullet-riddled Rolls-Royce is at the bottom of a castle moat?"

"I'll inform him. Don't worry, Charles was thinking of turning it in for a Bentley. He'll simply report it stolen." Her lips widened in her usual sunny smile. "Knowing Charles, I'd guess it was stolen to begin with." A dark cloud cast a shadow over her smile. "Do you believe what that poor Englishman Cavendish said? That the Fauchards started World War One and had at least some responsibility for the Second World War?"

Austin chewed on the question along with a bite of croissant.

"Dunno. It takes more than a few people to start a war. Hubris, stupidity and miscalculation play a big role."

"True, but think about it, Kurt. In 1914, the Great Powers were led by some of the most inept leaders in history. The decision to start war was in the hands of a few people. None were particularly intelligent. A tsar or a kaiser didn't have to ask his people for permission to go to war. Couldn't a small, wealthy and determined group like the Fauchards and other arms manufacturers manipulate these leaders, play off their deficiencies and influence their decisions? Then provide an event like the Grand Duke's assassination that would start the shooting?"

"Certainly possible. World War Two was a different situation, but you had the same volatile mixture waiting for a spark to trigger the explosion."

"Then you *do* think there is something to the charges?"

"Now that I've met the Fauchards, *mère* and *fils,* I would agree that if *anyone* could start a war, it would be them. The murderous way they reacted when Cavendish shot his mouth off speaks volumes."

She shivered as she recalled the Englishman's demise. "Cavendish claimed that Jules Fauchard was trying to stop the war," Skye said. "We know he got only as far as the Dormeur glacier. If he had made it across the Alps, he would have landed in Switzerland."

"I see where you're going. A neutral country where he could have revealed to the world what his family was plotting." He paused. "Let's think about it. Fauchard was rich and influential, but he would need proof to make his case. Documents or secret papers."

"Of course!" Skye said. "The *strongbox* that Jules was carrying with him. The Fauchards didn't want their dirty little family secret getting out."

"I'm still puzzled," Austin said, after a moment's thought. "Say we managed to exhume Jules's body and salvage incriminating documents. The Fauchards could weather the bad publicity. They would hire a high-priced PR firm to put spin on the story. They could say that the documents were forgeries. Outside of a few historians, I'm not sure if anybody would care so long after the fact."

"Then why did they resort to flooding the tunnel, killing Renaud and trying to killing us?"

"Here's another theory. Let's suppose Spear Industries is on the verge of a big deal. A merger. A new product. Maybe even a new war," he said with a wry grin. "Headlines about the family's unsavory past could spoil their plans."

"That would make sense," she said.

"What doesn't make sense is why Jules had the helmet with him."

"The Fauchards are eccentric," she ventured.

"You're being kind," Austin said, with a frown. "They are homicidal maniacs, but they don't act without a purpose. I think that the Fauchards were not simply worried about their family history being exposed. They desperately want to retrieve the helmet. There is something about that old steel pot that is of great importance to them. We have to find out what it is."

"Perhaps Charles has made progress in his examination. I must go see him as soon as I can."

A knock at the door interrupted their discussion. The maid had returned from her mission with shopping bags in hand. Austin had some cash and credit cards along with his passport in a neck wallet. He gave the maid a substantial tip, and then he and Skye tried on their new outfits. The red dress fit Skye's trim figure like a fine glove. Austin tried on his black slacks and white shirt. Conservative, but they wouldn't attract attention.

The desk clerk called a car rental for them, and while the Peugeot they rented was no Rolls, the drive back to Paris through the sunny countryside helped clear away the lingering cobwebs from the Fauchard catacombs. Austin kept a heavy foot on the gas. The more distance he put between them and the château, the better.

Austin almost launched into the "Marseillaise" when he saw the spike of the Eiffel Tower looming in the distance. A short while later, they were in Paris. Austin swung by Skye's apartment and she called the antiques dealer to let him know she was coming to Provence. Darnay was delighted to hear her plans, saying they had much to discuss. Skye packed an overnight bag and Austin dropped her off at the railroad station, where she kissed him on both cheeks before boarding a train south.

The hotel desk clerk smiled broadly when Austin came up for his key.

"Ah, Monsieur Austin. We're so glad to have you back. A gentleman has been waiting here for some time to see you." He glanced toward the lobby.

A figure was stretched out in a comfortable leather chair, apparently asleep. A copy of *Le Figaro* covered his face. Austin went over, lifted the paper and saw the dark-complexioned features of Joe Zavala.

Austin tapped Zavala's shoulder. "Hotel security," he said in an Inspector Clouseau accent. "You'll have to come along with me."

Zavala blinked his eyes open. "About time."

"Feeling's mutual, old pal. I thought you were in the Alps improving Franco-American relations."

Zavala sat up in the chair. "Denise wanted me to meet her parents. That's always a bad sign. Where have you been? I tried calling, but there was no answer on your cell."

Austin flopped down in a chair. "There's a good explanation for that. My cell phone is at the bottom of a castle moat."

"I must admit that's one excuse I've never heard before. Should I ask how it got there?"

"Long story. What was so urgent that you had to camp out in a hotel lobby?"

Zavala's face became uncharacteristically somber. "Rudi called me when he couldn't reach you." Rudi Gunn was Pitt's second-in-command. "There's been an accident at the Lost City site. Paul and Gamay dove in the *Alvin*. They never came up. There was a pilot aboard, too."

"Oh hell," Austin said. "What happened?"

"No one seems to know. There was an attack on the research vessel at about the same time they lost contact with the submersible."

"Doesn't make sense. Who would attack a peaceful scientific expedition?"

"You got me. I took a fast train to Paris last night, planted myself here and checked with the poor desk clerk every fifteen minutes."

"How long have they been missing?"

"More than twenty-four hours without contact."

"I assume Dirk and Rudi have been alerted?"

Zavala nodded. "Dirk wants us to keep him posted. He's called on the navy for help. I talked to Rudi a half hour ago. He sent the research vessel *Searcher* in so we could hear something at any minute."

"What's the life support situation on the *Alvin*?"

"About forty-eight hours of food and air left."

Zavala glanced at his watch.

Austin silently cursed. While he'd been dallying over croissants with Skye, the Trouts, if they were still alive, were in desperate need of help. "We have to move fast."

"There's a NUMA executive jet at De Gaulle airport. We can be in the Azores in a few hours and Rudi's arranged transportation for the next leg of the trip."

Austin told Zavala to stay put while he went up to his room. He shed his new wardrobe in exchange for his standard uniform of jeans and sweater, then threw some clothes in a duffel bag and was back in the lobby within minutes. The jet was warming its engines when they arrived at the airport. After a fast trip to the Azores, they hopped onto a seaplane and headed out into the Atlantic.

The NUMA research vessel *Searcher* had been on its way home from Europe when Gunn's call diverted it to the Mid-Atlantic Ridge. Austin was glad to learn that the *Searcher* was on site. The research vessel was only a few months old and it was crammed with state-of-the-art remote sensing equipment and undersea robots.

As the seaplane began its descent, Austin looked out the window and saw that the navy had lost no time reacting to Pitt's request. The NUMA vessel and the *Atlantis* had been joined by a navy cruiser.

The seaplane touched down on the water near the sleek-hulled NUMA vessel. Alerted by the seaplane pilot, the *Searcher* had a boat waiting to shuttle Austin and Zavala to the ship. The skipper, a tall, olive-skinned Californian named Paul Gutierrez, was waiting for them. Captain Gutierrez wasted little time and led them to the bridge. In the wheelhouse, Austin's coral-colored eyes stared off at the sea, where a powerboat was approaching the *Atlantis* from the navy ship.

"Looks like we're about to have company."

"The navy arrived within hours. They've been keeping

an eye out for further attacks. Let me show you what we've been doing." He spread out a chart of the area. Sections of the chart were crosshatched with a black grease pencil. "We've been lucky with weather conditions. This will give you an idea of the area we've covered. We've run sonar surveys and sent down our Remote Operated Vehicles."

"Impressive."

"Thanks. The *Searcher*'s gear can spot a dime at a thousand fathoms. We've covered the entire Lost City and some of the outlying areas where we discovered more fields of hydrothermal vents. The *Atlantis* has been checking out the ridge as well. The capabilities of the *Searcher* are awesome, if I say so myself." He shook his head. "Can't figure it. The *Alvin*'s one of the toughest little subs in the world. She's gone down hundreds of times without a problem."

"No sign of the submersible so far?"

"No *Alvin*, but that's not the end of the story."

Gutierrez handed Austin a printout showing the bottom as seen on the sonar monitor. "Once we covered the Lost City, we began to look beyond the immediate area. There are at least three other vent cities of comparable or larger size located on the ridge. Check out what we found in one of them, which we're calling 'LC II.' It's got us baffled as hell."

Austin borrowed a magnifying glass. Years of survey work had given him a skilled eye in reading sonar, but the markings he saw were puzzling. "What are these strange double lines?"

"We wondered the same thing. So we sent down an ROV and shot these pictures."

Austin studied the glossy eight-by-ten photos. The tall columns of the Lost City were clearly defined, as were the tracks that wound through the towers.

"They look like tread marks from a big bulldozer or a tank," Austin said.

"*Very* big," the captain said. "When we used the

columns for scale, we estimated that the treads must be at least thirty feet apart."

"What's the depth here?"

"Twenty-five hundred feet."

Zavala whistled. "A respectable engineering feat, but not impossible. Remind you of something, Kurt?"

"Big John," Austin said with a smile. In answer to the captain's quizzical expression, he explained that Big John was the nickname for a bottom-crawling vehicle NUMA had developed several years before as a moving deep-ocean lab. He pointed to a photo that showed the tracks coming to an abrupt end. "Whatever was down there seems to have lifted off. Unlike Big John, this mechanical turtle can swim as well as crawl."

"And my guess is that it took the *Alvin* with it," Zavala said.

"It seems too much of a coincidence having the *Alvin* disappear near these tracks," Captain Gutierrez said with a nod of his head.

"There is another strange coincidence," Austin said. "I understand you were attacked at about the same time as the *Alvin*'s disappearance."

"As we were starting to panic about the *Alvin*, we were approached by a strange ship," Gutierrez said. "It was an old rust bucket of a freighter. The name on the hull was the *Celtic Rainbow* and it was out of Malta. They called in a Mayday. When we returned the call there was no answer. Only the distress call, repeating over and over again. Then we sighted smoke, apparently coming from a hold."

"Did anyone try to abandon the ship?"

"That's what was crazy. *No* one. Not a soul on the deck. I was going to send a boat to investigate, but Captain Beck volunteered to go over with a party of his men."

"Beck?"

"He ran an ocean security outfit. As you may know, pirates have attacked or threatened research vessels around the world. The institution was working with Beck to set up security procedures for its research vessels. He had three men, all former SEALs like himself, on board for a training mission. They'd been teaching crew and scientists how to react to a pirate attack. He struck me as a very capable man."

"None better," said a man in a navy uniform who had stepped into the pilothouse. "From what I've heard, Beck was a real pro. I'm Ensign Pete Muller. That's my ship over there," he said, pointing to the cruiser.

Austin extended his hand. "Nice to meet you, Ensign."

"Always a pleasure to talk to folks from NUMA."

"What happened to Captain Beck and his men?" Austin said.

"I'm afraid they were all killed," the ensign said.

"I'm very sorry to hear that."

"We found the captain's body in the water, but no sign of his men or the ship," Muller said.

"How could a freighter simply disappear?"

"Our ship was the closest vessel when the *Atlantis* sent out the SOS. By the time we arrived, the attackers were gone. We secured the situation here, then we chased after the attackers. We knew their direction and with our superior speed we would have overtaken them. We had them on radar when the blip disappeared. We found debris and an oil slick, but no ship."

"I don't get it," Austin said. "SEALs are among the most highly trained special warfare people on the face of the earth. Boarding a potentially hostile ship is one of their specialties."

"I'm afraid they ran into something they never trained for." Austin noticed something in Ensign Muller's expression that he rarely saw in the face of a military man. It was the look of fear.

"I have the feeling that there is more here than I've been told. Maybe the captain can tell us about the attack."

"I can do better than that," Gutierrez said. "I'll let you *see* it."

27

THE SHAKY IMAGES on the video screen jumped spastically, making it obvious that they had been shot with a handheld camera under unsteady circumstances. The camera showed three men seen from behind. They were wearing bandannas wrapped around their heads and automatic weapons were slung over their shoulders. The men were in a moving inflatable boat, and the scene rose and dipped with the waves as the boat approached a rusty freighter of medium size. A hard-edged voice could be heard over the buzz of the outboard motor.

"Approaching target. Heads up, boys, this isn't a joy ride. We'll try a false insertion to see if we can draw fire."

The man closest to the lens turned and gave a thumbs-up. Then the picture froze.

Ensign Muller rose from his chair and stood beside the flat wall screen. He pointed to the dark-skinned man grinning into the camera lens.

"That's Sal Russo," he said to Austin and the others seated in the room. "Top-notch; savvy and tough as nails. Helped form SEAL Team Six, the antiterrorism unit.

Picked up a basketful of medals for his Persian Gulf service before mustering out to join Beck's company."

"And that must be Captain Beck's voice in the background," Austin said. He was seated in a folding chair next to Zavala and Gutierrez.

"That's right. Beck had a video camera on a chest harness. He used it as a training tool to show his teams where they made mistakes and what they did right. He was still wearing the camera when we plucked his body out of the water. Fortunately, it was in a waterproof housing. The picture gets a little jumpy from time to time, but it will give you a pretty good idea of what they encountered."

Muller punched the RESUME button on the remote control and returned to his chair. The man on the screen came to life and turned with his back to the camera again. The buzz of the outboard ratcheted up several decibels, the bow lifted as the boat rose on plane and headed directly toward the boarding ladder that hung down the starboard bow. A hundred feet from the ladder, the boat veered off and sped away from the freighter.

"Attempt to draw fire was unsuccessful," the voice said. "Let's check out the name on the stern."

The camera showed the boat coming around behind the ship, where the words CELTIC RAINBOW, and below that MALTA, were visible on the peeling hull. Then the boat moved alongside the larger vessel and headed back to the ladder. As they came up to the side, a man grabbed a rung and held the boat in place.

Everyone put gas masks on and two SEALs clambered up the ladder. The bow man pushed the boat off a few yards and brought his gun to bear on the deck, ready to pick off anyone trying to ambush the boarders. The two men climbed to the deck without incident. The point man waved the boat back in.

"Slick insertion with no resistance," Beck said. "Backup going in now."

With the boat tied up to the ladder, Beck and Russo began to climb. There was a jumpy picture of the side of the ship and the microphone picked up the sound of heavy breathing. Beck's voice could be heard muttering, "Getting too old for this crap. *Puff*. Hell of a lot more fun than sitting at a desk, though."

The camera panned the deck to show the SEALs crouched low, weapons at ready. Smoke drifted over the deck from the billowing cloud. As set out in their preplan, Russo took one man and made a heads-down dash to the other side of the ship, and then they worked their way toward the stern. Beck and the other SEAL did the same on the starboard deck and the team rendezvoused at the stern rail.

"Port side's clear," Russo said. He squinted at the smoke. "Looks like the fire's going out."

"You're right," Beck said. "Smoke is thinning. Remove your masks."

The men did as ordered, tucking their masks into belt bags.

"Okay, let's check the bridge to see who's sending that message."

The camera showed the men moving in leapfrog fashion, first one team then the others, so that the lead team was always covered. They climbed the companionways, pausing at each deck before going on, reaching the bridge wings with no incident.

The voice of someone calling "Mayday" was coming through the open door of the wheelhouse.

Speed, surprise and stealth are the essences of a SEAL mission. Having to board the ship in broad daylight ruled out two of those elements, so they wasted no time outside the wheelhouse. The camera followed them in and Beck's voice could be heard saying, "Good job. Hell. Damn place is empty."

The camera showed a 360-degree sweep of the wheelhouse, and then Beck went over to the ship's radio. A hand, obviously his, reached out and picked up a tape recorder next to the radio's microphone. The Mayday message they had heard was repeating over and over. The hand clicked off the recorder and the Maydays stopped.

"Goddamnit!" one of the men said. "What the hell's that *stink*?"

Beck's voice could be heard in the background, calm but with an unmistakable sense of urgency, ordering his men to cock their weapons, stay sharp and make their way doubletime back to their boat.

Then the gates of Hades opened.

Someone or something launched itself through the door, shrieking like an angry banshee. Then came the thundering blast of a shotgun at close range. More shrieks and lunging bodies and the rattle of automatic weapons fire. There were blurred flashes of dingy white hair or fur and glimpses of faces out of a nightmare.

"This way, Captain!"

Chip Russo had his back to the camera, blocking out most of the picture. More gunfire and hideous screams. Then a whole series of blurred images.

Beck was out of the wheelhouse and appeared to be half-falling, half-climbing down the companionways. His breath was coming out in great hoarse gasps. Russo could be heard in the background yelling:

"Move it, Cap, *move*! I nailed one of the red-eyed sons of bitches, but they're on our asses."

"My men—"

"Too *late*! Move. Aw hell."

Another blast of gunfire. Then a man screaming.

Beck had made it to the main deck. He was running now, huffing like a locomotive climbing a steep hill, his boots pounding. He was near the bow within a few feet of the ladder.

There was an inhuman scream from off-camera. More white hair and lunging bodies, then another shotgun blast. A glimpse of luminous red eyes. Then a gurgle and whirling sky and sea. The screen went dark.

Austin broke the stunned silence that followed. "Your video raises more questions than it answers."

"Beck almost made it back to the boat," Muller said, "but someone or something ambushed him as he was about to climb down the ladder. When his body was found his throat, had been torn open."

"Could you go back a few seconds in the video?" Zavala said. Muller complied. "Okay, freeze it right there."

The burning red eyes almost filled the screen. The image was fuzzy, but the vagueness didn't diminish the feral intensity. A silence ensued in the room, broken only by the hum of the ship's ventilator.

Finally, Austin said, "What do you make of this video, Ensign?"

Muller shook his head like a man who'd been asked to explain the mysteries of the universe. "The only thing I'm sure of is that Captain Beck and his men got themselves into a hell of a mess. Whoever, or *what*ever, ambushed them didn't expect to run into an armed SEAL unit."

"My guess is that they intended to attack the *Atlantis*, but changed their minds after the fight with Beck and his men," Austin said.

"That was my take on it, too," Muller said.

Captain Gutierrez rose from his chair. "I've got to get back to the bridge. You gentlemen let me know if there is anything further I can do to help."

Austin thanked Gutierrez and, after he left, turned to Muller. "I suppose you'll be going back to your ship."

"Not quite yet. A relief vessel is coming in to stand guard duty. Should be here in a few hours. I've got time. Now that the captain has gone, I'd like to talk about this situation if you don't mind."

"Not at all," Austin said. "From the little I've seen, there's a lot to talk about."

Muller smiled. "When I first heard this crazy story, I thought we might be dealing with pirates, although there was no evidence that they were operating in this part of the world."

"You've changed your mind about the pirates?" Austin said.

"I've discarded that theory. I neglected to mention that I'm an intelligence officer with the navy. After I saw the video, I contacted my staff in Washington and asked them to research everything they could on 'red-eyed monsters or fiends.' You should have heard the disrespectful replies I got, but they went through every source they could, from Dracula, photography, Hollywood movies. Did you know there's a rock group called 'Red-Eyed Demons'?"

"My rock education stopped with the Rolling Stones," Austin said.

"Me, too. Anyhow, I spent some time going over their reports and kept coming back to this."

Muller took a sheet of paper from his briefcase and handed it to Austin who unfolded it and read the headline.

TV CAST, CREW STILL MISSING
POLICE BAFFLED

It was a Reuters news story datelined London. He kept reading.

> Authorities say they still have no leads in the disappearance of seven participants and four technical crew members who were filming an episode of the *Outcasts* television show on a remote island off the coast of Scotland.
>
> Under the rules of the game, the other members of the so-called clan vote an "Outcast" off the island each week. A helicopter sent to pick up the latest exile found no sign of the others. Police, working with the FBI, found traces of blood, suggesting the possibility of violence.
>
> The lone survivor, who was found hiding, is recuperating at home. She has been quoted as saying the survivors were attacked by "red-eyed fiends." Authorities have discounted this account, saying that the victim was suffering from hallucinations brought on by shock.
>
> The popular TV show, a spin-off of earlier *Survivor*-type productions, has been criticized by some for encouraging even greater tension among participants and subjecting them to risky tests involving mental and physical stress. The network has offered a $50,000 reward for information.

Kurt handed the article to Zavala, who read the story and said, "How does this tie in with the *Alvin*'s disappearance?"

"It's a tenuous connection, I'll admit, but try to follow my convoluted line of thinking. I went back to those undersea tracks. It was clear that something was going on in the Lost City and *someone* wanted the activity kept a secret."

"That sounds right," Zavala said. "Whoever made those tracks wouldn't want anyone nosing around the thermal vents."

"If you had a secret like that, what would you do if a submersible loaded with cameras dropped into your backyard?"

"Simple," Zavala said. "The expedition was publicized, so I'd move my equipment out."

Austin said, "Not so simple. Someone was bound to see the tracks and ask questions. You'd have to eliminate the outside observers. And you'd have to take care of any witnesses."

"Then that would explain why a shipload of red-eyed freaks was unleashed on the *Atlantis*," Zavala said.

Austin said, "Suppose the *Atlantis* vanished. A while later the *Alvin* surfaced and when it sees the support ship has disappeared it calls for help. A massive search would be launched. There's always the chance that a search would pick up traces of the *Alvin* and attract more attention."

"Which means whatever made those tracks may have snatched the *Alvin*," Zavala said.

"Gutierrez says the submersible isn't down there, and I believe him," Muller said.

Austin glanced at the news article again. "Red eyes here. Red eyes there. As you say, a tenuous connection."

"I agree. That's why I ordered up a series of satellite photos of the waters surrounding the *Outcasts* island." From his briefcase, he took a stack of photos and spread them out on a table. "Most of the islands have small fishing villages that have been there for years. On others, the only inhabitants are birds. This one was unusual enough to catch my attention."

He slid a picture toward Austin. The photo showed several buildings, most of them clustered away from the shore, and some primitive roads.

"Any idea what these structures are?" Austin said.

"That island was originally owned by the British government, which operated it as a submarine station during World War Two and the Cold War. Later it was sold to a private corporation. We're still looking into that. Supposedly it was used for bird research although nobody knows for sure, because access to the island is barred."

"This could be a patrol boat to enforce the no-trespassing order," Austin said, pointing to a tiny white line that marked a wake.

"That's a good bet," Muller agreed. "I had the pictures taken at different times during the day, and the boat is always at some point around the island, following pretty much the same route."

As he examined the rocks and shoals guarding the island, Austin noticed a dark, oval object near the harbor opening. He saw it again in other photos but at different positions. It had a vague outline, as if it were underwater rather than on the surface. He turned the photos over to Zavala.

"Take a look at these and see if you see anything unusual, Joe."

As the team's expert on remotely operated and manned undersea vehicles, Zavala noticed the strange object immediately. He spread out the pictures. "This is an underwater vehicle of some sort."

"Let me see that," Muller said. "I'll be damned. I was so concentrated on what was above water that I didn't notice what was *under* it. I must have thought it was a fish of some kind."

"It's a fish all right," Zavala said. "Battery-operated and motorized. My guess is that it's an AUV."

"An Autonomous Underwater Vehicle?"

Originally built for commercial and research use, AUVs were the hottest development in undersea technology. The robot vehicles could operate on their own, guided by preprogrammed instructions, unlike Remote Operated Vehicles, which had to be guided with a tether.

"This AUV could have a sonar and acoustic instrumentation, and would be able to detect anything or anyone moving on or under the waters surrounding the island. It could send an alarm to land-based monitors."

"The navy has been using AUVs as replacements for the dolphins who sniffed out mines. I've heard that some AUVs can be programmed to attack," Muller said.

Austin stared at the photos and said, "It seems that we may have to make a fast decision."

"Look, I'm not telling you what that should be, and I know you're concerned about your friends," Muller said. "But there isn't much you can do here. Captain Gutierrez will continue the search and he can notify you if and when he finds something."

"You'd like us to check this place out?"

"The U.S. navy can't go busting in on this island, but a couple of highly trained and determined people could."

Austin turned to Zavala. "What do you think we should do, Joe?"

"It's a gamble," Zavala said. "While we're chasing creeps with bloodshot eyes, Paul and Gamay could be a million other places."

Austin knew that Zavala was right, but his instincts were pointing him to the island.

"We asked the seaplane to stand by," he told Ensign Muller. "We'll fly back to the Azores and catch a jet. With any luck we can take a close look at your mysterious island tomorrow."

"I hoped you'd say that," Muller said with a smile.

Less than an hour later, the seaplane lifted off from the water and climbed into the air. The aircraft circled once over the research vessel and the cruiser, and then headed toward the Azores, taking Austin and Zavala on the first leg of their journey into the unknown.

28

DARNAY LIVED IN a converted farmhouse of stucco and red tile that overlooked the historic old city of Aix-en-Provence. Skye had called the antiquities dealer from the train station to let him know she had arrived and Darnay was waiting at the front door when the cab dropped her off at his villa. They exchanged hugs and the perfunctory double cheek kisses, then Darnay ushered her onto a broad terrace that bordered a swimming pool surrounded by sunflowers. He seated her at a marble and wrought-iron table and poured two Kir cocktails of crème de cassis and white wine.

"You don't know how delighted I am to see you, my dear," Darnay said.

They clinked glasses and sipped the cold sweet mixture.

"It's good to be here, Charles." Skye shut her eyes and let the sunlight toast her face as she breathed in air tinged with the scents of purple lavender and the distant Mediterranean.

"You didn't say much when you called," Darnay said. "Your visit to the Fauchards went well, I trust."

Her eyes blinked open. "As well as could be expected," she said.

"*Bon.* And did Mr. Austin enjoy driving my Rolls?"

Skye hesitated. "Yes and no."

Darnay raised an eyebrow.

"Before I tell you what happened, you had better pour us another drink."

Darnay freshened their glasses and Skye spent the next forty-five minutes describing the events at the Fauchard château, from the time Emil greeted them at the front door to their madcap flight in the stolen airplane. Darnay's face grew graver with each new revelation.

"This Emil and his mother are monsters!" he said.

"We're very sorry about your car. But as you see, it couldn't be helped under the circumstances."

A broad smile replaced Darnay's grim expression. "What matters most is that you are safe. The loss of the Rolls is of no consequence. The car cost me a fraction of its worth. A 'steal,' as your American friend might say."

"I thought it was something like that."

Darnay paused in thought. "I'm intrigued by your description of the Jules Fauchard portrait. You're sure he was wearing the same helmet?"

"Yes. Have you made any progress with its identification?"

"A great deal of progress." He drained his glass. "If you are sufficiently refreshed, we will go see Weebel."

"What's a Weebel?"

"Not a *what*, but a *who*. Oskar Weebel is an Alsatian who lives in the city. He has the helmet."

"I don't understand."

Darnay rose from his chair and took Skye by the hand. "You will when you meet him."

Minutes later, they were in Darnay's Jaguar, speeding along a narrow, twisting road. Darnay casually wheeled the car around the switchbacks as if he were on a straightaway.

"Tell me more about your friend," Skye said as they entered the outskirts of the historic old city. Darnay turned off onto a narrow street between the Atelier de Cézanne and the Cathédrale Saint Sauveur.

"Weebel is a master craftsman," Darnay said. "One of the finest I've ever come across. He fabricates reproductions of antique weapons and armor. He farms out most of his production these days. But his own work is so good that some of the finest museums and most discerning collectors in the world are unaware that what they consider antique pieces were actually forged in his shop."

"Fakes?"

Darnay winced. "That's such an ugly word to come from such a lovely mouth. I prefer to call them high-quality reproductions."

"Pardon me for asking, Charles, but have any of these wonderful reproductions been sold to the museums and collectors who are your clients?"

"I seldom make claims about the authenticity of my wares. Something like that could land me in jail for fraud. I merely *imply* that the item in question may have a certain provenance and let the client connect the dots. As the American comedian W. C. Fields said, 'You can't cheat an honest man.' We're here."

He pulled the Jaguar up to the curb and led Skye to a two-story stone building of medieval architecture. He punched the bell and a moment later a short round man in his sixties, wearing a pale gray workman's smock, opened the door and greeted them with a wide smile. He ushered them into the house, where Darnay made introductions.

Weebel seemed to have been assembled of mismatched spare parts. His skull-bald head was too large for his shoulders. When he removed his old-fashioned spectacles, his kindly eyes were seen to be too small for his face. His legs were stumpy. Yet his perfect mouth and teeth could have come from a fashion model and his fingers were long and slender, like those of a concert pianist. He reminded Skye of Mole from the English classic *The Wind in the Willows*, by Kenneth Grahame.

Weebel shot a shy glance in Skye's direction. He said, "Now I know why I have not heard from you, Charles. You have been otherwise distracted."

"As a matter of fact, Mademoiselle Labelle arrived only a little while ago, my good friend. I have filled the time since her arrival telling her of your wonderful skills."

Weebel replied with a self-effacing tut-tut, but it was evident from his expression that the compliment pleased him. "Thank you, Charles. I was just brewing some hibiscus tea," he said, and led them into a neatly ordered kitchen, where they sat at a trestle table. Weebel poured the tea, then peppered Skye with questions about her work. As she patiently answered the questions, she had the feeling that Weebel was tucking her answers in tidy mental files.

"Charles has told me about your work as well, Monsieur Weebel."

When he became excited, Weebel punctuated his speech with a quick "Aha," spoken as one word.

"He has. Well then. Aha. I'll show you my workshop."

He led them down a narrow staircase to the basement, which was brightly lit with fluorescent lights. It was basically a blacksmith's shop equipped with a forge, anvil, chisels, specialized hammers and pincers, all tools geared for the amorer's basic task, which was beating out plates from hot metal. An assortment of breastplates, leg armor, gauntlets and other protective equipment hung from the walls. Darnay's practiced eye glanced at a shelf holding several helmets of various styles.

"Where is the piece I left here?"

"A special headpiece like that deserves special treatment," Weebel said. He went over to the suit of armor standing in the corner, flipped up the visor and reached inside. "This is a mass-produced item. Aha. I have them fabricated in China for the restaurant trade mostly."

He activated a switch inside the suit and a section of wall panel about four feet wide opened with a soft click to reveal a steel door. He punched out a number on the combination keypad. Behind the door was a room the size of a walk-in closet. The walls were lined with shelves stacked with wooden boxes of odd sizes, each marked with a number.

Weebel picked out a tall square case, which he brought

into the workshop. He set it on a table and lifted out the Fauchard helmet. Skye eyed the embossed face and thought back to the portrait of Jules she had seen at the Fauchard château.

"A remarkable piece. Remarkable. *Aha*." Weebel waved his hands over the helmet like a fortune-teller looking into a crystal ball. "I had my metallurgist look at it. The iron used to make the steel was most unusual. He believes it may have come from a meteorite."

Darnay smiled at Skye. "That was Mademoiselle Labelle's theory. Have you dated this piece?"

"Some of the design features were innovative, as you pointed out. I would place it in the fifteen hundreds, which is when the embossing of human or animal facial characteristics into the visor caught on. It is possible that the metal itself is much older, and that the helmet was recast from an earlier one. This dent is a proofmark, apparently made to test the vulnerability of the metal to a bullet. It did very well at stopping the projectile. Not so well with this hole. It could have been made at close range or by a firearm of great power, perhaps at a more recent date. Maybe someone used this for target practice."

"What about the manufacturer?"

"The helmet is one of the finest pieces I've ever seen. Look here on the inside. Not a hammer dimple mark to be seen. Even without the hallmark, I would know that there was only one armor maker that made such high-quality metal. The Fauchard family."

"What can you tell me about the manufacturer?" Skye said.

"The Fauchards were one of only three families that founded the guild that became what we know today as Spear Industries. Each family specialized in a certain area. One family forged the metal, the other fashioned the actual armor. The Fauchards were the sales arm, which sent agents traveling around Europe to sell their wares. They were well connected politically as a result. Normally they did not use their hallmark. They believed that the quality of their armor spoke for itself, which is why it is strange to see that they engraved their coat of arms into the crown of this piece. The helmet must have special significance to the family."

"Madame Fauchard told me that each eagle head stands for the original founding families," Skye said.

Weebel's eyes did a quick flutter. "You actually *spoke* to Madame Fauchard?"

Skye nodded.

"*Extraordinary.* It is said she is a total recluse. What was she like?"

"A combination of a scorpion and a black widow spider," Skye answered without hesitation. "She said the eagle in the middle represents the Fauchards, who came to dominate the company through death and marriage."

Weebel burst forth with a nervous laugh. "Did she tell you that many of these deaths were untimely and the marriages were mostly forced to cement their power?"

"Madame Fauchard is very selective when it comes to talking about her family. For instance, she denies the story that they were powerful enough to instigate World War One, and had a hand in promoting World War Two."

"Those rumors have circulated for many years. A number of arms merchants encouraged and facilitated the war. The Fauchards were in the thick of it. Aha. Where did you hear that story?"

"From an Englishman named Cavendish. He also said the Fauchards stole his family's process for making steel."

"Ah, Sir Cavendish. Yes, that's quite true. His family came up with a superior steel process. The Fauchards stole it." His fingers caressed the helmet. "Tell me, do you see anything unusual about the eagle design?"

She inspected the helmet and saw nothing she hadn't seen before.

"Wait. I see it. There are more spears in one claw than the other."

"A sharp eye, *aha.* I noticed the same thing and compared it to the Fauchard coat of arms. The number of spears in each claw is even in the original hallmark. When I examined the helmet more closely, I found that the extra spear was added long after it was fabricated. Probably within the last hundred years or so."

"Why would anyone do that?" Skye said.

Weebel smiled mysteriously and placed the helmet under a magnifying glass attached to a stand. "See for yourself, Mademoiselle Labelle."

Skye peered through the glass for a moment. "The spear shaft and head are actually writing of some sort. Numbers and letters. Come look, Charles."

Darnay took a turn at the magnifier. "It seems to be an algebraic equation."

"Yes, yes, *aha.* That was my feeling as well," Weebel said. "I have been unable to decipher it. A specialist is needed."

"Kurt said this helmet may contain the key that unlocks the Fauchard puzzle," Skye said. "I must get it back to Paris so I can show it to a cryptologist or a mathematician at the university."

"That's unfortunate," Weebel said. "I had hoped to reproduce this lovely piece. Later, perhaps?"

Skye smiled. "Yes, Monsieur Weebel. Maybe later."

He replaced the helmet in its case and handed it to Skye. She and Darnay thanked him and said their good-byes. She asked Darnay to take her to the train station. He was disappointed at her decision to leave, and tried to persuade her to stay. She said she was anxious to get back to Paris, but promised to return soon for a longer visit.

"If that is your decision I must respect it," Darnay said. "Will you be seeing Mr. Austin?"

"I hope so. We have a dinner engagement. Why do you ask?"

"I fear that you may be in danger and would feel better if I knew he was around to keep an eye on you."

"I can take care of myself, Charles." She kissed him on

the cheeks. "But if it makes you feel any better, I will call Kurt on my cell phone."

"That does make me feel better. Please give me a ring when you get home."

"You worry too much," she said. "But I'll call you."

True to her word, she tried to call Austin as the TGU train sped north. The clerk at Austin's hotel said he had left a message for her. "He said he had a matter of some urgency to attend to and would be in touch with you."

She wondered what was so urgent that he would leave on such short notice, but from what she had seen, Austin was very much a man of action, and she was not surprised. She was sure he would call her as promised. The trip from Aix took just under three hours. It was late evening when the train arrived back in Paris. She hailed a taxi to take her back to her apartment.

She paid her fare and was walking up to her door when someone said in a loud voice: "Excusez mwa. Parlay-voo Anglay?"

She turned, and in the illumination from the streetlight saw a tall, middle-aged man standing behind her. The smiling woman by his side had a *Michelin Green Guide* clutched in her hand.

Tourists. Probably American, from the atrocious accent. "Yes, I speak English," she said. "Are you lost?"

The man grinned sheepishly. "Are we *ever*."

"My husband hates to ask directions even at home," the woman said. "We are looking for the Louvre."

Skye tried not to smile, wondering why anyone would want to find the Louvre at night. "It's on the Right Bank. You are some distance from it. But it is a short walk to the Métro station and the train will take you there. I can give you directions."

"We have a map in our car," the woman said. "Perhaps you could show us where we are."

Even worse. Paris was no place for drivers who didn't know the city. She followed them to their car, which was pulled up at the curb. The woman opened the back door, leaned in, then pulled her head out.

"Would you reach across the seat and get the map, dear? My back—"

"Of course." Holding the bag with the helmet in her left hand, Skye leaned into the car but saw no map on the seat. Then she felt a pinprick on her right haunch, as if she had been stung by a bee. As she put her hand on the sting in reflex, she was aware that the Americans were staring at her. Inexplicably, their faces started to dissolve.

"Are you all right, dear?" the woman said.

"I—" Skye's tongue felt thick. The thought she was trying to express fell apart.

"Why don't you sit for a minute?" the man said, pressing her into the car.

His voice seemed to come from far away. She was too weak to resist when he took the helmet case from her hands. The woman slid in beside her and shut the door. Skye was vaguely aware that the man had gone around to the driver's seat and that the car was moving. She looked out the window but saw only blurred images.

Then a black curtain descended over her eyes.

29

TROUT WAS THE picture of scientific diligence as he checked the graph displayed on the spectrometer screen and jotted down his observations in a notebook. It was the third time he had analyzed the same mineral sample from the Lost City and the note taking had nothing to do with what was on the screen. Using his talks with MacLean as a guide, Trout was drawing a sketch of the island.

The laboratory didn't look like much from the outside. It was housed in three Quonset huts that had served as support crew quarters for the old British submarine base that once occupied the island. Two of the half-cylinder-shaped buildings of corrugated steel had been welded together end-to-end. A third hut was attached at the midsection so that the lab space was in the form of a large *T*. An entire hut was taken up by batching vats and the rest of the space was used for scientific analysis.

The dull-olive exteriors were patched with rust and projected a general air of neglect, but inside, the huts were warm and well lit. The spacious lab was equipped with state-of-the-art scientific tools, as up-to-date as anything

Trout had seen in a NUMA facility. The main difference was the addition of the guards, who idled near each door with automatic weapons slung over their shoulders.

MacLean said he had been brought in by plane, which had given him a bird's-eye view of the island. As the plane made its approach, he'd seen that the island was shaped like a teacup. High vertical cliffs ran around the perimeter of the island, broken in one place by a long, tapering harbor. A crescent-shaped beach about a half mile long was sandwiched between the harbor and low cliffs that rose sharply to a high wall whose face was snow-white with a swirling blizzard of seabirds.

The submarine pen was at the head of the inlet. A road ran from the crew quarters above the pen's entrance, along the cliffs that bordered the harbor. After the road passed an abandoned church and moldering graveyards and the ruins of an old fishing village, it merged with another way that led inland, climbing through a narrow pass, then descending to the island's interior, once the caldera of a long-dead volcano.

In contrast to the rocky ramparts that protected it from the sea, the interior was rolling moorland dotted here and there by small thickets of tenacious scrub pine and oak. The road eventually terminated in the former naval base that now housed the lab complex under Strega's command.

MacLean was walking across the lab toward Trout's station. "Sorry to interrupt your work," he said. "How is your analysis coming?"

Trout tapped the notepad with his pen. "I'm between a rock and a hard place, Mac."

MacLean leaned over Trout's shoulder as if they were conferring. "I've just come from a meeting with Strega," he said in a low voice. "Evidently the test of the formula was a success."

"Congratulations, I supppose. So that means we have outlived our usefulness? Why aren't we dead already?"

"Strega may be a murderous lout, but he's a meticulous organizer. He'll see to the details of wrapping up the operation on the island first, so he'll have time to enjoy himself without distraction. My guess is that tomorrow he'll take us on a lovely picnic and have us dig our own graves."

"That gives us tonight," Trout said. He handed the notebook to MacLean. "How does this jibe with your observance of the island topography?"

MacLean examined the map. "You have a skill at cartography. It's accurate in every detail. What now?"

"Here's how I see it, Mac. As Kurt Austin would say, K.I.S.S."

"Pardon me?"

"Keep it simple, stupid. We go through the pass, which so happens to be the only way out. Get to the harbor. You said there was a pier there."

"I couldn't be sure. We came in at dusk."

"It's a reasonable assumption. We'll assume that where there is a pier there's a boat. We borrow the boat. Then once we're at sea, we figure out where we are."

"What about contingencies in case something goes wrong?"

"There are no contingencies. If something goes wrong, we're dead. But it's worth a try when you consider the alternative."

MacLean studied Trout's face. Behind the academic features was an unmistakable strength and resolve. His mouth widened in a grim smile. "The simplicity appeals to me. It's the *execution* of the plan that's worrisome."

Trout winced. "I'd prefer to not use the word *execution*."

"Sorry for letting my pessimism show. These people have beaten me down. I'll give it everything I've got."

Trout leaned back in his chair in thought and stared across the room at Gamay and Sandy, who sat side by side examining specimens from the thermal vents. Then his eye swept across the lab, where the other scientists were immersed in their tasks, blissfully unaware of their approaching doom. MacLean joined him in his gaze. "What about these other poor souls?"

"Could Strega have embedded any of them to keep an eye on us?"

"I've talked to every one on the train. Their fear for their lives is as genuine as ours is."

Trout's jaw hardened as he realistically considered the complexities of an escape and the chances that any plan would go awry.

"It's going to be risky enough with the four of us. A large group would attract more attention. Our only hope is to make it out of the lab complex in one piece. If we can get control of a boat, it will have a position finder and a radio. We can call in help."

"And if we can't?"

"We'll all be on the same sinking ship."

"Very well. How do you propose to get us past the men guarding the electrified fence?"

"I've been thinking of that. We're going to have to create a distraction."

"It will have to be a big one. Strega's men are all professional killers."

"They might have their hands full trying to save their own skins."

MacLean's face turned gray when Trout outlined his plan.

"My God, man. Things could get completely out of control."

"I'm hoping that's exactly what happens. If we can't commandeer transportation, we'll have to go it on foot, which means we will need every minute we can gain."

"Don't look now, but one of the guards is watching," MacLean said. "I'm going to gesture and wave my arms as if I'm angry and frustrated. Don't be alarmed."

"Be my guest."

MacLean pointed to the spectrometer screen and scowled. He picked the notebook up, slammed it down, muttered a few curses, then stalked off across the room. Trout stood and stared at MacLean's back with a frown on his face. The guard laughed at the confrontation, then pulled a pack of cigarettes out of his pocket and stepped outside for a smoke.

Trout got up and walked across the lab to break the good news to Gamay and Sandy.

30

AUSTIN STEPPED through the front door of a noisy pub called the Bloody Sea Serpent and walked across the smoke-filled room to the corner table, where Zavala was chatting with a toothless man who looked like a Scottish version of the Old Man of the Sea. Zavala saw Austin enter and shook hands with the man, who then rejoined the crowd at the bar.

Austin sat down in the now-vacant chair and said, "Glad to see that you're making friends."

"It's not easy for a Mexican American boy like me. Their accents are as thick as chili, and as if things weren't tough enough, there isn't a single ounce of tequila in the whole town." He lifted his pint of lager to emphasize the terrible state of affairs.

"Appalling," Austin said, with a distinct lack of sympathy. He signaled a waitress, and a minute later he was sipping on a pint of stout.

"How did your mission go?" Zavala said.

In reply, Austin reached into the pocket of his windbreaker, pulled out a key ring and dropped it on the table.

"You see before you the key for the newest addition to NUMA's worldwide fleet of state-of-the-art vessels."

"Did you run into any problems?" Zavala said.

Austin shook his head. "I strolled along the fish pier and picked out the worst-looking boat I could find. Then I made the owner an offer he couldn't refuse."

"He wasn't suspicious?"

"I said I was an American TV producer doing a program on the *Outcasts* mystery and that we needed the boat right away. After I showed him the money, I could have told him I was from the Planet NUMA, for all he cared. He'll be able to buy a new boat with this windfall. We executed a quick bill of sale to make it legal. I pledged him to silence and promised him a bit part in the show."

"Did he have any theories about the disappearance of the missing *Outcasts* crew?"

"*Lots* of them. Mostly waterfront gossip. He said the police combed the island but the authorities have been keeping a tight lid on information. According to the scuttlebutt around the waterfront, the investigators found traces of blood and body parts. People don't seem overly disturbed about the whole thing. There's a rumor that it was all a publicity stunt and the missing crew will pop up on a tropical isle somewhere for a new show. They figure the lone survivor is an actress being paid big bucks to pony up a story about the red-eyed cannibals. What about your sources?"

"I picked up some of the same stuff from the guy I was just talking to. He's been around since kilts were invented and knows everyone and everything. I said I was a sport diver and bought a few rounds," Zavala said.

"Did your friend mention any connection between the *Outcasts* incident and the island?" Austin said.

"There was talk at first," Zavala said. "Then the publicity stunt rumor began to circulate and that was that."

"How far is the island from the *Outcasts* set?"

"About five miles. The locals think it's a semiofficial

operation, and that it's still owned by the government," Zavala said. "Given the place's history, it isn't far-fetched. The fishermen avoid the place. Armed patrol boats pop out the minute anyone even *thinks* of getting close. Some fishermen swear they've been tailed by miniature subs."

"That would fit in with what we know from the satellite photos," said Austin. "They must have encountered the AUV watchdog."

The pub's door opened and the fisherman who'd sold Austin his boat stepped inside. Austin figured the man would buy everyone in the house a drink, and didn't want to get drawn into any good luck celebration and the inevitable questions that would arise. He drained his mug and suggested that Zavala do the same. They left by the pub's back door and stopped off at their rooming house to pick up their gear bags. Minutes later, they were walking along a narrow cobblestone lane that took them to the fog-shrouded harbor.

Austin led the way along the line of boats and stopped in front of a vessel about twenty-five feet long. The lapstrake, or "clinker-built" wooden hull of overlapping planking, had an upswept bow built for rough seas. The deck was open except for a small wheelhouse near the bow. Even in the gauzy mists, they could see that the boat was being held together by numerous coats of paint.

"She's what the local fishermen call a 'creeler,' " Austin said. "The former owner says she was built in '71."

"Is that 1871 or 1971?" Zavala said, chuckling. "Can't wait to see Pitt's face when he gets the bill for this little luxury yacht."

"Knowing Pitt, I think he'd understand," Austin said.

Zavala read the name on the stern. *"Spooter?"*

"It's the local term for a razor clam. *Spoot* is supposed to have aphrodisiac qualities."

"Really," Zavala said, his interest piqued. "I suppose it makes about as much sense as rhino horn."

They climbed aboard the boat, and Zavala surveyed the deck while Austin poked his head into a wheelhouse about as big as two telephone booths put together. The cabin reeked of stale cigarette smoke and diesel fumes. When Austin came back out, Zavala stomped his foot on the planking.

"Feels solid enough."

"This old rust bucket is actually more seaworthy than she looks. Let's see if she has a chart."

Austin rummaged around in the wheelhouse and found a grease-smeared map that showed the island to be ten miles across the bay from the boatyard. Austin pointed to the island's harbor and explained the plan he had been mulling over to Zavala.

"What do you think of it?"

"A low-tech solution to a high-tech challenge. I think it can work. When do we go?"

"No time like the present," Austin said. "I persuaded the former owner to throw in a full tank of fuel."

He went into the pilothouse. In short order, they had the engine warming up, gear stowed and a compass course set. The boat had seen some hard times, but its electronics were fairly new and would allow them to navigate the unfamiliar waters in the night fog.

Zavala cast off the mooring lines while Austin took the helm and pointed the bow out of the harbor. The engine chortled and gasped as if it were on its last legs, but the *Spooter* pushed its way through the swirling mists and began its voyage to the mysterious island.

31

FOR A MAN who was nearly seven feet tall, Trout moved with uncommon stealth. Only the sharpest eye would have seen him slip out of the prisoners' compound shortly after midnight. He darted from shadow to shadow, staying away from the floodlights.

His excessive caution proved to be unnecessary. No guards patrolled the compound and the watchtowers were unoccupied. Drunken laughter and loud music drifted from the bunkhouse, where the guards were having a party. Trout surmised that the guards were celebrating the end of their boring duty on this lonely outpost.

The raucous noise grew fainter as Trout trotted along a dirt road away from the bunkhouse. No longer making an attempt to conceal himself, he covered the distance rapidly with his long-legged stride. He knew he was nearing his goal when the stench hit his nostrils. His resolve faltered as he considered the task he had set himself, but he set his jaw and pressed on toward the chamber of horrors Colonel Strega had facetiously referred to as the "Zoo."

Trout slowed to a walk as he entered the floodlit area around the concrete building and went directly to the front door. He ran the beam of his flashlight around the doorjamb, but saw no indication of alarm connections. No one could imagine the blockhouse being broken into, Trout mused, although that was exactly what he was about to do.

The double steel doors could have withstood a battering ram, but they were secured only with an ordinary padlock. Using a hammer and sharp-edged chisel borrowed from the lab, where the tools were used to chip rock samples, he made short work of the latch. He looked around, almost wishing someone would stop him, then opened the doors and stepped into the building.

The awful smell inside hit him like a baseball bat and he had to stifle his gag reflex. The big room was in semidarkness, illuminated by a few dim ceiling lights. His noisy entry must have alerted the Zoo's occupants because he heard faint stirrings in the darkened cells. Pairs of burning red eyes watched his every move. Trout felt like a clam at a clambake.

He ran his flashlight beam along the wall until he found a switch. As the room flooded with light, a chorus of snarls filled the air and the creatures retreated to the back of their cages. Perceiving after a moment that Trout was no threat, they crept back and pressed their nightmarish faces against the bars.

Trout sensed that these creatures were regarding him with more than feral hunger. They were curious, and their low growls and mutterings were a form of communication. He reminded himself that they had carried off a murderous raid on a neighboring island and it would be a mistake to think of these creatures as mere animals. They were once human, and they could think.

Trout tried to ignore their unwavering gazes and went about his inspection of the room. He found what he was looking for behind a metal wall panel and his fingers played over a rank of switches with numbers that corresponded to those painted over each cage. The numbers were labeled Alpha and Beta. He hesitated, thinking about the hell forces he was about to unleash. *Now or never.* He hit a switch labeled ALPHA as an experiment. A motor hummed and a cage door slid open with a metallic clank. The creature occupying the cell dashed to the back of his cage, and then it inched forward, pausing at the open door as if suspecting a trick.

Trout hit the other switches in rapid succession. Door after door clanged. Still, none of the creatures ventured out. They were gibbering and gesturing at each other in a primitive communication. Trout didn't hang around to tune in on the conversation. Having unleashed the demons, he ran for the door.

MACLEAN WAS waiting with Gamay and Sandy in a thick stand of trees about a hundred yards from the compound's gate. In outlining his plan, Trout had told them to slip away from their cottages as soon as he was on his way and to stay hidden until he rejoined them.

MacLean had heard the drunken party going on at the bunkhouse, but he was still nervous, having known the unpredictable guards longer than Trout. His worst fears were realized when he heard the sound of pounding feet. Someone was running toward him. He strained his eyes against the darkness, not knowing whether to run or fight.

Then someone called out "Mac." It was Trout.

Gamay stepped from the trees and grabbed him in a tight hug. "I am *so* glad to see you," she said.

"For godsakes, man," MacLean said. "I thought something had happened."

Trout caught his breath. "It was easier than I thought."

Trout tensed as a figure emerged from the trees, then another, until all six of their fellow scientists were gathered around.

"I'm sorry," MacLean said. "I couldn't leave them."

"It was my idea," Gamay said.

"Don't worry. I changed my mind and was about to go back for them myself. Is everybody here?"

"Yes," one of the scientists said. "No one saw us. But what do we do now?"

"We wait," Trout replied. He made his way though the trees and took up a post behind an oak where he had a clear view of the main gate. Two guards lounged in front of the sentry house. He returned to the others and told them to be patient.

Trout knew he had taken a calculated risk in releasing the creatures from their cages. Once they tasted freedom, they might simply bolt for the hills. He gambled that their urge to run would be tempered by an all-too-human emotion, a thirst for revenge against those who had tormented and imprisoned them.

He checked the gate again. The guards were smoking cigarettes and passing a bottle back and forth. If they couldn't join the party, at least they could have one of their own. He eased his way back through to the other side of the copse, where he had an unobstructed view of the Zoo.

In his hasty exit, he had left the doors of the blockhouse partially open. A sliver of light came from inside the building. He saw dark shapes begin to emerge from the building. They paused, went on, moving like a skirmish line toward the guards' quarters, and vanished into the shadows.

From the sounds of coarse laughter and music, the party was in full tilt, and for a moment Trout feared that he had miscalculated. Then, quite suddenly, the laughter stopped. It was replaced by shouted curses, a couple of gunshots, then screams of pain and terror.

Trout could only imagine the bloodbath that was going on, and he couldn't help but feel some pity for the guards. But he reminded himself that the guards were prepared to wipe out their prisoners at a word from Strega.

The sentries at the gate had heard the strange racket coming from their quarters. They conferred with each other, unsure of what to do. They seemed to be arguing. They halted their heated discussion when they saw headlights moving their way. They raised their automatic weapons and aimed at the fast-approaching vehicle, which was zigzagging and blowing its horn.

The vehicle entered the floodlit area near the gate and

Trout saw that it was Strega's convertible and the front and back seats were hidden under a mass of writhing bodies. More creatures hung onto the hood. Others dangled from the sides, resisting the driver's efforts to dislodge them with violent swerves.

The guards swept the oncoming vehicle with automatic gunfire. Two of the creatures dropped off the hood and rolled on the ground, splitting the night with their fearful screams, but the others hung on. The car made a violent turn, went out of control, and smashed broadside into the guardhouse. The impact dislodged the creatures, and the driver's door flew open. Colonel Strega emerged from the driver's side, pistol in hand. His razor-creased uniform was bloodstained and in tatters. Blood streamed from a dozen wounds to his head and body.

He staggered a few feet and fired off a wild round that killed one of the attackers, but before he could get off another shot the remaining creatures knocked the colonel to the ground. Trout could see his arms and legs flailing from under the thrashing bodies that swarmed over him and then the colonel stiffened and went still. The creatures dragged what was left of him into the shadows. The two guards had had enough. They fired a few shots, killing one or two of the creatures, and ran for their lives with a pack of red-eyed demons on their heels.

Trout rallied Gamay and the others and led them out into the open, stepping past the twitching bodies to the Mercedes. He got behind the wheel and threw the shift into reverse, but the vehicle was hung up on the wreckage of the guardhouse. He instructed the scientists to push and pull, and after a lot of grunts, the wheels were clear and they all piled into the convertible.

Trout practically stood on the accelerator. The vehicle lurched forward and smashed through the gates as if they didn't exist and barreled along the road that would take them to the sea, and what Trout hoped was freedom.

32

THE NEWEST ADDITION to the NUMA fleet began to spout leaks within minutes of clearing the harbor. The transition from virtually flat calm to seas of two feet in open water was not a severe change, but it was enough to open seams in the boat's elderly hull. Austin, who was at the helm, noticed that the wheel was responding sluggishly and that the boat was settling. He clicked the bilge pump switch, but the motor refused to start.

"They should have named this boat the *Busted Flush*," Austin grumbled.

"I'll check it out," Zavala said. At the heart of every brilliant engineer is a mechanic, and Zavala was no different. He was happiest when getting his fingers into grease. He slipped below through a deck hatch, and after a minute or two yelled up to Austin, "Try again." The pump started with a series of chortles and gasps. When he emerged, he looked like a dipstick, but he had a smile on his oil-smeared face.

"Engine repair 101. When all else fails, look for a loose wire," he said.

The repair hadn't come a minute too soon. The boat was

listing as if it had a flat tire. But the bilge pump worked heroically, keeping ahead of the leaks, and after a few minutes the *Spooter* got back on an even keel, more or less, and continued on its heading.

By then, Austin had discovered that when the *Spooter* wasn't sinking it handled quite well. The creeler was built for local conditions and its graceful, raised bow cut through the washboard sea as easily as a canoe on a pond. With a wind at their back, and the engine chugging along and only missing occasionally, they made good time across the bay.

Austin gave the radar screen a glance and saw that they were on course. He squinted through the spray-streaked windshield but saw only blackness. While Zavala took the helm, he stepped outside the wheelhouse. The cold damp air hit him in the face. He sensed rather than saw a dark mass rising from the darker sea. He went back into the warm wheelhouse.

"The island should be dead ahead," he said.

The boat chugged through the night, and before long the looming presence Austin had sensed earlier began to assume an outline. The island's silhouette was clearly visible against the blue-black of the sky. Austin moved the wheel over slightly to starboard and sheared off a few compass points. Odds were good that the boat had been under surveillance for some time and he wanted to create the impression for any watchers that the *Spooter* was going around the island.

The AUV's electronic eyes and ears would be less easy to fool with a feint. But it would not be impossible. Austin had studied the images on the satellite photos taken over several hours and he had computed the vehicle's timing, well aware that the formula was subject to natural and human vagaries. He had tracked the vehicle's position and figured the AUV's schedule. Periodically, the AUV went back to recharge its batteries.

He checked the time. The AUV should be on the far side of the island. Hoping to come in under the radar, he eased the wheel over, moving the boat closer to the sea cliffs, and prayed that his computations were right.

THE COMMAND center that protected the security of the island from nosy outsiders was housed in a squat, flat-roof, cinder-block building situated at the mouth of the inlet. Fifty percent of the building was crammed with electronic surveillance equipment. The other half served as a barracks for the twelve guards who manned the post.

The contingent had been broken up into four-man teams that worked three shifts. During the day, three guards patrolled the perimeter of the island by boat, while the fourth man stayed in the command center.

At night the routine changed. The patrol boat stayed on shore during the graveyard shift because the dangerous knife-edged rocks that lurked in the waters around the island were tricky to navigate in the dark. The boat was kept on standby, ready to respond if the AUV or radar picked up intruders. The night crew took turns recharging the AUV from an electrical station on the deck. The radar operator had seen the blip on his screen long before the boat approached the island and had watch it change course and come nearer.

The radar man was a German mercenary named Max. From experience, he knew that fishing boats rarely went out at night, but he relaxed when the blip moved past the island. He lit up a cigarette and leafed through the well-turned pages of a skin magazine for a few minutes, and then his eyes drifted back to the screen. It was blank. He let out a curse, mashed the cigarette into an ashtray and leaned forward, his nose practically touching the screen. He even tapped the glass with his knuckles as if it would do some good.

Still no sign of the target. The boat must have entered the radar's blind spot along the base of the cliffs while he was studying female anatomy. It was an annoyance, but not a catastrophe. There was still the AUV. He turned to another monitor that kept tabs on the AUV. As it made its rounds, the vehicle bounced signals off a series of floating transponders that ringed the island. The transponders relayed the hits to the command center, and the vehicle's location could be pinpointed at any time along its route.

The vehicle was twelve feet long, flat and wide, a combination of a manta and a shark in shape, and topped with a tall dorsal fin. One of the guards had said the menacing profile reminded him of his former mother-in-law, whose name was Gertrude, and the name had stuck. *Gertrude* cruised a few feet below the surface, its sonar scanning the water for one hundred feet on each side. Its TV cameras took in the underwater scene.

Commands could be transmitted back to the AUV as well. This was an invaluable asset, given the vehicle's dual function as an underwater watchdog and weapons carrier. The AUV carried four miniature torpedoes, each with the power to sink a destroyer.

Max commanded *Gertrude* to return at top speed to the area where he had last seen the boat. Then he punched an intercom button.

"Sorry to break up your game, boys," he said into the microphone. "We've got a boat inside the security zone."

The boat crew had been playing poker in the barracks when the wall speaker crackled with the news of an intruder. Two of the men were former French Legionnaires and the other a South African mercenary. The South African threw his cards down in disgust and went over to the intercom.

"Where's the target?"

"It entered the security perimeter on the north side, then slipped into the radar blind spot. I've sent *Gertrude* over to sniff around."

"What the hell," the mercenary said. "My luck stinks tonight."

The three men pulled on their jackets and boots and grabbed their compact FA MAS assault rifles. A moment later they trotted to the end of the fog-draped pier and climbed into a thirty-foot rigid inflatable boat. The twin diesels roared to life. The crew cast off the mooring lines, and before long the water jet system was kicking the boat along at nearly forty knots.

The boat had barely been at sea for a few minutes when the man in the command center reported that the target had reappeared on radar outside the mouth of the inlet. He guided the patrol boat to the target and watched as the two blips merged on the screen.

While two guards stood ready to blast anything that moved, the helmsman brought the patrol boat in close, until its spotlight could pick out every square inch of peeling paint. The South African lowered his rifle and began to laugh. The others joined in.

"*Spooter,*" he said. "We broke up our poker game for a *Spooter*?"

"What are you complaining about? You were losing your ass."

They roared with laughter again.

"Better board the old scow," the helmsman said.

The guards were all trained military men who didn't let their amusement get in the way of their caution. Their levity ended and their training came into play. The patrol boat edged up to the creeler and two men went aboard with weapons drawn while the other covered them with his rifle. They checked out the deserted wheelhouse, opened the hatch and looked below.

"Nothing," one of the mercenaries called back to the man on the boat. He leaned against the rail and lit up a cigarette.

His companion said, "I wouldn't perch there for too long, if I were you."

"Hell," said the other man. "Who died and made you king?"

The Legionnaire grinned and climbed back onto the patrol boat. "Suit yourself," he said. "Don't get your feet wet."

The South African looked at his boots. Water was rapidly flowing from the engine hatch and flooding the deck.

The boat was sinking. He let out a yell, which got his colleagues laughing. The helmsman pulled the patrol boat off a few yards, as if he were leaving his companion to his own devices, but he came back when the South African gave forth with a string of curses in Afrikaans.

The South African practically fell into the patrol boat, then he and the others watched as the water reached the gunwales. Then only the mast was visible and a few minutes later that was gone and the only evidence of a boat was a patch of bubbling water.

"Okay, so you bastards had a little joke," said the South African. "Let's go back and break open another bottle."

The helmsman got on the radio and reported to the command center.

"Doesn't make sense," the radar man said. "That thing was moving on a straight-line course when I picked it up on the radar."

"You been drinking?"

"Of course I've been drinking."

The shore patrol had been celebrating after hearing scuttlebutt from the guards at the complex that they might be closing down the island's operation.

"That explains it."

"But—"

"Currents are strong around the bloody island. She could have been caught up."

"I guess so," Max said.

"Can't help you there, mate. She's deep-sixed. We're coming in."

The voice from the command center said, "Watch out for *Gertrude*. She's in the area."

Seconds later, the huge fin cut the water near the boat. The men on the patrol boat were used to seeing *Gertrude*, but they had never felt comfortable when the AUV was in the area. They were nervous about its destructive potential and the fact that it operated largely on its own. The AUV stopped fifty feet away. It was matching the sound profile of the patrol boat with the information stored in its database.

"Make damned sure she's not armed."

Laughter. "I'll have the fish check around."

"You do that. We're getting the hell out of here."

The diesel engines rumbled, and the boat did a banking turn and headed back to its dock.

The fin went back and forth for several minutes, following parallel lines in a mow-the-lawn search pattern. The probing sonar picked up the fishing boat now lying on the bottom and transmitted a picture. The radar man watched the screen for several minutes and then commanded the AUV to resume its normal patrol.

Moments after the AUV moved off, two figures emerged from the cabin of the sunken boat. With strong rhythmic kicks that ate up the distance, they began to swim in the direction of the island.

33

TROUT HAD MASHED the accelerator to the floor after he blasted Strega's Mercedes through the compound gate. MacLean, who was in the passenger's seat with Gamay between them, had been staring at the speedometer as the car hurtled through the pass.

"Dr. Trout!" he said in a voice that was calm but assertive. "There's a sharp turn in the road ahead. If you don't slow down, we'll have to sprout wings."

Gamay put a hand on her husband's arm.

Trout glanced at the speedometer. They were doing more than seventy miles per hour. He pumped the brakes and switched the headlights on in time to see that the turn was more than sharp; it was *angular.* Off to the right was a drop-off with no guardrail.

The tires skidded close to the ragged edge of the cliff, but the Mercedes stayed on the road, which straightened and began a gradual descent. Trout let out the breath he'd been holding and relaxed his death grip on the steering wheel one finger at a time.

"Thanks for the warning, Mac."

MacLean compressed his lips in a tight smile. "I wouldn't want us to get stopped for speeding."

Trout glanced over his shoulder at the tangle of arms and legs in the backseat.

"Is everyone still with us?" he asked.

"We're not going anywhere unless you pry us out with a crowbar," Sandy said.

Trout allowed himself the luxury of a hearty laugh. In spite of his outer calm, he was wound as tight as a clock spring. MacLean's composed demeanor brought Trout back down to earth. The adrenaline pumping through his veins had helped him pull off the escape from the compound, but if they were to survive, he needed to be cool and deliberate. The road continued to descend until it was at sea level and ended at a junction with two roads.

Trout brought the Mercedes to a halt and pointed to the road on the left. "Is this the way we came in?"

"That's right," MacLean said. "The road runs along the edge of the inlet to the submarine pen. There's a garrison and guards' quarters there. If we turn right, we'll come to the mouth of the harbor. There's a command center and a dock there for the boat patrols."

Trout said, "You've done your homework."

"You're not the *only* one who's tried to figure out how to get off this blasted rock."

"Seems like a pretty clear choice. The patrol boat could be our ticket off the island."

"I agree," Gamay said. "Besides, if we're going to stir up a hornet's nest, the fewer hornets the better."

Trout nodded and wheeled the Mercedes to the right. The road ran for another half mile alongside a beach that bordered the inlet. He saw lights glowing in the distance and pulled off the road. He told the others where he was going and suggested that they get out and stretch, but to stay near the car. Then he started walking. The air was heavy with the smell of the sea and it felt good to be out of the compound. He had no illusions. His freedom was as ephemeral as the waves lapping the beach.

Trout saw that the lights were coming from a concrete-block building. The window shades were down. He gave the building a wide berth and kept on going until he came to a wooden pier that jutted out into the water. There was no patrol boat. Not even a rowboat. The cool breeze from off the sea was nothing to the cold he felt in the pit of his stomach. He trudged back to the Mercedes and slipped behind the wheel.

"The patrol boat is gone," he announced. "We can wait and hope it comes back, but once the sun comes up, all bets are off. I suggest that we scout out the submarine pen."

"It's the last place they'd expect us to be," Gamay said in support.

"It's the last place *I'd* expect us to be," MacLean said. "We're not what one would call a Special Forces contingent."

"There were only a hundred or so misfits at the Alamo."

"I know my American history, Paul. The Alamo defenders were massacred. And don't tell me about the Scots at Culloden. They were massacred, too."

Trout grinned. "Desperate times call for desperate measures."

"That's something I can understand. But I'm still not clear what measures you have in mind."

"I'll try to get aboard the sub and look for a radio. If that doesn't work, I'll figure out something else."

"I believe you will," MacLean said, examining Trout as if he were an interesting lab specimen. "You're a very resourceful man for a deep-ocean geologist."

"I try to be," Trout said, and turned the ignition key.

He drove the vehicle along the edge of the inlet until he came to the abandoned church and cemetery. He parked behind the ruined building and told the others to sit tight. Gamay insisted on going with him this time. They followed a gravel road that led to where the inlet narrowed to a rounded point.

Floodlights lit the perimeter around the barracks. The Trouts went to within a hundred feet or so of the barracks and studied the layout. The building was situated near the edge of the cliff with an observation platform cantilevered out over the inlet from the main structure. An enclosed ladder led down from the underside of the platform.

"Let's check out that ladder," he said.

"I don't think we'll have to worry. It sounds like a Klingon stag party is in progress," Gamay said.

Like the men in the compound, the sub guards must have learned that their duty was about to come to an end because a similar drunken celebration was under way in the guardhouse. Apparently, they hadn't learned the fate of their comrades in the lab compound area.

Gamay and Trout moved in until they were under the platform. The ladder dropped off the edge of the bluff. They climbed down the face of the cliff onto a narrow metal catwalk that was built a few feet above water level and followed a line of ankle-high lights into the yawning entrance of the sub pen.

The giant submarine that had kidnapped them loomed ahead. A few deck lights had been left on, so they were able to find the gangway and walk along the deck to the entry hatch. Trout lifted the hatch cover and poked his head inside. Low-level lights illuminated the sub's interior.

They descended a ladder and began to make their way through the sub as silently as shadows. Trout, who was in the lead, paused to peer around every corner, but he encountered no one. The control room was in semidarkness, lit by lights glowing on the various instrument panels. The radio shack was a small space off the control room. While Gamay kept watch, Trout sat in front of the communications console, picked up the radiophone, dialed the main number for NUMA and held his breath, not sure what would happen.

"National Underwater and . . . Agency," said a friendly female voice.

The faint transmission was broken up, probably by the walls and ceiling of the sub pen.

"Rudi Gunn, please. Tell him this is Paul Trout calling."

"One . . . ment."

The moment seemed like a day. In his mind's eye, he pictured the lobby of the NUMA building with its centerpiece globe. Then the voice of NUMA's assistant director came on the phone. He could picture the slightly built Gunn sitting in his big office, probably applying his genius to a complex logistical problem.

"*Trout?* Where in God's name . . . you? We've been looking . . . over Creation. Are you okay?"

"Fine, Rudi. Gamay's here, too. Got to talk fast. The *Alvin* was hijacked. We're on an island—I think it's in Scottish or Scandinavian waters. There are seven other scientists also being held prisoner. We've been working on some nutty experiment. We've escaped, but it might not last long."

"Having trouble hear . . . you, but understand. Can you stay on . . . radio?"

"We've got to get back to the others."

"Leave the radio phone on. We'll try to track you down through . . . signal."

Trout's reply was cut short by a whispered warning from Gamay. Someone was whistling a mindless tune. He carefully replaced the mike in its cradle and shut off the radiophone. Then he and Gamay dropped to their hands and knees and tried with limited success to cram their bodies under the console. The whistle came nearer. The whistler paused to peer through the glass pane in the door and apparently saw nothing amiss because the whistling grew fainter.

The Trouts pried themselves out of their hiding place. Paul called Gunn again and told him they were leaving the radio on. He checked the passageway, saw it was empty and they started back the way they came. They moved with even greater caution, keeping their ears cocked for a telltale whistle. They emerged from the deck hatchway, trotted along the catwalk and climbed the ladder that would take them back to the access road.

They returned to the church and were making their way through the graveyard when the night blazed with light.

Beyond the blinding glare, several forms could be seen rising from behind the gravestones like restless spirits. Then rough hands grabbed Trout and Gamay and guards hustled them into the church. A tough-looking guard stood in front of the altar, a grin on his face that didn't match the machine pistol held at waist level, its muzzle pointing toward Trout's belly button.

"Hello, mate," the man said, with a quick glance at Gamay. "This is the end of the road for you and your friends."

THE OWL had been perched in a withered tree near the edge of the sea, its keen hearing attuned to the scampering of a mouse darting among clumps of grass. The bird was about to swoop down upon the hapless creature when its round yellow eyes caught a movement on the beach. Something large and shiny had broken from a wave and climbed out onto the wet sand. The owl spread its wings and silently flew inland. The mouse scurried into the grass, unmindful of its reprieve.

A second figure with black skin emerged from the surf like a primitive creature crawling out of the primordial ooze. Austin and Zavala pushed their face masks up, unzipped their watertight packs and pulled out the SIG-Sauer 9-millimeter pistols the ill-fated SEAL team had left on board the research vessel. Seeing that they were alone, they took off their air tanks and stepped out of their dry suits.

They had slipped over the side of the *Spooter* as the patrol boat approached, first opening the petcocks to send the fishing boat to the bottom. They had watched from inside the wheelhouse as the AUV checked out the sunken boat. When the AUV had left, they'd started swimming for land. Currents had thrown them off course, but Austin was reasonably sure they had landed close to where they were supposed to be.

A glance at his watch told Austin they had six hours until daylight. He signaled to Zavala. After a five-minute walk in the sand, their feet crunched hard gravel. Austin took a minicomputer from his pack and examined the image the satellite photo had taken of the island.

"If we stay on this road, we'll come to the compound. It's about two miles through what looks like a pass."

Without another word, they started walking along the darkened road.

THE MAN pointing the gun at Trout had a face like a lizard, all teeth and no lips.

"We've been waiting for you," the man said in an Australian accent.

"How'd you know where we were?" Trout said.

The man laughed. "Guess you didn't know we've got surveillance cameras scattered around the island. If the boys hadn't been so drunk, we might have seen you earlier."

"Sorry to interrupt your party."

"Your friends didn't feel like talking," he said. "Where'd you get Strega's car?"

"The colonel wasn't using it, so we thought we'd take it out for a drive."

The man swung his rifle around and thrust the butt into Trout's midsection. Trout felt as if his heart had stopped. He doubled over, clutching his stomach, and dropped to his knees. When the waves of nausea had subsided, he staggered painfully to his feet. The man grabbed the front of Trout's jumpsuit and pulled him close. He reeked of whiskey.

"I don't like wiseass answers," he said. He pushed Trout away and leveled his gun at Gamay. "Where did you get the car?"

"Strega's dead," Trout said, still gasping for breath.

"Dead!" The eyes narrowed. "How'd he get dead?"

Trout knew that even if he told the truth, the man wouldn't believe him. "It's better if I show you."

The guard hesitated.

"What are you up to?" he said, raising his weapon.

"Nothing. We're in no position to hurt you."

The comment went to the man's ego, as Trout hoped it would. "Right about that, mate."

He and the other guards marched Trout and Gamay around to the back of the church where the Mercedes was parked. Sandy, MacLean and the other scientists were huddled near the vehicle under the watchful eyes of two more armed men. A long-bed pickup truck was parked next to the Mercedes. The prisoners including Gamay were ordered into the back of the truck. Some of the guards went with the truck while two others got into the backseat of the Mercedes. The Aussie told Trout to drive the car. Then he slid in next to Trout and ordered him back to the compound.

"This better be good," he said.

"Why don't you simply leave us?" Trout said. "The experiment has been completed."

"Nice try. We leave, and the next day some bloke comes along and finds you waving your undershirts on the beach. Things have a way of catching up with you in my business. Now drive and keep your mouth shut."

Trout did as he was told. When they arrived at the compound, the Aussie ordered Trout to stop. He yanked the keys from the ignition and got out to look around. The other guards jumped down from the truck and stared into the darkness with their weapons at ready.

The Aussie inspected the wreckage of the gate and the overturned gatehouse. There was an eerie quiet about the place. No night bird cries or insects humming. There was no sign of the carnage Trout had witnessed. He thought back to the rat-eating feast Strega had orchestrated and decided he didn't want to know what happened to the bodies.

The Aussie got back into the Mercedes. "What the hell is going on here?" he said.

"Did you know what we were working on in the labs?"

"Yeah. Germ warfare. Something to do with the stuff the sub was bringing in off the bottom of the sea. They never let us into the compound. Said we might catch something."

Trout laughed.

"What's so funny?" There was a dangerous tone to the Aussie's voice.

"They were lying," Trout said. "We were doing enzyme research."

"What are you talking about?"

"You ever heard of the Philosopher's Stone?"

The gun barrel jabbed Trout in the ribs. "*This* is my philosophy."

Trout winced, but stayed calm. "It was a secret formula supposed to change other material into gold."

"No such thing."

"You think the people who hired you would go through all this trouble if there were no such thing?"

Pause. "Okay, mate, show us this gold."

"I'll take you to the storehouse where they keep it. Maybe you'll rethink my suggestion about leaving us. "

The Aussie smiled. "I'll do that," he said.

Trout knew that he and his fellow scientists would be doomed, even if he were able to produce all the gold in Fort Knox. No other reason would have persuaded him to return to the Zoo. He drove up and parked in front of the wide-open front door.

"Here we are," he said.

They got out of the Mercedes and the Aussie took the ignition key and ordered his men out of the truck, leaving one behind, who was instructed to shoot anyone who got out of order. Then he told Trout to lead the way.

"*Jeezus*, what's that stink?" the guard said.

"That's the smell of gold," the Aussie said with a laugh.

Trout headed for the door as if he were in a trance. He knew he was taking a calculated risk, but he reasoned that the creatures who'd once been imprisoned in the building would return to the place that had been their home. He knew he had guessed right when he stepped into the fetid darkness, heard the sickening sound of bones being crunched and saw pairs of red eyes burning in the darkness. He ran his hand along the wall and flicked the light on.

The creatures were back in their cages with the doors open. They had been busy feasting on the remnants of Colonel Strega and his minions. As the light came on, they retreated to the back of their cages. There was a yell of revulsion and surprise from the Aussie guard.

The Aussie grabbed Trout and pushed him against the wall. "You and your friends are going to die for this."

Trout grabbed the barrel of the gun and tried to twist it out of the Aussie's hands, but his adversary had the advantage of being on the trigger end. He let off a shot that went wild, taking a chip out of the wall a few inches from Trout's neck. As they wrestled for the gun, the creatures came to the front of their cages. The sight of guard uniforms triggered a ferocious attack. The creatures leaped into the room in a howling mass of teeth and claws.

The guard got off a few rounds before being mowed down by the snarling onslaught. Two creatures jumped on the Aussie's back, pushing him to the floor. Another creature lunged toward Trout, but stopped halfway and stared. In that brief instant, Trout could swear that he saw a glimpse of humanity in the thing's face. When he saw Trout wasn't wearing a uniform, he pounced instead on the Aussie.

Trout bolted for the door and bowled over the man who'd been guarding the prisoners. One of the creatures who'd followed Trout out the door saw the fallen guard and made short work of him.

Trout yelled at Gamay to drive the truck. He slid behind the steering wheel of the Mercedes and reached for the ignition key. *Gone.* He remembered that the Aussie had taken it with him. Gamay called out that the truck key was missing as well. Trout jumped out of the car, grabbed Gamay and told everyone to run for their lives.

From the sudden quietness from the Zoo, Trout guessed that the creatures were enjoying having the guards over for dinner. He didn't want to be around at dessert time.

• • •

AUSTIN AND Zavala were about a mile from the compound when they heard feet pounding along the road in the darkness ahead. They scuttled off the gravel road and threw themselves belly-down in the tall grass.

As the footfalls approached, they were intermingled with the low murmur of voices and a wheezing that suggested that some of the people coming toward them were not in the best of physical condition. Then he heard a familiar voice pleading. "Please move it along, folks. We'll have plenty of time to rest later."

Trout stopped short as two figures materialized from the darkness.

"You're a long way from Lost City," Austin said.

"Kurt and Joe?" Trout said with relief. "Damn. This is like old home week."

Gamay threw her arms around her NUMA colleagues.

"These are my friends, Mac and Sandy," Trout said. "I'll introduce the others later. Do you have a boat?"

Austin said, "I'm afraid we burned our bridges behind us. We saw a patrol boat out on the water earlier. Do you know where they keep it tied up?"

"I know where it *might* be." Trout cocked his ear and he frowned. "We've got to get out of here."

Austin had heard the noise, like the distant howling of the wind. "What's that?" He listened again. "Sounds like a pack of wolves chasing a deer."

"I wish it were," Trout said. "Are you armed?"

"We've got handguns."

The howling was getting louder. Trout glanced back along the road again.

"Shoot anything that moves, especially if it's got red eyes," he said without further explanation. Austin and Zavala recalled the red-eyed furies from the video and didn't need any persuasion.

Trout took Gamay by the arm and called out to the others to get moving again. Austin and Zavala took up the rear.

The group walked in silence for fifteen minutes, urged on by the growing volume of the howling, until they could see the lights in the windows of the patrol boat barracks. Their pursuers were so close now that individual howls could be heard.

The noise must have penetrated the barracks walls because a couple of guards burst out of the building into the night as the fugitives were making their way around the blockhouse on their way to the dock.

The guards saw the faces reflected in the light coming from the door and yelled at the group to halt or be killed. One guard called into the building, and seconds later two more men emerged. One was half-dressed and the other, a big bearded man, must have been asleep because he was in his underwear. He grinned and said, "Looks like we caught ourselves a bonus from Strega."

His comrades roared with laughter, but their mirth was cut short, quickly turning to fear, as they heard the howling. The terrifying noise seemed to be coming from every direction. They huddled together, their guns facing outward, staring at the eyes that glowed like coals in the darkness.

The guard with the black beard sprayed the darkness with bullets. Cries of pain indicated that some bullets had hit a target. The gunfire triggered an onslaught. The creatures attacked from every direction, going after anyone wearing a uniform. The scientists and NUMA people took advantage of the bloody confusion and slipped away, with Trout showing the way to the dock where the patrol boat was tied up.

Austin got into the boat and started the engine. He climbed back onto the dock to help the others. MacLean was herding his fellow scientists into the boat. Then, as he was about to get in, shots rang out and he crumpled to the dock.

The shots had come from the bearded guard, who was running toward the boat. His slovenly lack of a uniform had protected him from being singled out by the creatures. Austin got off a quick shot that missed. The guard hadn't expected anyone to shoot back, but he quickly recovered, dropped to one knee and leveled his weapon.

A gunshot exploded in Austin's ear. Gamay had fired over his shoulder. She was an expert marksman, but in her haste her aim was off. The bullet caught the bearded man in the left shoulder. He screamed in rage and pain, but managed to swing his weapon around. Although he was deaf and dizzy from the shot near his ear, Austin stepped in front of his friends to shield them, raising his gun at the same time.

A chorus of howls came from behind the bearded guard. He turned and raised his gun, but he was buried under a pile of snarling creatures. Austin holstered his gun and he and Zavala were lifting MacLean into the boat when one of the creatures broke away from the others. It staggered toward the edge of the pier. Gamay raised her gun to shoot the creature. Trout, who was preparing to cast off the dock lines, stopped and grabbed her wrist. He recognized the creature as the one he had encountered in the blockhouse.

"He's wounded," Trout said.

The creature's chest was dark with blood. He stared at Trout, and then his legs buckled and he pitched forward, dead, into the boat. Austin yelled at Trout to take the wheel while he tended to MacLean. As soon as Gamay had cast off the lines, Trout gunned the throttle and pointed the bow into the darkness.

The boat sped from the island of horror at full throttle. Trout turned the wheel over to Gamay and went to MacLean, who was lying on his back. The other scientists had made room for him. Austin had tucked a life jacket under MacLean's head as a pillow and he was kneeling beside the mortally wounded scientist. His ear was close to MacLean's mouth. He raised his head when he saw Trout and said, "He wants to talk to you."

Trout kneeled down on the other side of the dying scientist.

"We got away, Mac," he said. "We'll get you to a doctor and get you fixed up in no time."

MacLean replied with a gurgling laugh and blood seeped out of the corner of his mouth. "Don't try to fool an old Scotsman, my friend."

When Trout went to reply, MacLean lifted a weak hand. "No. Let me talk." His eyes started to roll back in his head, but he pulled himself together.

"The formula," he said.

"What about it?"

MacLean's eyes went to Austin's face. And then he died.

34

GERTRUDE CAME OUT to say good-bye. The AUV picked up the sound of the departing patrol boat and intercepted it about a mile from the island. Zavala saw the vehicle first. He was probing the darkness with a spotlight, looking for rocks, when the tall fin came into view. He thought it was a killer whale, but as it grew closer he saw rivets in the metallic fin and knew exactly what it was.

The vehicle paced them for a few hundred feet, then peeled off and went about its routine patrol. No one aboard the patrol boat knew how close they had come to disaster. Back at the command center, Max had sent the AUV to pursue the escaping boat and had armed all four of the torpedoes. He had set the launch switch and was about to hit the FIRE button when his throat had been ripped out by a red-eyed demon.

The patrol boat continued blissfully on its way for another half hour before Austin decided to call the Coast Guard for help. Minutes later, the 110-foot British Coast Guard boat *Scapa* picked up the Mayday from a boat broadcasting a position. The *Scapa* responded with its full thirty-knot speed. Based on past experience, the boat's skipper thought the call was from a fisherman in trouble. As he gazed from the deck of the *Scapa* at the inflatable boat caught in the spotlight, Captain John Bruce thought that he had seen some strange sights in his twenty years of patrol in the Orkney Islands. But this was one for the books.

The rigid inflatable off the port bow was about thirty feet in length, Bruce estimated. Most of the shivering passengers on board were dressed in lime coveralls. The captain didn't know of any local prisons, but the circumstances, to say the least, were highly suspicious. Decades at sea had taught Captain Bruce to be careful. He ordered his crew to stand by with weapons ready.

As the patrol boat pulled alongside the inflatable, the captain raised an electric megaphone to his lips and said: "Please identify yourself."

A man came to the side and waved to get the captain's attention. He had broad shoulders, rugged bronze features and his hair was platinum, almost silver in color.

"Kurt Austin of the National Underwater and Marine Agency," he said, his voice carrying clearly without artificial magnification over the sound of boat engines. "These people are suffering from exhaustion and possible hypothermia. Can you help us out?"

The captain reacted with caution, despite the obvious earnestness in Austin's face. He had heard of NUMA, the far-reaching American ocean science organization, and had occasionally come across one of its vessels on a mission. But he couldn't reconcile the sorry bunch crowded into the small boat with the sleek turquoise-hulled research ships with which he was familiar.

Captain Bruce was a burly Scotsman with a freckled bald head, light blue eyes and a firm chin that correctly advertised the determination of its owner. He let his eye roam from stem to stern. There was no faking the weariness and anxiety he saw in the faces of those crowding the inflatable. Captain Bruce ordered a boat lowered and the passengers taken on board. He warned the deck crew to keep their weapons ready and a close eye on the boarders.

It took several trips to move the passengers from one boat to another. Seen from up close, it was clear that the bedraggled passengers were no threat. As they stepped onto the deck, the medic gave them a quick physical checkup. Then they were each given a blanket to wrap themselves in and directed to the mess hall for hot soup and coffee.

Austin took the last boat over, accompanied by an attractive red-haired woman and two men, one with a dark complexion and the other so tall he stuck out of the boat like a mast.

Austin shook the captain's hand and introduced the others. "This is Paul and Gamay Morgan-Trout and Joe Zavala," he said. "We're all with NUMA."

"I didn't know NUMA had any operations going in the Orkneys," the captain said, shaking hands all around.

"Technically speaking, we don't." Austin told the others that he would join them in the mess in a few minutes and he turned back to the captain. "The passengers were having a rough time and some of them are suffering from exposure. On top of that, we were lost in the fog, so we called for help. Sorry to bother you."

"No bother, lad. That's our job."

"Thanks anyway. I have another favor to ask. Could you radio a message to Rudi Gunn at NUMA headquarters in Washington? Tell him Austin and company are well and will be in touch."

"I'll have someone get right on it."

"In that case I could use some hot soup myself," Austin said with a smile. He turned around as he walked off and said casually, "By the way, there are two bodies on board the inflatable."

"*Dead* bodies?"

"*Very* dead. I wonder if your crew could bring them over before you put the boat in tow."

"Yes, of course," Captain Bruce said.

"Thanks again, Captain," Austin said. He wrapped a blanket around his shoulders like a Navajo Indian and strode off toward the galley.

The captain had an annoyed expression in his eyes. He was not used to having people usurp his command. Then he broke into a chuckle. After years at sea dealing with different crews and situations, he was a good judge of men. Bruce detected that what some might have seen as insouciance in Austin's carefree manner was a supreme self-confidence. He ordered his men to retrieve the bodies and take them to the dispensary. Then he told his crew to tie a towline on the boat.

He returned to the bridge and sent Austin's message off to NUMA. He had just finished filing a report with the Coast Guard command when the medic called on the intercom. The captain listened to the medic's excited voice, then left the bridge and went down to the dispensary. Two body bags were lying on gurneys. The medic gave Captain Bruce scented petroleum jelly to dab under his nostrils.

"Brace yourself," the medic said and unzipped one of the body bags.

The captain had seen and smelled dead bodies in various levels of sea decomposition, and the strong animal odor that issued from the bag didn't bother him as much as the sight that greeted his eyes. His ruddy face turned ash gray. The captain was a good Presbyterian who neither drank nor swore. This was one of those times when he wished he were less devout.

"What in God's name *is* that thing?" he said in a hoarse whisper.

"The stuff of nightmares," the medic said. "I've never seen anything like it."

"What about the other one?" the captain said.

The medic unzipped the second bag. The body was that of a handsome gray-haired man in his fifties or sixties.

"Zip them both up," the captain ordered. When the medic complied, the captain said, "What did they die of?"

"Both these, er, men were killed by gunshots."

Captain Bruce thanked the medic and then headed to the mess hall. The frightened faces he had seen earlier were smiling, thanks to generous infusions of food and rum. Austin sat at a table talking with Paul and Gamay.

Austin had been listening, deep in thought, as they took turns filling him in on their kidnapping and imprisonment. He saw Captain Bruce and gave him a warm smile. "Hello, Captain. As you can see, your hospitality has not gone unappreciated."

"Glad to hear that," the captain said. "I wonder if I might have a word with you in private, Mr. Austin."

Austin took in the seriousness of the captain's expression. He had a good idea of why the captain wanted to see him. "Of course."

The captain led him to a ready room near the mess hall and told him to take a seat.

"I've got some questions to ask you."

"Go right ahead."

"It's about those bodies. Who or *what* are they?"

"One of them is a Scottish chemist named MacLean. Angus MacLean. I'm not sure who the other one is, or *was*. I've been told that he is a mutant, the result of a scientific experiment gone wrong."

"What kind of experiment could produce a monster like that poor devil?"

"I'm not privy to the details."

The captain shook his head in disbelief. "Who shot them?"

"They were killed trying escape from an island, where they were being held prisoner." He gave the position.

"The *forbidden island*? I've patrolled these waters for two decades and have never set foot on the place. What in God's name were you doing there?"

"My colleague Paul Trout and the pilot of the submersible *Alvin* were being held against their will. We went ashore on a rescue mission and ran into a little trouble."

"Who was keeping them prisoner?"

"I don't know. I suggest that we straighten it all out when we get back to shore."

A young crewman came into the room and handed Captain Bruce a sheet of folded paper. "These just came in, sir."

"Thank you," the captain said. He excused himself and read the messages and handed one to Kurt. It was from Rudi Gunn.

"Glad all are well. Details soon? Rudi."

The captain read the other note and raised his eyebrows.

"It seems that you have what Americans call 'clout,' Mr. Austin. The central Coast Guard command has been contacted by the Admiralty. We are to treat you with the utmost courtesy, and to give you anything you want."

"Do British vessels still stock grog?" Austin said.

"I don't have any grog, but I have a bottle of fine Scotch whiskey in my cabin."

"That will do just fine," Austin said.

35

A WELCOME OF A different sort greeted the *Scapa* as it sidled up to the dock at Kirkwall, Orkney's capital. Lined up on shore, waiting for the Coast Guard boat to arrive, were a bus, a hearse and about two dozen figures dressed in white hooded contamination suits.

Austin stood at the rail of the boat with Captain Bruce. He eyed the welcoming committee and said, "That's either a decontamination team or the latest in British fashion."

"From the looks of things, my crew won't be going on shore leave anytime soon," the captain said. "The *Scapa* and its crew have been quarantined in case you and your friends have left any nasty bugs behind."

"Sorry to cause you all this trouble, Captain."

"Nonsense," Captain Bruce said. "Your visit has certainly enlivened what would have been a routine patrol. And as I say, it's what we do."

Austin shook hands with the captain, then he and the other refugees from the island walked down the gangway. As each passenger set foot on land, he or she was asked to don a clear plastic suit and cap and a surgical mask. Then they were escorted onto the bus and the dead were loaded into the hearse. The passengers were asked not to raise the window blinds. After a ride of five minutes, they stepped off the bus in front of the large brick building that once could have served as a warehouse.

A huge bubble tent had been set up inside the building to serve as a decontamination lab staffed by more people in white suits. Everyone who had been on the island was asked to shower and their clothes were stuffed in plastic bags and taken off to be analyzed. When they were finished showering, they were given cotton hospital outfits that made them look like mental patients, poked and prodded by a phalanx of plastic-wrapped doctors and pronounced fit to rejoin the human race. Despite the indignities, they were treated with the utmost politeness.

After being examined, Austin and his NUMA colleagues were given back their neatly folded and newly laundered clothes. Then they were taken into a small, mostly bare room furnished with several chairs and a table. At their entry, the man in the pin-striped suit who sat behind the table stood and introduced himself as Anthony Mayhew. He said he was with MI5, the British domestic intelligence service, and asked them to take a seat. Mayhew had finely chiseled features, and an upper-class accent that led Austin to say, "Oxford?"

"Cambridge, actually," he said with a smile. Mayhew talked in clipped sentences, as if he had taken verbal shears to extraneous words. "Distinction is hard to catch. My apologies for the folderol with the sawbones and those lab people in the space suits. Hope you weren't inconvenienced."

"Not all. We were badly in need of showers," Austin said.

"Please tell whoever does our laundry to use a little less starch in our collars," Zavala added.

A chuckle escaped Mayhew's thin lips. "I'll do that. MI5 are well acquainted with the work of NUMA's Special Assignments Team. But once the brass heard from Captain Bruce about dead bodies, secret experiments and mutants, they simply panicked like the good civil servants they are.

They wanted to make sure you wouldn't contaminate the British Isles."

Austin grimaced. "I didn't think we smelled *that* bad."

Mayhew gave Austin a blank look, and then broke into laughter. "American humor. I should have known. I spent several years on assignment in the States. My superiors were less worried about odor than having a deadly virus be unleashed."

"We wouldn't dream of contaminating our English cousins," Austin said. "Please assure your superiors that this has nothing to do with biological warfare."

"I'll do that as well," Mayhew said. He looked from face to face. "Please, could *some*one please explain what the devil is going on?"

Austin turned to Trout. "Paul is in the best position to fill you in on island life. The rest of us were only there for a few hours."

Trout's lips tightened in a wry grin. "Let me start by saying that the island is not exactly a Club Med."

He then laid out the story, from the *Alvin*'s aborted dive on the Lost City to his escape and rescue.

Austin expected a snort of disbelief when Trout described his work on the Philosopher's Stone, but instead, Mayhew slapped his knee in an un-British display of emotion. "This fits like a glove. I *knew* there was something big behind the scientists' deaths."

"I'm afraid you've lost us," Austin said.

"Pardon me. Several months ago, my department was called in to investigate a bizarre series of deaths involving a number of scientists. The first was a fifty-year-old computer expert who went out to his garden toolshed, wrapped bare electrical wires around his chest, stuck a handkerchief in his mouth and plugged the wires into an outlet. No apparent motive for killing himself."

Austin winced. "Very creative."

"That was only the beginning. Another scientist on his way home from a London party drove off a bridge. The police said his blood alcohol level far exceeded the legal level. But witnesses at the party said he had not been drinking and his relatives said the man never drank anything stronger than port. He'd throw up if he did. On top of that, someone had put old worn-out tires on his meticulously maintained Rover."

"You're starting to interest me," Austin said.

"Oh, it gets better. A thirty-five-year-old scientist ran a car filled with gas cans into a brick wall. Apparent suicide, the authorities said. Another chap was found under a bridge. Suicide again, the police said. Evidence of alcohol abuse and depression. Family said he never drank alcohol in his life, out of religious conviction, and that there was no depression. Here's another. Chap in his twenties ties one end of a nylon cord around his neck, the other end to a tree, gets back in the car and speeds off. Decapitation."

"How many of these strange deaths did you investigate?"

"Around two dozen. All scientists."

Austin let out a low whistle. "What's the connection to the forbidden island?"

"None that we knew of at the time. A couple of the scientists were American, so we had a request from the U.S. embassy to look into it. Some MPs have asked for a full-scale inquiry. I was told to nose around and given a very small investigative staff, not to make a big thing of it, and report my findings directly to the prime minister's office."

"Sounds as if the brass wasn't anxious to stir things up," Austin said.

"Exactly my impression," Mayhew said. "Talked to the relatives and learned that all the dead men had formerly worked for the same research lab."

"MacLean's former employer?" Trout said.

"That's right. When we couldn't find MacLean, we assumed he had met an untimely end or had something to do with the deaths of his colleagues. Now here he turns up on your island, dead unfortunately, thereby establishing the connection to the lab."

Trout leaned forward in his chair. "What was the nature of the research?"

"They were supposedly doing research into the human immune system at a facility in France. It was apparently a subsidiary of a larger, multinational corporation, but they did a good job of hiding ownership in layer after layer of straw companies, dummy corporations and overseas bank accounts. We're still trying to trace the line of ownership."

"And if you do, you'll charge them with murdering those scientists," Austin said.

"That's the least of it," Mayhew said. "From Dr. Trout's account, it seems that the work they were doing created those mutants and condemned them to a living death."

"Let me sum up what we have so far," Austin said. "This lab employs scientists to work on a project to come up with the so-called Philosopher's Stone, an elixir based on ocean enzymes from the Lost City. The scientists are apparently successful in producing a formula that prolongs life, thereby ensuring their own premature deaths. MacLean escapes, but is brought back to lead a reconstituted scientific team to correct flaws in the formula. Flaws that produce awful mutations. Paul blunders into their mining operation and is drafted to work in their lab."

"The pieces fit together like clockwork," Mayhew said. "May I ask you a question, Mr. Austin? Why didn't you contact the British authorities immediately with this information?"

"Let me answer that with a question of my own. Would you have believed me if I showed up at your door raving about red-eyed fiends?"

"Absolutely not," Mayhew said.

"Thanks for being honest. You must know that it would have taken time going through regular channels. We felt that any delay might be fatal. Paul Trout is a friend as well as a colleague."

"I can understand that. As I said, I'm acquainted with the work of your Special Assignments Team and know you were probably more than up to the task. I had to ask you the question because my superiors would ask it of me."

Gamay said, "Is anyone in your government going to investigate the island?"

"A naval ship is on its way," Mayhew said. "It's carrying a contingent of Royal Marines who will be sent ashore. They'll attempt to find this submarine, seal off the labs, and neutralize the guards and these mutants."

"From what I saw, I doubt you'll find much left of the guards," Trout said.

There was a moment of silence as Trout's words sank in, then Mayhew said, "You had the most experience with these mutants, Dr. Trout. What was your impression?"

"They are savage, cannibalistic and incredibly strong. They are able to communicate, and judging from their raid on the *Outcasts* island, they can plan." He paused, thinking about his encounter with the mutant in the Zoo. "I don't think their essential human qualities have all been eliminated."

Mayhew replied with an enigmatic smile. "Fascinating. I think we're done here, but I wonder if you could spare a few more minutes. I have something of interest I'd like to show you."

Mayhew led them through a labyrinth of corridors until they came to a chilly room that had been set up as a medical examiner's lab. A plastic sheet covered a form that lay on a metal table illuminated by a spotlight. A middle-aged man in a white lab coat was standing next to the table.

Mayhew signaled the man and he pulled the sheet back to reveal the ravaged face of the red-eyed creature that had been shot aboard their boat. He didn't seem so terrible with his eyes closed. His face had lost its permanent snarl and seemed more in repose.

"A little rough around the edges," Mayhew said. "Not bad-looking for a Frenchman."

"Are you displaying your Anglo bias or do you know for a fact that he's French?" Austin said.

Mayhew smiled and reached into his pocket, producing a thin metal tab with a chain attached. He handed the object to Austin. "This was around this gentleman's neck. It's a little timeworn, but you can read the writing."

Austin held the tab under the light and read the words: *Pierre Levant Capitaine, L'Armee de la Republique de France, b. 1885.*

"Looks like our friend here stole someone's dog tag."

"I had the same thought at first, but the tag actually belongs to this chap."

Austin responded with a quizzical look. Mayhew was not smiling as he would if he meant the wild assertion as a joke.

"That would make him more than one hundred years old," Austin said.

"Close to one hundred and twenty, to be exact."

"There must be some mistake. How can you be sure this is the man whose name is on the dog tag? Millions of men were lost during World War One."

"Quite true, but the armies did a tolerably good job of keeping records despite the chaos. Men were often identified by their comrades or officers. As the fighting moved on, bodies were cleared by special units and the director of graves registration took over, aided by the unit chaplain. There were cemetery maps drawn, information filtered through a casualty clearing station, hospitals and grave registrations and so on. That information has been put on a computer. We learned that there was a Pierre Levant, that he served as an officer in the French army and that he disappeared in action."

"A lot of men disappeared in action."

"Oh, you skeptical Americans," Mayhew said. He reached into his suit and pulled out a pocket watch, which he handed to Austin. "We found this in his pocket. He was quite a handsome devil at one time."

Austin examined the inscription on the back of the watch. "*À Pierre, de Claudette, avec amour.*" Then he flipped the watch open. Set into the cover was a picture of a young man and woman.

He showed the watch to the other members of the NUMA team. "What do you think?"

Gamay examined the tag and the watch. "One of the first things I learned in marine archaeology was the importance of establishing provenance. For instance, a Roman coin found in a Connecticut cornfield could mean that a Roman had dropped it, but it's just as likely the source was a Colonial-era coin collector."

Mayhew sighed. "Perhaps Dr. Blair can convince you."

"I didn't believe it either," said the white-frocked pathologist. "We did an autopsy on the gentleman. The cells in this individual are comparable to those of a man in his late twenties, but the brain sutures, the joints of the skull, indicate the gentleman is—" He cleared his throat. "Ah, more than a hundred years old."

"That would mean the work on the life extension formula goes back much further than we've assumed," Austin said.

"An incredible yet reasonable assumption," Mayhew said. "There were rumors during World War One of attempts to develop a "berserker," a super-soldier of sorts who would charge enemy trenches in the face of fierce fire."

"You're thinking that it's related to the life extension research?"

"I don't know," Mayhew said. He drew the sheet back over the creature's face.

"Poor hombre," Zavala said, glancing at the happy couple in the watch photograph. "What a waste of a hundred years."

"We may only have uncovered the tip of the iceberg," Mayhew said. "Who knows how many have died to keep this terrible secret?"

"I don't blame them for not advertising failures like the one on that table," Gamay said.

"It goes beyond that," Mayhew said. "Suppose this elixir has been perfected. What kind of a world would we have if some people could live longer than others?"

"A world that will be very much off balance," Gamay ventured.

"My feelings exactly, but I'm a lowly detective. I'll leave that for the analysts and policymakers to deal with. Do you plan to stay long in the UK?" he asked Austin.

"Probably not," Austin said. "We'll talk about our plans and let you know what we decide."

"I'd appreciate that." Mayhew produced a business card with his name and phone number and handed it to Austin. "Please call. Night or day. In the meantime, I can't overemphasize the importance of keeping this to yourselves."

"My report will go only to Dirk Pitt and Rudi Gunn. I'm sure the Woods Hole Oceanographic Institution will be interested in the fate of its submersible."

"Fine. I'll let you know what our marines find on the island. Maybe we can track down the people behind this thing. Murder, kidnapping, hijacking, slave labor," he mused. "Immortality is a potent motive for evil. I'd wager that anyone in this room would sell his firstborn rather than pass up the chance to live forever."

"Not everyone," said Austin.

"What do you mean? Given the chance, who wouldn't want to live forever?"

Austin gesturing toward the sheet-draped gurney. "Ask the old soldier lying on that table."

36

"I HATE TO THROW cold water on this warm-hearted reunion," Gamay said. "But with all this talk of red-eyed monsters and the Philosopher's Stone, we've forgotten we have some unfinished business to attend to."

After the meeting with Mayhew, they had gone to their hotel lounge to discuss strategy. Sandy, the *Alvin* pilot, had been anxious to leave, and Mayhew had put her on a flight to London where she could catch a plane home. The scientists were still being debriefed.

"You're right," Zavala said, lifting his glass to the light. "I'm way behind in my goal to drink all the top-shelf tequila in the world."

"That's very laudable, Joe, but I'm more interested in the *survival* of the world, not its tequila supply," Gamay said. "May I sum the problem up in one word? Gorgonweed."

"I haven't forgotten," Austin said. "I didn't want to spoil your reunion with Paul. Now that you've brought the subject up, what's the situation?"

"Not good," Gamay said. "I've talked to Dr. Osborne, the infestation is spreading faster than anyone imagined."

"The mining operation has been stopped. Won't this halt the spread of Gorgonweed?" Austin said.

Gamay heaved a heavy sigh. "I wish. The mutated weed has become self-replicating and will continue to spread. We'll see harbors clogged along the east coast of the U.S first, then Europe and the Pacific coast. The weed will continue its spread to other continents."

"How long do we have?"

"I don't know," Gamay said. "The ocean currents are moving the stuff all around the Atlantic."

Austin tried to picture his beloved ocean turned into a noxious saltwater swamp.

"Ironic, isn't it?" Austin said. "The Fauchards want to extend their lives, and in doing so they will produce a world that may not be worth living in." He looked around the table. "Any idea how we can stop this thing?"

"The Lost City enzyme holds the key to halting the weed's spread," Gamay said. "If we can figure out the basic molecular makeup, we may be able to find a way to reverse the process."

"My body is covered with bumps and bruises that tell me the Fauchards don't give up family secrets easily," Austin said.

"That's why Gamay and I should go back to Washington to set up a conference at NUMA with Dr. Osborne," Trout said. "We can try to get a flight out of here the first thing in the morning."

"Go to it." Austin looked around at the weary faces. "But first I suggest we all get a good night's sleep."

After bidding his friends a good-night, Austin found a computer room off the hotel lobby, where he did an abbreviated report for Rudi Gunn and sent it off by e-mail with the promise to follow up with a call in the morning. He rubbed his eyes a few times as he was typing and was glad when he pressed the SEND button and sent the message winging across the ocean.

He went up to his room and noticed that someone had

called his cell phone. He returned the call, which turned out to be from Darnay. He had located Austin through his NUMA office.

"Thank God I have found you, Monsieur Austin," the antiquities dealer said. "Have you heard from Skye?"

"Not lately," Austin said. "I've been on the move or out at sea. I thought she was with you."

"She left here the same day she arrived. We had discovered what looked like a chemical equation etched into the crown of the helmet and she wanted to show it to an expert at the Sorbonne. I saw her off at the train. When I didn't hear from her after that night, I called the university the next day. They said she hadn't been in."

"Maybe she's been sick."

"I wish that were so. I called her apartment. There was no answer. I spoke to her landlady. Mademoiselle Skye never returned to her home after visiting me in Provence."

"I think you had better call the police," Austin said without hesitation.

"The *police*?"

"I know you have an understandable aversion to the authorities," Austin said in a firm voice, "but you must do this for Skye. Make an anonymous call from a pay phone if you'd like, but you must call them and report her missing. Her life may depend on it."

"Yes, yes, of course. I'll call them. She's like a daughter to me. I warned her to be careful, but you know how young people are."

"I'm in Scotland now, but I'll return to France tomorrow. I'll call you again when I get to Paris." He hung up so Darnay could notify the police and stared into space for a few moments, trying to make sense of Skye's disappearance. His cell phone rang. It was Lessard, the manager of the glacier power plant.

"Austin? Thank God. I've been trying to get you," he said.

"Sorry. I've been away from the phone," Austin said. "How are things at the glacier?"

"The glacier is as it always is," Lessard said. "But there are some strange things going on here."

"What do you mean?"

"A few days ago, a boat came with divers on the lake. I wondered whether NUMA had come back to finish its survey, but the boat was not the color I remember."

"The survey is over," Austin said. "There was no NUMA activity planned that I know of. What else is happening?"

"An incredible thing. The tunnels under the glacier are being drained."

"I thought you said that was impossible."

"You misunderstood. It would have been impossible to do it in time to save the people who were trapped in the tunnel. It has taken a few days to divert and pump water, but the observatory tunnel is almost dry."

"Was this a decision of the power company?"

"My superiors hinted to me that the decision was the result of some influence at a very high level. The work is funded by a private scientific foundation."

"Is Dr. LeBlanc involved?"

"I thought so at first. His little car Fifi is still here, so I assumed he was coming back. One of the men who had been diving in the lake came to the plant, showed me the authorization, and his men have taken over the control room. They are a hard-looking bunch, Mr. Austin. They watch my every move. I am afraid for my life. I am talking now at great risk. I've been told not to intervene."

"Have you told your boss of your feelings?"

"Yes. He told me to cooperate. The decision is out of his hands. I didn't know where else to turn. So I called you."

"Can you leave?"

"I think it will be difficult. They sent my crew home, so there is only me. I will try to shut down the turbines. Maybe headquarters will take me seriously when the power stops."

"Do as you see best, but don't take any chances."

"I'll be careful."

"What was the name of the man who came to you?"

"Fauchard. Emil Fauchard. He reminds me of a snake."

Emil Fauchard.

"Behave as if everything is okay," Austin said. "I'll be at Le Dormeur tomorrow."

"*Merci beaucoup,* Mr. Austin. It would not be wise for you to show up at the front door, so how will I know when you've arrived?"

"I'll let you know."

They hung up and Austin pondered the turn of events. Then he picked up the hotel phone and called Joe and the Trouts to say that there had been a change of plans. When they showed up at his room, Austin told them about the phone calls.

"Do you think the Fauchards have kidnapped Skye?" Zavala said.

"It's a reasonable assumption, given their previous interest in the helmet."

"If they have the helmet, why would they need Skye?" Gamay asked.

"One guess."

Light dawned in Gamay's face. "I get it. They're using her as bait to lure you into a trap."

Austin nodded. "My first impulse was to go directly to Château Fauchard," Austin said. "But then I thought that is exactly what they would expect me to do. We should do the unexpected and go after Emil instead. He might be able to give us some leverage, and I'm worried about Lessard, too. I think he may be in immediate danger. They'll keep Skye alive until I take their bait."

"What would you like us to do?" Paul said.

"Probe the defenses around the château. See if there is a way in. But be careful. Madame Fauchard is much more dangerous than her son. He's a violent sociopath. She's smart as well as murderous."

"Charming," Gamay said. "I can hardly wait to meet her."

They bid each other good-night and returned to their rooms. Austin called the number on the card Mayhew had given him, told the intelligence agent that he needed to get out of Scotland as soon as possible and asked for his help. Mayhew said he was leaving the next morning on an executive jet and would be glad to give Austin and the others on the NUMA team a ride to London, where they could catch a shuttle to Paris.

Austin thanked him and said he would return the favor one day, and then went to catch a few hours of sleep. He lay in bed on his back and brushed aside distracting thoughts so he could concentrate on the task at hand, which was to rescue Skye. Before long, he fell into a restless sleep.

37

THE EXECUTIVE JET lifted off at daybreak the next morning, but instead of heading toward London's Heathrow airport it set a direct course for Paris. Before the plane was in the air, Austin had talked Mayhew into changing his flight plan. He said he didn't have time to go into details, but that it was a matter of life and death.

Mayhew asked only one question: "Does this have anything to do with the matter we discussed last night?"

"It could have everything to do with it."

"Then I should expect that you will keep me up-to-date as to the progress of your investigations?"

"I'll give you the same report I send to my superiors at NUMA."

Mayhew smiled and they shook hands on the deal. By late morning, they were at Charles De Gaulle airport. The Trouts split off and headed to château country and Austin and Zavala hopped aboard a charter flight to the quaint alpine village nearest the glacier.

Zavala had called his friend Denise in the French parliament. After extracting a promise from Zavala to see her again, she arranged to have a fast eighteen-foot powerboat waiting for them at the village. They had traveled up the twisting river all afternoon and arrived at Lac du Dormeur at dusk. Not wanting to announce their arrival, they kept their speed low as they crossed the misty, mirror-still lake waters and wove their way around the miniature icebergs that spotted the surface. The four-stroke outboard motor was whisper-quiet, but to Austin's ears it was like someone shouting in a cathedral.

Austin steered the boat toward a single-engine float-plane that was anchored a few feet off the beach. The boat pulled alongside the plane and Austin climbed onto a float to peer inside the cockpit. The plane was a de Havilland Otter with space for nine passengers. Three seats were stacked with scuba gear, confirming Lessard's observation that the plane was being used as a dive platform. Austin got back in the boat and surveyed the beach. Nothing moved in the gray light. He ran the boat farther along the shore, pulled it behind a rock outcropping, and then he and Zavala made the long hike up to the power plant.

They traveled lightly, carrying water, power bars, hand-guns and extra ammunition. Even so, it was dark when they reached the plant. The door to the portal building was unlocked. The interior of the building was hushed except for the hum of the turbine. Austin slowly pivoted on his heel as he stood in the power plant lobby, his ears tuned to the beehive humming that issued from the bowels of the mountain. His coral-blue eyes narrowed. "Something's wrong," he said to Zavala. "The turbine is working."

"This is a power plant," Zavala said. "Isn't the generator *supposed* to be working?"

"Yes, under normal circumstances. But Lessard told me on the phone that he would try to shut down the turbine. The power loss would start bells clanging at the main office and they'd have to send someone in to investigate."

"Maybe Lessard changed his mind," Zavala said.

Austin shook his head almost imperceptibly. "I hope it wasn't changed *for* him."

After exploring the office and living quarters, Austin

and Zavala left the lobby and made their way to the control room. Austin paused outside the door. All was quiet, but Austin's sixth sense told him that there was someone in the control room. He drew his pistol, signaled Zavala to do the same and stepped inside. That's when he saw Lessard. The plant manager looked as if he had fallen asleep, but the bullet hole in his back proclaimed otherwise. His right arm was outstretched, his fingers inches away from the blood-spattered line of switches that would have stopped the generator.

A look of barely restrained rage came to Austin's face. He silently vowed that someone would pay for killing the gracious Frenchman whose expertise had enabled Austin to rescue Skye and the other scientists trapped under the glacier. He touched Lessard's neck. The body was cold. Lessard was probably killed shortly after he called Austin.

The fact that it would have been impossible to save the Frenchman gave Austin little solace. He went over to the computer monitor that displayed a diagram of the tunnel system and sat down in front of the screen to study the flow of water through the tunnels. Lessard had done a masterful job of diverting the water from the glacial streams away from the observatory tunnel using a complex system of detours.

"The tunnels are color-coded," he explained to Zavala. "The blinking blue lines show the tunnels that are wet and the red lines indicate the dry water conduits." He tapped a red line. "Here's the tunnel we used in the rescue."

Zavala leaned over Austin's shoulder and with his finger traced a convoluted route from the observatory access tunnel back to the power plant. "Quite the maze. We'll have to double back a few times and make a couple of jogs."

"Think of it as a cross between a fun house and a water park," Austin said. "We should come out where our pal Sebastian blew off the sluice gate. From there it's a short walk to the observatory. Now for the bad news. We've probably got ten to fifteen miles of tunnels to navigate."

"It could take hours, longer if we get lost."

"Not necessarily," Austin said, recalling something Lessard had said about Dr. LeBlanc.

He ran off a printout of the computer display and cast a sad glance at Lessard's body, and then he and Zavala left the control room. Moments later, they were on the observation platform where Lessard had shown Austin the power of the glacier's melt water. The torrent that had reminded Austin of the Colorado River rapids had become a narrow stream a few yards wide and a foot deep.

Satisfied that the tunnel had been drained, he and Zavala went back through the lobby and out the front door of the plant. They walked a couple of hundred yards from the plant's entrance to a sheet-metal garage butted up against the mountain wall. The garage housed two vehicles, the utility truck that had picked Austin up on his first visit to the power plant, and, under a plastic cover, Dr. LeBlanc's beloved Citroën 2C.

Austin removed the cloth. "Meet Fifi," he said.

"Fifi?"

"It belongs to one of the glacier scientists. He has a thing for her."

"I've seen prettier women," Zavala said, "but I've always said that it's personality that counts."

With its humped back and sloping hood, the tough little Citroën 2C was one of the most distinctive cars ever produced. The auto's designer had said he wanted "four wheels under an umbrella," a car that could cross a plowed field without breaking eggs carried in a basket. Fifi had seen some hard miles. Her half-moon rear wheel covers were dented, and the faded red paint almost pink and pitted by sand and gravel. Yet she had the jaunty air of a woman who was never beautiful but infinitely sure of her ability to cope with life.

The key was in the ignition. They got in the car and started the engine with no problem. Then he and Zavala drove along a gravel road that followed the base of the mountain wall until they came to a set of high double doors. Austin consulted the map and saw that they were at the site marked *Porte de Sillon.* He wasn't sure of the correct translation, but he reasoned that the huge drilling machines that bored out the tunnels must have had a way to get in and out of the mountain.

The doors were made of heavy steel, but they were well balanced and opened easily. Austin drove Fifi through the opening into the tunnel, where the whine of her tiny engine echoed off the walls and ceilings. The tunnel went straight into the mountain past the turbine room and entered the main system. They would have been lost in the maze of intersecting tunnels if not for the map. Zavala did yeoman service as a navigator, despite Austin's heavy foot and his quick turns. Fifteen minutes after they had entered the tunnels, Zavala told Austin to take a left at the next intersection.

"We're almost at the observatory tunnel," he said.

"How far?"

"About a half of a mile."

"I think we'd better leave Fifi and walk from here."

Like the rest of the system, the tunnel had a string of lights running along the ceiling. Many of the bulbs had burned out and not been replaced. The sporadic lighting intensified the blackness of the unlit sections between the pale circles of light. As the two men trudged along, the dripping orange walls gave off a damp raw cold that numbed their faces and the chill tried to sneak in around the collars of the down jackets they had found in the crew quarters.

"They told me that when I joined NUMA I would go places," Zavala said. "But I didn't know I'd have to *walk* there."

"Think of it as a character-building experience," Austin said cheerfully.

After a few more minutes of character building, they came to a ladder that ran up the side of a wall to a catwalk. A section of the walkway was enclosed by plastic and glass. Austin remembered Lessard mentioning satellite control rooms scattered throughout the tunnel system. They kept on walking and had just turned into a new tunnel when Austin's keen ear picked up a sound that was loud enough to drown out the ongoing chorus of gurgles and drips.

"What's that?" he said, cupping his hand to his ear.

Zavala listened for a moment. "Sounds like a locomotive."

Austin shook his head. "That's no ghost train. *Run!*"

Zavala was transfixed. He stood in place, as rigid as a statue, until Austin's voice pulled him out of his trance. Then he took off like a sprinter at the starting gun, keeping a step behind Austin. They splashed through puddles, ignoring the spray that soaked their clothes from the waist down.

The rushing grew louder and became a roar. Austin made a quick right-angle turn into another tunnel. Zavala tried to follow, but skidded on the wet floor. Austin saw Zavala fall. He went back and pulled his friend up by the wrist and they were off again, running from the unseen menace. The floor seemed to vibrate under their pounding feet as the noise reached a mind-numbing level.

Austin's frantic eyes saw the metal ladder that ran up the wall to the catwalk. He grabbed onto the first rung and pulled himself up like a circus acrobat. Zavala had hurt his knee in his fall and was having trouble climbing with his usual agility. Austin reached down and pulled his partner onto the catwalk and they dove into the control booth.

Just in time.

A second after they had slammed the watertight door shut, a huge blue wave cascaded through the tunnel. The catwalk disappeared under the rushing, foaming water that battered the windows like seas slamming into a ship in a storm. The catwalk shook from the impact, and for a moment Austin feared that the whole structure, control booth and all, would be washed away.

After the first shock, the torrent moderated, but the height of the river still reached the bottom of the catwalk. Austin went over to the control panel and stared at the diagram. He was worried that a sluice gate had given way, allowing the full force of the glacial melt water to pour through the tunnel. If that were the case, they would be stuck in the control room until they died or the glacier melted entirely.

The tunnel line was still red, indicating that it was dry. He saw this as a ray of hope because it meant that the flow of water came from a pocket of water and might have a beginning and an end.

It turned out to be a very *large* pocket. Five minutes that seemed like five years went by before the flow of water began to abate. Once the water level started to drop, it did so with great rapidity until they were able to go out onto the catwalk without danger of being washed off.

Zavala watched the still-formidable torrent and yelled over the sound, "I thought you said this would be like a fun house. Some fun. Some house."

"I think I said something about a water park, too."

It took another ten minutes for the water flow to diminish to a point where it was safe to descend the ladder. Austin considered the possibility of other pockets bursting open, but put the thought out of his mind and led the way through the maze of tunnels. On one occasion, a tunnel that was supposed to be dry proved to be otherwise. They would have become dangerously wet instead of uncomfortably damp if they had tried to ford the stream, and chose to detour around it.

According to the map, they were within minutes of the access tunnel to the glacial observatory. Eventually, they came to a massive steel door that was similar to the sluice gates they had seen in other tunnels. This one was different from the others they had encountered. The thick steel was peeled back like the skin of an orange.

Zavala went over and gingerly touched the twisted steel. "This must be the door that Fauchard's goon blew off its hinges."

Austin borrowed the map and pointed to a tunnel line. "We're here," he said. "We go through the door and take a right and the observatory is about a half a mile walk. We'd better stay alert and keep the noise down."

"I'll do my best to keep my teeth from chattering, but it won't be easy."

Their lighthearted bantering was deceptive. Both men were well aware of the potential danger they faced, and their concern was evident in the care they used to check their firearms. As they entered the main tunnel, Austin gave Zavala a whispered description of the lab setup. He told him about the lab buildings, then the staircase leading to the observatory tunnel and the ice chamber where Jules Fauchard was entombed.

They were nearing the lab trailers when Zavala started limping again. His injured knee was giving him trouble. He told Austin to go ahead, and he'd catch up in a minute. Austin thought about checking out the trailers, but the windows were dark and he assumed that Emil and his men were in the observatory itself. He learned that he was wrong when a door swung quietly open behind him and a man's voice told him in French to get his hands in the air. Then he was ordered to turn around, slowly.

In the murky light, Austin could make out a hulking figure. Although the tunnel was dim, stray shafts of light reflected off the gun pointed in his direction.

"Hello," Sebastian said in a pleasant voice. "Master Emil has been waiting for you."

38

THE ROADSIDE BISTRO was like a desert watering hole to the Trouts, who had been on the go for most of the day. They beat a path to the door of the converted farmhouse and were soon seated in a dining room that overlooked a formal flower garden. Although the stop was motivated by hunger and thirst, it proved to be a stroke of luck. Not only was the food excellent, the bistro's handsome young owner was the equivalent of a chamber of commerce information booth.

He overheard Paul and Gamay speaking English and he came over to their table to introduce himself. His name was Bertrand, "Bert" for short, and he had been a chef in New York City for a few years before returning to France to open his own place. He was pleased at the chance to talk American English and they answered his queries about the States with good-natured patience. As a Jets fan, he was particularly interested in football. As a Frenchman, he was intrigued as well by Gamay and her unusual name.

"C'est belle," he said. *"C'est très belle."*

"My father's idea," she explained. "He was a wine connoisseur, and the color of my hair reminded him of the grape of Beaujolais."

Bert's appreciative eyes took in Gamay's long swept-up coif and her flashing smile. "Your father was a lucky man to have such a lovely daughter. And you, Monsieur Trout, are fortunate to have a beautiful wife."

"Thank you," Paul said, putting his arm around Gamay's shoulder in an unmistakable male gesture that said, You can look but don't touch.

Bert smiled in understanding as the subtle message sunk in and again became the professional host. "Are you here on business or for pleasure?"

"A bit of both," Gamay replied.

"We own a small chain of wine shops in the Washington area," Paul explained, using the cover story he and Gamay had cooked up. He handed Bert one of the business cards he and Gamay had hastily printed up at an airport copy shop during their Paris stopover. "As we travel about, we like to keep an eye out for small vineyards that might be able to offer something special for our discerning customers."

Bert clapped his hands as if in light applause. "You and your wife have come to the right place, Monsieur Trout. The wine you're drinking is from an estate not far from here. I can get you an introduction to the owner."

Gamay took a sip from her glass. "A robust red. Precocious and lively. It has high notes of raspberry."

"There's a hint of mischievousness to it that I like," Paul said. "Combined with low notes of pepper."

Both Trouts tended toward microbrewery beer, and their knowledge of wine was gleaned mostly from the labels, but Bert nodded sagely. "You are true wine aficionados."

"Thank you," Gamay said. "Do you have any other vineyard suggestions?"

"*Oui*, Madame Trout. Many." Bert jotted down several names on a napkin, which Paul tucked into his pocket.

"Someone mentioned another vineyard," Gamay said. "What was that name, dear?"

"Fauchard?" Paul said.

"That's it." She turned back to Bertrand. "Do you carry the Fauchard label?"

"*Mon Dieu.* I wish I did. It's a superb wine. Their production is very limited and their wine is bought by a select group of wealthy people, mostly Europeans and rich Americans. Even if I could get it, the wine is much too expensive for my customers. We're talking a thousand dollars a bottle."

"Really?" Gamay said. "We'd love to visit the Fauchard estate and see what sort of grapes can fetch prices like that."

Bert hesitated and a frown came to his handsome face. "It's not far from here, but the Fauchards are . . . how can I put it? Odd."

"In what way?"

"Not very friendly. Nobody sees them." He spread his hands. "They are an old family and there are stories."

"What sort of stories?"

"Old wives' tales. Farmers can be superstitious. They say the Fauchards are *sangsues.* Bloodsuckers."

"You mean vampires?" Gamay said with a smile.

"*Oui.*" Bert laughed and said, "I think they simply have so much money they are always afraid people will steal it. They are not typical of the people who live here. We are very friendly. I hope the Fauchards don't give you the wrong impression."

"That would be impossible after enjoying your fine food and hospitality," she said with a sly smile.

Bert beamed with pleasure and, using another napkin, wrote down directions to the Fauchard estate. They could get a glimpse of the vineyards, he said, but the NO TRESPASSING signs will warn them when they get closer to the estate. They thanked him, exchanged hugs and cheek busses in the French manner and got back in their car.

Gamay broke into laughter. "A *mischievous* wine? I can't believe you said that."

"I'd rather have a mischievous wine than a *precocious* vintage," Paul said with a haughty sniff.

"You must admit it had high notes of raspberry," she said.

"And low notes of pepper, too," Paul replied. "I don't think Bert noticed our viticultural pretensions. He was fixated on you. 'You 'ave a beeyootiful wife,' " Trout said in an accent like that of the old film star Charles Boyer.

"I think he was quite charming," Gamay said with a pout.

"So do I, and he was completely right about how lucky I am."

"*That's* more like it," she said. She consulted the map Bert had drawn on the napkin. "There's a turnoff that goes to the château about ten miles from here."

"Bert made it sound like Castle *Dracula*," Paul said.

"From what Kurt told us, Madame Fauchard makes Dracula look like Mother Teresa."

Twenty minutes later, they were driving down a long dirt road that ran through rolling hills and neatly terraced vineyards. Unlike the other vineyards they had passed on the way, there were no signs identifying the owners of the grapevines. But as the surrounding countryside changed to woods, they began to see signs on the trees warning in French, English and Spanish that they were on private property.

The road ended at a gate in a high chain-link electrified fence topped with razor wire. The sign at the gate had an even sterner warning, again in three languages, saying that trespassers venturing farther would encounter armed guards and watchdogs. The threat of bodily harm to unauthorized persons was unmistakable.

Paul read the signs and said, "It appears that Bert was right about the Fauchards. They're not the warm-and-fuzzy type."

"Oh, I don't know," Gamay said. "If you look in your rearview mirror, you'll see that they sent someone out to greet us."

Paul did as Gamay suggested and saw the grille emblem of a black Mercedes SUV through the window of their rented Peugeot. The Mercedes blocked the road behind them. Two men got out of the vehicle. One was short and stocky and had a shaved head shaped like a bullet. He held the leash of a fierce-looking Rottweiler who wheezed as he strained against his choke collar. The second man was tall and dark-complexioned and had the fleshy nose of a prize-fighter. Both men wore military-style camouflage uniforms and sidearms.

The bald man came over to the driver's side and spoke in French, which was not Paul's strong suit, but he had no problem understanding the order to get out of the car. Gamay, on the other hand, was fluent. When the bullet-headed man asked what they were doing there, she handed him a business card, produced the napkin Bert had given them and showed them the vineyards listed on it.

The man glanced at the names. "This is the Fauchard estate. The place you want is that way," he said, pointing.

Gamay seemed to get agitated. She burst into a nonstop stream of French, gesturing frequently at Paul. The guards started laughing at the husbandly harangue. Bullethead gave Gamay a head-to-toe body sweep with his eyes that was more than casual. Gamay returned his unabashed interest with a coy smile. Then he, his companion and the dog got back into the Mercedes. They moved the SUV out of the way so that Paul could back out. As the car drove off, Gamay gave the guards a wave that was eagerly returned.

"Looks like we met Kurt's skinhead friend Marcel," Trout said.

"He certainly fits the menacing description," Gamay said.

"He was a lot friendlier than I expected," Trout said. "You even had the dog smiling. What did you say?"

"I told them that you were an idiot for getting us lost."

"Oh," Trout said. "And what did baldy say?"

"He said he would be glad to show me the way. I think he was flirting with me."

Trout gave her a sidelong glance. "This is the second time you've used your feminine charms. First with Bert, then on Bullethead and his mutt."

"All's fair in love and war."

"It's not the *war* I'm worried about. Every Frenchman we meet seems to have bedroom eyes."

"Oh, shush. I asked him if we could drive around and look at the grapes. He said that was all right, but to stay away from the fence."

Trout turned off at the first dirt road and they bumped along through acre after acre of vineyards. After a few minutes, they pulled over and got out of the car near a crew of grape pickers who were taking a cigarette break by the roadside. There were about a dozen dark-skinned workers talking to a man who seemed to be in charge. Gamay introduced themselves as American wine buyers. The man frowned when she explained that Marcel had given them permission to drive through the vineyards.

"Oh, *that* one," the man said with a frown. He said his name was Guy Marchand and he was the foreman of the work crew.

"They are guest workers from Senegal," he said. "They work very hard, so I go easy on them."

"We stopped at the bistro and talked to Bertrand," Gamay said. "He told us the wine produced here is wonderful."

"*Oui. C'est vrai.* Come, I'll show you the vines."

He waved the grape pickers back to work and led the Trouts down a line of vines. He was a voluble talker and enthusiastic about his work, and the Trouts had no need to do their wine snob act. They had only to nod their heads as Guy went on about soil, climate and grapes. He stopped at a vine trellis and plucked a few grapes, which he handed to Gamay and Paul. He squeezed the grapes, sniffed them and tasted the juice with the tip of his tongue. They followed suit, clucking with admiration. They headed back to the road and saw that the workers were dumping grapes into the back of a truck.

"Where is the wine bottled?" Paul said.

"On the estate itself," Guy said. "Monsieur Emil wants to make sure every bottle is accounted for."

"Who is Monsieur Emil?" Gamay said.

"Emil Fauchard is the owner of these vineyards."

"Do you think it would be possible to meet Monsieur Fauchard?" Gamay said.

"No, he keeps to himself."

"So you never see him?"

"Oh yes, we see him," Marchand said. He rolled his eyes and pointed toward the sky.

Both Trouts looked up. "I don't understand," Gamay said.

"He flies over in his little red plane to keep watch."

Guy went on to explain that Emil personally dusted the crops. He told them that Emil had once dusted one of the work crews with pesticides. Some workers became violently ill and had to be transported to the hospital. They were all illegal immigrants, so they didn't complain, but Marchand threatened to quit and the workers were given paltry gifts of money in compensation. He'd been told the dusting was an accident, although it was clear from the tone of his voice that he thought Emil had done it on purpose. But the Fauchards had paid him well and he didn't complain.

While Marchand talked, the workers finished loading the truck. Paul's eyes followed the truck as it trundled along the dirt road. After going about a quarter of a mile, it took a left-hand turn and headed toward a gate in the electrified fence. As a fisherman, Paul had developed a keen eye for detail and he could see a couple of guards standing in front of the gate. He watched the truck slow down, then it was waved through and the gate closed behind it.

Paul tapped Gamay's shoulder and said, "I think it's time to go."

They thanked Marchand, got in their car and headed back to the main road that would take them out of the vineyards.

"Interesting conversation," Gamay said. "Emil sounds just as lovely as Kurt described him." Paul only grunted in return. Gamay was used to Paul's sometimes taciturn nature, a trait he had inherited from his New England forebears, but detected something deeper in his monosyllabic reply. "Is there anything wrong?"

"I'm fine. The story about the 'accidental' dusting got me thinking again about all the misery Emil and his family have caused. They're responsible for the death of Dr. MacLean and his scientific colleagues, and that Englishman, Cavendish. Who knows how many more they've killed through the years?"

Gamay nodded. "I can't get those poor mutants out of my mind. They've had to endure a living death."

Paul whacked the steering wheel with the palm of his hand. "It makes me want to punch someone in the nose."

Gamay was surprised at the uncharacteristic outburst. She arched an eyebrow. "We'll have to figure out a way to get past that fence and guards before we do any nose punching."

"That may be sooner than you think," Paul said with a smile, and he began to describe his plan.

39

SEBASTIAN SEARCHED Austin with a rough hand, relieving him of his gun, and then ordered him to move toward the stairs. They climbed the stairway and went along the Y-shaped passageway and up the wooden ladder to the ice cavern. A loud hissing came from the cavern and a steam cloud obscured its opening. Austin closed his eyes against the hot swirling steam and when he opened them he saw a silhouette in the mist.

Sebastian called out to the figure. Emil Fauchard materialized from the steam cloud like a magician making his appearance onstage. When he saw Austin, his lips contorted in rage and his pale features writhed into a Greek mask of fury. Wrath boiled within him like hot oil and he seemed barely able to contain himself. Then his mouth softened into a mirthless smile that was even worse. He closed a nozzle valve on the hose he was holding and the steam dissipated.

"Hello, Austin," he said in a knife-edged voice. "Sebastian and I hoped we'd meet again after you left our costume party without saying good-bye. But I must admit I expected you to go to the château to rescue your lady friend."

"I couldn't resist your warm snakelike personality," Austin said, his voice cool. "And I never did thank you for the loan of your plane. Why did you kill Lessard?"

"Who?"

"The plant manager."

"He had outlived his usefulness as soon as he drained the tunnels. I let him live until the last moment, letting him think he could stop the turbine and bring in outside help." Fauchard laughed at the memory.

Austin smiled as if he appreciated Fauchard's evil humor. He had to use all the self-discipline at his command to resist the fatal urge to tear the Frenchman's head off. He bided his time, knowing that he was in no position to take revenge.

"I saw your plane on the lake," Austin said. "It's a little cold for scuba diving."

"Your concern is appreciated. The Morane-Saulnier was exactly where you said it would be."

Austin glanced around the cavern. "You went through a great deal of trouble to flood this place," Austin said. "Why drain it again?"

The smile dissolved into a frown. "At the time, we wanted to keep Jules locked away from the prying eyes of the world."

"What changed your mind?"

"My mother wanted Jules's body back."

"I was unaware that the Fauchard family was so sentimental about its kinfolk."

"There's a lot about us you don't know."

"Glad I could make it to his coming-out party. How is the old boy?"

"See for yourself," Emil said, and stepped aside.

A section of wall had been melted and chipped away to create a blue grotto. Jules Fauchard lay on the raised platform like a human sacrifice to the god of the glacier. The body was on its side, curled up in a fetal position. Jules was still wearing his heavy leather flying coat and gloves, and his black boots were as shiny as if they had just been polished. He wore a parachute harness, but the actual parachute had been ripped off by powerful glacial forces. Although the corpse had been locked in the ice for nearly a century, the cold had kept it well preserved. The skin on the face and hands had a burnished copper look and the heavy handlebar mustache was coated with frost.

The hawk nose and firm jaw on the frozen face matched the features of the man in the Fauchard family gallery. Austin was especially interested in the hole that had punctured the fur-trimmed leather aviator's cap.

"Nice of your sentimental family to give Jules a going-away present," Austin said.

"What are you talking about?"

Austin gestured toward the hole. "The bullet in his head."

Emil sneered. "Jules was on his way to see the pope's emissary when he was shot out of the sky," Emil said. "He carried documents that would prove our family's complicity in starting the Great War. He also wanted to offer the world a scientific discovery that would be a boon to all mankind. He hoped to avert war with his actions."

"Laudable and unusual goals for a Fauchard," Austin said.

"He was a fool. *This* is where his altruism landed him."

"What happened to the documents he carried with him?"

"They were useless, ruined by water."

"Then it was all a big waste of time."

"Not at all. Look. You are here. And you will wish that you were chained in the château catacombs when I am through." Emil pointed to the ragged edge of ice that framed the opening to the grotto. "See? The ice is already re-forming. In a few hours, the tomb will again be resealed. And this time you will be inside, keeping Jules company."

Austin's mind was racing.

Where the hell was Zavala?

"I thought your mother wanted the body."

"What do *I* care about the body? My mother won't always be in power. I intend to lead the Fauchards to their greatest achievements. Enough stalling. I'm not going to indulge your pathetic effort to forestall the inevitable, Austin. You stole my airplane and treated it shabbily, and have caused me a great deal of trouble. Get over there next to Jules."

Austin stayed where he was. "Your family didn't give a rat's ass about being blamed for the war. It was an open secret that you and the other arms merchants wanted the bullets to fly. It was something bigger than any war. Jules was carrying the formula for eternal youth."

A startled expression flashed across Emil's face. "What do you know?"

"I know that the Fauchards will destroy anyone who stands in the way of their goal of living forever." He glanced at the frozen corpse of Jules. "Even a family member proved to be expendable when it came to the fountain of youth."

Emil studied Austin's face. "You're an intelligent man, Austin. Wouldn't you admit that the secret of eternal life is *worth* killing for?"

"Yes," Austin said with a wolfish grin. "If *you're* the one being killed."

"Your civilized veneer is wearing thin," Emil said with a chuckle. "Think of the infinite possibilities. An elite group of immortals imbued with the wisdom of ages could rule the world. We'd be like gods to the life-deprived."

Austin glanced at Emil's henchman. "What about Sebastian over there? Does he fit in with your group of elites? Or will he join the rest of the 'life-deprived,' as you call them?"

The question caught Emil by surprise. "Of course," he said after a moment. "Sebastian's loyalty will earn him a place in my pantheon. Will you join me, old friend?"

The hulking man opened his mouth to reply but said nothing. He had caught the hesitation in Emil's voice and there was confusion in his eyes.

Austin twisted the verbal knife. "Don't count on living forever, Sebastian. Emil's mother wants you out of the picture."

"He's lying," Emil said.

"Why would I lie? Your boss here intends to kill me, no matter what I say. Madame Fauchard told me at the masquerade ball that she had ordered Emil to get rid of you. We both know Emil always does what his mother tells him to do."

A doubtful expression came to the bland face. Emil saw himself losing control of the situation.

"Shoot him in the arms and legs," he barked. "Make sure you don't kill him. I want him to *beg* for death."

Sebastian stood there, unmoving. "Not yet," he said. "I want to hear more."

Emil uttered a curse and snatched the gun from Sebastian's hand. He aimed at Austin's knee.

"You'll soon find that your life is all *too* long."

Austin's ploy to turn Sebastian against Emil had bought him a little time, but it had failed, as he knew it would in the end. The master-and-servant bond between the two men was too strong to be dissolved by a few doubts. He braced himself for the shattering pain. But instead of a gunshot, he heard a sharp hissing sound from the passageway outside the ice cave. Then a hot cloud of steam surged into the chamber.

Emil had turned his head in reflex toward the source of the noise. Austin lunged forward in a low boxing stance and drove his right fist into Fauchard's midsection. Fauchard let out an explosion of air and his legs buckled. The gun flew from his fingers.

Sebastian saw his master under attack, and he tried to grab Austin by the neck. Instead of trying to elude Sebastian, Austin bulled right at him, using his palm to straight-arm the big man under the chin. As Sebastian reeled from the attack, Austin shouldered him aside and then sprinted through the blinding steam.

He heard Zavala calling. "Kurt, over here!"

Zavala stood in the passageway holding a cutoff section of hose that was spewing hot water onto the walls to create the cloud that rolled into the ice cavern. Zavala dropped the hose, grabbed Austin and led him through the steam cloud. They could hear Emil shouting in incoherent rage.

Gunfire raked the passageway. Austin and Zavala were racing down the stairs and the bullets went high. Hearing the gunfire, the rest of Fauchard's men emerged from the lab trailer. They saw Austin and Zavala and gave chase. As they made their way into the tunnel, Zavala got off two quick shots to give their pursuers something to think about. He was still limping, but managed a loping run, and they made it back to the sluice gate Sebastian had blown off. They plunged through the opening a second ahead of a hail of bullets.

Austin searched his pockets for the tunnel map. It was nowhere to be found. He remembered he had left it in the Citroën. They must get back to Fifi. He pictured the system in his mind. The flow in the system could be manipulated in the same way electricity pulses through the grid on a circuit board.

They headed back to the Citroën, only to halt at the sound of voices echoing along the passageway ahead. Austin led the way into another tunnel and he and Zavala were able to make their way in roundabout fashion back to their intended route. The detour cost them precious minutes that allowed Fauchard to organize the chase, and Austin wasn't surprised when they heard Emil's voice behind them eerily exhorting his men on.

Austin and Zavala had been proceeding with haste tempered with caution, but they picked up the pace, following a bewildering course of lefts and rights. Austin was acting mostly on gut instinct, trusting the internal compass that he carried around in his head and using a crude form of land-based dead reckoning.

Despite Austin's fine-tuned sense of direction, the detours took their toll. He lost his bearings completely. Emil's voice was getting closer. Austin was as close to despair as he had ever been when they came to an intersection of four tunnels. Austin's coral-blue eyes probed the gloom.

"This looks familiar," Zavala said.

"We're near the midstation control booth," Austin said.

They entered the right-hand tunnel that would take them back to Fifi, only to stop after taking a few steps. Rough male voices could be heard coming in their direction. They ran back to the intersection and tried going straight, but a sluice gate barred their way. They came back to the intersection. The distant sound of booted footfalls was coming from the passageway at the left.

"We're surrounded," Zavala said.

A desperate plan was hatching in Austin's brain. He turned into the left-hand tunnel.

Zavala held back. "Hold on, Kurt. Fauchard's goons are coming that way, too."

"Trust me," Austin said. "But do it fast. We don't have a second to spare."

Zavala shrugged and sprinted into the dimly lit passageway a step behind Austin. He mumbled to himself in Spanish as they splashed through the puddle-covered floor. He had worked with Austin on many missions since joining the NUMA Special Assignments Team. Zavala had developed an abiding faith in Austin's judgment. There were times, however, like the present, when Austin's behavior seemed completely irrational, and that confidence was put to the test.

Zavala pictured them bumping into Fauchard's thugs in a deadly version of a Keystone Kops silent movie. But they reached the control booth unimpeded and scrambled up the ladder onto the catwalk. Fauchard's men materialized in the dim tunnel and gave out with a hoarse cry of triumph at having brought their game to roost. They unleashed a blistering attack on the booth.

Bullets *ping*ed and ricocheted off the metal catwalk, the tunnel walls amplifying the racket to D-day proportions. Austin dove into the control booth, pulled Zavala in behind him and slammed the door shut. The rest of Fauchard's men heard the gunfire, came running and joined in the turkey shoot. They peppered the booth with hundreds of rounds. The windows disintegrated and the sustained barrage of lead threatened to punch through the steel walls.

Austin crawled across the shards of glass littering the floor, got up on his knees and, keeping his head low, ran his hands onto the control panel keyboard. A diagram of the tunnel system appeared on the screen. The racket of bullets slamming into the booth was deafening and Austin tried to stay focused. He typed out several commands and was gratified when he saw the colors change on the diagram.

Zavala started to rise, hoping to get off a shot or two, but Austin pulled him down.

"You'll get your head shot off," he yelled over the sound of gunfire.

"Better than getting my *ass* shot off," Zavala said.

"Wait," Austin said.

"Wait? For *what*?"

"Gravity."

Zavala's reply was drowned out by a new volley. Then the gunfire stopped abruptly and they could hear Emil's mocking voice.

"Austin! Are you and your friend enjoying the view?"

Austin put his finger to his lips.

When Austin didn't answer, Emil taunted, "Don't tell me you're shy. I want you to listen to the plans my mother has for your lady friend. She's going to give her a face-lift. You won't recognize her when she's through with the transformation."

Austin had had enough of Fauchard. He signaled for Zavala to hand over his gun and moved closer to the control booth wall. Disregarding his own advice, he squeezed the trigger until it was a feather's touch away, then he popped up like a hand puppet, fired once and ducked down. He had honed in on Fauchard's voice, but his aim was off. Fauchard and his men scattered in search of cover. Once they saw that there was no follow-up attack, they again sprayed the booth with lead.

"You really showed them that time," Zavala yelled over the racket.

"Emil was starting to irk me."

"Did you get him?"

"Emil? Unfortunately, no. I missed Sebastian, too. But I nailed the guy standing next to him."

"That *is* unfortunate," Zavala said, raising his voice a few decibels. "Brilliant strategy, though. Maybe they'll run out of bullets."

Bullets were starting to punch through the floor of the booth. Austin knew he had to stop the shooting and buy time. "Do you have a white hanky?" he asked Zavala.

"This is a funny time to be blowing your nose," Zavala said, ducking as a round ricocheted off the wall. He saw from Austin's face that he wasn't joking and said, "I've got my Mexican 'do-rag.' " Zavala fished his multipurpose red bandanna out of his back pocket and handed it over.

"This will do," Austin said, tying the bandanna to the gun barrel. He poked the impromptu flag out the door and waved it.

The gunfire again stopped. Emil's sharp-edged laughter echoed throughout the tunnel.

"What is that rag, Austin?" he said. "I'm no bull to be taunted by your antics."

"I didn't have a white flag," Austin shouted down.

"A *white* flag? Don't tell me you and your friend are prepared to come to terms with your fate?"

Austin cocked his ear, listening. He thought he heard a distant whispering, like the surf along the shore. But his ears were still ringing from the gunfire and he couldn't be sure.

"You misunderstood, Fauchard. I'm not ready to surrender."

"Then why are you waving that ridiculous piece of cloth?"

"I wanted to say good-bye before the freight train comes through."

"Have you gone mad, Austin?"

The whispering had become a low rumble.

Emil gave the order to start firing again.

Bullets whined and splattered around their heads in a

nonstop crescendo. The concentrated gunfire was punching through the walls. In another few minutes, the booth would be no more protection than the slice of Swiss cheese that it was starting to resemble.

Then the firing stopped abruptly.

The gunmen had felt the vibration. With the guns silent, they, too, had picked up the rumble of distant thunder.

Austin got to his feet and stepped out onto the catwalk. Emil had a puzzled look on his face. He looked up, saw Austin staring down at him and knew he had been bested.

"You've won for now, Austin," he yelled up, shaking his fist in defiance, "but you haven't heard the last from the Fauchards."

Austin grinned, stepped back into the booth, grabbed onto one of the metal legs supporting the console table and told Zavala to do the same.

Emil shouted one last oath, and then he turned and he and his gang of thugs ran for their lives. Sebastian lurched after the others.

It was too late.

Seconds later, the wave hit Fauchard and his men with an explosion of blue water that swept them away like a giant broom. Heads bobbed for an instant in the cold foam, arms flailed ineffectually. Sebastian's face was pale against the dark water. Then he was gone along with Emil and his men.

Unlike their previous experience, when Austin and Zavala stayed high and dry inside the undamaged watertight booth, this time the cascading water flowed in through the broken windows, flooded the control room and tried to pull Austin and Zavala from their anchor. They hung on with every ounce of strength.

Just when their lungs were ready to burst, the main force of the wave spent itself and the water began to subside.

They stood on shaky legs and peered through the jagged-edged framework, which was all that was left of the window.

Zavala looked down on the river flowing under their feet, amazement on his dark features. "How did you know that high tide was coming?"

"I opened and closed a few sluice gates in another part of the system and diverted water this way."

Zavala grinned and said, "I hope that Fauchard and his pals are all washed up."

"My guess is that they're feeling a bit flushed by now," Austin said.

Miraculously, the control monitor was in a secure housing and had escaped damage. Austin punched in some keyboard commands.

The water level dropped until the rushing river became a narrow stream. Both men were shivering in their wet clothes by then. They had to get out of the tunnels to someplace dry and warm before hypothermia set in. They climbed down the ladder. This time, no one tried to stop them.

They plodded through the tunnels with no idea of where they were going. Their teeth had started to chatter from the cold. The batteries in their flashlights were getting low, but they kept on because they had no alternative. Just when they were about to give up all hope, they saw an object ahead.

Zavala yelled with joy. *"Fifi!"*

The Citroën had been picked up by the wave and deposited sideways in the tunnel. It was covered with mud and the paint was scraped off in a dozen places where it must have banged against the walls. Austin opened the door. The map was floating in a few inches of water on the floor. The key was still in the ignition. He tried to start the car but the engine wouldn't turn over.

Zavala fiddled around in the hood and told Austin to try it again.

This time the motor started.

Zavala got in and said, "Loose battery cable."

It took a half hour of driving through the tunnel grid before they figured out where they were, then another half hour to find their way back through the system. The car was running on gas vapors when they saw gray daylight ahead, and moments later they drove out of the mountain.

"What next?" Zavala said.

Austin didn't even have to think about it. "Château Fauchard."

40

WHEN SKYE WAS a girl her father had taken her to the Cathédrale de Notre Dame and she had seen her first gargoyle. The grotesque face leering down from the ramparts looked like a monster from her worst nightmares. She had calmed down after her father explained that gargoyles were nothing more than rainspouts. Skye had wondered why such talented sculptors could not have fashioned things of beauty, but she had put aside her childhood fears. Now, as she blinked her eyes open, the gargoyle of her restless dreams was back. Even worse, it was talking to her.

"Welcome back, mademoiselle," said the cruel mouth only inches away. "We have missed you."

The face belonged to Marcel, the bullet-headed man in charge of the private army at Château Fauchard. He spoke again.

"I'll be back in fifteen minutes," he said. "Do not keep me waiting."

She closed her eyes as a wave of nausea swept through her body. When she looked again, he was gone.

Skye glanced around and saw that she was in the chamber where she'd changed into the cat costume for the Fauchard masquerade ball. She recalled walking up to her apartment building. She dug deeper into her recollection and remembered the lost American couple, the bee sting on her backside and the slide into oblivion.

Dear God, she had been kidnapped.

She sat up in the bed and swung her legs over the side. There was a brassy taste in her mouth, probably the remnant of the chemical that had been injected into her veins to render her unconscious. She took a deep breath and stood up. The room began to swirl around her. She staggered into the bathroom and vomited into the sink.

Skye gazed at her reflection, hardly recognizing the face in the mirror. Her face was ghostly pale, her hair lank and straggly. She felt better after she had rinsed her mouth and splashed cold water on her face. She brushed her hair back with her fingers and patted the wrinkles out of her clothes as best she could.

She was ready a few minutes later when Marcel opened the door without knocking and beckoned for her to follow. They walked down the long carpeted corridors, eventually passing through the gauntlet of faces lining the walls of the portrait gallery. She looked for the painting of Jules Fauchard, but it was gone, leaving only blank wall in its place. Then they were standing outside Madame Fauchard's office.

Marcel gave Skye an odd smile, and then he knocked gently and opened the door. He pushed Skye inside. Skye saw that she was not alone. A blond woman with her back to Skye sat at Madame Fauchard's desk, staring out the window. She swiveled around in the chair at the click of the door shutting and stared at Skye.

The woman was in her forties, with creamy skin set off by probing gray eyes. She parted her red, almost voluptuous lips. "Good afternoon, mademoiselle. We've awaited your return. You left in such a spectacular fashion."

Skye's mind reeled. She wondered if she were still feeling the aftereffects of the knockout drug.

"Sit," the woman said, pointing to a chair in front of the desk.

Skye obeyed, moving like a zombie.

The woman regarded Skye with amusement.

"What's wrong? You seem distracted."

Skye was more confused than distracted. The voice that came from the woman's mouth was that of Madame Fauchard. It had lost its cracked, old lady quality, but there was no mistaking the hard-edged words. Crazy thoughts ran through Skye's mind. Did Racine have a daughter? Maybe this was a clever ventriloquist.

Finally, she found her own voice.

"Is this some sort of trick?"

"No trick at all. What you see is what there is."

"Madame Fauchard?" The words came out falteringly.

"One and the same, my dear," she said with a wicked smile. "Only now I am young and you are old."

Skye was still skeptical. "You must give me the name of your plastic surgeon."

Heat came to the woman's eyes, but only for a moment. She rose from her chair and came around to the other side of the desk with silken movements. She leaned over, took Skye's hand and placed it on her cheek.

"Tell me if you *still* think this is the work of a surgeon."

The flesh was warm and firm, and the skin was creamy without a trace of wrinkles.

"Impossible," Skye said in a whisper.

Madame Fauchard let the hand drop, then stood upright and returned to her chair. She tented her long, slender fingers so that Skye could see that they were no longer gnarled.

"Don't worry," she said. "You're not going mad. I am the same person who invited you and Mr. Austin to my costume party. He's well, I trust."

"I don't know," Skye said, guardedly. "I haven't seen him in days. How—"

"How did I turn from a cackling old crone into a young beauty?" she said, a dreamy look in her eyes. "A long, long story. It would not have been so long had it not been for

Jules absconding with the helmet," she said, spitting out the name with bitterness. "We could have saved decades of research."

"I don't understand."

"You're the antique arms expert," Madame Fauchard said. "Tell me what you know about the helmet."

"It's very old. Five hundred years or possibly older. The steel was of extremely high quality. It may have been made with iron from a meteorite."

Madame Fauchard arched an eyebrow.

"Very good. The helmet was made with star metal and this strength saved the lives of more than one Fauchard in battle. It was melted and recast through the centuries and was passed down through the family to the *true* leaders of the Fauchards. It rightfully belonged to me, not my brother Jules."

The words took a second to sink in, but when they did, Skye said, "Your *brother*!"

"That's right. Jules was a year younger than me."

Skye tried to do the calculation, but her thoughts were whirling around in her head. "That would make you—"

"Never ask a lady her age," Madame Fauchard said, with a languid smile. "But I'll save you the trouble. I'm past the century mark."

Skye shook her head in disbelief. "I don't believe it."

"I'm hurt by your skepticism," Madame Fauchard said, but her expression belied her statement. "Would you like to hear the details?"

Skye was torn between her scientific curiosity and her revulsion. "I saw what happened to Cavendish because he knew too much of your business."

"Lord Cavendish was a bore as well as a blabbermouth. But you flatter yourself, my dear. When you're as old as I am, you learn to keep things in perspective. You're no good to me dead. Live bait is always more effective."

"Bait. For what?"

"Not what. *Whom.* Kurt Austin, of course."

41

SHORTLY AFTER FIVE O'CLOCK, the workers at the Fauchard vineyards ended the day that had started with the rising sun. As the men headed back to their crude dormitories, a fleet of dump trucks laden with newly picked grapes rolled along the dirt roads that ran through the rolling hills and converged on the gate in the electrified fence. A bored guard waved the line through the gate and the trucks headed to a shed where the grapes would be off-loaded for crushing, fermentation and bottling.

As the last truck slowed to a halt near the shed, two figures jumped off and darted into the woods. Satisfied that they had not been seen, Austin and Zavala brushed the dirt off their clothes and tried to wipe the grape juice off their faces and hands, but it only made the stain worse.

Zavala spit out a mouthful of damp earth. "That's the last time I let Trout talk me into one of his crazy schemes. We look like a purple version of the Blue Man Group!"

Austin was picking twigs out of his hair. "You must admit it was a stroke of genius. Who'd expect anyone to disguise themselves as a bunch of grapes?"

Trout's plan was deceptively simple. He and Gamay had

taken another tour of the vineyards. This time Austin and Zavala were hunkered down in the backseat. The Trouts stopped and got out to say hello to Marchand, the foreman they had met on their first visit to the Fauchard vineyards. As they chatted, the dump truck pulled up in front of the car. Austin and Zavala waited until the truck was loaded, then they slipped out of the car, climbed onto the back of the moving vehicle and burrowed into the grapes.

The dark woods were like something out of a Tolkien novel. Austin carried a device Gandalf the wizard would have envied. The miniaturized Global Positioning System could put them within yards of the château. Using a compass in the initial stages of their journey, they struck out through the woods in the general direction of the château.

The woods were thick with clawing brambles and foot-catching underbrush, as if the Fauchards had somehow extended their malevolence into the flora surrounding their ancestral home. As the sun sank lower in the sky, the woods grew darker. Traveling in the dusky light, the two men stumbled over roots, and needle-sharp thorns caught at their clothes. Eventually, they broke out of the forest onto a dirt path that led to a network of well-used trails. Austin frequently consulted the GPS and it proved its worth when he saw a glow through the trees from the turrets of Château Fauchard.

At the edge of the woods, they crouched in the trees and watched a lone guard make his way along the edge of the moat. When the guard rounded the far wall of the château, Austin set the timing mode on his watch.

"We're in luck," Zavala said. "Only one sentry."

"I don't like it," Austin said. "Nothing in my brief acquaintance with the Fauchard family leads me to believe that they treat their own security lightly."

Even more suspicious, the drawbridge was down and the portcullis up. The water in the strange war-themed fountain tinkled musically. The tranquil scene stood in stark contrast to his last visit, when he'd driven the Rolls into the moat under a hail of bullets. It seemed all too inviting.

"You think it's a trap?" Zavala said.

"All that's missing is a big hunk of cheese."

"What are our options?"

"Limited. We can turn around or keep moving and try to stay one step ahead of the bad guys."

"I've had my fill of grapes," Zavala said. "You didn't say anything about an exit strategy."

Austin clapped Zavala on the shoulder. "Here you are, about to take an exciting tour of Château Fauchard, and you're already thinking of leaving."

"Sorry I'm not as blasé as you are. I was hoping for a more dignified exit than driving a Rolls-Royce into a moat."

Austin cringed at the memory. "Okay. Here's the plan. We will offer to trade Emil for Skye."

"Not bad," Zavala said. "There's only one little hitch. You flushed Emil down the drain."

"Madame Fauchard doesn't know that. By the time she finds out, we will be long gone."

"Shame on you, bluffing an old lady." Zavala pursed his lips in thought. "I like it, but what if she doesn't bite? Is that when we call in the *gendarmes*?"

"I wish it were that easy, old pal. Picture this. The cops knock on the château door and the Fauchards say, 'Search all you want.' I've been in those catacombs, you could hide an army in that labyrinth. It could take weeks to find Skye."

"And time isn't on our side."

A thoughtful look came to Austin's eyes. "An hour is worth a hundred years," he murmured, checking his watch.

"Is that from one of your philosophy books?" Zavala said. Austin was a student of philosophy and the bookshelves in his Potomac boathouse were crammed with the works of the great thinkers.

"No," he replied thoughtfully. "It's something Dr. MacLean said to me."

The guard emerged from the other side of the château,

cutting their discussion short. Austin clicked his watch again. The sentry had taken sixteen minutes to perambulate the château.

As soon as the guard started on another round, Austin signaled Zavala. They dashed across the open space and followed the moat to the arched stone bridge, then sprinted across the drawbridge into the courtyard. In their black clothes, they were almost invisible in the shadows along the base of the wall. Lights glowed in the first-floor windows of the château, but no guards patrolled the grounds, further raising Austin's suspicions.

He was sure his instincts were on target when he and Zavala came to the gate guarding the staircase to the ramparts. When he and Skye had inspected the gate, it was locked. Now it was wide open, an invitation to climb to the wall and cross over a narrow bridge to the turret. Austin had other plans. He led the way across the cobblestones to the rear of the château and descended a short stone staircase to an ironbound wooden door.

Austin tried the handle. The door was locked. He extracted a portable drill and a handsaw from his pack, drilled several holes in the door and sawed out a circular section. He reached in through the hole, raised the bar and opened the door. The putrid mustiness of the catacombs welled through the doorway like the exhalation of a corpse. They switched on their electric torches, stepped inside and closed the door behind them.

They went down several short flights of stairs. Austin paused briefly at the dungeons, where Emil had paid his bloody homage to Edgar Allan Poe. The pendulum hovered over the wooden table, but there was no sign of the unfortunate Englishman, Lord Cavendish.

Austin blundered down a few blind alleys, but his mariner's sense of direction held him in good stead. Before long, they passed through the bone-filled ossuary and followed the route to the armory. Again, a door was unlocked. Austin pushed it open and he and Zavala stepped into the altar area. The armory was in darkness except for a glow that came from the far end of the nave. The flickering yellow light glinted off the highly polished armor and weapons.

Zavala glanced around at the display. "Cozy. I like the combination of Gothic and heavy metal. Who's their interior decorator?"

"Same guy who worked for the Marquis de Sade."

They made their way along the long nave past the lethal relics that were the foundation of the Fauchard fortune. The light grew brighter as they came up behind the mounted knights. Austin went first, and as he stepped around to the front of the display he saw Skye.

She was seated in a sturdy wooden chair that was flanked by braziers, facing the charging figures on horseback. Her arms and legs were bound tightly with rope and a piece of duct tape had been stretched across her mouth. Two shiny suits of armor stood at her sides, as if ready to defend Skye against the fierce onslaught.

Skye's eyes widened. She shook her head vigorously, becoming more frantic as Austin drew nearer. He was reaching for his sheath knife so he could cut Skye's bindings when out of the corner of his eye he detected motion. The armored suit on his right was on the move.

"Oh hell," he said for want of a better reaction.

Clanking with each step, the suit raised its sword hand and advanced on Austin like an antique robot. He backed away.

"Any suggestions?" Zavala said, doing the same.

"Not unless you brought a can opener."

"How about our guns?"

"Too noisy."

The other suit had sprung into life and was advancing as well. The armored figures closed in with unexpected speed. Austin realized that the knife he had in his hand would be about as effective as a toothpick. Skye was struggling in her chair.

Austin wasn't about to be sliced up like a salami. He put his head down, charged toward the nearest suit and threw a football body block across the jointed knees. The suit teetered, dropped the sword and, with arms flailing, toppled over backward and hit the stone floor with a horrendous crash. The suit's occupant gave a feeble jerk of his legs and arms and then he was still.

The other suit hesitated. Zavala duplicated Austin's body block with equal effectiveness. The second suit of armor crashed to the floor. While Austin cut away Skye's ropes, Zavala bent over one fallen figure, then the other.

"Out cold," he said with pride. "The bigger they are, the harder they fall."

"It felt like tackling a Bradley fighting vehicle. All those misspent hours watching NFL football weren't a waste of time after all."

"I thought you were worried about the noise. That little dustup sounded like a couple of skeletons making love on a tin roof."

Austin shrugged and carefully peeled back the duct tape covering Skye's mouth. He helped her rise from the chair. She stood on shaky legs, threw her arms around Austin and gave him one of the longest and warmest kisses he had ever experienced. "I never thought I'd see you again," she said.

A silvery laugh issued from the shadows of a nearby cloister. Then a tall slender figure whose face was obscured by a gauzy veil stepped into the flickering light from the braziers. The diaphanous fabric covered her form down to her ankles. Light filtered through the veil, outlining her perfect figure.

"Charming," she said. "How utterly charming. But must you always be so dramatic in your comings and goings, Monsieur Austin?"

Marcel stepped out behind the woman, a machine pistol cradled in his hands. Then six more armed men melted from dark corners. Marcel relieved Austin and Zavala of their weapons.

Austin glanced at the motionless suits of armor. "From the looks of that pile of tin, I'm not the only one with a flair for the dramatic."

"You know I like the theater. You were at my masquerade ball."

"Masquerade ball—"

She slowly unwound the veil from her face and head. Hair that looked as if it had been spun from gold thread tumbled to her shoulders. Slowly, seductively, she removed the rest of the veil as if she were taking the wrapping off a precious gift and let it drop from her body to the floor. Underneath the veil, she wore a long, low-cut gown of pure white. A gold belt with a three-headed-eagle design encircled her slim waist. Austin peered into the cold eyes and felt as if he'd been struck by lightning.

Even though Austin knew about the mysterious workings of the Lost City enzymes, the logical part of his mind had never fully accepted them. It was easier, somehow, to believe that the formula for the Philosopher's Stone, misused, could produce ageless nightmarish creatures than to imagine that it could create a mortal of such astonishing godlike loveliness. He had assumed that the formula would extend life, but not that it could roll back the effects of fifty years of aging.

Austin found his tongue. "I see that Dr. MacLean's work was far more successful than anyone could have imagined, Madame Fauchard."

"Don't give MacLean too much credit. He was the midwife at the birth, but the formula for the life that burns within me was created before he was born."

"You look a lot different from a few days ago. How long did this transformation take?"

"The life-extending formula is too powerful to be taken at once," she said. "It calls for three treatments. The first two doses produced what you see before you within twenty-four hours. I am about to take the third."

"Why do you need to gild a lily?"

Racine preened at the unlikely comparison to a delicate flower. "The third dose makes permanent the effects of the first two. Within an hour of completing the treatment, I will begin my journey through eternity. But enough talk of chemistry. Why don't you introduce me to your handsome friend? He seems unable to put his eyes back into his head."

Zavala had not seen Madame Fauchard in her former, older incarnation. He knew only that he was in the presence of one of the most dazzling females he had ever encountered. He had muttered words of amazement in Spanish. Now a slight smile cracked the ends of his lips. The guns pointed in his direction did nothing to cool his appreciation for a woman who was apparently perfect in every physical way.

"This is my colleague, Joe Zavala," Austin said. "Joe, meet Racine Fauchard, the owner of this charming pile of stone."

"Madame Fauchard?" Zavala's mouth dropped down to his Adam's apple.

"Yes, is there a problem?" she said.

"No. I just expected someone different."

"Monsieur Austin no doubt regaled you with descriptions of me as a bag of bones," she said, her eyes flashing.

"Not at all," Zavala said, absorbing Madame Fauchard's slim figure and striking features with wondering eyes. "He said you were charming and intelligent."

The answer seemed to please her because she smiled. "NUMA evidently chooses its people for their gallantry as well as their expertise. It was a quality I saw in you, Monsieur Austin. That's why I knew you would try to rescue yon fair maiden." She eyed their purple-stained skin. "If you wanted to sample our grapes, it would have been far less trouble to buy a bottle of wine than to bathe in them."

"Your wine is out of my price range," Austin said.

"Did you really think you could enter the château without being detected? Our surveillance cameras picked you up after you crossed the drawbridge. Marcel thought you would climb to the outside wall and come in that way."

"It was kind of you to leave the stairway gate unlocked."

"You were obviously too smart to take the bait, but we never dreamed that you could find your way through the catacombs. You knew the château was well defended. What did you hope to accomplish by coming here?"

"I had hoped to leave with the mademoiselle."

"Well, you have failed in your romantic quest."

"So it seems. Perhaps, in the interests of romance, you would offer me a consolation prize. At our first meeting, you said you would tell me someday about your family. Here I am. I'd be glad to tell you what I know in exchange."

"You could never equal what I know about you, but I admire your audacity." She paused a moment, crossed her arms and lightly pinched her chin. Austin remembered seeing the old Madame Fauchard make the same gesture of thought. She turned to Marcel and said, "Take the others away."

"I wouldn't do that if I were you," Austin said to Marcel.

He stepped protectively in front of Skye. Marcel and the guards moved in but Madame Fauchard waved them away.

"Your chivalry appears to know no bounds, Monsieur Austin. Have no fear; your friends will only be taken a short distance away where you can see them. I want to talk to you alone."

Madame Fauchard motioned for him to sit in Skye's vacated chair, and snapped her fingers. Two of her men brought over a thronelike chair of heavy medieval construction and she settled into it. She said something in French to Marcel, and he and some of his men escorted the prisoners a short distance, but still in view, while others dragged away the suits of armor.

"Now there are just the two of us," she said. "Lest you entertain any illusions, my men will kill your friends if you do anything foolish."

"I have no intention of making a move. This encounter is much too fascinating to end so soon. Tell me, what's with the high priestess outfit?"

"You know how I enjoy costumes. Do you like it?"

Austin couldn't take his eyes off Madame Fauchard in spite of himself. Racine Fauchard was stunning in the way a finely crafted wax figure is perfect in every feature considered important, except one. Her soulless eyes held all the warmth of the cold steel that the Fauchards had used to fashion their swords and armor.

"I find you absolutely enchanting, but—"

"But you don't readily consort with a hundred-year-old woman."

"Not at all. You've aged quite well. I don't usually consort with a cold-blooded killer."

She raised a finely arched eyebrow. "Monsieur Austin, is this your strange way of flirting with me?"

"Far from it."

"Too bad. I've had many lovers in the last hundred years, but you're a very attractive man." She paused and studied his face. "Dangerous, too, and that makes you even more attractive. First, you must fulfill your part of the bargain. Tell me what you know."

"I know that you and your family hired Dr. MacLean to find the elixir of life he called the Philosopher's Stone. In the process, you killed anyone who got in your way and created a group of wild-eyed mutants."

"A cogent summary, but you've only scratched the surface."

"Scratch it for me, then."

She paused, letting her memory drift back through the years.

"My family traces its ancestry back to the Minoan civilization that flourished before the great volcanic eruption on the island of Santorini. My ancestors were priests and priestesses in the Minoan snake goddess cult. The snake clan was powerful, but power rivals drove us off the island. A few weeks later, the volcano erupted and destroyed the island. We settled in Cyprus, where we went into the arms business. The snake evolved into the Spear, then to Fauchard."

"How did you get from spears to mutants?"

"It was a logical outgrowth of our arms business. Around the turn of the century, Spear Industries set up a laboratory to try to design a super-soldier. We knew from the American Civil War that trench warfare would make future battles a stalemate. First one side would charge, then the other, with little gain in ground. They would retreat in the face of the automatic weapons that were being developed. We wanted a soldier who would charge the trenches without fear, like a Viking berserker. In addition, this soldier would have super endurance and speed, and fast-healing wounds. We tried the formula on a few volunteers."

"Like Pierre Levant?"

"I don't recall the name," she said with a frown.

"Captain Levant was a French officer. He became one of the first mutants your research created."

"Yes, he seems vaguely familiar. A dashing, handsome young man, as I recall."

"You'd never recognize him these days."

"Before you condemn me, you must know that they were all volunteers, soldiers who were excited at the prospect of becoming supermen."

"Did they know that along with these superhuman powers, their appearance would change rather drastically?"

"None of us did. The science was crude. But the formula worked, for a time, anyhow. It gave the soldiers superhuman strength and quickness, but then they deteriorated into uncontrollable, snarling beasts."

"Beasts who could enjoy their new bodies forever."

"Life extension was an unexpected by-product. Even more exciting, the formula promised to reverse aging. We would have succeeded in refining the formula if not for Jules."

"He turned out to have a conscience?"

"He turned out to be a fool," she said, with undisguised vehemence. "Jules saw our findings as a boon to mankind. He tried to persuade me and others in the family to stop the march toward war and release the formula. I led the family against him. He fled the country in his airplane. He carried papers that would have implicated the family in the war plot and intended to use them as blackmail, I suppose, if he had not been intercepted and shot down."

"Why did he take the helmet?"

"It was a symbol of authority, passed down to the family leader of each generation. He lost his right to the helmet by his actions, and it should have passed to me."

Austin leaned back in his chair and put his hands behind his head. "So Jules is gone, along with the threat that the family's war scheme will be exposed. He was in no position to stop your research."

"He had already stopped it. He destroyed the computations for the basic formula and etched them into the helmet. Clever. *Too* clever. We had to start all over again. There were a million possible combinations. We kept the mutants alive with the hope that one day they might reveal the secrets of the formula. The work was interrupted by wars, the Depression. We were close to succeeding during World War Two when our laboratory was bombed by Allied planes. It set back our research by decades."

Austin chuckled. "You're saying that the wars you promoted hurt your research. The irony must not have escaped you."

"I wish it had."

"In the meantime, you got older."

"Yes, I got older," she said with uncharacteristic sadness. "I lost my beauty and became a crackling old crone. Still, I persisted. We made some progress in slowing aging, which I shared with Emil, but the Grim Reaper was catching up with us. We were so close. We tried to create the right enzyme, but with limited success. Then one of my scientists heard about the Lost City enzyme. It seemed to be the missing link. I bought the company doing research on the enzyme, and enlisted Dr. MacLean and his colleagues to pursue round-the-clock research. We built a submarine that could harvest the enzyme and set up a testing laboratory."

"Why did you have the scientists at MacLean's company killed?"

"We're not the first to dispose of a scientific team so they won't talk about their research. The British government is still investigating the deaths of scientists who worked on a Star Wars missile defense project. We had created a new batch of mutants and the scientists threatened to go public with the news, so we got rid of them."

"The only problem with your scientists is that they hadn't really finished their work," Austin said. "Pardon me, but this operation sounds like a clown convention."

"Not an inaccurate analogy. I made the mistake of letting Emil handle things. It was a big mistake. Once I took control again, I brought back Dr. MacLean to reconstitute a research team. They managed to recoup much of the work."

"Was Emil responsible for flooding the glacier tunnel?"

"Mea culpa again. I had not brought him into my confidence about the true significance of the helmet, so he never tried to find it before flooding the tunnel."

"Yet another mistake?"

"Luckily, Mademoiselle Labelle removed the helmet, and it is now in my possession. It provided the missing link and we closed down the lab. So you see, we make mistakes, but we learn by them. Apparently, you don't. You escaped from here once, yet you came back to certain disaster."

"I'm not certain that's the case."

"What do you mean?"

"Have you heard from Emil lately?"

"No." For the first time there was doubt in her face. "Where is he?"

"Let us go and I'll be glad to tell you," Austin said.

"What are you saying?"

"I stopped off at the glacier before coming here. Emil is now in custody."

"A shame," she said with a flip of her fingers. "Too bad you didn't kill him."

"You're bluffing. This is your son we're talking about."

"You needn't remind me of my familial obligations," she said coldly. "I don't care what happens to Emil or his cretinous friend Sebastian. Emil planned to usurp me. I would have had to destroy him myself. If you've killed him, you did me a favor."

Austin felt as if he had just been dealt a pair of deuces in a high-stakes poker game.

"I should have known that mother snakes sometimes eat their eggs."

"You can't insult me with your silly taunts. Despite its internal friction, our family has grown ever more powerful through the centuries."

"And created a river of blood in the process."

"What do we care for blood? It is the most expendable commodity on earth."

"Some people might argue with that."

"You have no idea what you have gotten yourself into," Madame Fauchard said, with a sneer. "You think you know us? There is layer upon layer invisible to you. Our family has its origins in the mists of time. While your forebears were clawing at rotten logs searching for grubs, the first Spear had already fashioned a flint point, attached it to a shaft and traded it to his neighbor. We are of no nation and every nation. We sold weapons to the Greeks against the Persians and the Persians against the Greeks. The Roman legions marched across Europe wielding broadswords of our design. Now we will forge time, bending it to our will as we once did steel."

"And if you live another hundred or even a thousand years, then what?"

"It is not how *long* you live but what you do with your time. Why don't you join me, monsieur? I admire your resourcefulness and courage. Maybe I could even find a place for your friends. Think of it. Immortality! Deep down, isn't that your most fervent wish?"

"Your son asked me the same question."

"And?"

A cold smile crossed Austin's face. "My only wish is to send you and your pals to join him in hell."

"So you *did* kill him!" Madame Fauchard clapped her hands in light applause. "Well done, Monsieur Austin, as I would expect. You must have known I wasn't serious with my proposal. If there is one thing I have learned in a century, it is that men of conscience are always a danger. Very well, you and your friends wanted to be part of my masque, so it will be. In return for removing my son, I will not kill you right away. I will allow you to be present at the dawn of a new day on earth." She reached into the bodice of her dress and extracted a small amber phial, which she held above her head. "Behold, the elixir of life."

Austin was thinking about something else: MacLean. His eyes glimmered with a faint light of understanding as he pondered the scientist's last words.

"Your mad scheme will never work," Austin said quietly.

Racine glared at Austin and her lips curled in contempt. "Who is going to stop me? You? You dare to pit your puny intellect against the lessons of a hundred years?"

She uncorked the phial, which she put to her lips, and drank the contents. Her face seemed to glow with an aura. Austin watched in fascination for a moment, aware that he was witnessing a miracle, but he quickly snapped out of his spell. Racine noticed him push the timing button on his watch.

"You might as well throw that timepiece away," she said derisively. "In my world, time will have no meaning."

"Pardon me if I ignore your suggestion. In my world, time still has a great deal of meaning."

She regarded Austin with an arrogant tilt of her head, then signaled Marcel, who came over. Together with the other prisoners, they marched to the door that led down to the catacombs.

As the thick wooden door swung open and Austin and the others were prodded into the depths at gunpoint, the warning from the French pilot flashed through his mind.

The Fauchards have a past.

Then he looked at his watch and prayed to the gods who look over fools and adventurers, often one and the same. With any kind of luck, this evil blight of a family might not have a future.

42

RACINE GRABBED a torch from the wall and plunged through the doorway. Reveling in the freedom of her newfound youth, she bounded gracefully down the stairs leading into the catacombs. Her schoolgirl enthusiasm stood out in sharp contrast to the morbid surroundings, with their dripping walls and lichen-splotched ceilings.

Behind Racine came Skye, followed by Austin and a guard who watched his every move, then Zavala and another guard. Last in line was Marcel, ever watchful, like a trail boss keeping his eye out for straying cattle. The procession moved past the boneyard and the dungeons, and then it descended staircases that plunged guards and prisoners ever deeper into the catacombs. The air grew more stale and hard to breathe.

A narrow, barrel-roofed passageway about a hundred feet long led off from the last set of stairs and ended at a stone door. Two guards rolled the door aside. It opened quietly, as if the rollers had been well oiled. As the prisoners were marched along another corridor, Austin assessed their options and decided that they had none. At least for now. The Trouts had instructions to stand by until he called.

He could kick himself for assuming too much. He had miscalculated badly. Racine was ruthless, as shown by the fact that she had had her brother killed, but he never dreamed she would be so callous about the fate of her son. He glanced ahead at Skye. She seemed to be bearing up well, too busy brushing cobwebs out of her hair to dwell on her long-term prospects. He only hoped that she would not have to pay for his miscalculation.

The passageway ended in another stone door, which was also rolled aside. Racine stepped through the opening and waved her torch in the air so that the flame crackled and snapped. The dancing torchlight illuminated a stone slab about two feet wide that seemed to jut out into empty space from the edge of a precipice.

"I call this the 'Bridge of Sighs,'" Racine said, her voice echoing and reechoing off the deep walls of the chasm. "It's much older than the one in Venice. Listen." The wind wailed up from below like a chorus of lost souls and tousled her long flaxen hair. "It's best not to pause."

She dashed across the slab with seemingly reckless abandon.

Skye hesitated. Austin took her hand and, together, they shuffled across the narrow bridge toward Racine's fluttering torch. The wind tugged at their clothes. The distance was about thirty feet, but it might as well have been thirty miles.

Zavala was a natural athlete, who had boxed in college, and he strode across with the sure-footedness of a high-wire walker. The guards, and even Marcel, took their time as they made their way across and it was obvious they didn't like this part of their duty.

The guards unlocked a thick wooden door and the procession stepped out of the catacombs into an open space. The air was dry and heavily scented with a strong piney smell. They were in an aisle around a dozen feet across.

Racine walked over to a low wall between two massive square columns and beckoned for the others to follow.

The walkway was actually the top tier of an amphitheater. Three more tiers of seats lit by a ring of torchlight descended to an arena. The seats were occupied by hundreds of silent spectators.

Austin gazed through an arch at the vast open space. "You never cease to surprise, Madame Fauchard."

"Few strangers have ever seen the sanctum sanctorum of the Fauchards."

Skye's fears had been momentarily overshadowed by her scientific curiosity. "This is an exact replica of the Coliseum," she said with an analytical eye. "The orders of columns, the arcade, everything is the same except for the scale."

"That should come as no surprise," Racine said. "It's a smaller version of the Coliseum, built by a homesick Roman proconsul for Gaul who missed the amusements of home. When my ancestors were searching for a site to build the château, they thought that by having the great house rest on a place where gladiators shed their blood they could fuse with the martial spirit. My family made a few modifications, such as adding an ingenious ventilation system to bring air to this place, but otherwise all is as they found it."

Austin was puzzled by the spectators. There should have been a murmuring of voices, a rustling or coughing. But the silence was palpable.

"Who are all these people?" he asked Racine.

"Let me introduce you," she replied.

They descended the first of several crumbling interior staircases. At ground level, a guard unbolted an iron gate and the group passed through a short tunnel. Racine explained that it was the access for the gladiators and other entertainment. The tunnel led to a circular arena. Fine white sand covered the floor.

A carved marble dais about five feet high stood at the center of the arena. Steps had been cut into the side of the rectangular platform. Austin was studying the stolid faces of a contingent of guards who stood at attention around the arena's perimeter when he heard a gasp from Skye, who hadn't let go of his hand since crossing the chasm. She squeezed his fingers in a viselike grip.

He followed her gaze to the lowest row of seats. The yellow torchlight fell upon skeletal grins and parchment yellow skin and he realized he was staring at an audience of mummies. The dried bodies filled row after row, tier after tier, staring down at the arena with long-dead eyes.

"It's all right," he said evenly. "They won't hurt you."

Zavala was awestruck. "This is nothing but a big tomb," he said.

"I'll admit I've played to livelier audiences," Austin said. He turned to Madame Fauchard. "Joe's right. Your sanctum sanctorum is a glorified mausoleum."

"To the contrary," Racine replied. "You're standing on the family's most sacred ground. It was there on that podium that I challenged Jules in 1914. And here is where he stood and told us that he would abide by the wishes of the family council. Had not Emil failed, I would have placed my brother's body with the others so he could see my triumph."

Austin tried to imagine Racine's brother making his case for mankind to deaf ears.

"It must have taken a great deal of courage for Jules to defy your murderous family," Austin said.

Racine ignored his comment. She pirouetted on her heel like a ballerina, seemingly at home in this dread place of death, and pointed out several family members who had rejected Jules's appeal so long ago.

"Pardon me if I don't get misty-eyed," Austin said. "From the look on their faces, they still haven't gotten over your brother's defection."

"He was not just defying us; he was going against five thousand years of family history. When we returned to France with the Crusaders, we moved our ancestors here to be with us. It took years, with long caravans of the dead winding their way thousands of miles from the Middle East, until, at last, the mummies were brought to this place of rest."

"Why go through so much trouble for a bunch of skin and bones?"

"Our family has always dreamed of eternal life. Like the Egyptians, they believed that if the body were preserved, life would go on after death. Mummification was a crude attempt at cryogenics. The early embalmers used pine resin rather than liquid oxygen as they do now." She looked past Austin's shoulder. "I see our guests have begun to arrive. We can begin the ceremony."

Ghostly figures dressed in white robes were filing into the arena. The group was equally divided between men and women. There were about two dozen people, and their white hair and wrinkled faces seemed only decades removed from the silent mummies. As the figures came into the arena, they kissed Madame Fauchard's hand and gathered in a circle around the dais.

"You already know these people," Racine said to Austin. "You met them at my party. They are the descendants of the old arms families."

"They looked better in costume," Austin said.

"The ravages of time are kind to no one, but they will be the elite who will rule the world with me. Marcel will be in charge of our private army."

Austin let out a deep laugh. Startled faces turned in his direction.

"So *this* is what this insanity is all about? World domination?"

Racine stared at Austin like an angry Medusa. "You find this humorous?" she said.

"You're not the first megalomaniac to talk about taking over the world," Austin said. "Hitler and Genghis Khan were way ahead of you. The only thing they accomplished was to shed a lot of blood, nothing more."

Racine regained her composure. "But think of how the world would be today if they had been immortal."

"It's not a world most people would care to live in."

"You're wrong. Dostoyevsky was right when he said mankind will always strive to find someone new to worship. We will be welcomed as saviors once the world's oceans have been turned into fetid swamps. Surely someone from NUMA must know about the undersea plague that is spreading through your oceanic realm like a green cancer."

"Gorgonweed?"

"Is that what you call it? A colorful name, and most apt."

"The epidemic is not general knowledge. How did you hear about it?"

"You pathetic man! I *created* it. Long life alone would not give me the power I desired. My scientists discovered the mutant weed as a by-product of their work. When they brought their findings to me, I knew it was the perfect vehicle for my plan. I turned the Lost City into a breeding ground for this noxious weed."

Austin had to admire the complex workings of her villainous mind. She had been one step ahead of everyone.

"That's why you wanted the Woods Hole expedition wiped out."

"Of *course*. I couldn't have those blundering fools jeopardizing my plans."

"You want to become empress of a world in chaos?"

"That's the point. Once countries are in bankruptcy, suffering from famine and political anarchy, their rulers impotent, I will come to remove this scourge from the world."

"You're saying you can kill the weed?"

"As easily as I can kill you and your friends. The 'deathbound' will come to worship the immortals who will be created here tonight. These people will go back to their respective countries and gradually assume the mantle of power. We will be superior beings whose wisdom will be a welcome relief to democracy, with its fickleness and demands on the ordinary people. We will be gods!"

"Demigods who live forever? Not an appetizing prospect."

"Not for you and your friends. But cheer up. I might let you live in a somewhat altered state. A pet, perhaps. It only takes a few days to turn a human being into a snarling beast. Quite a remarkable process. It would be amusing to let you watch the changes in your lady friend and see if you still want to hold her in your arms."

"I wouldn't count on it," Austin said. "Your miracle elixir may be in short supply."

"Impossible. My laboratories will continue to supply as much as I need."

"Have you been in contact with your island recently?"

"There has been no need to be in contact. My people there know what to do."

"Your people are no more. Your island laboratories have been destroyed. I was there to witness it."

"I don't believe you."

Austin smiled, but there was a hard look in his coral-blue eyes. "The mutants escaped and made short work of Colonel Strega and his men. They wrecked your labs, but they would have been useless to you anyway, because the island and your submarine are now in the hands of British marines. Your star scientist MacLean is dead, shot by one of your own men."

Racine hardly blinked at the news. "No matter. With the resources at my command, I can build other labs on other islands. MacLean would have been disposed of with the others in any case. I have the formula and it can be replicated easily. I have won and you and your friends have lost."

Austin glanced at his watch. "Too bad you'll never see your utopia," he said, with renewed self-confidence.

"You seem fascinated by the passage of time," Racine said. "Are we keeping you from an appointment?"

Austin stared into Racine's eyes, which now glowed with ruby-red intensity.

"You're the one who has the appointment."

Racine seemed puzzled at Austin's reply. "With whom?"

"Not with whom. *What.* The thing that you fear the most."

Racine's features hardened. "I fear nothing and no one." She whirled away and strode over to the raised platform.

A white-haired couple had stepped forward from the encircling group. The woman carried a tray that held a number of round-bottomed amber phials similar to the one Racine had drunk from in the armory. The man held a carved wooden box of dark wood inlaid in ivory with a triple eagle.

Skye's grip on Austin's hand tightened. "Those are the people who kidnapped me in Paris," she whispered. "What should we do?"

"Wait," he said. He glanced at his watch, even though he had checked it a minute before.

Events were moving too fast. Austin began to formulate a desperate plan. He exchanged glances with Zavala to put him on alert. Joe gave a slight nod, indicating that he understood. The next few minutes would be crucial.

Racine reached into the box and extracted the helmet. There was a soft round of applause as she mounted the stairs to the platform. She raised the helmet high and then she placed it on her head and glanced around, her face wreathed in a triumphant smile.

"You have had a long journey to this holy of holies, and I am glad to see that you all made it across the Bridge of Sighs."

There was muted laughter from the crowd.

"Never mind. You will find the strength to *leap* across the chasm on the way out. Soon we will all be gods, worshipped by mere mortals unable to fathom our power and wisdom. As you are, I once was. As I am, you soon will be."

Racine's acolytes drank in her beauty with hungry, yearning eyes.

"I took the final phase of the formula only an hour ago. Now, my honored friends, who have done so much in my service, you are next. You are about to drink the true Philosopher's Stone, the elixir of life that so many have sought in vain for centuries."

The woman with the tray walked around the dais. Eager hands reached for the phials.

Austin was waiting for Marcel and the guards to step forward. There would be a narrow window of opportunity when attention switched from the prisoners to the prospects of the wonderful new age that lay ahead. He was gambling that even Marcel would succumb to the excitement of the moment. Austin had been moving in barely noticeable side steps closer to the nearest guard. The guard was already transfixed by the spectacle on the dais and had lowered his weapon to his side.

The phials were being passed to Marcel and his men.

Austin planned to jump the guard and wrestle him down. Zavala could grab Skye and run for the tunnel. Austin knew it was a sacrifice bunt at best, but he owed it to his friends for getting them into this mess. He signaled Zavala with his eyes again and tensed his body for a leap, only to check his move as a murmur ran through the crowd.

Racine's followers had put the flasks to their lips, but their eyes were directed toward the stage.

Racine had raised her hand to her slender neck, as if something were caught in her throat. There was a puzzled look in her eyes. Then her hand moved up to her cheek. Her fair skin seemed to be withering. Within seconds, it was yellow and wrinkled as if it had been hit with acid.

"What's happening?" Racine said. She touched her hair. It could have been the light, but her long locks seemed to have gone from gold to platinum. She plucked gently at her hair with a clawlike hand. A tuft came out loose in her fingers. She stared at the clump with horror.

The wrinkles on her face were spreading like cracks in a drying mudflat.

"Tell me what is happening!" she wailed.

"She's getting old again," someone said in a whisper that had the impact of a shout.

Racine stared at the speaker. Her eyes were losing their reddish glow and were sinking deeper into their sockets.

Her arms were withering to sticks and the helmet weighed on her thin neck. She began to hunch over and curl up like a shrimp, seeming to shrink in on herself. Her beautiful face was a ruin, the marble skin flecked with age spots. She looked like a victim of a rapid-aging disease.

Racine realized what was happening to her. "No," she said, trying to shout, but her voice came out as a croak. "Nooooo," she moaned.

Racine's legs lost their ability to hold her up and she sank to her knees and then fell forward. She crawled a foot or so and reached out to Austin with a bony hand.

The horror of the moment was not lost on Austin, but Racine had been responsible for countless deaths and misery. He gazed at her with pitiless eyes. Racine's appointment with death was long overdue.

"Have a nice journey to eternity," he said.

"How did you know?" she said, her voice a harsh cackle.

"MacLean told me before he died. He programmed the formula so that it would eventually accelerate age rather than reverse it," Austin said. "The trigger was the third shot of elixir. It compressed a century of aging into one hour."

"MacLean," she said, the word trailing out to a hiss. Then she shuddered once and lay still.

In the stunned silence that followed, Racine's acolytes lowered their drinks as if the contents had turned to molten glass and dropped the containers onto the sand.

A woman screamed, precipitating a mad rush for the exit tunnel. Marcel and the guards were swept aside by the panic-stricken exodus.

Austin lunged for the nearest guard, spun him around and dropped him with a knuckle-crunching right cross. Zavala grabbed Skye by the arm, and with Austin in the lead, they formed a flying wedge through the geriatric melee.

Marcel saw the prisoners bolting for safety. He was like a man possessed. He fired his gun from waist level, spraying the crowd with bullets. The fusillade cut a swath through the white-robed gods-in-waiting like an invisible scythe, but by then Austin and the others had gained the shelter of the tunnel.

While Skye and Zavala dashed for the stairs, Austin shot the bolt, locking the gate, and raced after his friends. Bullets splattered against the iron bars and the racket of metal on metal drowned out the cries of the dying.

Austin paused at the first level and told the others to keep moving. He ran into a passageway that led to the seating sections. As he feared, Marcel and his men had wasted little time trying to knock the gate down and were taking a more direct route. They had scaled the wall that separated the first row of seats from the arena.

Austin backtracked and climbed to the next level. Zavala and Skye were waiting for him. He yelled at them to keep moving, and then dashed through a passageway that took him out to a higher row of seats. Marcel and his men were halfway up the first tier, rapidly climbing higher, knocking aside mummies that exploded into dust.

Marcel glanced up, saw Austin and ordered his men to shoot. Austin ducked back out of sight. The hail of bullets peppered the wall where he'd been standing. Marcel would catch up within minutes. He had to be stopped.

Austin stepped boldly back into view. Before Marcel and his men could bring their weapons to bear, he snatched a blazing torch from its bracket, brought his arm back and threw the torch in a high sputtering arc. The flaming trajectory ended in a shower of sparks when the torch landed in a row of mummies.

Fueled by the resin used to preserve the mummies, the ancient remains ignited instantly. Flames leaped in the air and the grinning corpses exploded like a string of Chinese firecrackers. Marcel's men saw the amphitheater erupting into a circle of fire and they tumbled down the rows of seats in their haste to escape. Marcel stood his ground, his face contorted in rage. He kept firing until he disappeared behind a wall of flame and his gun went silent.

The conflagration enveloped the bowl-shaped stadium in seconds. Every tier was ablaze, sending up billowing black clouds of thick smoke. The inferno created in the confined space was incredible in its intensity. Austin felt as if he had opened the door to a blast furnace. Keeping his head low, he ran for the stairs. The smoke stung his eyes and he was practically blind by the time he reached the top tier of the amphitheater.

Zavala and Skye were waiting anxiously at the opening to the passageway that led back to the catacombs. They all plunged into the smoke-filled tunnel, groping their way along the walls until they emerged at the chasm spanned by the Bridge of Sighs.

Zavala carried a torch, but it was practically useless, its light sapped by the black plumes that poured from the tunnel. Then it went out completely. Austin got down on his hands and knees and groped in the darkness. His fingers felt the hard, smooth surface. He told Skye and Zavala to follow. Using the stone edges as guides, he inched his way forward across the narrow span in total blackness.

The hot wind that howled from the chasm was thick with choking smoke. Glowing cinders whirled around them. Coughing fits triggered by the smoke slowed their progress, but slowly and laboriously, they made their way to the other side.

The trip back through the catacombs was a nightmare. Smoke filled the labyrinth and made navigation confusing and dangerous, but they had picked up a couple more torches on the way and followed the torturous route back to the ossuary. Austin never thought he would be glad to see the Fauchard bone repository. The route to the courtyard would take them outside the château, but he wasn't sure he could find it. Instead, he opted to follow the passageway to the armory.

He had hoped that the air in the armory would be fresher than that in the catacombs, but when he stepped through the door behind the altar area, the atmosphere in the huge chamber was gray with a misty pall of smoke. Noxious fumes were pouring into the armory from a dozen heat gratings. Austin remembered what Racine had said about the ventilation system that served the subterranean amphitheater and surmised that the air flow must be tied into the main system.

The visibility was still relatively clear, and they sprinted the length of the nave and dashed through the double doors into the corridor. They made their way through the château in fits and starts, eventually coming to the portrait gallery. A thick layer of roiling smoke obscured the painted ceiling and the temperature in the gallery approached Saharan levels.

Austin didn't like the way the smoke seemed to glow with a scorching heat and he urged the others to move faster. They came to the front door, found that it was unlocked and ran out into the courtyard, where they took fish-like gulps of air into their oxygen-starved lungs.

Fresh air rushed into the château through the open door. With a new source of oxygen, the superheated smoke in the portrait gallery ignited with a loud *whump*. The flames flowed along the walls, feeding on the fuel provided by oil portraits of generations of Fauchards.

Figures could be seen running across the smoke-filled courtyard. Racine's guards. But they were intent on saving their own skins and no one bothered Austin and his friends as they crossed the drawbridge and the arched stone bridge. They paused near the grotesque fountain and ducked their heads in the cool water to wash the cinders from stinging eyes and soothe throats made raw by irritation.

The fire had grown in intensity in the few short minutes they took to revive themselves. As they continued along the driveway that would take them to the road leading through the forest, they heard a loud grumbling noise, as if tectonic plates were grinding against each other. They looked back and saw that the great house visible above the protective walls was fully enveloped, except for the turrets, which rose defiantly from the glowing gray-black billows.

Then the turrets were hidden behind the smoke. The noise repeated, louder this time, to be followed by a great muffled roar. Flames shot high in the sky. The air cleared for a second above the château, and in that instant Austin saw that the turrets had vanished.

The château had fallen in on itself. A greasy mushroom-shaped cloud obscured the site. Showering the grounds around the château with glowing cinders, the slag-hued cloud writhed and twisted like a living thing as it climbed toward the heavens.

"Dear God!" Skye said. "What's happened?"

"The House of Usher," Austin said with wonderment.

Skye wiped her eyes on the edge of her blouse. "What did you say?"

"Poe's story. The Usher family and their house were both rotten to the core. Just like the Fauchards, they collapsed under the weight of their deeds."

Skye gazed at the place where the château had been. "I think I like Rousseau better."

Austin put his arm around her shoulders. With Zavala leading the way, they started on the long walk that would take them back to civilization. A few minutes after they had emerged from the tree tunnel, they heard the sound of a motor. Moments later, a helicopter came into view. They were too tired to run, and only stared dumbly at the helicopter as it landed in front of them. Paul Trout stepped out of the cockpit and loped over.

"Need a ride?" he said.

Austin nodded. "I wouldn't mind a shower, too."

"And a shot of tequila," Zavala said.

"And a long hot bath," said Skye, getting into the swing of things.

"All in due time," Trout said, leading them back to the helicopter, where Gamay sat at the controls. She greeted them with a flashing smile.

They belted themselves in, and a moment later the helicopter rose above the trees, circled around the dark smoldering hole where Château Fauchard had been and headed for freedom.

No one on the aircraft looked back.

43

THE LINE OF SHIPS was stretched out from Chesapeake Bay to the Gulf of Maine along the edge of the Continental Shelf off the Atlantic coast of the United States.

Days before, the fleet of NUMA vessels and naval warships had moved into place from all points of the compass and established their original defensive perimeter a hundred miles to the east of the shelf, in the hope of repelling the invasion far from shore. But they had been swept back by the inexorable advance of the silent enemy.

The turquoise NUMA helicopter had been in the air since dawn, following a course that took it over the elongated armada. The helicopter was east of Cape Hatteras when Zavala, who was at the controls, looked out the window and said, "It's like the Sargasso Sea on hormones out there."

Austin lowered his binoculars and he smiled thinly. "The Sargasso Sea is like a rose garden compared to this mess."

The ocean had developed a split personality. To the west of the ships, the water was its normal dark blue, flecked here and there by whitecaps. To the east, beyond the picket line, the dull sea was an unhealthy yellow-green, where interlocking tendrils of Gorgonweed had formed a mat on the surface as far as the eye could see.

Austin and Zavala had watched from the helicopter as various ships tried different techniques in an effort to halt the relentless drift of the weed. The warships had fired broadside salvos with their big guns. Soggy geysers erupted, but the holes the shells punched in the mat closed up within minutes. Planes launched from aircraft carriers attacked the weed with bombs and rockets. They proved as ineffectual as a mosquito biting an elephant. Incendiary devices fizzled on the top of the thick mat, whose main bulk lay below the surface. Fungicide sprayed from planes was washed away as soon as it hit the water.

Austin asked Joe to circle over two ships that were trying to stop the movement of the weed with the use of pipe booms that were strung between the vessels. It was an exercise in futility. The surface barrier worked—for about five minutes. Pushed by the enormous pressure from a moving mass that extended back for miles, the weed simply piled up against the booms, surged over the pipes and buried them.

"I've seen enough," Austin said in disgust. "Let's go back to the ship."

Racine Fauchard was dead, nothing but shriveled flesh and brittle bones buried under the ruins of her once-proud château, but the first part of her plan had exceeded far beyond her dreams. The Atlantic Ocean was becoming the big swamp that she had promised.

Austin took consolation in the fact that Racine and her homicidal son Emil would not be around to take advantage of the chaos they had caused. But that still didn't solve the disaster the Fauchards had set into motion. Austin had encountered other human adversaries who, like the Fauchards, embodied pure evil, and he had managed to deal with them. But this unnatural, mindless phenomenon was beyond his ken.

They flew for another half hour. Austin saw from the wakes of the ships below that they were drawing back to avoid being caught up in the advancing weed.

"Stand by for landing, Kurt," Zavala warned.

The helicopter angled down toward a U.S. navy cruiser, and moments later it landed on the deck helipad. Pete Muller, the ensign they had met when his ship was guarding the vessels at the Lost City, was waiting to greet them.

"How's it look?" Muller yelled over the *thrump* of the rotors.

Austin was grim-faced. "About as bad as it gets."

He and Zavala followed Muller to a briefing room belowdecks. About thirty men and women were seated in rows of metal folding chairs drawn up in front of a large wall screen. Austin and Zavala quietly slipped into a couple of chairs in the back row. Austin recognized some of the NUMA scientists in the audience but knew only a few of the uniformed people from the armed forces and the suits from various governmental agencies charged with public security.

Standing in front of the screen was Dr. Osborne, the Woods Hole phycologist who had introduced the Trouts to the Gorgonweed menace. He was wielding a remote control in one hand and a laser pointer in the other. Displayed on the screen was a chart showing the circulation of water in the Atlantic Ocean.

"Here's where the infestation starts, in the Lost City," he said. "The Canaries' current carries the weed down past the Azores, flows westward across the Atlantic Ocean where it joins the Gulf Stream. The Gulf Stream moves northerly along the continental shelf. Eventually, it joins the North Atlantic current, which takes it back to Europe, completing the North Atlantic gyre." He swirled the red laser dot in a circle to make his point. "Any questions?"

"How fast does the Gulf Stream move?" someone asked.

"About five knots at its peak. More than a hundred miles a day."

"What's the present state of the infestation?" Muller asked.

Osborne clicked the remote and the circulation chart disappeared. A satellite photo of the North Atlantic took its place. An irregular yellowish band that resembled a great deformed donut ran in a rough circle around the edge of the ocean, close to the continents.

"This real-time composite satellite photo gives you an idea of the current areas of Gorgonweed infestation," Osborne said. "Now I'll show you our computer projection of the further spread." The picture changed. In the new photo the ocean was totally yellow, except for a few dark blue holes in the central Atlantic.

A murmur ran through the audience.

"How long before it gets to that stage?" Muller asked.

Osborne cleared his throat as if he were having a hard time getting the words out. "A matter of days."

There was a collective gasp at his answer.

He clicked the remote. The picture zoomed in on the eastern seaboard of North America. "This is the area of immediate concern. Once the weed reaches the shallower waters of the continental shelf, we're really in trouble. For a start, it will destroy the entire fishing industry along the east coast of the United States and Canada and northwestern Europe. We've been trying various measures of at-sea containment. I saw Mr. Austin enter the room a few minutes ago. Would you like to bring us up-to-date, Kurt?"

Not really, Austin thought as he made his way to the front of the room. He scanned the pale faces in front of him. "My partner, Joe Zavala, and I just completed an aerial survey of the picket line that has been established along the edge of the continental shelf." He described what they had seen. "Unfortunately," he concluded, "nothing made a dent."

"What about chemicals?" a government bureaucrat asked.

"Chemicals are quickly dissipated by water and wind," Austin said. "A little seeps down, and it may kill a few tendrils, but Gorgonweed is so thick that the chemical doesn't go all the way through. We're talking about a vast area. Even if you were able to cover it you'd end up poisoning the ocean."

"Is there anything that could destroy a large area?" Muller asked.

"Sure. A nuclear bomb," Austin said, with a bleak smile. "But even that would be ineffectual with thousands of square miles of ocean. I'm going to recommend that booms be erected around major harbors. We'll try to keep our major ports clear so we can buy time."

A beefy four-star army general named Frank Kyle stood and said, "Time for *what*? You've said yourself that there is no defense against this stuff."

"We've got people working on genetic solutions."

The general snorted as if Austin had suggested replacing his soldiers' rifles with flowers. "*Genetics!* DNA stuff? What the hell good is that going to do? It could take months. Years."

"I'm open to suggestions," Austin said.

The general grinned. "Glad to hear that. I'm going to pass your suggestion about nuclear bombs along to the president."

Austin had dealt with military types when he was with the CIA and found that they were usually cautious about using force against any enemy. General Kyle was a throwback to another nuclear general, Curtis LeMay, but in a climate of fear his recommendation might prevail.

"I was not suggesting it," Austin said patiently. "As you'll recall, I said a nuclear bomb would make a relatively small dent in the weed."

"I'm not talking about *one* bomb," General Kyle said. "We've stockpiled thousands of them that we were going to use against the Russians. We carpet bomb the ocean, and if we run out we can borrow more from the Ruskies."

"You're talking about turning the ocean into a nuclear waste dump," Austin said. "A bombing campaign like that would destroy all ocean life."

"This weed of yours is going to kill all the fish anyhow," Kyle replied. "As you know, shipping has already been disrupted and there is a loss of billions of dollars by the hour. This stuff is threatening our cities. It's got to be stopped by any means. We've got 'clean' nukes we can use."

Heads were nodding in the audience. Austin saw that he was getting nowhere. He asked Zavala to sit in on the rest of the strategy session while he went to the bridge. A few minutes later, he was in the wheelhouse, using the ship's radiophone to call the Trouts, who were on the *Sea Searcher*, over the Lost City. He made quick contact with the NUMA research vessel and a crewman tracked down Paul, who had been directing a Remote Operated Vehicle (ROV) from the deck.

"Greetings from the wild weird world of Dr. Strangelove," Austin said.

"Huh?" Trout replied.

"I'll explain in a minute. How's your work going?"

"It's *going*," Trout said, with no real enthusiasm. "We've been running an ROV to collect samples of algae and weed. Gamay and her team are busy in the lab doing analysis."

"What's she looking for?"

"She hopes they can find something in the weed's molecular structure that might help. We've been sharing information with NUMA scientists back in Washington, and with scientific teams in other countries. How about you?"

Austin sighed. "We've tried every trick we can think of, but with no success. The offshore wind is giving us a little reprieve. But it won't be long before every harbor on the east coast will be clogged up. The Pacific is showing patches of infestation as well."

"How long do we have?"

Kurt told him what Osborne had said. He could hear Paul suck his breath in.

"Are you having any problem navigating in the stuff?" Austin asked.

"The area around the Lost City is relatively clear. This

is where the infestation starts, and it thickens as it goes east and west of here."

"That may be the only clear patch in the ocean before long. You'd better plot an escape route so you don't get caught up in the weed yourself."

"I've already talked to the captain. There's a channel open south of here, but we're going to have to leave within twenty-four hours if we expect to get out. What was that you said about Strangelove?"

"There's a general here by the name of Kyle. He's going to tell the president to nuke the stuff with every bomb in our arsenal."

Trout paused in stunned silence and then found his voice. "He's not serious."

"I'm afraid he is. There is tremendous political pressure on leaders around the world to do something. *Anything.* Vice President Sandecker may be able to stall him. But the president will be forced to act, even if the scheme is foolhardy."

"This is more than foolhardy! It's crazy. And it won't work. They can blow the weed to pieces, but every stray tendril will self-replicate. It could be just as disastrous." He sighed. "When can we expect to see mushroom clouds over the Atlantic?"

"There's a meeting going on now. A decision could come as early as tomorrow. Once the machinery is set in motion, things could start moving fast, especially with the Gorgonweed lapping at our shores." He paused. "I've been thinking about MacLean. Didn't he tell you that he could come up with an antidote for the weed using the Fauchard formula?"

"He seemed fairly confident that he could do it. Unfortunately, we don't have MacLean or the formula."

Austin thought about the helmet buried under tons of rubble. "The key lies in the Lost City. Whatever caused the mutation in the first place came from the Lost City. There's *got* to be a way to use something from down there to fight this thing."

"Let's think about this," Trout said. "MacLean knew that his life-extension formula was flawed, that it would reverse aging, but as Racine Fauchard learned the hard way, the formula was unpredictable. It also *accelerated* growth."

"That's what I was getting at. Nature is always out of balance."

"That's right. It's like a rubber band that snaps back after being stretched too far."

"I don't know if Racine Fauchard would like being compared to a rubber band, but it makes my point about nature seeking equilibrium. Mutations happen every day, even in humans. Nature has built a corrective device into the system or we'd have people running around with two or three heads, which might not be all that bad. When it comes to aging, every species has a death gene that kills off the old to make room for the new generation. Gorgonweed was stable until the Fauchards introduced the enzyme into the equation, tipping things out of balance. It's got to snap back eventually."

"What about the mutant soldiers who lived so long?"

"That was an artificial situation. Had they been on their own, they probably would have devoured each other. Equilibrium again."

"The constant here is the enzyme," Trout concluded. "It's the precipitating factor. It can retard aging or it can accelerate it."

"Have Gamay look at the enzyme again."

"I'll see how she's coming along," Trout said.

"I'm going back to the meeting to see if I can discourage General Kyle from a nuclear carpet bombing of the Atlantic Ocean, although I'm not optimistic."

Trout's head was spinning. The Fauchards were dead, but they were still managing to inflict harm on the world from their graves. He left the bridge and went down to a "wet" lab where Gamay was working with a four-person team of marine biologists and those from allied marine sciences.

"I was talking to Kurt," Paul said. "The news isn't good." He outlined his conversation with Austin. "Have you turned up anything new?"

"I explored the interaction between the enzyme and the plant, but I didn't get anywhere, so I've been looking into DNA instead. It never hurts to revisit previous research."

She led the way to a table where a series of about twenty steel containers were lined up in a row.

"Each one of these containers contains a sample of Gorgonweed. I've exposed the samples to the enzymes that the ROV collected from the columns to see what would happen. I wanted to see if there would be any reaction if I overloaded the weed with various forms of enzyme. I've been busy following other avenues and haven't looked at the samples recently."

"Let me see if I understand what happened," Trout said. "The Fauchards distorted the molecular makeup of the enzyme during the refinement process, when they separated it from the microorganisms that created the substance. The irregularity was absorbed into the genetic makeup of the weed, triggering its mutation."

"That's a pretty good summation."

"Stay with me. Up until that time, the weed coexisted with the enzyme in its natural state."

"That's right," Gamay said. "Only when the enzyme was modified did it interact with the nearest life-form, which happened to be obnoxious but perfectly normal seaweed, transforming it into a monster. I hoped that an overdose of the stuff would speed up the aging even more, just the way it did with Racine Fauchard. It didn't work."

"The premise sounds logical—there's something missing here." He thought about it for a moment. "What if it isn't the enzyme but the *bacteria* that are the controlling influence?"

"I never thought about that. I've been fooling around with the chemical, thinking that was the stabilizing factor here, rather than the bugs that produce it. In extracting the enzyme from the water, the Fauchards killed off the bacteria, which may have been the governing factor that kept things on an even keel."

She went over to a refrigerator and extracted a glass phial. The liquid contents had a slight brown discoloration.

"This is a culture of bacteria we collected from under the Lost City columns."

She measured off some liquid, poured it into a Gorgonweed container and made a note.

"Now what?"

"We'll have to give the bacteria time to do their work. It won't take long. I haven't eaten. What say you get me some food?"

"What say you get out of here and we have a real meal in the mess hall?"

Gamay brushed the hair back from her forehead. "That's the best invitation I've had all day."

Cheeseburgers had never tasted so good. Refreshed and full, the Trouts went back to the lab after an hour. Trout glanced at the container with the bacteria. The complex tangle of tendrils looked unchanged.

"Can I take a closer look at this stuff? It's hard to see in this light."

Gamay pointed to a long pair of tongs. "Use those. You can examine the specimen in that sink basin."

Trout extracted the glob of weed from its container, carried it to the sink and dropped it into a plastic tub. By itself, the clump of Gorgonweed looked so innocent. It was not a pretty plant, but it did have an admirable functionality, with spidery tendrils hooked onto other pieces of weed to form the impenetrable mat that sucked nutrients from the ocean. Trout poked it with the tongs, then lifted it up by a tendril. The tendril broke off at the stem and the weed plopped wetly back into the tub.

"Sorry," he said. "I broke your weed sample."

Gamay gave him a peculiar look and took the tongs from his hand. She plucked at another tendril and it, too, came off. She repeated the experiment. Each time, the thin appendages broke off easily. She removed a tendril and took it over to a bench, where she sliced it up, put the thin sections on slides and popped them under a microscope.

A moment later, she looked up from the eye piece. "The weed is dying," she declared.

"What?" Trout peered into the sink. "Looks healthy to me."

She smiled and plucked off more tendrils. "See. I'd never be able to do this with a healthy weed. The tendrils are like extremely strong rubber. These are brittle."

She called over her assistants and asked them to prepare microscope slides from different parts of the sample. When she looked up from her microscope again, her eyes were red-rimmed, but her face was wreathed in a wide grin.

"The weed sample is in the first stage of necrosis. In other words, the stuff is dying. We'll try it with some of the other samples to make sure."

Again she mixed the bacteria in with the weed, and again they waited an hour. Microscopic examination confirmed their original findings. Every sample subjected to the bacteria was dying.

"The bacteria are essentially eating something in the Gorgonweed that it needs to survive," she said. "We'll have to do more research."

Trout picked up the phial with the original bacteria culture. "What's the most effective way to use these hungry little bugs?"

"We'll have to grow large quantities, then spread the bacteria far and wide and let them do the work."

Trout smiled. "Do you think the British government would let us use the Fauchard submersible to spread this stuff around? It's got the capacity and speed that we need."

"I think they'll bend over backward to keep the British Isles from being cut off from the rest of the world."

"MacLean saved our hash again," Trout said, with a shake of his head. "He gave us the hope that we could beat this thing."

"Kurt deserves some credit."

"His instincts were on the nose when he said to go back to the Lost City and to think in terms of equilibrium."

Trout headed for the door.

"Are you going to tell Kurt the good news?"

Trout nodded. "Then I'm going to tell him that it's about time we had a send-off for a proper old Scottish gentleman."

44

THE LOCH WAS several miles long and half as wide and its cold, still waters reflected the unblemished Scottish sky like a queen's mirror. Rugged, rolling hills carpeted with heather held the loch in a purple embrace.

The open wooden-hulled boat cut a liquid wake in the tranquil waters as it headed out from shore, gliding to a drifting stop, finally, at the deepest part of the loch. The boat held four passengers: Paul and Gamay Trout, Douglas MacLean, and his late cousin Angus, whose ashes were carried in an ornate Byzantine chest the chemist had picked up on his travels.

Douglas MacLean had met his cousin Angus only once, at a family wedding some years before. They had hit it off and vowed to get together, but as with many a well-meant plan made over a glass of whiskey, they'd never met again. Until now. Douglas was the only living relative Trout had been able to track down. Equally important, he played the bagpipe. Not well, but loudly.

He stood in the prow of the boat, dressed in full MacLean tartans, his kilted legs braced wide to give himself a steady platform. At a signal from Gamay, he began to play "Amazing Grace." As the haunting skirl echoed off the hills, Paul poured Angus's ashes into the loch. The gray-brown powder floated on the calm surface for a few minutes and gradually sank into the deep blue water.

"Ave atque vale," Trout said softly. Hail and farewell.

About the same time Trout was saying his good-bye, Joe Zavala was among the pallbearers carrying a simple wooden casket along a dirt path that ran between the moldering headstones in an ancient churchyard near the cathedral city of Rouen. The other pallbearers were all descendants of Captain Pierre Levant.

At least twenty members of the extended Levant family surrounded the open grave set next to the headstones that marked the final resting place of the captain's wife and son. The gathering included a contingent of men and women representing the French army. As the country priest intoned the last rites, the army people saluted briskly and Captain Levant was lowered into the grave, given the rest that had been denied him for so long.

"Ave atque vale," Zavala whispered.

By prearrangement, high above the Fauchard vineyards, the small red biplane circled like a hungry hawk. Austin checked the time, banked the Aviatik slightly and, by prearrangement, dumped out the ashes of Jules Fauchard, whose body had been removed from the glacier.

There had been some discussion whether Jules should be cremated, a practice frowned upon by the Catholic Church. But since there were no living relatives, Austin and Skye took the matter into their own hands, deciding to return Jules to the soil that nurtured his beloved vineyards.

Like Trout and Zavala, Austin, too, gave the old Latin funeral salutation.

"Well, that does it for Jules," Austin said, speaking into the microphone that connected him with Skye, who was in the other cockpit. "He proved the best of the bunch. He deserved better than being frozen like a Popsicle under that glacier."

"I agree," she said. "I wonder what would have happened if he had made it to Switzerland?"

"We'll never know. Let's imagine that in a parallel time stream he was able to stop the bloody war."

"That's a nice thought," Skye said. Then, after a moment, she added, "How far can we fly in this thing?"

"Until we run out of fuel?"

"Can we make it to Aix-en-Provence?"

"Wait a minute," he said. He tapped the keys on the GPS and programmed in a route that showed airport fueling points. "It will take a few hours and we'll have to stop to refuel. Why do you ask?"

"Charles has offered us the use of his villa. He says we can even use his new Bentley if we promise not to drive it into the swimming pool."

"Tough condition, but I guess I can agree to that."

"The villa is a wonderful place," Skye said with growing excitement. "Quiet and beautiful with a well-stocked wine cellar. I thought it might be a good place to work on my paper. I must thank the Fauchards, for one thing. Using what Racine said about their family background, I'll be able to prove my theory linking Minoans with early European trade. We can talk about your theory that they went as far north as the Faroe Islands. Maybe even to North America. What do you say?"

"I didn't bring any clothes."

"Who needs *clothes*?" she said in a laugh that was ripe with promise. "That's never stopped us before."

Austin grinned. "I think that's what they call a deal clincher. We're picking up a tailwind. I'll try to get us to Provence in time for dinner."

Then he glanced at his compass and pointed the nose of the plane south, on a course that would take them toward the beckoning shores of the Mediterranean Sea.